LIEUTENANT KUROSAWA'S ERRAND BOY

LIEUTENANT KUROSAWA'S ERRAND BOY

A Novel of
Forgiveness

WARRAN KALASEGARAN

EPIGRAM BOOKS
SINGAPORE · LONDON

Epigram Books UK
First published in 2017 by Epigram Books Singapore
This Edition published in Great Britain in July 2018
by Epigram Books UK

Copyright © 2017 by Warran Kalasegaran
Cover Design by Yong Wen Yeu

A CIP CATALOGUE RECORD FOR THIS BOOK IS AVAILABLE FROM THE BRITISH LIBRARY.

ISBN   978-1-91-209858-3

PRINTED AND BOUND IN   Great Britain by Clays Ltd, St Ives plc
                                Epigram Books UK
                                55 Baker Street
                                London, W1U 7EU

10 9 8 7 6 5 4 3 2 1

www.epigrambooks.uk

For my family

Remember December 8th,

The day world history changed.

The day Anglo-Saxon power

was denied across the land and sea of East Asia.

It was our Japan that denied them,

the small country in the Eastern sea,

the Land of the Gods, Nippon.

Ruled over by a living God.

The power of Anglo-America,

monopolists of global wealth,

was denied in our own country.

Our denial was our justice.

We only demand the return of East Asia to East Asia.

Our neighbours grow thin from their exploitation.

It is we who will break those claws and fangs.

We who build our strength and rise up.

Young and old, men and women: soldiers all.

We fight until our great enemies see the error of their

ways.

World history has been severed in two.

Remember December 8th.

—"December 8th" ("*Jūnigatsu yōka*"), Takamura Kōtarō

1

Dedicated to Papatti

I was born in the year Showa 9 by the Japanese calendar, the year 1934 by British convention, and although I was born in Singapore, raised a Hindu and speak Tamil, I know of no other metric of time that mattered. That was the world I was born into.

My father worked as a coolie on His Majesty's Naval Base in the north of Singapore, then a lucrative British colony. The Englishman, not content with his gunboats and Bible, or perhaps spurred on by them, borrowed the title "coolie" and the indentured labourer from South India to fatten out his dictionary and Treasury, and returned neither. That my father, at the age of seventeen, said *sayonara* to his parents in Tamil Nadu and bought a one-way meal ticket across the Indian Ocean for any work in an unknown country is testament to his faith, infinite as faith must be, that life could only get better. And a repudiation of the hierarchy of the Indian caste system, where rich Indian Brahmins repressed other Indians before the Englishman came along and repressed them all, and at whose bottom my father would have found himself ingloriously squashed in either scenario.

My father's ship moored at Tanjong Pagar Harbour in the south of Singapore during the April of 1928, where a few Tommies herded him and other young healthy males onto a pickup truck bound for the north, an experience that vindicated my father's religious distaste for eating cow meat. Used to the torrid heat, he slept thinking the journey across the country would take a few days. He woke up delirious when soldiers shouted at him to get off, and he realised barely an hour had passed. They put him to work immediately, instilling in him the industry of the Protestant (because only Protestants could be industrious in those days) and rewarding him with the pay of an Asian.

King George's Naval Base in Sembawang was then half-constructed and the white man taught my father to operate a mechanical crane so he could lay the final stones to cement the Royal Navy's dominance east of Suez. Having accomplished this worthy endeavour, my father swept the Naval Base's pink-cobbled parade square, repainted its white bungalows, fixed the lights in the barracks, and unloaded crates from the ships and stocked them in the warehouses. He did anything the white soldier didn't want to do and reported to him after that. That was a "coolie". But my father loved his occupation and he was a British man—or possession—through and through. At the end of ten years of service, his supervisor, whom we called "Corporal Gibraltar", presented him with a copy of *The Jungle Book*, perhaps unaware that my father and I didn't read, but my father proudly placed the cover of the Indian boy in his loincloth next to our mini statue of Ganesha, even remarking that we looked alike. He called Corporal Gibraltar a "good man".

My mother migrated from the Tamil-speaking north of Sri Lanka and cooked in the Naval Base canteen, where she had the fortune of meeting the hero that was my father. They say necessity breeds invention, which I suppose is the only way I can explain their union. Being the only two civilian Tamil speakers on base, they were naturally drawn to each other. He kept turning up at her stall without money in hand but plenty of love in his eyes, and she kept giving him dollops of rice and beef rendang (that he learned to eat for the higher virtue of love), until finally *she* had to ask for *his* hand in marriage.

My mother died giving birth to me and I never got to know her and thus cannot say much except this: sometimes, I think I killed her clawing my way out to take my first breath. It was a tragic fact of my world that new beginnings were often sought through violent exorcisms. My father never spoke about my amma except to say that she lived on inside me. He, like any person, spoke his share of crap that held a deeper truth. But from the beginning, it was just Appa and me. He was a hardworking and humble man and I respected him for that. I merely think that whatever courage and pluck I have, I must have inherited from Amma.

I must stop here, for my grandson who is writing this down on his foolscap paper tells me that I cannot talk like this about Protestants and Englishmen and Indians, that people are one and the same. This is all fine and well. But I have had more salt than my grandson has had rice. He doesn't know oppression or division, militarily and hierarchically enforced, where the colour of your skin and the employment of your father decided from birth whether you lived in a brown congested room in a demarcated zone called Little India, or a white bungalow facing the snot-green sea. Where a Briton hurled racist slurs like "Hurry up you *keling!*"

while you polished his shoes, and you just scratched the difficult dirt away with your fingernails and called him "Sir" as you stood up with blackened hands. My grandson does not know how it is to feel humiliated, backward and lesser every day, and think that this is your fate in life and that you must accept it. I must treat such a past with a little anger and a little irony, for without the first, the world would never move on, and without the second, I never would. But my grandson lives in a different world and I haven't even started on the best bits of my story yet.

I was eight years old when I encountered War. He was a calculating and unbridled man. The Japanese invaded Singapore from the north in the February of 1942, raining bombs on a city of bazaars. Appa never thought the Japanese, an Asian army, would dare attack a British colony, so we had barely fled before they liberated him of this fantasy and captured Sembawang. We took with us a second-hand army haversack stuffed with spare clothes, our cash savings wrapped in underwear, a two-kilo sack of white rice, a mess tin cradling some sour mango achar to embellish the rice, a robust iron pot, matchboxes and *The Jungle Book*. We trekked south and southeast towards Singapore city with the battle to our backs, trudging by the edge of long roads rutted by Bren gun carriers and Lanchester armoured cars, ready to dive face-first into the long grass if War flew over us or lobbed an artillery shell, our hands protecting the back of our heads against explosives and metal shrapnel.

One night, Appa and I slept under a stilted kampung house in what would now be called Bishan. I stared up at brown wooden planks with iron nails the size of my eyes and hoped the nails wouldn't transform into missiles and shoot down at us.

Appa had always called me "Thambi" or "younger brother" in Tamil. He had said we were more than father and son;

we were brothers and best friends. I had liked that idea. "Thambi. Are you awake?"

I closed my eyes and pretended to sleep.

He patted the dry, packed earth between us. The stray mongrel lying at our feet perked its head. Flies scattered, swollen lumps of black diptera hovering over my skin. You would think that War would at least kill these parasites, but War was unsparing. "Thambi?" Appa said again.

"What, Appa?" I opened my eyes.

"I want you to know—this is the last time we'll run. The British are going to make one big advance tonight and we'll kick the Japanese out by tomorrow morning. You wait and see. God willing, when morning comes, we'll walk back to Sembawang and Appa will go back to work. Okay?"

I kept quiet, knowing he had been wrong before. He had been wrong too many times. Now, whenever he spoke of War as if he knew it, as if he were some Brigadier-General, I felt ashamed of him, and I felt even more ashamed and angry when we quietly packed our things and walked south and southeast every morning. I wished he would just be quiet.

Instead, he said, "The British are fighting hard, Thambi. They'll win, you'll see. How about this? Tomorrow, when we start work, I'll let you climb onto the ships, shimmy up the top deck and jump into the water. Your super dive. What do you say? You can swim in the sea for as long as you want. I'll ask Corporal Gibraltar to let you. I know he will. What do you say, Thambi?"

"I want to sleep, Appa."

"Don't talk like that, Thambi; just pray and it will all work out. Okay?"

"I said I want to sleep, Appa."

He stopped talking, stung. I closed my eyes, unbothered. In the quiet between Appa and me, I heard gunfire and grenade explosions. I no longer knew if I imagined it and I certainly didn't bother praying. *Om Shanti Shanti* wasn't going to save us and if the meek really did inherit the earth, my father would have been Emperor by now.

The next morning, we woke up and walked south and southeast again.

Appa and I finally reached Kallang, a warren of two-storey shophouses ringed by the brown and sullen Kallang River and the bumboats congesting its banks. Colourful bamboo laundry poles jutted out of the shophouses, their paint peeling. The roadside coffee shops were littered with cigarette butts and broken glass bottles and black footprints. A few wooden benches lay on their sides. A rickshaw was missing its wheels, sitting on the road like a duck. Over these, the Sultan mosque with its beautiful golden dome rose, its minarets piercing the sky. Near it was the gated colonial palace the Sassenach had built for the old Malay Sultan.

A Chinese man was trekking south to Tanjong Pagar with his family, and had heard the news from a teashop playing the Malayan Broadcasting Corporation radio. Face to face, he was a carbon copy of Appa, despite Appa's swarthiness. Their faces were tanned and beaten from heavy labour under the sun, and their hair dirtied by sleeping in the jungles. Their singlets and shorts were muddied. They wore slippers, smut caking their toes and spattered on their calves. The Chinese man said in Malay, "They surrendered. In two weeks. Two weeks! They forgot how to fight. They said they won't lose, they said they can't lose, then they surrendered. They only know how to talk. Talk and talk only. They only look out for themselves, because they are fighting in Europe also. But still, two weeks!" He swore in Hokkien, a language whose lewd vulgarity sparkles with its own delight. "They did not even send tanks. Did you see a tank here? There were no tanks, right or not? *Kan ni na!*"

Appa was shaking his head, stunned, as if he had been the one fighting and shell-shocked. "No, they can't lose. They said they can't lose."

"Lose? What lose?" The man spat. A wad of saliva burst onto the sand like a bomb. "Surrendered! My grandma can fight better than them. *Na bei*! It's our fault. We never should have trusted them. You lost your wife already? Go save your son. Okay okay, enough rest. Come, let's go! Come!" He shoved his wife, whose eyes were closing and head was drooping, and she stumbled forward. He carried his youngest son in one arm and prodded her further. The older son, my age, dragged the family's sole portmanteau the way he dragged his feet, and I thought: all over the world, our fathers are leading us to our demise.

Appa chased him. "Wait, are you sure? Are you sure? Where are you going?"

The man didn't stop. "I lie for what! It's over! What more you want? Go save yourself. We are *mati*."

We are dead.

Appa turned. His eyes, disbelieving black orbs, met mine. The family disappeared behind him. "I can't believe this, Thambi. They gave up. How could they surrender?"

Surrender. The word still echoes in my head. To stop trying. But what's the word for not trying in the first place? I am not sure if I thought this then or realised it after, but that Chinese man was right. It was our fault. Appa never fought. I never fought. We never even learned to fight. We just ran and ran from the Japanese like cowards and trusted the British to defend us. We had given up first.

That evening, Appa and I snuck onto an abandoned bumboat on the Kallang River to sleep. The floor bobbed with a deceptive gentleness. There were no gunshots. There were no missiles. Instead, an empty silence hung over Singapore, brooding with the uncertainty of tomorrow, a terrifying sky to sleep under.

At midnight, glass shattered and a baby cried. A saw shrieked through metal as looters tore shutters apart and hammered down doors. I rolled against the damp wooden starboard side and cupped my ears as a man screamed and another man yelled at him. A thump. Then a woman begging. Appa started talking into my ear and I pushed him away. Although the bumboat owner didn't return, I didn't sleep that night.

The next morning, a light blue sky dawned on quiet and empty streets, but the night revealed itself in the brown bloodstains congealed on the road, the crusted glass bits and broken metal jewelling the asphalt, and a parang lying in a drain, crimson-tipped. Watch shops and pawn shops and mama shops were laid open, missing shutters and doors. Their shelves were empty, glass cabinets broken, tin containers toppled over, and leftover rice grains and biscuits trampled over. The people of Kallang had boarded themselves inside the tenement houses above the shops and shut the windows, and no sound came from them. The bamboo poles had been emptied of clothes. Only a few men like Appa roamed the street in wide-eyed amazement. One carried a butcher's knife. I reached for the parang but Appa told me to toss it back into the drain.

We walked up to Jalan Besar and I tugged his arm. A mama shop stood across the street, four jumbo Chinese characters emblazoned across its peeling iron signboard. Inside the mart, three men hauled a fourth away from his cash register. They wrestled him against a cupboard stacked with Chinese alcohol bottles, and spread his arms like a crucifixion. They stuffed his mouth with cloth and punched him in the gut. His eyes bulged and they punched him and punched him until he sat. A looter booted his privates and his eyes rolled up into his head. They started pulling an empty rice sack over his body.

Appa said, "Mind your business and walk." As if reading my mind, he clasped my mouth and picked me up. Muffled, I slapped his arms and kicked at air as he dashed down the road. He turned into an alley between the shophouses and only put me down in the middle of it. The alley was empty except for a pile of rubbish buckets, cardboard boxes and a grey mattress leaning against the wall at the end. Two alley cats coiled amidst the rubbish and watched us. Appa grabbed my arms. His bushy eyebrows sat heavily above large deep eyes.

I spoke before he could. "Why did you do that, Appa? Why didn't we help him?"

"Help him? How? We would have ended up dead. This is no time to be a hero, Thambi."

"We could have tried. Now he's going to die. For sure." I kicked a loose stone at the cats. They did not move.

"Thambi, stop fooling around. Please."

"I am not fooling around! He's going to die! We must help him, Appa!"

"Stop shouting. Please, Thambi."

I quieted. "I'm not scared. Not like you."

"Well, you should be. There is no law, no police, nothing to save us now. You saw what those thieves were doing, right? You think anyone is going to punish them for it? You think they would have just done a *namaskaram* for you and said sorry and left if you had told them to stop? Be smart, Thambi."

"Stop talking like you know everything, Appa. You don't know anything. That man is dead because of you. We are homeless because of you. We lost everything because of you. Because of you!" I stuck a finger into his face.

His eyes widened. "So you are going to behave like a little child? You're not my thambi anymore, right? You're a child, right?"

I glared back. I refused to be emotionally blackmailed like this and I shouted, "I am not scared!"

His hands bolted over my mouth. Then a spondaic pulse throbbed under my feet. The street shivered. *Tennō heika banzai! Tennō heika banzai!* Leather boots beat against the tarred road. The sounds grew louder and closer. Locks latched into the doors and clicked into the windows around us as Kallang sprang to life for one second. Then it died away. Appa said, *"Jappankarran."*

The Japanese.

He grabbed my hand and we sprinted to the end of the alley to see if it was true. The cats, the smarter creatures, slipped past us and ran off towards Jalan Besar.

The Japanese soldiers were marching onto Kallang Road in four columns. The soldiers wore earthy uniforms with peaked caps and gripped long and polished rifles high and still over their shoulders. A blood-red band wrapped each cap and a gold star in the centre of the band glinted in the sun. Rows and rows of thin bayonets stuck out like a field of luminescent silver grass. The soldiers swung their left fists in swift jerks, up and back, up and back. They marched as one disciplined leviathan called War, boots crunching together, advancing furiously. A fluttering flag led this parade, white with a large crimson ball in the centre, a big pottu, burning brightest of all.

Migi! Hidari! Tennō heika banzai!

These were the men who had chased me from my home. These were the men who had made Appa look like a fool. A fury came into me as they advanced closer: anger at them and at Appa. I wanted to show Appa that we didn't need to be afraid. So I stalked onto the street.

Appa yanked me back. I struggled even more furiously against him, and he wrestled me into the rubbish, sitting, pulling me into his clutch, a bucket upturning its waste, the stench of rotten fish and manure rising around us. He hissed, "Thambi. Stop this. Please. *Please*. Listen to me for once. Please, I'm begging you." I could not speak because his hand covered my mouth. Still I struggled to escape and throw myself at the enemy as the drumming under my feet grew louder and louder, as if the earth itself was churning, and wanted to erupt against the oncoming army. I didn't care what happened to me.

The commands boomed inside the alleyway. The soldiers filed past the entrance and the timed beat of their boots shook the hutong. Left, right. Left, right. Every second, a new soldier marched past the entrance. But he could have been the same tanned clean-shaven face, cropped hair, clenched jaw, pinched eyes, left arm swung to ninety degrees, leg kicked out to forty-five, cold, ruthless, relentless. They looked the same and marched the same. They had no differences. They were one machine.

Then a soldier turned his head. His sharp eyes met mine for an instant, and a cold fear gripped me. He turned back and disappeared.

Appa's grip had become painful, but I had also stopped struggling.

It was an endless parade of soldiers. When the last trooper marched past, desert-green light tanks thundered after him, the same Japanese soldiers standing at the turrets, saluting the flag, proud and confident. Then armoured jeeps and lorries camouflaged in green netting rolled after the tanks. This time, I let Appa cover my ears.

The procession lasted forever. Even after the victory parade moved on to the Municipal Building that is now City Hall, it felt like Japanese soldiers and tanks still rumbled through Kallang and the ground still shook. As I let the aftershock subside, Appa took a long breath. We knew who was in charge now.

Appa sensed the difference in me and did not press the point. "Are you okay, Thambi?" he said.

I nodded. "What do we do now, Appa?"

"Survive," he said, reaching for the mattress.

Appa and I built a house on a patch of grass and sand between Kallang Road and the river. We propped thin sheets of rusted zinc and tin, cardboard and wood to resemble the four walls of a container, a little shorter than Appa, and nailed them into place. Then we leaned the ramshackle concoction against a tree and nailed it to the tree. We used the spare sheets and enormous attap leaves that had drifted down the river from the mangrove swamps to make a roof. I sat on Appa's shoulders and thatched the roof, alternating long logs below and above the layers of metal and leaves to hold the roof in place. Appa smacked it a few times to make sure it wouldn't collapse under rain. There was no door, only a sheet to be dragged aside for us to enter and leave our new home. It was a small house and it took us two days to cobble it together.

The Japanese patrols started the next day. The soldiers were sharply dressed and carried themselves with arrogance. They strutted in pairs in the middle of Kallang Road, rifles hung in front like warning signs saying "Behave", fingers near the trigger saying "Do not give me an excuse to kill you". They stared disdainfully at the underclothes that had started hanging from the bamboo poles again, at the rubbish thrown outside and at the few boats that had started plying the river in search of work.

The locals started trickling out of their houses to go to

work and pretend life could continue as usual. When they saw the patrols, they squirmed even as they tried not to look uncomfortable. Once, a man broke and ran; the soldiers hollered and chased after him and they disappeared around the bend. A brief breakout of chaos, quickly replaced by the veneer of peace where everyone pretended nothing had happened in the hope that nothing would happen.

Appa noted that the soldiers patrolled Kallang Road at nine in the morning and four in the afternoon, making one pass in the direction of Jalan Besar. During those hours, he hid in a corner of our house and left the door open to show we had nothing to hide. He held me to make sure I didn't do anything stupid, but as the days passed and the patrols continued, I needed less and less warning.

A week after Surrender, I realised our small rice sack was almost empty and waited for nighttime to retrace my steps to the mama shop on Jalan Besar Road. No one had cleaned the dried blood that had spilled onto the street, and I imagined the shopkeeper's assailants dragging out his body in the sack to dispose of it, the blood soaking through the canvas.

I followed the red trail into the shop and it led to an emptied cash register. There were still spare rice grains that had spilled onto the ground. I thought we could boil the dirt away, so I took off my shirt and swept the grains into it, careful to avoid any blood-soaked rice.

I rolled up my shirt and took it back to Appa. When I showed him the rice, he frowned. "Did I raise a thief?"

The Mahatma was balancing the iron pot on four jagged stones, a slapdash stove. He had lit a fire with the broken branches underneath and only its weak orange glow and the moonlight shone upon the dark walls of the house. The haversack lay crumpled behind Appa. A few extra stones, a mound of red nails, a corroded hammer, and our leftover pickles sat listlessly on it. We had lain out the lumpy mattress beside the haversack and piled our clothes at its end. Appa had buried that useless weight of *The Jungle Book* the moment he accepted that the Japanese had won. The house stank of us and the river, but we had become used to it.

I said, "Appa, our rice is running out. I was hungry and I wanted to help you."

"We can find a kopitiam or a market or something. We still have money. We are not a family of thieves. Put that down."

I put my shirt filled with rice on the grass. "Appa, all the shops are shuttered." He touched the pot to feel it warm up and I pushed my case. "And there was no one in this shop. It was empty. The rice doesn't belong to anyone."

"Did you pay for it?"

"No, but everyone else is taking from the shops too."

"Thambi, what are you saying? So if everyone does something, that makes it okay? If everyone kills their fathers for food, will you stab me too?"

"Of course not, Appa."

"I raised you to be better than that."

"Then we should have helped the shopkeeper instead of worrying about stealing from him after he's dead!"

"What shopkeeper?" His eyes widened. "You went back to that mama shop. Thambi, that was different."

"Why?"

"What could we have done?"

"We could have tried. We didn't even try."

"Try? You're an eight-year-old boy. You must know your limits. How could we have fought off three armed men, all grown up? They would have killed you and me and strung our bodies upside down outside the shop. My job is to look after you. You are my first and only priority. What does the *Gita* say? We must all do our duty. My duty is to you."

"Why are you always scared? Why are you always running away?"

"Are you not afraid of the Japanese soldiers when you see them?"

"No."

Appa smiled. "Okay. You are more man than me. And I'm proud of you. But maybe one day when you have your own son to look after, you'll be afraid for him. Sit. I want to tell you something."

"What?" I sat cross-legged.

"Don't be rude, Thambi." Even his admonishingly arched eyebrow was kind. He was never angry with me. "Thambi, these Japanese are a different species from the British. You heard them going around with their loudspeakers telling the Chinese men to report for screening, for an examination. People say that the Japanese are looking for anyone who opposed them. And some people don't come back from the screening. You know Appa used to work for the British. Do you think they'll be kind to me if they find out? The Japanese are ruthless, Thambi. I want us to keep a low profile. This is serious. You cannot go around stealing or attracting any kind of attention, or we are both dead. You must listen to me. Will you do that please?"

The water started to bubble. I was tired of his excuses. "You didn't help the British fight. You didn't even help a dying man. And now you don't want to take free food when you can't even feed us. Why would the Japanese want you?"

Appa looked wounded that I thought the Japanese wouldn't want him. I bit my lip. I had not meant to hurt him. He said, "I know what I can and cannot do. You must too." He extended his hand, producing a packet of pandan leaf wrapped around rice.

He must have hoped to surprise me before we

started arguing. I hated myself then. I turned my head away and said, "I'm not hungry." I didn't deserve it.

"Take it. I know you are." He put on his fake parent smile, pretending to be unhurt and encouraging.

"You?" I asked.

"I've eaten."

For as long as I can remember, he never ate without me. "I don't believe you," I said. "I'll only eat if you take some."

His smile broke out more sincerely. In the end, he was my Appa, and when we got along I felt better. He said, "Okay. But will you behave?"

I nodded.

By erecting our makeshift home on grass, we had also effectively laid claim to some of the land around it, a mini-colonisation, so to speak. But over the next weeks and months, we shared this riverside property with other dwellers who arrived but never left, and I assumed they had fled their homes too. They constructed their shacks around ours and I started calling our shared land Garden Country.

And Appa and I were grateful for the other Garden Country residents. For one, our home blended into a maze of jerry-built houses that blocked our views of Kallang Road, which meant the Japanese soldiers couldn't see us from the road either. What's more, Appa didn't want to collect ration cards from the Japanese administrators because they would ask him many questions. So we planted sweet potato sprouts into the soil and let it rain and shine on it and we urinated on it and shat on it. After two months, we boiled and ate the potatoes. But we and the other residents could never know when our potatoes, tapioca, or anything else we reared in our commons would run out and so we shared our food. The farmers Wong and Chin kept chickens and Uncle Malik fished in the Kallang River. Appa occasionally bartered a potato for an egg or a small tarpon.

This was our banana money. And we helped each other to keep an eye on these chickens and vegetables in case robbers had any ideas, and warned each other if a Japanese patrol approached.

However, Appa did not trust the Garden Country dwellers, or anyone or anything for that matter. I sometimes caught cockroaches and grasshoppers, collecting them in glass bottles and giving them to Uncle Wong as chicken feed, in exchange for the tapioca crisps I heard his wife fry. But I lied to Appa that Aunty Wong gave me the crisps for free and did not tell him that I had climbed into the canal near Rochor Road and wandered among the homeless sleeping under sarongs to catch bugs. He would have banned me from leaving our house altogether.

Appa did not even like me talking to Uncle Wong. But knowing interaction was inevitable within Garden Country, he reminded me to talk as little as possible. Which is in general good advice. He said at every dinner, "Thambi, you remember that kampung house that we slept under? Remember, we used to live there. I reared chickens and farmed spinach and we lost everything during the war. Are you listening to me?"

"How do you grow spinach, Appa?"

"You put it in the soil and wait. One day, it grows up and never listens to you and asks you a thousand questions. Now, remember this. Don't say anything to anyone unless you are asked. Okay, Thambi?"

"Yes, Appa."

"And if you are asked…"

"We lived in a kampung and farmed spinach that talks back to their fathers."

"You rascal." He tried to pull my ear but I leaned away. He laughed. "But Thambi, no joking. There are informants everywhere and we cannot take the risk. Be careful what you say. These guys are scoundrels. Traitors. If I lay my hands on one, I will strangle them myself. Bastards." His eyes widened and he bit his lips. I was also taken aback by his vehemence. I hadn't imagined him capable of such intensity of feeling, let alone violence, even towards quislings.

Appa rubbed his callused legs miserably. "I'm sorry, I shouldn't have spoken like that. In fact, I shouldn't speak about these things to you at all. You are my thambi, yes, but sometimes I forget that you are also still a young boy. A big boy, but a young boy. And I should frighten you less with my scary stories. It's just that I want to protect you. But still, I'm sorry, Thambi."

"I'm big enough, Appa. Don't worry."

Quite frankly, I didn't see why any of our neighbours would care, and who would tell? I loved and respected Appa, but he was no hero. Why would the Japanese wander through the squalid smelly slum I had euphemistically named Garden Country to find him? Nevertheless, I promised Appa that I would keep my mouth shut and till today I am certain I kept that promise. I have no culpability for what happened next, beyond the fact that Appa and I had been too weak to stop it.

Seven months into the Occupation, Appa and I sat around the "stove" eating sweet potatoes boiled in coconut milk and water for dinner. We had lost much weight these months. Every time Appa shaved, it revealed a smaller and smaller visage, and his aquiline nose grew more and more bulbous on his face. His rib cage jutted out of his skin like the prongs of a fork and his stomach and arms curved inwards like spoons. But one advantage of being constantly hungry was that our appetites shrank too, so our stomachs required less food to feel full, and on average our state of hunger stayed miserably constant despite the food we had. After we ate, Appa dipped a finger into the pot. Satisfied it had cooled, he said, "Here.

Drink the water." I drank the saccharine liquid, careful not to waste a drop. After three regulated sips, I handed the pot to Appa.

In Garden Country, we were used to slippers and bare feet. So when thick leather boots crunched into the soil with strength and conviction, crushing our sweet potatoes and Kipling, our breaths caught.

An army of boots had swarmed onto our garden. Appa glanced at the shut door. Rising, he placed a finger on his chapped lips before carrying me to the corner farthest from the door, stepping onto the mattress. He sat, sinking into it, holding me in his lap, and we watched the door.

Through the tin wall, men spoke in hushed tones. But one soldier spoke loudly; deep, clear and assertive. He spoke in the guttural harsh chopping tempo of the Japanese language and I was clueless as to what he actually said, but understood that he was broadcasting his authority and impatience for Garden Country to hear. He went on for minutes until it became worse. It became quiet.

There was only the dark. We had thatched the roof so well by this time that even moonlight did not enter the house. I heard only our hearts beating, sensed that beat connecting all of us in Garden Country, throbbing with one question: Who did they come for? It was a waiting game where trying to pre-empt anything would guarantee us the fate we wanted to avoid in the first place, and so we waited. Appa hugged me tighter and his bones pressed against me. His breathing had become straggled over these months and it grew louder in my ear. He said, a whisper, *"Kadavule."*

God.

A lightning sound sprang from the door. The scrap metal sheet fell back. The house shook and a few loose leaves fell, but the house held. Japanese soldiers poured into the doorway and fanned outwards, yelling and screaming in guttural Japanese. White torchlight burst into my eyes, bright and blinding.

By the time my vision cleared, five soldiers had encircled Appa and me, their round helmets shaking, jabbing their rifles at us, angrily spitting out words, cautioning us, as if *we* threatened *them*. Appa shielded my eyes with one hand and I squinted through his fingers. Two troopers stalked towards us, one foot after another, barrels squared at Appa's face, shouting at him.

A soldier grabbed his left arm and Appa let go of me right away. The soldier pulled him on his side, away from me. The Arisaka rifles swivelled to follow Appa and I was suddenly released and alone in the cacophony of light and shouting. Before I knew it, I was running towards Appa. He shouted at me louder than all the Japanese soldiers combined, screaming in Tamil, "Stay there! Thambi! Don't come! Stay there, Thambi!"

The soldier dragging Appa let go and shoved his muzzle into Appa's face. He barked in Japanese, out-shouting Appa into shutting up. Appa sat on the ground with his legs splayed out and only stared at me and extended a hand. "Stay there! Thambi! Don't come!"

The other soldier let me run past him but grabbed my neck from behind and lifted me up. My windpipe clenched shut and my feet kicked air, trying to kick backwards into his groin. Appa's eyes widened and he tried to stand but the soldier kicked him in the stomach and he sprawled on the ground. The soldier pressed his boot onto his chest, standing on top of him like a statue of Vishnu destroying a rakshasa, the archangel Michael standing over Lucifer. Appa tried to shove that leg off, shouting in Tamil at the soldier, "Let him go! Let him go! Thambi!" He craned his neck to look at me and his words grew strained and breathless as the boot pressed deeper into his chest. The soldier thrust his barrel into Appa's face and yelled back at him. Appa's head fell back against the floor.

I bit into the forearm of the soldier holding me, tasting sour uniform, sweaty meat, the metallic twang of blood. He screamed and dropped me and I ran towards Appa, but another soldier blocked my way. He clenched me just below the neck, fixed me to the spot. I tried wrestling his hand off, twisting away, but his grip never wavered.

Two soldiers sat Appa up from behind and dragged him by the armpits, backwards and on his bum, towards the open door. Appa twisted his torso, bucked his hips, thrashed his legs in all directions, shouting, "Let him go! Let him go!" But the soldiers' faces were dour and uncaring, as if Appa wasn't writhing at all, as if they were just towing the fallen dead log of a tree to the side of the road so a car could pass. They had stopped shouting at him, given up trying to communicate with him.

Then Appa's eyes met mine, the only human relationship in the house. They grew large and worried and he was crying. He said, "Don't do anything, Thambi! Don't do anything, okay! It will be fine! It will be fine!" He said in English: "I love you, Thambi!"

I bit the hand holding me. But it slipped behind my head and grabbed a fistful of my hair and yanked it. I screamed and found myself staring up at the soldier.

He wore a peaked cap instead of a helmet. His black eyes, hawklike, contemplated me. At the edge of his right eye, a little scar had healed into a soft, white furrow. He had a bridge-like nose and a flat broad moustache and lips so thin they accentuated the contempt in his mien. His mouth sneered to the right in contemplation, enhancing his arrogance. He said in English, slowly and loudly as if it pained him to say it, but intended to be clear with his message. He was the man who had spoken so loudly and boldly outside. He said it in English but they were basic words and I caught them: "This is not your war."

Then he raised his pistol in his right hand, holding it by the butt high above my head. It gleamed, self-assured in all its power. It was as if the pistol had turned on a light and shone on all of us to reveal our strange equality at the bottom, this soldier, me, Appa being dragged away on his bum and shouting my name faintly in the distance. We were nothing without the favour of the gun. I shut my eyes and made to turn my head away, and felt the butt crash down on my nose.

...

When I woke up, I lay horizontal, staring at the blank ceiling. Everything seemed serenely orange. It was quiet. To remind me that I was alive, my nose throbbed. I put two fingers to it and pinched gingerly upwards from the nostrils. At the bridge bone, a sharp pain flared and I cried out. I focused on my breathing to let the pain subside. I could still breathe normally and assumed it was a benign bruise. A face entered my vision, blocking out half the ceiling, peering at me.

He was as bald as the sun on the Japanese flag, with predatory black eyes, a black moustache and a cut by his right eye. I kicked with hands and feet, scrambling backwards until my head hit a wall. I cried and held the injured balakkoo with one hand and looked around me. On my right, a rice-straw tatami mat blanketed the cement floor, a stony bed. Uniforms and white shirts hung on nails above it, the nails drilled in the straightest of lines, the uniforms pressed flat into the wall like posters. A greenish ochre military fieldpack sat at the head of the tatami, compact and ready to go. A shiny aluminium mess tin lay on its right with a rolled-up tissue like leftover food mopped up inside. On my left, a wide timber board rested on four standing bricks. The papers and pens on top suggested it was a desk that he sat on the floor to use. On the left of the desk lay a Type 99 Arisaka rifle, shortened to suit the close quarters of jungle fighting, cleaned and polished so the brown wood and black bolt gleamed. A pyramid of rolled-up papers rose next to it. On the other side of the desk there were a few patterned sake bottles and ceramic cups smaller than my fists. It was still dark outside and the orange light above us was on.

The Japanese soldier watched me, a shadow of amusement dancing on his lips. He knelt on one leg, leaning an elbow on it. He had removed his boots and had strikingly flawless white socks. A long *guntō*, sheathed in dark brown, hung from his left hip, declaring him to be an officer. He holstered the black automatic pistol he had slugged me with on his right hip, wrapped safely (for my sake) in russet leather. A white armband circled his left bicep and two red Japanese characters were emblazoned on it. I did not need to know Japanese to know what they meant: the Kempeitai—the Japanese Secret Military Police, the ghoulish all-powerful guardian of Japanese Fascism, its power honed into ruthlessness by racial supremacism and religious fervour. The Kempeitai wrote and enforced its own laws while it operated above them. They organised the screening centres Appa had been afraid of, led the pogroms of Chinese nationalists and British loyalists, massacred anyone who disagreed with them, and methodically ran everything in Japan-occupied Singapore from torture chambers to brothels—often using the threat of one to bolster the power of the other. Everyone knew the Kempeitai.

The night came back to me unsequentially, in one rush,

beginning with this soldier bashing me with the pistol, the soldiers invading my home, dragging Appa out, the harsh Japanese yelling, the lights flashing. Memory didn't need to order time and space to know what happened, it just did. But memory couldn't tell me where Appa was. Before I realised it, I had barked at him, my questions sounding braver than I felt. "Where is Appa? Where is Appa?"

He frowned at me and his lips sneered to the right again. "Indo-jin?" he said and I remembered his voice. It rang clearly. He said again, feeling the word as he pronounced it, "Indian?"

I nodded and said again with restraint, "Where is Appa?" I sounded like a beggar.

He tilted his head to the right. "Engurish?" he said.

I had learned a little of the language from the soldiers on Sembawang base. "Father where?"

"Mm." He lifted a hand high above his head, palm faced down as if he gripped a ball from its top. He was indicating a taller person and he said a word in Japanese and I knew it referred to father.

I nodded. "Father where?"

He put on a crestfallen face, more to communicate his message than to express his feelings. He brought his hand down and shook his sad face. Then he raised his eyebrows and shoulders, and lifted his palms upwards. It seemed like his torso had detached itself from his hips and ascended towards heaven. He looked around wonderingly, as if a toy was missing, as if looking for it, and puzzled and sorry, shook his head at me.

I nodded. "You know." Then I said in English, "You know."

He shook his head and raised his palms and searched around again. I needed him to know that I didn't believe him, that I deserved the truth, that I wanted Appa back.

I shouted in Tamil, finger accusingly pointed at him, "You know! Don't lie! You know!"

He shook his head sadly. I yelled, a throaty, pitiful war cry of a prepubescent boy. Scrambling to my feet, I charged him. What I was hoping for or expecting, till today I don't know. I didn't find out either. He calmly gripped my arms to my sides and held my body as I ran on the spot and screamed into his face. His grip was firm and strong and he watched me coolly, as if he were a father waiting for his child to calm down, which enraged me even more—that he presided over me so patronisingly, in a way I had not even allowed Appa to. I screamed louder and thrashed harder to break out of his hold. Tears ran down my face. I felt angry at the unfairness of my impotence. I believed then as a child, as strongly as I believe now, that I had done no wrong and wanted to do no wrong to anyone, whereas he had committed many atrocities and wanted to steal more fathers from their sons. Yet life had granted him power over me. It wasn't fair.

Soon, I stopped flailing and crying. He pushed me downwards, so I sat. He used a strong finger to lift my chin. I slapped it away and looked down, saying in a quiet mumble, "No touch me."

He touched my chin again and I slapped his finger. He pinched my nose at the bridge and pain seared through me. I screamed and swatted at his hands until he finally let go. Then I breathed heavily, exhausted from the pain and effort. He raised a finger at me, like a flagpole stuck out that said, "I am warning you." He lifted my chin again.

I let him and found myself gaping into his eagle eyes. The stinging in my nose ebbed but I was too afraid to touch it. He pointed at his chest and said, "*Rikugun* Kurosawa *desu.*" He articulated it slowly and with emphasis, thrice. He pointed at my lips and quacked his fingers.

I said, *"Rikugun* Kurosawa *desu."*

He shook his head. His hand wiped away at the air. *"'Desu' ga chigau."* He said in English, "No *desu*. No." He pointed at his chest again. *"Rikugun* Kurosawa."

Later, I learned that *"desu"* was a form of "I am". I had called myself, *"Rikugun* Kurosawa". Having corrected this, he quacked his fingers at my lips again.

I must have pronounced it right because he broke into a smile, flashing narrow white teeth. He nodded gleefully. *Rikugun* Kurosawa.

Lieutenant Kurosawa. Henceforth, I would call him that.

Kurosawa poked my solar plexus. He converted the poke to a questioning open palm. I told him my name. He frowned at me and I said it again. We spent a few minutes where he butchered and mangled my name and I half-heartedly repeated it. Finally, he smiled and nodded. He pointed at himself and said, "Lieutenant Kurosawa." He pointed at me and said, "Nanban."

I presumed he meant "friend" and I did not want to be his friend. I did not want him to baptise me like this. I told him my name again but he shook his head. "No. Nanban."

I shook my head and said my name.

He frowned strictly and crossed his wrists into an X. He brought both hands down and across each other like two katanas. He pointed at me. "Nanban." That was his name for me. No more discussion. What's in a name? Only people with power over others, like colonisers over subjects, slave-owners over slaves, parents over babies, can name them. I was Nanban because he said so. To accept it was to submit to him.

I nodded and he looked satisfied. Later, I learned "Nanban" meant "southern barbarian" in Japanese, which is ironic because I had thought it meant "friend", as "nanban" does in Tamil.

Anyway, perhaps pleased we had settled this matter and not ready for the frustrations of further communication, he stood up, towering over me with his hands on his hips, as if finalising our arrangement. Without irony, he said in English, "You safe here." He grabbed his rifle and left the house and I watched sadly as the Arisaka departed with him. Even if I did not know how to use it, it felt like an opportunity was slipping away into the night. I looked around the room and its alienness and emptiness made me feel lonelier.

But Kurosawa returned shortly, holding a wooden broom my height. He held it out and waited, and I took the broom from him. It was light. He gestured around the stony floor, which appeared clean to me. He grabbed the back of my neck and shoved it downwards, a quick firm jerk. Under the desk, at the back, a diaphanous cobweb adorned the eave like stage curtains. Kurosawa pointed at the web and the room and drew his slung rifle out. He made a sweeping motion with it and I hoped he would shoot himself in the foot. He said, "*Sōji. Sōji.*" He stopped and stared at me. "*Wakatta ka?*"

We had learned to say "*wakarimasen*" after the Surrender because that meant "I don't understand" in Japanese. It was a handy phrase, but also useful for bootlicking because it demonstrated that we had tried to learn our new lords and masters' language. Power, by its existence, simply demands. I assumed from Kurosawa's questioning face that he was asking if I understood him and swept the floor to demonstrate that I did.

He didn't say anything else. I asked, "Father?"

He shook his head. We were not to discuss this anymore. "*Sōji,*" he said and pointed at the table.

Giving up for now, I crawled onto my belly and stuck the broom into the saturnine crevice between the table board and floor. I heard Kurosawa step out of the room. I was alone again. The broom's bristles dragged the silvery cobweb away from the wall and the board jumped a little. Dust and gossamer swarmed towards my face.

"Appa," I said into the cranny, "where are you?"

I wanted to hear him say, "Thambi."

Nothing.

Appa?

I hated my father. He had deserted me. He always justified his actions, telling me it was for the best, it was for my safety. But now, I was in the hands of a Japanese Kempeitai Lieutenant. If only Appa had fought, fought for the 44th Indian Infantry Brigade, manufactured explosives for the Malayan People's Anti-Japanese Army, anything, we might have been better off. If only he had tried harder. After all, it could not have been worse than this.

I became angry, at Appa, at the lieutenant, at the world. I wanted to escape, to rescue Appa, and build a new life for us. One that I would control. One that would be *right*. I hated him.

I was alone and terrified.

I wiped the tears that started running from my eyes. As much as I hated Appa, I missed him very much too.

2

After the War

Her name was Papatti, pronounced Papa with a T, with the stress on the second "pa". It was 1952, seven years after the Japanese Occupation. Papatti didn't remember the Occupation, and the British ruled Singapore again now.

She was ten years old and tall for her age, but despaired that she still needed to take two steps for each of her father's to match his stride. Papatti marched between him and her mother along Jalan Besar Road. She was dressed in an azure tunic that matched the free sky, collar stiff to her chin. She had thrown a dark blue shawl over her left shoulder. Her baggy pants were dark blue too. Her snowy socks and shoes, which she had washed and dried twice to be immaculately free of dust, glimmered like the light. Papatti felt older and more dignified in her uniform.

She sidestepped the owner of the Kwong Soon Lights and Fans store coming out to spit phlegm, and almost knocked into a barber shaving a man's beard. The man sat slouched, falling asleep on the chair installed into the pavement outside the store as the razor stroked his chin. Papatti automatically placed a finger straight over her nose to make sure the pottu on her forehead remained centred between her eyebrows. She checked out the uniforms awash around her as other children hurried to school—polka-dotted white shirt on black skirt, beige shirt and pants tied with a maroon belt. She recognised a convent school's blue pinafore with regret. Like Papatti, the smaller children were chaperoned by their parents. The few older teenagers walked alone or in posses, chattering excitedly while their feet led the way they knew so well. Papatti wrinkled her nose at one puffing a cigarette, but envied their independence. One day, she would be one of them.

Ahead on Jalan Besar Road, a boy sat *à cheval* on the main bar of a tottering bicycle. His father sat on the rubber seat and cycled with legs pointed outwards so as not to knock his son onto the road, and Papatti felt relieved her father had not subjected her to that discomfort, even if he loved to cycle.

Some short boys had buzzed their heads bald for the new school year. Papatti understood that schools had strict rules governing hair length, but did these boys have to buzz their heads like Buddhist monks? Papatti released her mother's hand and reached for her hair. She had pulled her long, ramrod-straight black hair into a thick plait that shone with the oil her mother massaged into it every night. Her ribbon at the end had not fallen off.

"What are you doing, Papatti?" her mother said in Punjabi, hand stretched towards her.

Papatti elbowed a passing man's briefcase out of the way with a little violence. Body odour sledgehammered her. He peered at her queerly, tripped and hurried onward. The man's shirt was so damp a singlet showed underneath. She seized her mother's hand again.

Ahead, a woman was squatting and pouring water from

a pail over her two naked little sons, and Papatti and her mother raised their hands like a bridge as the younger boy hollered and ran between them, wetting the corridor with his footprints. Like them, there were other children not going to school. Two girls carried long sticks across their shoulders, rattan baskets hanging off them filled with clothes for the dhobi, the baskets swinging wildly. Another girl squatted beside her mother, plucking off the tails of beansprouts and pooling them on a newspaper like a mound of white tadpoles, along with water spinach, celery and brinjal. A boy grilled skewers on a low cart, the s-shaped smoke rising. She was glad not to be them.

Papatti's mother was a skinny Tamil woman called Lalitha, who wore a purple saree that captured the light tightly with a golden hue. The other women walking on Jalan Besar also wore darker shirts—or lighter materials—to thwart the tropical weather from besmirching their modesty. Despite the heat, Lalitha had wrapped a purple shawl around her head like a hood. Papatti's father was a tall, broad-shouldered Punjabi man called Rajpal, big but lanky. He was unnaturally fairer than her mother, and wore a short-sleeved white shirt and black pants over brown chappals. Papatti had selected, washed and ironed her parents' clothes the past week with all the diligence she believed a schoolgoing child should muster.

An old man dressed in brown shorts and a smeared white shirt like an overgrown schoolboy pushed a three-wheeled street cart of nasi lemak beside Rajpal and shouted his one-item menu at the oncoming cars, motorbikes and trishaws, and they honked back and swerved around him angrily. His son, of Papatti's age, was swinging his legs from the top of the cart and shouting Hokkien curses back at the vehicles. Ignoring him, Papatti said in Punjabi, "Amma, Appa,

I'm memorising the way already. By next week, you won't have to walk me to school anymore, okay? I can go myself. I won't walk close to the road. I won't talk to anyone. I won't even talk back to anyone. I promise. Amma please. I won't. I'm only talking back to you, not to a stranger! This is different. Amma!"

The eponymous Bencoolen Primary School on Bencoolen Road, where classes were taught in the Punjabi language, was a twenty-minute walk from Papatti's house on Serangoon Road. By the time they reached its campus, Papatti's sweat had mixed with the talcum powder on her face to form a creamy lather. Papatti wished she had talked less, a constant refrain from her amma that she never heeded until she was panting, as she was now.

Black iron gates sprung open onto a vast pink-cobbled courtyard. At the end, a three-storey polished white façade rose like a cliff face. Boys and girls in the blue hues of her uniform streamed in, noise billowing in their wake. Papatti had begged her parents for two years for this opportunity and finally, they had given her the chance. Soon, Papatti would attend classes independently, ask intelligent questions, find her clique, and walk between Serangoon and Bencoolen roads without parental supervision. In school, children ruled children.

Her appa knelt before her. Below his black turban, he had hefty round eyes, a voluminous nose that she liked to pull and a thin black beard that she loved rubbing. Papatti skirted his bear hug and pecked him quickly on his cheek. His open eyes and arms implored her still, but Papatti was more worried that her soon-to-be schoolmates had seen the sentimental kiss. He said, "You don't want to hug your appa?"

Her amma, Lalitha, not one for hugs and kisses, tapped her feet. Her round and fierce eyes, prominently hooked nose and strong cheekbones protruded out of a small, round, tight face. It would have been tight even if the heavens broke and God declared himself to her. A thick ring studded her nose, a bulkier version of Papatti's. She handed Papatti a tiffin box that shimmered in the torrid sun, reflecting Papatti's effort the night before to polish it. The tin felt warm and she had done a good job. Rajpal stood and held up a boxy backpack like a jacket for her to sling her arms into.

Lalitha said, "Behave, Papatti."

"Okay. You can go home now. See you!"

Before her appa could ask for another hug, Papatti ran through the gate and into the swelling throng of new schoolmates. In the courtyard, a turbaned, bespectacled teacher with a sage's thick beard was saying in Punjabi, "Quietly now children. I said *quietly*! Jaswinder, you know where to go. Go." He held a clipboard. A line of ten students had formed in front of him. Jaswinder, clearly a senior student, raised an eyebrow at Papatti and headed straight for his classroom.

At her turn, Papatti said, "Good morning teacher. I am Papatti, daughter of Rajpal."

"Who? Ah. You are Rajpal's daughter. Is he outside?"

"Yes teacher."

"Of course he is. You are all he talks about. Okay, wait." He unfurled a few papers and thumbed one victoriously. "Here." He turned and pointed at a block of tinted windows on the second floor. "Class 1B. It's that one. Can you see it?"

"Yes. Thank you teacher."

"You are tall for your level, aren't you?"

Papatti said, "Yes teacher. I—"

"I know, girl. Don't worry. It's not unusual for students to start late. Go and meet your new friends. I will see you shortly. Remember, have fun."

He winked and she liked him already. "Thank you teacher."

Papatti's tiffin box swung as she skipped to the staircase. From the second-floor corridor, she saw her appa slouched like a forlorn bear, waving meekly, while her amma had started walking off. Papatti waved once and entered her classroom.

Class 1B was filled with three rows of wooden tables and chairs painted in grey. Students had filled out the back row and sides and stared at Papatti with the hostility of strangers. Avoiding their gazes, Papatti found the table front and centre, as she had planned. She parked her bag against the table leg, pulled out a notepad and arranged two pencils at the head of the table before sitting, vision of propriety. A cinema-screen-like blackboard canvassed her view. A white metal-bladed fan swirled above her uselessly, clicking loudly after every full turn. Papatti puffed air downwards to cool herself. She would not compromise her primness by removing her shawl.

She glanced at the grey-rimmed doorway, anticipating her teacher's arrival. Then she turned to assess her new classmates, to see if she could make friends. They still stared back hostilely. Papatti tried a smile, lips closed and meek, and turned back to face the blackboard.

"Oi, you," she heard in Malay.

A rangy boy with white socks up to his knees sat beside her. She smiled nervously, her way of saying "hello".

The boy said, "Why are you here?"

"I don't understand."

"Oh. You speak Punjabi? How come?"

Papatti had grown up knowing she was adopted but not realising it, the way a child grows up knowing there are things such as clouds and a sun without actually stopping to stare and wonder what they were and what they were doing in the sky, until an adult said not to stare at the sun. At which point they stopped and stared at the sun, acknowledging the sun, and forever living consciously with the sun hanging over them.

The boy's question in Class 1B, her first encounter with that flat set of opinions sliced out of time called society, awoke her dormant consciousness and reminded Papatti that she was adopted. But she didn't feel comfortable stating this fact and, unsure how else to respond, for once did what Lalitha had taught her was the smartest thing to do. She kept quiet.

A girl behind her said, "Why do you have a bindi?" She had an equally meticulous plait that tossed from side to side with the cadence of her words. She pointed, but Papatti knew the Punjabi word for it.

"Why can't I?"

"You can I guess, but you're not Punjabi. What are you?"

The boy said, "Where are you from?"

"How do you pronounce your name?"

"Pa-Pa-Tee?"

"So you speak Tamil also?"

A round-faced girl with two pigtails hunched at the back with one foot on her seat and said, "You've got small eyes."

A few children laughed. Papatti could not help think that her amma always said never to put shoes on chairs. Lalitha would say, "Did I raise a gangster?"

The other girl with the plait said, "Don't be mean."

"It's just the truth. She's weird."

Papatti said, "You're weird."

"What did you say?" The gangster put her foot down and leaned forward, eyes flashing menacingly.

She had broader shoulders than Rajpal. The gangster said, "Say that again, small eyes." Papatti didn't want to say it again now that she had appraised the gangster's bulk.

Thick rubber-soled shoes clapped the concrete outside. The teacher with the clipboard drifted like a wraith across the windows. He emerged into the doorway and the students stood up, at attention. Relief flooded Papatti.

"Good morning class," he said in Punjabi.

"Good morning teacher."

He took off his glasses. His grey eyes twinkled as he smiled. "Let's see if that energy lasts till the end of the year. You can call me Mr Singh."

"Good morning Mr Singh."

"Good morning. Sit. Sit. I'll be your form teacher and English teacher. Sorry I'm late."

After Mr Singh left the classroom, the gangster, whose name was Kareena, said, "Oi, you. Small eyes. Did you understand him?"

Papatti didn't turn around. Her amma had said, "Don't talk back to anyone. Don't get into trouble. Keep your head down, study hard, and get a good reputation. Okay, Papatti?" Besides, Kareena, a stocky Hanuman-like gangster, was bigger than Papatti.

Kareena said, "Well if you didn't, I won't help you!"

More laughter.

"Small eyes."

The next day, Papatti first learned about the problems that arise from the democratic freedom of choice when Kareena sat behind her. Papatti would have preferred everyone to be forced to sit in the seats they had chosen on the first day, as she had. Mrs Dhillon, a portly middle-aged woman in a long, swishy skirt, wrote addition equations on the blackboard for them to practise. As Papatti bent forward to write, pain tore at her hair roots and her head was yanked back. Kareena released her plait immediately. A few snickers erupted.

Mrs Dhillon glanced up from three rows down, where she was tutoring Manjeet. "What's happening? Papatti, stop playing with your hair and write your sums."

She crimsoned. "Yes, Mrs Dhillon."

Then her hair was yanked again and she yelped.

"Papatti. What's wrong with you? If you cannot behave you will sit outside and do your sums, do you understand?"

"But Mrs Dhillon—"

"No buts. Now, finish your work."

"Yes, Mrs Dhillon."

The shame of being scolded stung more than her roots. Papatti had wanted to show Mrs Dhillon that she was studious and trustworthy, a class topper. From behind, a whisper, "Small eyes." More stifled chuckles.

Over the next weeks, the gangster teased Papatti. Kareena's sheer loudness and sass and all-round gangsterishness won the admiration of their classmates. Trying to endear themselves to Kareena, to be part of her gang, they called Papatti "weird" and "small eyes". They asked if she was contagious, told her to go home, told her she didn't belong. Papatti became the scapegoat for Kareena's popularity and class solidarity.

Papatti maintained a partially stoic, partially fear-induced silence, trying to focus on classes instead, feeling better for her progress in understanding the symbols on the board and in deciphering equations. She loved Mr Arvinder's art lessons. He drew a tombstone on the board at the start of class and inscribed the time left till the final bell inside it. He said, "Are we dead when we stop learning or do we stop learning when we are dead?" and they all laughed thinking he was silly. Under Mr Singh's patient tutelage, she started reading entire English words at a go. At home, she rewrote her math homework thrice so it flowed in her best handwriting without cancellation marks, even if her teacher eventually planted a giant red cross on the bottom of the page.

But it was the jabs that hurt. She wanted friends too.

Only the plait-pruning girl called Jaspreet ate with her during recess. They played hide-and-seek and hopscotch after school before walking home together, since Jaspreet lived in a shophouse on Tessensohn Road, past Serangoon Road.

On the eleventh week, Jaspreet and Papatti walked to the playground near school. They wiped the white pigeon poop from the black rubber swings before competing to see who could swing the highest, judging by the tip of their toes. Jaspreet whooped as her equally scrubbed white shoes nipped past Papatti's, poked a cloud in the sky, and Kareena said, "It's the weirdo! And the weirdo's friend! Weirdo Two? Big eyes?"

The gangster encroached onto the playground with Simran, Jessie and Aksha. Papatti grounded her feet to halt the swing, lurching to a stop. She tightened her grip on the metal chains carrying the seat tighter.

Jaspreet said, "Stop it. Leave us alone."

"Or what?"

"I'll tell Mr Singh."

"I'll tell him you started it. Will he believe the four of us or the two of you? Plus, you have the weirdo on your side. Who'll believe her?"

Papatti said, "Stop calling me that. Why don't you just leave?"

"No. You leave and give us the swings."

Jaspreet stuck her chin out. "We were here first."

"This playground is ours," Kareena planted herself in front of them, hands on stocky hips.

"Says who?" said Jaspreet.

"Me."

Papatti wanted to be just as brave as her friend. She said, "You are not the owner of this playground. Go away. Leave us alone."

"Is that so?" Kareena pounced and grabbed Papatti's ankles.

"Stop it!" Papatti said, trying to kick, but Kareena clenched Papatti's legs snug to her waist, which was when Papatti realised with mortal fear that her assessment had been right, and that Kareena was indeed far stronger than she was. She was doomed to die that day. Kareena wrenched backwards with a heave and Papatti's bum lifted off the black saddle. She tightened her hold on the creaking chains and became suspended horizontal in mid-air. "Let. Go. Of. Me!"

"Leave her alone!" Jaspreet leapt off her swing but Simran and Jessie blocked her path. Jaspreet slapped at them, and they punched and kicked back, and in the catlike flurry Jaspreet tripped backwards over the swing and tumbled to the ground, shouting, "Stop it! Stop it! Help!"

Papatti yelled for help too, bucking her hips to try and throw Kareena off.

Aksha tried to prise Papatti's fingers off the chains but Papatti wiggled her fist up and down the metal links. Then Aksha's slimy wet teeth bit into Papatti's hand, and with a scream Papatti let go and fell to the ground, head banging against the stony floor, Kareena also falling. The bigger girl climbed onto her and raised a hand. A hard slap landed on Papatti's left cheek before she brought her arms up to cover her face. More slaps rained on her arms. Then Kareena pulled her hair up and down and beat her stomach and all Papatti could do was jerk and writhe on the floor and scream.

"Who's that? What's happening there?" It was a deep voice. Hurried footsteps nearing. The weight lifted and Papatti blinked. She saw a high and clear blue sky. Kareena and her gang had disappeared. Jaspreet sobbed by the swing, curled around their schoolbags.

Papatti crawled to her hands and feet, and as the

adrenaline left, her cheek burned, her stomach ached, her hair felt like nettles, and deep down, in her soul, in that place that belonged to her and only her, she felt as if someone had violated her. She was humiliated. "I'm sorry, Jaspreet. This is my fault."

"Papatti. Jaspreet. What happened to you two? Were you fighting?"

Mr Singh's familiar, concerned eyes gazed at her.

"Come, girl. Stand. I'll walk the two of you home. Slowly now. We can talk later."

...

Two lines of two-storey shophouses with sloping roofs fenced in and watched over Serangoon Road. The Sri Veerakaliamman Temple and the Masjid Angullia interrupted the shophouses at different junctions, religious guardians of that concentrated Indian community. The open-air Tekka Market marked the beginning of the road, where it shared a junction with Sungei Road. Papatti and her parents lived in a white house with maroon-painted wooden shutter windows and maroon awnings (covered with cardboard and littered with a fallen shirt belonging to Rajpal) on 111 Serangoon Road. The first floor had been converted into Govinda's Textiles Emporium, so named to convey scale and options and grandeur, even though it was just a small business. On the second floor, Papatti's family occupied one room of five, and a kitchen and dining table in the middle of the rooms constituted the living room.

When Rajpal returned home, Papatti was slumped over the dining table, hair frazzled, puffy-eyed, dried tears on her cheeks like wax. A warm, pink handprint shone on her left cheek. Lalitha sipped tea and contemplated her daughter from the stove. Rajpal's eyes widened. "What happened?"

At the distress in his voice, Papatti cried and ran to hug him.

Lalitha said, "Your beiti got into trouble."

"My beiti? No. Beiti, let me see your face. Did someone hit you? What is this? Lalli!"

"Sit, dear. She'll tell you."

He whisked Papatti to the dining table. Between snivels, Papatti recounted Kareena's bullying and assault on her at the playground. Rajpal pulled up her shirt and saw the purple-blue splotches on her waist. His chair fell back with a deafening thud as he stood. Rajpal quivered, fists clenched, and Papatti realised that she had never seen him angry. But his anger comforted her, made her feel like she was in the right, made her even feel better. "Did you see that?" He glared at Lalitha, as if it were Lalitha's fault.

"Yes, I did."

"And you're not angry?"

"Of course I am!"

"Then why aren't you doing something about it?"

"What do you expect me to do?"

Rajpal started pacing between the table and a metal cabinet set against the wall. The doors of the cabinet were removed and it had been converted into an altar that Papatti prayed at (or more precisely, asked a thousand wishes in front of) every morning. Small but elaborately sculpted ceramic statues of Krishna and Radha, Ganesha, Saraswathi, and other Hindu gods stared out of the cabinet. In the centre of the statues, a white wick stuck its head out of a bowl of oil, a curious snake with a fiery head. Behind the statues, larger, faded pictures of these gods stood alongside lifelike prints of Sikh gurus with long, white beards and scarves wrapped around their heads. Above the gods and gurus hung murky grey photos of Lalitha's and Rajpal's parents. The men in the photos wore smart jackets while the women wore their best sarees, which all only appeared black and white in the photos. Holy ash and vermillion, vibhuti and kungumam, were rubbed onto the glass frame, onto the middle of their foreheads as blessings. Rajpal inspected the photos. "I'll tell you what I'm going to do. I swear on my parents' heads. Your parents too."

Lalitha said, "Don't bring *my* parents into this."

"I will go over to that school, and I will find that Kareena girl and chop her hands off. You mark my words. How dare she touch my daughter! How dare she bully her? Who does she think she is, that little Japanese tyrant? And that Aksha girl. I will rip her teeth out one by one."

Rajpal's rage continued to gratify Papatti, and she felt ever more in the right. She could see Aksha toothless, see Kareena handless, and it felt so right and sweet and good. She felt better. Lalitha said, "Don't talk rubbish dear. You don't mean that. We will go and see the teachers and find out what's happening first."

Papatti only wished her amma would support her more vociferously. When Lalitha had first seen Papatti, she had cursed. Then she shouted at Mr Singh, wagging her finger furiously at him, and Mr Singh nodded and took the scolding like a good obedient student. Only then did Lalitha collect herself and give Mr Singh some tea before sending him on his way. She ordered Papatti to take a warm bath and nap until her appa came home. In this interlude, Lalitha seemed to have calmed down, back into her tight, emotionless self.

"For what?" Rajpal thumbed his fist up and down at Lalitha. Papatti's hope rose, though she did not know what to hope for. "This is my daughter we are talking about. My daughter! I have never hit her my whole life. How dare someone lay a hand on her? How dare she? What kind of school are they running? I will burn the whole compound to the ground. She is my daughter!"

"Dear, you are talking nonsense. This is not the Occupation and you are not Sivaji Ganesan."

Papatti wished it were the Occupation if it meant her father would be allowed to slice Kareena into pieces like that expensive Japanese food. Rajpal said, "Racists! They are racists! Just like the Occupation."

"They are children. Dear, sit down, please."

"How can I sit calmly after seeing that? What did Mr Singh say? Where is that bugger?"

Lalitha said, "He called an hour ago. The other girls— Kareena and her gang. They said Papatti and Jaspreet started the fight. They were in the playground when Papatti and Jaspreet shouted at them and dragged them off the swings. They fought back and ran off. They said Papatti has been calling them names and pinching them and whatnot since the first day of school."

"I have not, Amma! That's a lie!" Tears bubbled up again. The impotence of her truth hurt more than anything.

"Well it's your word against theirs. I am taking your side. Their mothers will take their side. Mr Singh is a good man but he cannot take any side, right or not? What to do?"

Rajpal said, "Well maybe if I knock his head a few times at the kopitiam he will come to his senses. What kind of institution is he running?"

He pounded the cement in quiet, and after long moments, Rajpal righted the chair, sat and released a long breath. "If we file a complaint, the teachers will scold that Kareena girl and our Papatti but after that the students will only pick on Papatti more. The teachers can watch out for her in school, but what if they bully her after school again? At the playground? On the way home? We both have work. We cannot pick her up from school every day. What happens if that Kareena girl decides to go beyond punching next time? And that poor Jaspreet. How is she?"

Papatti didn't understand. Why had her appa mellowed? Why was he admitting defeat? She yearned to see him yell and rage and threaten Kareena. Lalitha said, "Her parents came over just now. They are okay, but..."

"But what?"

Lalitha glanced her way. "I'll tell you later."

"What Amma?"

Rajpal shook his head. "Their daughter has more heart than them."

"What Appa?"

Lalitha said, "Nothing. Keep quiet."

"They don't want her to play with me?"

Rajpal said, "You don't care about them, Papatti. None of this is your fault. Okay? What do you want to do?"

"I don't want to move schools again."

Two years ago, Papatti's parents had sent her to the Convent of Holy Infant Jesus on North Bridge Road, an all-girls' school where she wore a blue pinafore and classes were taught in English because Rajpal had wanted the best education for his daughter, and the closer it sounded to a British education, the better it was supposed to be. Five months in, during one lesson, Mr Johnson had said, "Come Papatti, you're always so quiet. What's the answer to number two?" He pointed at the blackboard, that perennially imposing screen. Cinemas were so much more fun, and cheaper than studying too.

Mr Johnson was her short spritely English-language teacher who liked to wear chequered shirts. He spoke with a lilt and flair, and grinned at Papatti encouragingly.

She scrutinised the second line on the board, with a long

dash running in the middle of it. She scoured it for clues, a T here, an E there. She counted the letters and discovered the first word: *The*. Her classmates watched her, impatient. The rest of the letters were like Chinese characters that she needed to unlock. She leaned forward to demonstrate she was trying, narrowed her eyes, bit her lips. *Ummed* and *ahhed*. Finally ...

"I-I don't know, Mr Johnson."

Two hands shot up, the show-offs.

Mr Johnson's smile widened. "No, no, give Papatti a chance. Take a guess, Papatti. So many words are available. Try."

She shook her head. "I-I'm sorry. I'm sorry. I don't know, Mr Johnson."

"You must at least try."

Papatti took a deep breath. She focused on the white words. *Su..Tuu..Da..Eh..*

A classmate cleared her throat. Another tapped her table. Papatti was holding the class back, restraining their progress. "I'm sorry. I don't know Mr Johnson."

Mr Johnson's grin vanished, replaced by a blacker frown. The tapping quieted. An icy, brittle silence filled the classroom and the hands went down. "We've been covering adjectives for two weeks now. Have you been daydreaming the whole time, girl?"

His displeased scowl. His jarring tone. Papatti nodded to appease him.

A few girls chortled. A few girls glowered at her even more reproachfully, angry on Mr Johnson's behalf. Mr Johnson said, "Oh for the love of— If you don't want to learn then don't come to school. It's as simple as that. No one's forcing you to be here. Some of the girls have quit. Why don't you?"

"I-I'm sorry, Mr Johnson. I-I want to learn. I want to learn." She had tried reading her second-hand textbook every day at home. But her parents couldn't help her. They spoke Punjabi and Tamil but not English, and read none. So she would stare at the textbook, hoping that flipping the pages and identifying random letters would somehow and someday produce a grand clarity. She wanted to ask questions in class, but that would attract this very type of attention, and she didn't want to be the class idiot. She sank into the chair and bowed her head. "I'm sorry, Mr Johnson."

"Ladies. Can someone educate Ms Papatti here on the answer?"

More hands speared the air. Stephanie Vijendran Anthony didn't wait for Mr Johnson to select her. "A *dumb* student, Mr Johnson!"

Uproar in the classroom. Chair legs screeched back. Students clutched their stomachs and laughed, pointing at her. Papatti's eyes pricked with embarrassment. She shut them. Tsu Ting said, "Stephanie was rude, Mr Johnson."

"Yes Stephanie, that was rude. Oh no. Papatti, don't cry. It was just a joke. You poor thing. I'm not angry anymore. See? Come, why don't you take a break? Go to the toilet and freshen up." He was in front of her, smiling sympathetically, pointing at the door. He circled his hands to pretend to wash his face and said, "Toilet? Wash face? Don't worry child. Go on now."

She swept her notebook and pencils into her boxy bag and sprinted out, a wet film blurring her vision, a glimmer of Mr Johnson's amazed countenance, flashes of faces staring at her in shock. She didn't return.

Papatti had asked her parents to send her to a Punjabi or Tamil school instead. She begged, whined, pulled her hair and cried for two years. She wanted to study. She wanted to learn about the world. She wanted to have friends and play catch and share secrets with them. Her amma didn't see the need for her to attend school, especially since she had already failed once. Finally, Rajpal had coaxed Lalitha to let Papatti attend the school his friend taught in. Now, after her second disastrous attempt, Rajpal said, "Do you want to try the Tamil school on Victoria Street, Beiti?"

"You spoil her," Lalitha said.

"No Appa, it will be the same thing."

Rajpal said, "What same thing? This Kareena girl won't be there."

"No one there will know me either. They will call me weird and tease me. I don't want it." Papatti shook her head.

"You are special, Beiti. Come, sit on Appa's lap."

Lalitha rolled her eyes. "Yah yah so special she must go to school. None of the neighbours' children went to school. Why does she need to? She'll wait another year to enrol and if she quits again then *I'll* be the laughing stock. She might as well stay at home and be useful."

"Who cares about you, woman? Come, Beiti. Don't listen to your amma."

Papatti hopped off her chair and Rajpal picked her up tenderly. "Does it hurt?"

"No Appa. But Amma is correct. If I fail again, people will call me stupid. And if I wait another year, I'll be a giraffe in class."

Her amma grunted affirmatively. Rajpal laughed. "A very pretty giraffe. Beiti, don't care about what people think. That's your amma's bad habit. Do what you want. Do you want to stay in Bencoolen Primary School?"

"No."

"Why?"

Papatti slumped. "If Jaspreet won't play with me anymore, I will have no friends. Why doesn't anyone like me?"

"They are silly children. What's more important is that

you enjoy studying. You stood on one foot demanding to go to school. I come home and see you poring over your papers like my own little scholar. I am so proud of you. If you want to study, study. We'll figure a way around this Kareena girl. I will pick you up every day from school if that's what it takes."

"But Appa, I want people to like me."

"They do, Beiti. Your amma and appa do."

"That's not the same."

"Why?"

"You have no choice."

He chuckled. "Beiti, people will come and go. Forget them. The only important people are those who stay. And the only important thing is that you follow your heart. Now, what do you want to do? Do you want to study?"

She caressed his beard gently and felt better. "It's okay, Appa. It wastes your money."

"You are too young to be worrying about money."

Lalitha said, "Eh. Listen to your beiti. She's got more brains than you. We are not printing money in this house. We've tried, two times. Nothing's come of it. She doesn't like it anymore either. Let it go. Why does a girl need to go to school anyway? What will a book teach her about marriage and housework and making money? She can be a good girl and stay at home and help me."

Rajpal gently tilted Papatti's chin up. "Beiti?"

His large eyes beckoned. His soft smile said be not afraid. "What do you say?"

She couldn't find the words to express this conflict within her, between the ease of giving up and letting go, and the feeling that the right thing to do was to stick it out in school. To grit her teeth and confront the bullying and the seeming impossibility of acquiring an education. Her bruises still throbbed. She just didn't know. Papatti toyed with her fingers. She wanted her parents to make the right decision for her, insist she stay in school, tell her they would support her fight through it, like her appa had been defending her all this while. After all, they were the only ones who cared about her and she couldn't do it without them.

Lalitha said, "That's it. She will stay home. No one will touch my daughter in my house."

Papatti frowned. It felt easy when Lalitha said it, but also wrong. A dulcet whisper surrounded Papatti. Rajpal's voice. "Beiti. Are you sure?"

Papatti started crying. She wanted to go to school, but she was scared.

"Uh oh. Uh oh." Rajpal hugged her, made soothing noises. "Don't cry, Beiti. Don't cry. You don't need to go to school. It's okay. I love you, Beiti. Don't worry. No one will hurt you. I'm sorry I pushed the matter. It's okay now. I love you."

She hugged him.

Lalitha stood up. "Come, I will teach you something they won't teach you at school."

Papatti perked up. She dried her eyes against her appa's pocket, sniffing. Rajpal was caressing her hair, singing a Punjabi folk tune into her ear. She asked, "What's that, Amma?"

"How to survive." Lalitha went into their bedroom and Papatti followed, chucking academics at the door.

A primrose yellow wardrobe stood opposite the door, three rolled-up rattan mats leaned against it. Every night, Papatti unfolded the mats for her family to sleep on and their three bodies would fill up the small floorspace. Next to the cupboard, a single maroon shutter window had been set into the wall, slats of white moonlight falling upon the grey floor.

Lalitha turned on the light. A wooden Singer sewing

machine stood at the end of the room, with a low wooden stool before it like a temple and devotee. The machine consisted of a swivelling pedal beneath to control the speed of the needle, a chestnut wooden tabletop in the middle to lay cloth upon, and an L-shaped instrument above that stapled down the needle. A row of square, pocket-sized drawers lined the front of the tabletop, holding bobbins, needle sets, pincushions, a measuring tape, spare buttons and endless stacks of safety pins that were the house's back-up plan for every contingency. A yellow wooden metre rule jutted out from behind the machine.

Lalitha walked to the stool. She said, "Sit."

"Amma, you'll let me touch your sewing machine?" The Singer looked intimidating in that big and confident American way.

"Can you do one thing without talking back? Now sit. This is what you do. Listen carefully and don't talk back."

...

Every day, first thing before a dosai or uppuma breakfast, Papatti sat in front of the Singer sewing machine, and Lalitha trained her in the basic stiches and principles of needlecraft. After breakfast, she went to the shop below to observe Lalitha help Govinda with tailoring, alterations and repairs for his textile business—an individualised vocational training programme.

From Lalitha's long ruler, Papatti learned the conversion ratio from centimetres to inches and honed a surgeon's eye for marking and cutting length. Her vocabulary expanded to include technological nomenclature like "take-up lever" and "presser foot", and she talked back to her amma in these terms too. Within weeks, Papatti learned the physics behind the basic lockstitch so well that she could subconciously time the milisecond in which the hidden rotating hook of her machine caught the thread from the needle and carried it one full circle around the bobbin case before pulling it up into the fabric with a satisfying click. Progress.

Downstairs, in the violet-curtained fitting room, Papatti learned that an armscye should end right over the shoulder and men's trousers should fall at the anklebone to sit weightlessly on shoes. She observed that women were varyingly comfortable about the amount of skin they showed on the back of their bodices. Whampoa athai liked a "window", Rani liked a "door", and Veena kept an "open house". She also learned never to tell Veena this, but Lalitha had already lost a customer by then. Nevertheless, within a few months, Lalitha and Govinda deemed Papatti competent enough to let her poke her needle into garments that would actually be sold, and Govinda paid Papatti a commission (and Lalitha, of course) for helping with his "Emporium".

When Papatti turned 11, Govinda walked her around his shop like they were touring an art gallery. Rolls and rolls of bright saree fabric covered the walls, with wooden counters in front of them to spread the sarees out in layers so customers could compare them, feel the materials and inspect the colours. At the entrance, three female mannequins showed off Punjabi suits. Two rows of hangers ran down the middle of the store, with readymade shirts, pants and Punjabi suits hanging off them. Papatti tended to linger at the back during working hours, where the cashier and fitting room were. Govinda took one roll of carrot-orange garment from the shelves. He placed the triangular end over a roll of deep cobalt blue. It looked like an early sunrise. Govinda said in Tamil, "These are complementary colours. They contrast and create space and depth in between the colours. This captures your gaze in this space, in this depth. Do you see?"

Papatti nodded, wide-eyed and indeed captured. She made a mental note to stitch a turned hem that would reproduce this delightful contrast for her appa. Govinda took a pink shirt off the rack and laid it over his lap behind the cashier. "This is a good example. It's not ours, but I use it to explain how high our quality is to customers." Papatti appreciated that he now called the shop, "ours". Govinda's dark bony finger followed an inseam from the waist up to the armpit, and stopped. He had a tailor's sure and steady hand. At the ring around the armpit, the seam zig-zagged an inch before running down the sleeve. Govinda slotted two dark fingers into this mismatching inch. "Do you see? Obvious right? Look at this."

He deftly inverted the shirt. The inner seams were red instead of pink. "They think no one will know. But it's in the places no one knows that you discover the true quality of a garment. Tsk. See. I just noticed this." A thread was loose and he pulled it out. He shook his head. "These details make our shop better than the rest. Including those fellows on Buffalo Road. Ah, a customer. Time to make money, eh Papatti."

Papatti rose from her stool to be polite. But this time, Govinda stayed seated. "Papatti, why don't you talk to the customer?"

"Really, Govinda mama?" Uncle.

"Yes. Why not? I've prepared you for this, right?"

"I don't know, Govinda mama."

"Yes, I have. You can do it. Can you do it?"

Hesitantly, she nodded. "Yes, Govinda mama."

"Remember, no colour, pattern or design matters if…"

"The clothes don't fit you perfectly."

He clapped. "That's my girl. I told you you're ready. Now, go. Shoo." He waved his hands like chasing away mynahs.

A lithe lady had stepped in, fingers flicking through the dresses on the rack, eyes running across the saree walls. She was so tall, so fashionably dressed, so independent. Papatti felt that this woman must be a somebody who had plenty of somebody friends. She nimbly stepped around the cashier, walked up to her and gave her best smile. The lady looked at Papatti curiously, but Papatti said in Malay, "Welcome. My name is Papatti. Can I help you?" The lady beamed and her smile lit a warm glow within Papatti.

It struck Papatti then that this lady could actually like her, that her somebody friends and other people could also like Papatti, if she was useful to them, and that sewing could empower Papatti to be useful to them, to help her be liked and accepted by the strange world that lay beyond 111 Serangoon Road and Govinda's Textiles Emporium, a world that she had only had unfortunate glimpses of at school. Whatever her heritage, whatever her lack of education or riches, people would flock to her for sartorial ideas and to see these ideas materialise in cotton and polyester thread counts, because she would attend to them with diligence and a practised genius. Even Kareena would one day knock on her door to apologise and ask to be friends with Papatti and have a baju fitted. So as Papatti guided the lady across the gallery of fabrics the way Govinda had toured her, she determined that once she made this sale, for she would make this sale, she would throw herself even more earnestly into her needlecraft and brand a name for herself in the rag trade.

She sold the lady not one, but two sarees, and became even more confident that she could learn and improve every gram of value that Govinda's Textiles Emporium offered its patrons. So when Papatti watched customers argue with Govinda about paying extra to return their clothes to their original sizes, Papatti asked her amma to teach her to weave the hem stitch such that it tucked away the excess cloth instead of cutting it out, so that if her customers put on weight or their children grew older, she could just unpick the stitches with a needle's tug. When coolies like Rahim complained to Govinda that they were losing wages per hour away from work because they had to keep getting their tattered work clothes darned, Papatti scoured the markets for thick interfaces to back and strengthen the clothes so they ripped less easily. At night, she sketched new saree designs on her old school notebooks to propose to her customers, depending on their skeletal frames. Govinda praised her initiative, and for the first time, someone who was not Rajpal had complimented her. Govinda then followed this by giving Papatti a larger commission, and she took it as affirmation that she had won her first fan and was on the right track.

In between, when Lalitha chastised her for not holding the loose thread as she started pedalling the machine, or when Lalitha brought idli downstairs for their short lunch break, or when they discussed how Papatti could have haggled better with a sarcastic customer, Papatti also managed to ask her amma the questions she had wanted to ask at school. Like:

"Amma, how does the first bus driver go to work?"

"Amma, why are they burning the buses?"

"Amma, the Indian philosopher who said that a mother is happiest hearing her son praised—why doesn't he mention the daughter?"

"Amma, did you want a daughter?"

"Amma, why am I adopted?"

"Amma, where is Japan?"

3

Dedicated to Papatti

I swept Kurosawa's room, gathering the dust and trash into a knoll by the door. Then I went outside. A soldier sat on the porch, inspecting his nails, his squished peaked cap resting on a knee. He was a shorter, portlier version of Kurosawa, with a rounder face and stubble staccato over his head, and he wore no sword. Kurosawa was nowhere in sight.

I realised where I was: Jalan Besar, not a few hundred metres from Garden Country, and down the road from the mama shop that Appa and I had argued over, an incident that now made me feel so foolish. Kurosawa's house stood at the end of Jalan Besar Road. The road and its adjoined pavement curved into a kerb around his house, and while the road transformed into Perak Road and drove east again, the kerb melded into a grassy patch like a backyard. A few Angsana trees festooned the patch, thunder-trunked and crowned with thick bushy leaves, obscuring Perak Road from Kurosawa's house, which I assumed was a relief for the people staying on Perak Road.

My chappals lay by the side of the door, next to two pairs of straw slippers and dark brown military boots, all lined in strict attention, toes to the wall. Above the doorway, a dark cedar structure was set into the wall. The structure resembled a mini Japanese mansion, with a gable pagoda-like roof on top of two small, ornate and open doors. Three small steps led up to the doors. A polished round mirror was safely embedded into the centre of the doors and lightning-white strips of paper hung from the roof. On the table, sprigs of sasaki plants stuck out of two white ceramic vases. A white bowl of sticky white rice, a white jar of water and two unlit white candles were also placed as offerings. It was a Shinto altar, or as I would later learn, a *kamidana*, emblem of my destruction.

I bowed to the soldier and he jerked up. He rose and said, "Nanban." He pointed at himself. "Corporal Yamashita *desu*."

I understood and bowed again. Then I made a sweeping motion with my right hand into a cupped left hand, hoping Yamashita understood my request for a dustpan.

They say the Greeks invented Asia by declaring everything eastwards of Anatolia one and the barbaric same, as if Iran and India and China could be summarily understood through these four sibilantly connected letters, flowing as one breath— Asia. Of course, sitting in their Parthenon, the Greeks coined the moniker long before the first European traders and Jesuits set out east, or the American Wright brothers invented the aeroplane, or the Chan Brothers sold tourism packages, but the label has stuck. Thousands of years later, the Kempeitai appropriated it, claiming that Japan would rescue us from white colonialists and build an Asian empire, an Asia for Asians as they called it, a big happy non-Greek family where of course, Japan was the Appa. But thinking back to that day, when Yamashita stared confusedly at me, struggling to decipher my sign language, I still wonder if he bought into his own propaganda. It goes without saying (and hence must be emphasised) that a Japanese master turned out to be very different from a British one, but just as different as the Japanese soldier was from me. But here I digress.

At that moment, I pointed at the mound of dirt and rubbish and Yamashita's eyes lit up in a fleeting moment of inter-Asian understanding. He nodded and crossed Jalan Besar Road, disappearing into a shophouse. Then he returned with a dustpan cut from a golden tin biscuit container, with a long wooden handle attached. I scooped up the rubbish and was about to dump it into the uncovered drain running along the road when Yamashita said, "Eh!"

He waved his fingers in front of his nose.

The drain was cluttered with soggy, black detritus and smelled of urine. I didn't see the difference but Yamashita shook his head firmly. Seeing no dustbin in sight, I decided to dump everything into the Rochor River nearby. The roads were wide and empty then and I walked with the dustpan held before me and faced up to the stygian sky like a metal detector.

Yamashita followed me. I suspected that his orders were to watch over me until Kurosawa returned. I also suspected that he preferred simply to follow me instead of trying to communicate another way for me to dispose of the rubbish. It felt creepy walking along a dark empty road knowing a Japanese soldier was trailing me. Whenever I turned, Yamashita just stopped and stared back as if our arrangement was completely normal, as if we had agreed to this routine like two Cold War spies. Then when I walked, he walked too. I could not help think, if this was what having a bodyguard or servant was like, why did the rich want one?

On the trek back from the river, I decided to be practical and study my whereabouts. Jalan Besar wasn't your typical military outpost. Kurosawa had billeted a four-square, single-storey house at the end of Jalan Besar by himself. More Japanese soldiers, including Yamashita, billeted two shophouses across the road from Kurosawa. There were no military jeeps or trucks waiting by the road. There were no barbed wire fences or sandbag encirclements or artificial trenches guarding the houses. The only signs of a military presence, an occupying force, were a sentry and a few men in military fatigues lolling outside Kurosawa's house, spouting Japanese as they ate supper. In fact, the "Japanese" shophouses connected seamlessly into the shophouses along Jalan Besar Road, as if trying to fit in. However, the bright orange lights of the Kempeitai houses dazzled while the rest of the houses were unlit, veiled in black shadow like a fugitive drug street with two working lampposts. In a way, it was the most frightening display of power, confident enough to be low-key and unaggressive, but there. It was unmistakeably Kempeitai.

The next morning, I learned that the other shophouse tenants had stayed on, despite knowing they lived next to the Japanese Secret Military Police. As the sun rose, they trickled quietly and nervously onto the street to collect rations or hustle to work and in the evenings, they hurried home and barred themselves inside, shrouded in darkness and quiet till the morning. They often returned when the sentries changed shifts or before the soldiers' dinnertime.

I wondered what Kurosawa or Yamashita wanted of me now. I approached Yamashita and tilted my head to rest on closed hands and yawned deliberately to see if it was time to sleep. I was also exhausted and wanted to escape everything. Sleep was the only reprieve I knew. He brought me to the toilet inside Kurosawa's house. A large metal pail was half-filled with water, a gayung cup floating atop. He pointed at the pail and me and left. I had not expected this. I squatted and took my first bath in months before wearing my clothes again.

Yamashita sniffed at my attire, sighed and shook his head with a resigned look. He patted the porch next to him. My day was not over.

I sat farther away and leaned against the cold white wall. The breeze curled around me and I hugged my legs to my chest. I wondered where Appa was, telling myself he was okay. I missed him and Garden Country, missed the comforting predictability of living with Appa. Here, I didn't know what I was allowed to do, what Kurosawa and Yamashita wanted me to do, and what I would be punished and hurt for doing. Thinking endlessly about this, my eyes drooped. I jerked awake intermittently, and fell asleep again.

Kurosawa arrived, carrying a rolled-up rattan mat under his left arm. He spoke a few words to Yamashita, seeming cheerful, and then pointed into the room to tell me to enter. Yamashita saluted him and strutted away, taking out a cigarette, while I went inside. Kurosawa unfurled the rattan mat next to his desk and, looking at me empathically, he used two outstretched hands to draw a path over the mat, like pushing a swing over it. He said, *"Nero. Koko.* Sleep."

I lay down on the hard rattan weaves to show I understood. Kurosawa nodded and turned away and I watched the orange bulb above flicker with mosquitoes. In this humidity, it was a nightly ritual to be lathered with bites and bumps. Sleep overcame me fast.

Then he woke me up, gabbling in Japanese.

"Appa?" I was bleary. The day seemed like a reverie continuing, until Kurosawa wrenched me upright. He shoved his mess tin into my face, jabbing into the emptiness of the metal container and showing me his open palm. I shook my head to convey that I didn't understand. His eyes were wide and maniacal and he clasped my shoulders to stop me pulling away. Fear woke me up properly.

I tried hard to understand him but he kept talking furiously, shaking my shoulder, and pushing my head into the mess tin, as if roughing me up into understanding. But he only frightened me more. I said in Tamil, "Stop. Stop, please." He talked over me, pushed and tugged. It hit me that I had cleared the tossed-out tissue of dinner remnants from the mess tin. But Kurosawa's desperation suggested that the tissue contained more than leftover food or bones. I stood up to avoid his yanking and barely escaped a grasping hand. I quickly demonstrated that I had swept the tissue up with the rubbish, hoping that would make him stop.

His hands went to his baldpate, forming indents around his fingertips. His mouth mumbled mutely, before he opened both palms upwards to say, "Where?"

He followed me silently in his white socks, sword clinging to his side, Arisaka rifle slung onto his back. The sewage stench of the river attacked us before it came into view. It was brown, and empty bottles, cardboard, dead cigarettes and broken fishing lines drifted aimlessly on it. From the net- and glass-strewn embankment, I jumped onto the first slimy bumboat. I ducked around its canopy and from its bow, jumped onto the stern of another. Kurosawa watched from shore. Once I reached the fifth bumboat, farthest into the river, I showed where I had stretched out the handle of the dustpan and upturned everything.

Across the bumboats and river, Kurosawa's face contorted. He was on some tipping point, a man about to go mad. He covered his face, breathed loudly into his hands, and this laborious attempt at quelling his anger scared me even more.

He whipped out his rifle and aimed it at me. In one strong jerk, he pushed the barrel down to my feet and I needed no second reminder to sit on the bow deck to keep my head.

Kurosawa tightened his rifle sling so the long black weapon hung higher from his neck, at chest-level. He unstrapped a torchlight from his gear belt and shone a white circle, like a nimbus of milk, on the brown turbid water. He waded into it and the water burped and plopped at his stamping until it reached his pistol and sword hilt and settled quietly lapping about his waist. He pushed a drifting log aside.

In his uniform, Kurosawa merged into the liquid, like a dark roaming beast of the river. With his left hand, he shone the torch and water striders skated away on water. With his right, Kurosawa dug into the river, pulled out a silver hook or can and tossed it onto land. Sometimes, he muttered to himself and groaned. I watched in the company of the murmurs of crickets and frogs, too frightened to feel sleepy anymore. I considered hightailing it and running off. But every time I gathered the guts to almost stand up, Kurosawa glanced in my direction and squashed my nascent courage.

After wandering the middle of the waterway, Kurosawa combed the embankment. He swept the dike from left to right, plunged his hand into the soil, excavated fistfuls of seeds, swivels, a sinker, and threw them at shore with increasing desperation. At the farthest right, after three hours of searching, he threw everything into the water with an agonised splash. He ducked out of sight for one second. Quiet.

I jumped from boat to boat, not caring about the cracking sounds my landings made. My feet hit the embankment and a stone cut into my bare foot and Kurosawa had reappeared on shore, dripping wet. Our gazes met in moonlit shadow, recognising without seeing, and I sprinted off.

Wet clomping behind me squelched faster, more frequently, closing in. I ran harder, panicked and afraid. Then a wet hand grabbed my neck and tightened like it was about to strangle me, and I shouted. Water dripped down my back. Kurosawa pushed my head forward; my legs kicked at the ground to keep up as we scrabbled back to Jalan Besar. The sentries turned their heads the other way as we disappeared into Kurosawa's house.

He shoved and I barely broke my fall against the wall. His hand fixed my neck to the wall like a tightened noose, my cheekbone pressed against wall, my cornea next to stone.

Something tore a laceration through my shorts, cutting skin on my buttocks, drawing blood. I screamed but Kurosawa's grip didn't budge. He struck again on the same line, with all the stereotypical precision and diligence of the Japanese worker channelled into the worst extremity. The pain doubled up in waves. I shouted "Stop! Please!" in Tamil, in English, tears and saliva leaking down the wall, but he caned me a third time. My shorts felt soaked and I didn't care if I had peed in them. A fourth. A fifth. Then he released me. The pain had become a constant stinging, my bum was shaking, and I rested my forehead on the wall, blubbering and ashamed of it. I realised that I had been calling for Appa.

He took two steps back and said something in Japanese, harsh and guttural. I kept quiet, letting the pain etherise, waiting for him to say something that would help me understand. He said, "*Wakaru? Wakaru?*" The wooden rotan smashed against the wall next to my head and clattered to the floor, making me jump. It was not actually a rotan or cane, but a stick used to scratch your back, a long thin wooden rod with a baby-like hand at the end. I looked at him and he barked again, "*Wakatta?*"

"No," I said in English, shaking my head. "No. No understand."

His fists were clenched into tight balls and he glared at me. Time slowly neutralised his loud and angry breathing. Finally, his hands unclenched and he said in English, a clipped, "Go sleep."

He marched out of the house.

With no other choice, I fell forward on the mat, trying to figure out what I did wrong, wondering if he beat me because of the mess tin or because I tried to escape. Only later he would tell me the grave mistake I had unknowingly made. How could I have known? But at that moment, I realised that Appa was right, that the Japanese master was far more cruel and unpredictable than the British, and that the Greeks were right about barbarism in the East. I decided that I would try to escape again, even if I risked a hundred canings from the backscratcher.

When stuck in a situation, we locals tell each other to "suck thumb"—suck it up and get on with it. I am no hypocrite and I told myself to suck thumb too, wait it out, use the time I had to learn where Appa was, lull Kurosawa into a false complacency and then escape. Few people are as good at putting up and shutting up as we were in those days. We were like the land, stubbornly and silently enduring. Most of my friends are now dead and if I could resurrect them we would survive another hundred years as a nation. Today, if a teacher spanks a student, people whine and moan about it and the newspapers carry the story like it heralds the end of the world. Trust me, for I have seen world's end, and we are far from it.

4

1962

Growing up had narrowed Papatti's chin, thinned her lips and sharpened her nose. Her eyes were as fiery as the vermillion on her forehead. She tied her hair into a professional bun and she was taller and curvier than Lalitha now, which she liked to remind her amma of by unexpectedly emerging at her side, her shoulders a few inches above her amma's, and staring around wondering where the midget was. She would mime this performance until Lalitha threatened to slap her and they would fight over her amma's language.

A swathe of viridescent polyester cloth straddled the left side of Papatti's sewing table, spilling over the desk, ends hanging evenly above the floor and rippling in obedient graceful swishes whenever Papatti's right leg pedalled the machine. She found the rippling of cloth calming, and suspected that it was like meditation for some.

Rajpal sat beside her, on the old stool that Papatti once used. She had since invested her earnings in a second-hand chair with a disjointed wooden slate that Rajpal had broken off before it could poke into his precious daughter. A stump was all that was left. Rajpal's eyes had started drooping and white hairs had emerged in his beard that Papatti occasionally pointed out for the fun of it. Her appa's gangly legs stuck out like a praying mantis' because the stool was too short for him. He struggled not to lean back against the small table, newly installed in the corner, for Papatti had piled saree fabric on it and he didn't dare upset her work. A newspaper and pencil lay on his right lap, and he opened his mouth to ask for something.

Papatti raised a long skinny finger, dotted with pink pin marks. "Oh oh. What did she say? Tailor it tighter, Papatti. I plan to lose weight by Deepavali. Now what does she say? Loosen it, Papatti, I cannot breathe. I'm a fat, demanding woman who shouldn't have eaten so many laddoos and kuehs! And she wants *pound* gold on green, that golden hippo! *Pound* gold."

Papatti puttered and pressed the pedal with the ball of her right foot. Her soft sole sank into the gaps between the iron shafts and the lever gently seesawed forward. The needle jabbed down into the forest-green fabric, made a click like a stapler and lodged a gold stitch into it. Papatti held the cloth down on either side of the needle and the feeder dog advanced the fabric away from her. The needle jabbed continuously, and the thread nipped in and out of the green fibers like a flying golden fish. Papatti just needed to make sure the line travelled straight. The end hanging closest to Papatti rose. She glanced at Rajpal, whose mouth remained half-open at her sudden interruption. She stopped pedalling, lifted the silver presser foot and pulled the broad drape off the table. She held it out, blocking out Rajpal's face, only his legs showing underneath. "Mm. The gold does look good on green."

She lowered the fabric to reveal Rajpal's face, now eager, sensing an opportunity to jump in. Sighing, she gave him a pittance: "What, Appa?" She slid the cloth back between the presser foot and table, cracked her neck and started singing. The needle punched down and the table shivered and green inched forward.

"Beiti, she doesn't have much. You have a chance to make her happy so make her happy. Isn't that what we are all in this world for? To help each other and make each other happy and be happy ourselves? Don't scold her. Okay? Help her. Now, can you give me some of your precious time? Please?"

Rajpal did not need to tell her this. Whatever Papatti's frequent complaints about her customers, she would much rather have a weight-fluctuating, fastidious, niminy-piminy customer than no customer at all. All Papatti had wanted since young was to fit in, and she fit in by being a useful, in-demand, sought-after seamstress. Of course, people also annoyed her by praising Muthu & Co., that small garments store that operated out of Buffalo Road and had over-optimistically abbreviated itself as Singapore's first MNC. But this merely motivated Papatti to redouble her efforts at honing her arsenal of stitches and learning new weaves.

Sewing had become Papatti's identity. She was consumed by a paranoia that if someone else could offer the same value for money that she did, they would not just undercut her business and steal her livelihood, but throw her back into a past where she would just be a poor, uneducated woman with a peculiar heritage. A woman that people could ignore, or worse, bully, leaving only Rajpal and Lalitha by her side. Sewing had become a way for Papatti to stand on her own two feet and be somebody in society. Or as Lalitha had impressed upon her since she was ten, it was her way to survive.

Hence, Papatti had recently settled on a new resolution—

she wanted to be the best seamster, boy or girl, on Serangoon Road, and she was happy for every additional customer and order that came her way to help her get there.

It just so happened that the only way she could express this sense of satisfaction and pride in being in demand, in being wanted, was to complain about the hordes of customers and lengths of fabric that demanded her attention, a humble bragging of sorts. She was also highly selective of whom she whinged to—only her appa and amma. What was family if not people whose affection she could take for granted? Especially Rajpal, who could not stand to see his daughter hurt. But she didn't need to admit this to her appa. No, she had the privilege of grunting to indicate that he could carry on speaking.

Rajpal held up the hoary newspaper and the black letters ran in illegible line upon illegible line. A thick red circle looped around a large alphabet in the capitalised headline. She briefly wondered if her appa was teasing her. But he never would dare and he said, "In the referendum, I can choose from three letters: A, B and C. I will obviously choose 'A', but I need to learn to recognise the alphabet before the referendum, Beiti. I don't want to circle the wrong option."

"And you are asking me because?"

"Beiti, I want you to help me memorise the letter. You went to school for a bit. And you studied a bit of English. You should know this better than me. Do you think one month is enough to memorise? I've never memorised anything, except 4D numbers. Like when I saw that accident take place on Bras Basah Road last month, I slowed down cycling and memorised the car number right away. Just missed it by one number too." He snapped his fingers.

Before he could embark on his story for the umpteenth time of how he had missed winning the national lottery by *just* one number, which was to Rajpal as narrow as the snap of his fingers had been brief, as if in a permutation of four numbers picked at random, that one number 3 instead of 9 was *just* a small margin of error, a close call, that a different accident on a different road would perhaps have brought him more prosperity, Papatti said, "Appa, I went to school so long ago. I forgot everything already. Why are you dredging that up now?"

"Beiti, you and your amma never forget anything. I know that better than anyone. Anyway, in the worst case, we can learn together. I want you to write the three letters and hold them up and I will tell you which is 'A'. What do you think? Sounds fun?"

Papatti released the pedal and the needle shuddered to a halt. It did not sound fun at all. She sighed. "Appa, I'm working. Someone needs to make money in this house."

The newspaper fell onto the floor with a thwack. The pencil clattered on top of it and rolled away. "Eh. What's this now my little Chettiar? You put the food on the table for this family, is it?"

She stared up at the ceiling, seeing past the cement to plead to the ethereal heavens beyond. "Yes. If not me, then who will do it? Who?" she demanded of the gods embedded beyond that stone sky.

Rajpal stood up and his towering shadow fell on her. Before she knew it, his thick, hairy arms hugged her to him and her chair's legs lifted off the floor and she toppled into his wide chest, her left cheek pressed against him. Immediately, Papatti released the cloth and raised her legs into the air above the pedal, completely disconnecting herself from the Singer machine to keep her opus safe. She grabbed and pulled at Rajpal's arms. "Appa! Stop it! Let go of me or I'll pinch you!" Her muffled echoes rebounded, stifled by his arm.

"Appa! Please!"

His voice blossomed above. "So, you're a big girl who earns money for this family eh? Me and your amma are good-for-nothing bums. Is that it, my little Chettiar? You put the roof over our heads? The food on the table? You're the money-maker?" He rubbed his knuckles on her head like a buzzing machine, a thousand itches.

She shrieked. "Appa! No!"

"Ouch! Stop that you mad girl!" She had pinched her nails into his arm, digging them in like claws. "Beiti! Don't! It hurts!"

"You let go first!"

"No, you let go first!"

"What's going on inside there?"

Quiet. Her amma, termagent woman, was in the kitchen. Papatti and Rajpal stopped moving, turning into two statues transfixed in silence and anticipation, Papatti easing the pressure of her nails. Moments elapsed. Still silence. Then Papatti tilted her head back and shouted, "Nothing!"

Water dripped from a tightly twisted rag. Clanking of a metal pan. The danger had passed.

"Ouch!"

She had bit into Rajpal's arm. He sat down, rubbing his forearm sorely, and picked up the newspaper and pencil.

"Next time I'll use this." She raised her bodkin viciously.

"You are a gangster, not a girl."

She stabbed at his stomach with the needle. He fenced with the pencil. "Yes," she said. "I have learned to defend myself. With this." She lunged with the needle again.

"Beiti," he said, swatting her tiny sword away, "Do this for your country. Do you want us to be an independent country or not?"

Papatti set the weapon down and retied her bun.

"Appa, I can't even vote yet. And I don't even understand this whole thing properly."

"After all these years of British rule, and that horrid Japanese Occupation in between, we will finally be able to run our own country properly. How's that for a start?"

Papatti frowned. "I thought they said the Federal government will be in KL?"

"Yes, it will. But we will have representation in that government. And we will have our own local government in Singapore, led by our own boys. And we get to vote on the terms of our merger. So our boys are telling us to vote 'A' to support them and merger and I want to vote 'A'. I want to support our boys."

"What about girls?"

"And hopefully girls too. And we won't have to listen to lectures from some Colonial office or Parliament in London."

"What's a parliament?"

"It's this big white place where big white men meet and talk about the future."

"Why don't you join the Parliament then?"

He guffawed and slapped the newspaper against his thighs, which was all a newspaper was normally good for in their house. "That's a good one. I'm neither big nor white enough, Beiti. I'm not even literate. I need your help memorising my vote."

"Appa, if you are good enough to vote, why won't you be good enough for Parliament? And if people don't think you are good enough for Parliament, why do they let you vote? I'll vote instead. Maybe I'll run. I will win everyone over to support me and big women can talk about the future of the country."

"Of course you will. And I will be the number one Papatti-ist."

She was pleased by his answer. But then she felt guilty for usurping the conversation and making it about her. "Anyway, what must you memorise?"

He held the paper up like a tout showing a movie poster, except it was grey and bland and had no recognisable faces. "Ravi helped me circle the letter 'A' but I told him that I want to practise with my beiti. It'll be fun, my princess. We haven't had time together in so long."

"I am always in the house! We have too much time together! Here, let me see that." She snatched the newspaper and inspected the red halo around the familiar letter. "This letter that's circled, this is the one?"

"Yes, it must be."

"Appa, so you do know. Why do you need to practise some more?"

"Eh, because I want to be safe. This could jolly well be the most important vote I ever cast in my life. What if I get it wrong because I circled the wrong letter? What if one vote made all the difference? I'll never live down the shame. No, no. I won't allow it. We must practise."

"Ugh! You are such a pain sometimes." Having issued this decisive statement, because this one-line judgement was all that mattered in her conversations with Lalitha and Rajpal, Papatti pulled one wooden drawer out of the sewing table. It was stacked to the brim with spools of fine thread—sapphire, cerise, oak and other colourfully wrapped cylinders. She dug her fingers in like chopsticks, rolled spools under one another until an off-white reel bobbed to the top. Taking it and her silver needle, she said, "Come here, Appa." She pushed herself towards her father in three huffs, three screeches of chair legs against cement.

"What's happening inside there?" Lalitha asked. She had stopped scrubbing maniacally with the tight rag.

"Nothing, Amma. Stop shouting for every little thing!"

"I'm not shouting!" The rag dipped into a pail with a splosh.

Rajpal was wearing a white polyester button-up shirt with short sleeves that had passed her approval before he bought it. Papatti turned over an end of the shirt, inches below the last button. He sighed as she examined it. "Beiti, what are you doing? I asked you to help me memorise the alphabet and you want to fix my shirt. You always find something wrong with my clothes. What's wrong with it now? Come, stop it, put it down and help me with this first. Please, Beiti." Rajpal reached for the newspaper behind her and she smacked his hand.

"Be still, Appa. Quiet. Let me do this first."

"Beiti." The word breathed and died on its own, unheard.

Rajpal was used to this. She had an absolute authority over him that drove Lalitha crazy, an effect Papatti put down to plain jealousy. Amma just needed to work on being a more likable person instead of interjecting with shouts from the kitchen all the time. Papatti dipped her needle into Rajpal's shirttail, swooping it in and out of the fibers with ease, as if the shirt were butter. Her perceptive eyes always found rents, holes, mismatched seams and uncut dangling threads on his clothes that Rajpal and Lalitha never noticed. It was the Govinda training. Sometimes, she scolded them for being so oblivious in their old age and threatened not to support them when they became decrepit, at which point Rajpal would become so dramatically hurt that she would have to admit that it was a joke and hug him.

As she sewed, Rajpal began talking and she pretended not to hear, focused as she was on guiding her needle, absorbed in stitching. But secretly, Papatti enjoyed listening to the soothing quality of her appa's voice, like a flute playing happy tunes around her even if she didn't catch every note.

"You know, Beiti, about what you said. About whether I should be allowed to vote if I could not join the Legislative Assembly. I never really thought about it that way. But I think, that's what this independence movement is about isn't it? You see, I used to admire my boss, a Mr John Stevenson. I think he was the Vice-President of the paper then. He would wear a white hat and suit with a tie as pink as his face and come into the distribution centre with his long walking stick and plant a hand on his hip like Stamford Raffles and talk for the whole company to hear his strong English accent, telling us about the power of newspapers and the direction he was taking the company in and his favourite brand of Chinese tea. He promised to organise classes for us to learn to read English as well. Then when the rumours started spreading that the Japanese would attack Singapore, he came in and said confidently that we should not believe the rumours for no one would dare attack a British colony, and that even if the rumours were true, the Japanese could not fight or win because their eyes were too small for them to see with."

"What nonsense," she said. But she wished she hadn't blurted out.

"I knew you were listening!"

"Appa, I'm working. I can't help listening if your words keep *pouring* into my ears."

"Fine. Okay. You're not listening. Anyway, while you are *not* listening, I agree. Utter nonsense. He was all talk, no action. But I only know that now. Back then, we thought, so much confidence and pomp in a man. He must know what he's talking about. Besides, he was white. Of course, soon the Japanese came along and proved otherwise. But you know what Mr Stevenson did right before the Japanese even attacked Malaya? He caught a flight for London and took off. Just like that. He didn't even stand by his own words, couldn't even put his money where his mouth was. Cowardly swine. Sorry.

"But when my Supervisor at the centre told me that Mr Stevenson had flown off, fled, I realised then and there that if you don't speak for yourself, if you don't rely on yourself, some bugger like Mr Stevenson will tell you what's good for you, decide for you, and then go MIA and run for the hills when it's time to pay the bills. And you will end up paying all the debt. Right? What do you think? Isn't that why I should be allowed to vote? To decide for myself?"

Unprovoked by comments on eye sizes, she didn't answer, knowing Rajpal would continue in his garrulous reverie. "Yes. Yes. I think so. You know, after the Japanese Occupation—and trust me, the Japanese were also more than happy to tell us what to do—guess who walked into the office again, like nothing had happened? Lo and behold, it was Mr Stevenson in his same white suit and pink tie, carrying his walking cane in one hand and holding his hat in another, grinning from ear to ear as if he had just came back from vacation at Port Dickson. He opened his mouth, his confident voice soaring above us, saying how the world had returned to normal and the British were back to save us, and we all walked out. We just marched out like soldiers. The way his mouth hung open in shock, like a big black hole, you could have stuffed your sewing table into it, I tell you!" Rajpal tittered and then stopped just as suddenly with a guilty look when Papatti glared at him. No matter how tickled or enamoured he was, he should know that his laughter was disrupting her sewing, and that he should leave her sewing instruments out of Mr Stevenson's mouth, thank you very much.

"Sorry, sorry," he said. "I think all this referendum talk is getting to my head. I sound like one of those journalist or politician types. Maybe I should have gone to school. But it's not good for a man to think too much. Yes, it applies to women too. Don't poke me for that, it was a mistake. Mr Stevenson would call it a 'fou par'. Ah, you are surprised, even if you are pretending not to listen. Ah, a smile. You see, you might be the intelligent one in the family, but your appa has a few surprises up his sleeve too. Anyway, they transferred Mr Stevenson out the next day, because I don't know if white men actually get fired like the rest of us, but either ways *Hare Rama Hare Krishna* I never saw the bugger again. What do you think about that? Do you understand what I'm trying to say? Beiti? Are you really not listening to me? What are you doing?"

"I am…" she drew her head back, taking a wider view of her handiwork, "Finishing…" and she narrowed her eyes, swooped in, checked again, "Finished." She scrubbed the lint away, pulled the shirt taut and leaned back. Arms crossed, smug, Papatti beamed at Rajpal. She took the newspaper and victoriously tossed it on the heap of garments and said, "You can return the paper. Now you don't have to worry about the referendum. Just wear this same shirt when you go to vote."

"Beiti, what are you talking about?"

She sighed aloud. It was so blatantly obvious, how could he not have noticed, this Mister "Fou Par"? She pinched the end of his shirt, below the last button, and turned it up so its inside faced him. The springy hairs on his stomach popped out. On the backing, the off-white stitch stood out, embossed, but only because her finger hung like a cursor over it. Otherwise, he wouldn't have noticed it at all, just like he hadn't noticed the mismatched seams and loose threads. It would have melted into the rest of the white shirt. But seeing it, understanding dawned on Rajpal's face, and wondrous, he beamed, seeing that she had stitched the letter 'A' into the underside of his shirt.

"You are a genius! Lalitha! Come see this." She felt a lift. Her appa had inadvertently handed her an opportunity, a way to make others living on both sides of Serangoon Road see and acknowledge that she was indeed the best seamster in the neighbourhood. Her mind was already searching for how to make the most of it.

Rajpal twirled like a bharatanatyam dancer in a new frock across the room, knowing he would have to go and show it off to his wife and running out of the room, saying, "We are going to start a revolution!"

Lalitha said, "Stop yelling and tell your daughter to go downstairs. Karnan needs his shirt fixed before his next shift."

5

Dedicated to Papatti

I was shaken awake the next morning. I had been sleeping on my front and turned my head. Yamashita knelt by my side, hand still holding onto my shoulder, staring blankly at me. He stood and waited for me to do the same. I jumped to my feet, noticing that Kurosawa's mat was abandoned. Yamashita ordered me to roll up my mat and lean it against a corner before we went outside. The sear across my bum came alive.

It was five in the morning. They had turned the clocks forward to match Tokyo time, so it was actually four, far before sunrise. The sky was an inky dark purple, as if the sun had pummelled and bruised it overnight when no one was watching too. It was chilly because of the dawn wind, and I wrapped my arms around my body while waiting to build up sufficient body heat.

Yamashita stood before the Shinto altar perched over the door, the *kamidana*. He clenched his fists by his sides and bowed twice. He bowed so deeply I thought he was about to bang his head against the concrete. He straightened up with a robotic jerk, clapped twice and robotically bowed once more. Then he looked at me and empathically pointed at the shrine and performed the ritual again, but this time, slower. I understood that I was to copy him, that I owed my life to his Creator now. Taking my place beside Yamashita, I replicated his prayer and Yamashita looked satisfied by this. Through significant theatrics, he managed to explain that I was always to bow to the *kamidana* when I walked past it, the way appa used to touch a hand to his forehead whenever he saw a temple.

Yamashita spread a newspaper on the stony floor and wanted me to sit on it. I shifted from cheek to cheek as my bum flared, trying to even out the pain. He took a heavyset pair of scissors, like garden shears, to chop off my mop of thick hair. It had flown over my eyebrows and ears like a soldier's helmet since the War began. He cut my hair in his image, cropping it close to stubble all over, but my head ended up more like the uneven turf behind Kurosawa's house, patchy and potholed, with four or five lonesome strands falling over my eyes that I tore out the next day with my fingers. It goes without saying that I looked hideous, but the Occupation was not a time to worry about things like this.

After my epilation, Yamashita ordered me to gather my hair, which lay in shambles on the newspapers, stripped of any relation to me. I wrapped them inside the newspaper and this time he let me toss it into the drain. I suspected that he knew about the previous night.

We crossed the road to the Jalan Besar soldiers' houses and Yamashita entered the first. There were numerous elevated cots planted around the house, set against the walls to create a common space in the middle. Each black cot was identical, field packs stowed underneath, next to straw slippers and dark brown boots, toecaps facing me. Uniforms hung flattened into the walls, like Kurosawa's. A few small family portraits and photographs of smiling women were also tacked to the walls, aligned with the precision of a ruler. I couldn't understand why the soldiers would choose to be so far away from their families.

A well-ordered kitchen waited at the back of the house. I noticed a long drying rack where large pots, woks and spatulas had been towel-dried and then arranged neatly to avoid watermarks. A worn rag was neatly folded and hung on the rack, next to a narrow closet door. An adjacent storeroom, dark as a bomb shelter, had been stocked with wooden crates of brown ration bags, woven rice-straw kegs of sake, towers of canned food like compressed salmon and sardine, and boxes of vitamin tablets. I could see that everything had been segregated and had its place in the storeroom, just like people did in the colonial world. Yamashita disappeared into the bomb shelter and returned with a sack of rice.

He taught me to boil green tea and to make rice balls with a tuna centre for breakfast. By the time we finished, I heard the soldiers noisily re-enter the house after their morning run, yakking away. Shoes fell to the floor and slid back under the cots. I heard a few soldiers plop loudly onto their cots. Yamashita passed me a tray and I put the round rice balls on it and took it out to the soldiers.

The soldiers were tall and sinewy and well fed, something hunger and fear trained me to recognise. They were also confident and raucous. When their eyes fell on me, the clamour died into a moment of quiet frowns and glances. Then someone rattled off something in Japanese and the laughter and smiles reappeared. The chatter returned to normal and the bunk seemed to have forgotten I was there as the soldiers changed out of their wet white T-shirts.

A soldier with a runway of curly hair above his buzz cut sides waved his hand over at me. Nakamura.

I presented the rice ball the way Yamashita taught me. I presented the tray before me and bowed. Taking one, he gently patted the side of my head to send me off. The irony did not escape me that I had inherited my appa's servitude, if only for a different lord, and as much as I detested it, I could do nothing about it. I continued to the next soldier, careful to execute the routine correctly each time.

In fleeting glances, and in earshot of their conversations, the soldiers came to seem less and less like the identical cogs of a machine that I had presumed they were. As with the British soldiers on Sembawang base, I noticed differences in height. Some soldiers were more tanned, some broader-shouldered, some had deeper voices and one threw his rolled-up socks at another. I didn't understand the words they said, but I understood who asked questions, who was being made fun of, who was the bunk clown, and who was the introvert who read a book on his cot while the rest gabbled on. Truly, my greatest surprise was how loquacious the Japanese soldiers were when they were together. But they were still different from me, beginning with the simple fact that they had guns.

After the tray emptied, I walked backwards to the kitchen, bowing before turning my back to them, and Yamashita finally handed me a rice ball. I bit into it and the rice was stickier and sweeter than the Thai rice I was used to. I was hungry and finished the rice ball in seconds. Yamashita smiled at this, baring crooked uneven teeth. Then he opened the closet.

The dustpan and broom I had used the day before stood alongside a mop, all gathered inside a large metal pail like the one in Kurosawa's toilet. There was a smaller metal pail and some scrubs nearby. Yamashita gave me the metal pail and a rancid smell struck me. It was familiar. We went to the toilet.

That first time, he watched and made sure I cleaned the toilet properly with my bare hands. The griminess of picking up a stranger's excrement and dumping it into the tin pail has never left me. I finished the job and scrubbed the toilet clean as fast as I could.

By the time I finished, the soldiers had left for their morning briefing. I cleaned their houses under Yamashita's quiet and attentive supervision. Then we went to Kurosawa's house. He was briefing the soldiers on his porch while they knelt on the ground, and he didn't notice us. We cleaned his house and toilet and I gladly returned the cleaning materials to the closet. Yamashita let me wash my hands.

He gave me two pairs of white T-shirts and khaki shorts, neatly folded and pressed. They were enormous but I understood that I was to wear a pair the whole day. Yamashita tucked the shirt in all the way, pulling it down so flat he exposed half my chest. I was surprised its hems didn't stick out of the bottom of my shorts, which billowed beneath my knees. Yamashita tied a brown string around the waist like a belt and I understood that the string always had to be visible. This was my new uniform. But I was to use my chappals because it was far harder to move around in oversized footwear handed down from soldiers.

After this, Yamashita led me to the Kempeitai Headquarters at Dhoby Gaut, a ten-minute brisk walk. I ran after him, holding my shorts up, afraid the belt would come undone and let my shorts fall.

I will never forget the Young Men's Christian Association building that I saw that day. It remained the three-story colonial mansion we knew, overly majestic for our slummy island. Its walls were chequered in red and white that glowed orange with the sunrise. Arched bay windows, like a cathedral's, ringed its corridors and a portico jutted out to guard over the entrance. White stairs ran up to resplendent white doors. But the Kempeitai had converted the YMCA building into their Military Police Headquarters, and it served as the East District Branch. Barbed wire was stacked underneath each window, to prevent people from jumping out rather than sneaking in. The windows were covered with black curtains so I couldn't see into them. They had dug trenches at the corners of the building and filled the rice sacks with sand to protect the soldiers from air raids. Soldiers in fatigues manned these foxholes, circled the corridors and the perimeter, carrying their Arisaka rifles before them. Platoon-sized troops marched on the road, arms and legs swinging and chanting loudly. Over time, I would start recognising the more popular songs. A few soldiers with white armbands braceleting their biceps strode in and out of the porch, and their lackeys chased nervously after them, reminding me—ashamedly—of myself.

A dark military jeep swerved past Yamashita and me and lurched to a halt inside the portico. Four soldiers unloaded a white woman, unconscious, hands and feet bound, mouth taped. A soldier shouted, and in unison they lifted her up the stairs and carried her into the building. The jeep drove away, and after its dust settled and the resplendent white doors closed behind the white woman, it was as if nothing had happened. Everyone went about their day again. She wasn't just forgotten; she had never existed.

In front of Headquarters, there rose a silver flagpole, with a stockier podium by its base. An empty courtyard unfolded before the pole, swept of all leaves and dirt so the white concrete was like a large polished mirror. In the middle of the courtyard, a white drape covered a pyramidal structure, revealing traces of wooden scaffolding.

Then I looked across the courtyard properly, and I stopped.

In front of the Cathay Building, the Japanese had impaled heads on stakes. The heads were severed at the neck and hoisted onto the stakes. Some heads were slanted, others upright. The blood ringing their necks had dried and cracked in the sun and fallen in brown bits onto the floor. The faces were sandy, stained by birds, and wore open wounds that had rotted black. Their hair was also dirty and I concluded that the Japanese military's assiduous eye for cleanliness and propriety did not apply to these heads. I still cannot understand how a man has the stomach to chop another's head off, pick up his head, and then stuff its neck onto a rusty iron spike while blood drips down onto his toes. And how could a man do this while their two eyes, wide open in shock and horror from the moment of death, stared back, the way this row of eyes stared at me across the silver courtyard? Placards that I could not read hung underneath these heads. Later I was told they said: *This is an example for those who disobey the Imperial Japanese Army.* Velvety black crows took no heed and sat on the skulls, cawking and gnawing at the ears.

I ran to the drain and barfed. When I stood up for air, Yamashita was walking back for me. He looked impatient and gestured at me to hurry. Then he turned around again. I wiped my mouth and ran after him, trying not to look at the Cathay Building, trying to forget, but unable to unsee what I had seen.

Yamashita directed me to stand in the courtyard, facing the flagpole. Slowly, more and more people joined us, filling the plaza: Japanese soldiers, Singaporean men, white men. I did not see Kurosawa. The sun had ascended and flung dancing bayonets across the shining floor. Heat encased itself within the swelling crowd and made the courtyard feel like an oven. I felt even more nauseated. But everyone around me waited still and quiet and I made sure to stand with my feet together, hands by my side, lips shut.

A soldier climbed onto the podium and began making announcements in Japanese. He sounded impassioned and what he said sounded important. Later I learned it was a daily news and proclamation reel. Then he uttered a command and everyone turned to an angle. I followed suit. He shouted another command. We all bowed deeply. We were bowing northeast, to Tokyo, to the Imperial Palace, to the Emperor. On command, we faced the flagpole again and music trembled loudly over the speakers, an escalating din as the *Kimigayo* played and a bright flag ascended the pole. Yamashita sang loudly, his voice suddenly resonating with gusto. The crowd around me sang too. We became a great choir. I did not know the Japanese National Anthem then and I refused to learn or sing it, so I kept my mouth closed. Even in this minute defiance I hoped that no one would notice and tell Yamashita. I squinted as the flag rose above the crowd and went higher and higher until it disappeared into the sunlight and the music died.

The crowd dispersed and I took a deep breath. Yamashita tapped me on the shoulder. I hurried after him, ducking through the crowds, keeping him in sight. I leapt up the stairs to the Headquarters building two at a time to keep up with him. Two guards checked his pass and they opened the doors and bowed to him as we swept through.

Headquarters' interior was like a hospital, sanitised and clinical, as if not a single germ, bacterium or unwanted person could survive the building. Three long empty halls stretched ahead and around me. The tiles gleamed, freshly mopped, and the varnished walls were empty. Typewriters clicked furiously and men talked in hushed voices in the rooms. Occasionally, a phone rang, a long piercing drill of terror, until someone picked it up. Yamashita pointed at the stairs at the ends of the halls, pointing upstairs on them. He made an X with his hands and I nodded.

As we walked ahead, I glanced into a room. A Japanese military man with a white armband stood over a table, dictating while a seated clerk scribbled away. The man looked up and glared at me, mouth talking angrily still, and I turned my head away and scurried after Yamashita, who turned into the second room on our right.

Four mahogany desks were neatly arranged, two in front and two behind. They were exact replicas, with a paper tray in one corner, a black phone in another and a typewriter set in the middle. Clerks in military uniform sat behind the tables, young faces perking up as we entered. Cupboards with files and books lined the sides of the room, codes written longhand on their spines in Japanese. The thick black drapes behind the soldiers were drawn to shut the sun out and they had turned on the artificial white office light above instead.

The soldiers rose and bowed to Yamashita and then remained standing while he spoke to them. They nodded along in oleaginous unison, saying, "*Hai, hai, hai.*" Yes, yes, yes. They never interrupted or asked him to repeat himself. Then a soldier dialled his phone. Another opened his drawer and took out a pocket-sized white card. He rubber-stamped it on his desk and gave it to Yamashita, who passed the card to me, stamp facing up. He said in English, "*Passu. Passu.*" He pointed at the main entrance and said, "*Passu.* Come in. Go out. Everywhere. *Wakatta?*"

I nodded and Yamashita slid the card into my humongous side pocket and patted it in place. He pointed at each of the soldiers and recited his name. He quacked his fingers at me and I repeated after him. Today, I only remember the names of Private Uchida and Private Sugiura. Then he nodded, *Good*. I assumed that these deskbound soldiers were somehow to be important to me. The soldiers stared at me impassively, stiff at attention, until Yamashita left and I followed him. Muffled whispers trailed us, whispers that died as we reached the entrance. As we left Headquarters, I thought I heard a woman screaming from above.

Another jeep waited in the foyer, the metal door in the back open. I grew nervous, fearing Yamashita would tie me up like the white woman. But he grabbed my armpits and lifted me onto the jeep and climbed on after. Two benches lined either side of the jeep; Yamashita sat on one, and I took the other. I could only trust that I was "safe". After all, I had prayed to the right God today. I watched through the open back as the jeep's engine revved and it spun out of the porch and drove off. Strangely enough, this was my first car ride.

By day's end, Yamashita had shown me two more Kempeitai offices. The Central Police Station at South Bridge Road and another discreet house on Smith Street were also being used as Military Police Posts. I learned the names of more soldiers sitting before typewriters. Later, I came to understand that these soldiers were secretaries or assistants to officers of the Kempeitai. Uchida from Headquarters was Kurosawa's secretary.

We returned to Kurosawa's house at dusk. After a whole day of constant orientation and re-orientation, I actually felt grateful to see something familiar. Yamashita taught me to batter and deep-fry a few fillets of pork until it turned tough and brown like cutlets. We minced the pork, mixed it in with rice and emptied the rice into a bucket (not the one used for the toilets). I went around scooping rice into the soldiers' mess tins. This time, they paid me no mind, continuing their own Japanese chatter as I bowed and finished my job quietly. Yamashita brought Kurosawa's dinner to him.

After this, I was allowed to sit outside and eat alone from a mess tin that Yamashita gave me. I had never eaten pork before and found it chewy and tasty. I sat at a distance from the soldiers but still in everyone's sight.

With time to think, I considered whether Appa was on the third floor of Headquarters, if they had knocked him out and tied him up like the white woman, if they were torturing him in prison. It suddenly occurred to me that Appa could become a head on a stake too. My mind panicked. That day I learned that fearing an outcome could be just as agonising as realising it, for fear had no end to its madness. I decided to stop thinking about things I could not control, decided that the Kempeitai was not torturing Appa in its Headquarters or beheading him. I told myself that this was because in all honesty Appa would know nothing that was of value to the Japanese and you do not make an example of men like Appa. He was safe in some normal civilian prison and I just needed to find out where that was.

After dinner, Yamashita returned me to Kurosawa's custody. I bowed into the open doorway and said loudly, as Yamashita had taught me, *"Ojama itashimasu."* In response, Kurosawa told Yamashita something. I learned over the next days that Kurosawa had no more inclination to speak to me, which suited me then. Yamashita handed me a packet of dog biscuits and pushed me towards the door to indicate that I should enter. Then he saluted Kurosawa and left.

Inside, Kurosawa sat cross-legged, writing at his desk, ignoring me. I sat by the door and watched the birds flit from branch to branch in the trees outside. I munched on the biscuits, which were crunchy like British digestives, and after an hour, Kurosawa stood up to turn the light off. I took that as my signal to sleep. He had placed the backscratcher next to my mat as a warning to behave, a panopticon. I wondered if Kurosawa had carried the backscratcher all the way from Japan or bought it at a thieves' market here, like the one at Sungei Road. But I could not imagine Kurosawa, with his grave demeanour and strict self-control, visiting a thieves' market. Besides, he was a Japanese officer and I presumed he could order the damn thing without stepping foot out of the house if he wanted to. I spread my mat and lay on my front and waited for sleep to find me.

...

The Jalan Besar unit comprised a platoon of soldiers belonging to the Imperial Guards Division of the Imperial Japanese Army. They were infantrymen, foot soldiers. The Imperial Guard was one of three divisions that had invaded Singapore, but they were apparently disappointed because they had not been the first to enter the city. The Fifth Division had beaten them to this important milestone in an Imperial soldier's life, and so these poor sods had been stuck in second place and trying to redeem themselves ever since. This platoon was attached to the Kempeitai to support Kurosawa's operations in the city, like conducting house raids and sending men like Appa to prison. Corporal Yamashita was a Section Commander and in charge of the platoon's logistics and administration, from controlling their rations to enforcing bunk tidiness to assigning sentry duty to the soldiers. Now, he took charge of me too, like I was another piece of equipment or a routine chore that needed to be managed.

To avoid being woken by a kick to my gut, I woke up at five every morning of my own accord, by which time Kurosawa had usually gone for his morning run. Some days, he shadowboxed in the yard, punched and kicked at the air, ducked and weaved, fighting an invisible, dynamic adversary. Yamashita later explained to me that Kurosawa's family owned a martial arts gym, or a dojo as he called it, in Hiroshima in Japan. They taught a martial art called *kyoshokan* that his father had invented. When Kurosawa returned to Japan, he wanted to continue teaching at his dojo. I did not ask when he would return to Japan.

In the mornings, I prepared breakfast for the Jalan Besar unit and cleaned their houses and toilets. When he supervised me, Yamashita invested much effort into teaching me the Japanese language. The language had a strict and formal hierarchy, governing how a subordinate should speak to a superior, and vice versa. Hence, the street-smart side of me cottoned on to the most formal and polite expressions swiftly. I did not want to be caned or kicked for having accidentally offended a soldier, and so I used *onegai itashimasu* to say please, and *mōshi wake gozaimasen deshita* to express my deepest apologies. I used these terms, particularly the apology, liberally, most liberally when I was not sure what to use.

I would later learn that Kurosawa spent his time in his house meeting informants, writing his reports, planning his missions, and going out for raids and inspections and anything else the Kempeitai found vital to running a city. He only went to Headquarters for the odd meeting at night.

In the day Yamashita normally dropped me off at Headquarters after the flag-raising ceremony, where Uchida took over my supervision. He was a skinny soldier with a round face and round spectacles and never spoke in the office unless it was work-related. Sometimes, he would call me over in his high-pitched shrill voice, which made me understand why he preferred not to speak. He would write Japanese characters on scrap paper and send me off to Kurosawa's house to find a folder or document with matching characters. I was expected to do this without help from anyone and soon realised that I was the perfect messenger boy: I couldn't understand the message and had no one else to give it to. Other times, Uchida made me memorise the name of some soldier at Jalan Besar and ordered me to fetch him to Headquarters or collect a duffel bag from him. I would nervously ask around and then hesitantly approach a "Private Nakamura" or "Lance-Corporal Osagawa", but the soldiers would automatically know what Uchida needed.

The Cathay Building across the courtyard, one of the few air-conditioned buildings in Singapore then, housed the Kempeitai's Propaganda Department—the Hōdōbu. Its office was smaller, noisier and less disciplined than Headquarters, with people in civilian shirts and trousers racing and shouting across each other. Sometimes, Uchida ordered me to loop around the barrier of impaled heads to hand over orders or collect documents and film tapes at the Cathay Building. When I did this, the Propaganda people always stared and pointed at me and then talked about me loudly like I wasn't there, like they were being visited by a circus monkey.

If I had no more tasks, I would sit cross-legged in a corner of Uchida's office. He gave me a Japanese book and we pretended I was reading it. Sometimes, I watched the secretaries bent over their clunky typewriters. Sometimes, I covered my ears as a woman or man screamed from above and tried not to imagine what the Kempeitai was doing to that person, convincing myself that it was not Appa's voice.

One day, Sugiura tired of my presence and hissed at Uchida, his pale finger stabbing at me accusingly. They had a brief discussion and Uchida came out from behind his table, which was a rare occurrence during working hours. He was very short, which made me feel he was better off seated too. Nevertheless, I scrambled to my feet, almost his height, and Uchida motioned for me to follow him. We walked to the entrance, where he opened the white doors and pointed outside. He showed me on his watch that he expected me back in an hour, and I realised then that the other Secretaries didn't want me inside their office all day either. I had truly become a pet dog, allowed to roam on my owner's humiliating confidence that I would always return.

Despite what I told myself, I wanted to make certain that Appa had not been beheaded. So this time, I gathered the courage to inspect the heads in front of the Cathay Building, scanning them in a line the way a Japanese officer reviewed a Guard of Honour contingent, walking briskly from right to left, eyes fixed on the dead faces, stopping occasionally to get a close-up. Even if I held my breath, it took me a few times to get my vomit out of the way.

Later, Yamashita told me that the heads belonged to thieves, looters and other petty criminals. But the Kempeitai had an elastic definition of what was considered "criminal" and I would not take at face value any excuse they gave to kill a man. So I assiduously inspected the heads every time a new one appeared, often miraculously overnight, as if heads on stakes could simply be bought from Cold Storage and planted to decorate the Cathay Building for Deepavali. I even learned to distinguish heads that were cut off before and after the person's death, because the former left more blood running down the stake. Slowly my mind could imagine what Kurosawa's sword was being used for on the beaches of Singapore.

It is necessary to point out that most of the heads belonged to young Chinese men. It was no secret that the Japanese military was specially prejudiced against Chinese males and much of its operations, including the Kempeitai screening centres, were fronts for rounding up these men to destroy their bodies. It was a Far-Eastern holocaust. People talk about mind-control and brainwashing, but there is something so sinisterly urgent about the threat to one's body, so much easier and swifter to destroy, knowing that the mind or *athma* will be destroyed along with it, leaving nothing of the man behind. The Kempeitai were horrible at propaganda but terrific at targeting our bodies.

Then one day I saw a familiarly shaped head, dark and brown. Long black hair hung over it, obscuring its eyes and nose. I stopped, knowing that the hair was longer than Appa's, unsure if hair could grow after a man died. But I recognised the gaunt strong jaw and stepped closer. A crow stood on the scalp and didn't fly away as I approached. Its territorial black eye watched me, head rotating as I circled. I inched closer and smelled death, and could not believe that this was what Appa might have been degraded to. I extended an arm to part the hair, and the crow bit my ear with its marble beak. I swatted at it and fell to the ground as the bird flew up and resettled on the head, victoriously claiming its territory. I scrambled away, the blood warm on my ear.

But I needed to know and I didn't allow myself to be afraid, even if I was. I scoured the grass for a stick before I returned, wielding the branch like an amateur kendo fighter. I swiped at the black predator and it jumped up, catching air in its pinions, claws poised. Then it flew off and I felt foolish at the ease of it and for being scared of a bird. But I tucked the stick under my armpit just in case. Gingerly, I used my fingertips to part the man's hair and took a deep breath, taking in that death smell, letting it fill me with fear. Lifeless, soulless eyes stared through me, unfamiliar, surrounded by peeling raw skin and beak bites that had ripped off the flesh of the cheeks. But it wasn't Appa. Relief overwhelmed me. The hair fell back like curtains as I threw the stick onto the grass and wiped my hands on the leaves, crying. When I returned to Headquarters, the guards were watching me amusedly, but I didn't care anymore.

...

There were other Singaporeans around Headquarters: Chinese, Malays, Indians, present at the flag-raising ceremonies and bustling about during the day. They tended to look at me strangely, perhaps wondering at my age. But they also viewed me with sympathy, for we were in the same quandary. I did not know their names and they did not know mine, but we did not need to know these details to know what our lives must be like. As I was normally accompanied by Yamashita and sometimes sat in Uchida's office, they did not approach me. They kept their chins tucked in, fixed their eyes before their toes and moved from A to B quickly. Whenever they spoke in Malay, I eavesdropped to find out what they did, and to listen for clues of Appa's whereabouts.

A few were translators for the Japanese. Some helped the Kempeitai coordinate with the *Gunseikanbu*—or Central Military Establishment—and *kumiai* guilds and local district heads to check if each district had sufficient stocks of rice, oil, sugar and water rations (and whether to cut them), or to check whether the district crime rates had decreased. They updated the Japanese if the trams faltered or if an electricity shortage broke out somewhere in the city. They processed applications from people to travel outside of Singapore. By and large, they seemed to do the administrative and menial functions the Japanese soldiers hadn't signed up for when they joined the war. I realised that they never spoke about their homes or families around Headquarters, as if that would keep them safe.

There were other Singaporeans around Headquarters, but they were there to be tortured. These men were stripped and made to lie in their underwear on the sizzling courtyard for days and nights, without food and water, pleading for leniency, then growing ill and moaning, until they curled up in silence. Sometimes a Japanese soldier laughed or spat at them as he strode past. The rest of us tried not to stare, which was all we could do to help them. Before long, more amputated arms and legs hung from the lampposts and signboards along the major streets . Everywhere, the local body was under threat.

I wish I could say I shared the same empathy with the British prisoners of war. The Japanese loved making the white soldier work in the streets in his old military uniform, on display for everyone. The soldiers were as hollow-cheeked and skeletal as Appa had been, their uniforms stained and torn and baggy, and I could see why they called them fatigues. Their brown shirtsleeves, rolled up to the elbows, hung like hula hoops, and their shorts billowed as airily as mine. I saw a soldier missing an arm, his sleeve like a flag flapping whenever he moved. These soldiers wiped the courtyard with wet rags. They stood inside the drains running along its perimeter and cleaned it with their bare hands. Some crawled around the grass with a pair of scissors, trimming it one blade at a time. I learned that the unfinished scaffolding in the middle of the courtyard was a memorial the British prisoners of war were building for the Japanese war dead, the only dead that mattered now. After we sang the National Anthem, they pulled away the white drape and I guessed that its final shape was to be a tall marble tablet sitting atop a stone block foundation, with Japanese names to be scrawled around it. A few Japanese soldiers supervised them, looking far cleaner, stronger, sharper, carrying their Arisaka rifles, visually impressing this new hierarchy upon us.

I did pity the Anglos. But I remembered how they used to shout at my father, calling him "Sinkie" and "Blackie". I remembered that they used to saunter around their base and suddenly order him to fetch a soldier or mop up a splotch of oil on the wharf or grab a shoeshine to clean their boots with. All this had been fine, we had accepted it as part of life as long as they had seemed superior. Then they lost the war. Surrendered. Now, our inevitable masters did the same dirty work that had been reserved for Appa and me. I had never seen a white man do manual labour before and felt a smug satisfaction. I admit that it was a shameful thought, indulging in the pleasure of seeing another man fall beside me. Given a choice, I would not have wished defeat or subjugation upon these soldiers. In fact, I had wanted them to win for all our sakes. But seeing that subjugation was their *fait accompli*, I could not help but feel schadenfreude.

...

In the evenings, I cooked dinner, made tea and served the soldiers. After that, I returned to Kurosawa's house and had "free time" as the soldiers called it, though I felt anything but free. Kurosawa normally worked at his desk. Sometimes, he reclined on his mat and read a book, or poured himself two cups of sake and closed his eyes and meditated, although I never knew about what. Occasionally, he hummed a tune. He never glanced my way. So I loitered on the yard outside, ate biscuits if Yamashita gave me any, and even taught myself to climb the Angsana trees. One thing that all the colonialists had in common was that they all ended up moulding me into some form of jungle boy.

Some nights, Kurosawa brought a woman back to the house. Or a woman would come to the door and say, "*Ojama itashimasu.*" Each time, it was a different woman,

Dutch, Korean, Chinese, Indian, but they wore tight-fitting uni-coloured dresses that ended high above their knees, high heels to match the colour of the dress and bright red lipstick. Their hair was either pulled back and tied into a bun or cascaded over their shoulders. For all their differences, they could have been the same woman with the same fake smile.

The women mostly smiled kindly at me and walked me outside, escorting me to a more appropriate place so I wouldn't see what followed when they locked the door. A few were mean and ordered me out with harsh tones and snappy fingers while they smiled at Kurosawa like he was an old friend they were glad to see again. But I was happy to leave. At that age, I first assumed from the whimpering noises behind the door that he was beating the women the way he caned me. I became disquieted thinking that the sentries smirked just as much whenever Kurosawa hit me. But after a few weeks, it struck me that he wasn't beating them, and I just knew that he was doing what I had seen the dogs do near the Sembawang base.

I did not understand what many of the women said. But I remember one woman, a Singaporean. After the deed was over, she came outside and stood over me. I was lying on the grass, staring at the high and cloudless night sky. The woman wore a black dress and heels and took a cigarette from her purse. She took a drag and the slate-grey smoke whistled through my sky. A thick infusion of tobacco and musky perfume settled on me and I wrinkled my nose, but didn't say anything. It was quiet behind us and I assumed that Kurosawa was asleep.

She put her cigarette hand on her hip and considered me from above. Finally, she said in Malay, "What are you doing here?" For some reason, her voice reminded me of mango, young and sweet and warm.

I sat up and waved at the air around me, trying to clear the smoke. Then I saw her face. Her thin eyes were bored and unconcerned, and I could tell she didn't care what I said in return. Her nose was pointy and she wore dark purple lipstick. Her face reminded me of mango too, the type that old aunties left out on rattan baskets to dry under the sun, dried but still sweet. I decided that I liked her. "I don't know," I said, sniffing the air to see if its purity had been restored. It still smelled of tobacco and strong perfume. "Working for Lieutenant Kurosawa, I guess."

She nodded and continued smoking, obviously unimpressed by my answer, likely not even having heard it. I gave up trying to clear the fumes. I asked her, "What are you doing here?"

She smiled at me. Then she cooed, pretending to be me, and her voice chimed sweetly. "Working for Lieutenant Kurosawa," she said.

I remained quiet.

As if reading my mind, she said, "Do you want to know what I do, little man? Are you curious?" She fingered the hem of her dress. "Do you want to know where I get my cigarettes from?"

I shook my head furiously, red-faced, and she laughed. Then she toked on her cigarette. "We were not that different once, little man. They like us for the same reason, you know that? Do you want to know what that reason is?"

I kept quiet.

"We were young and virginal." She laughed. "You see, we were not that different once."

I kept thinking, *mango, mango, mango.*

The next week, I saw the girl go into the soldiers' houses, wearing the same black dress. The soldiers jumped up and catcalled and whooped from the kerb as she came down the road, clearly having been briefed about the night's recreation. One got down on his knees and raised two hands up to the sky and said, *"Tennō heika banzai!"* Long live the Emperor! They laughed but quickly picked their comrade up in case Kurosawa came out and sent the girl back, at which point they would have had to join the long queue for the Comfort Station at Cairnhill Circle instead. Mango girl waved at me and gave a mischievous wink as she passed Kurosawa's house and I waved back, meekly. I felt proud that she had noticed me, that she had bestowed me with a wave and a wink. She had a cool calmness that I admired. She went into the first house and all the soldiers followed her inside, like a vacuum had sucked them all in. I only learned later that Mango girl was called a comfort woman, and that she had filled two days of her quota that evening. She couldn't have been older than sixteen.

On a less amorous night, two desert-green jeeps pulled up along Jalan Besar Road. The soldiers formed three rows on the road and Platoon Sergeant Takagi led an equipment check. They laid out their magazines, bullets, grenades, torchlights, battering rams and more on the asphalt, the orange of the houses acting as floodlights while the rest of the street stayed dark and hidden. Yamashita and two other Section Commanders counted the soldiers and then barked at them to stand at stiff attention. Takagi reported the status of the troops to Kurosawa and if the officer was satisfied, Takagi shouted at the soldiers and they gathered their belongings, armed themselves and poured into the waiting jeeps. The officer was always satisfied. Kurosawa sat next to the driver, prerogative of the highest-ranking commander in the vehicle, and the jeeps drove off for their next night raid in the city or in Johor. Sometimes, they went up to Malacca too. I wanted to follow, to see where they brought the men and women they arrested and to see if Appa was amongst them. But I had to sit with the sentries until Kurosawa and Yamashita returned.

...

The Japanese military had a strict social hierarchy, based on gender, rank, age and race, all of which tended to correlate. The older Japanese men were more highly ranked and the younger ones, lower. Then there were the rest of us, civilians, Singaporeans, women, floating around like ducks around warships. The higher up the hierarchy, the better you were treated. The Kempeitai were treated the best of all. The lower ...

Two weeks into my capture, a soldier shouted, "Nanban! Come here!"

Saito, a wiry soldier who looked no older than a teenager, sat on the kerb with other off-duty troopers, drinking weedsoup. He had a wide face that reminded me of the broad flanges of an orangutan, with beady eyes and a stout nose and thin lips. He waved his hand at me and I crossed Jalan Besar Road to stand before him. He eyed me up and down and said, "Wait here." He went into the house and came out with a four-kilogram sack of rice. "Here," he said and swiftly lifted it onto the top of my head.

Instinctively, my arms reached up and grabbed the sack and there I stood, holding a rice sack overhead, the sagging weight pressing down on me. "*Susume*," he said, pointing at my legs. At first, I didn't understand the word. Standing opposite me, Saito marched on the spot, lifting his knees and slamming the balls of his feet down onto the road. "*Susume. Susume.*" March. A few soldiers snickered.

Tentatively, I raised my knees to march. Saito pushed my arms in so they straightened and lifted the sack higher overhead. "Sing the *Kimigayo*," he said.

I only knew a few words of the Japanese National Anthem and shook my head. I hadn't memorised it yet, partly because I had been getting away with not singing it in the mornings. He chuckled and shook his head. "Sing. Sing. When you sing, you can go. You must learn the *Kimigayo*."

I murmured a few words and faltered. I tried humming the tune instead.

"Again. Keep trying. Say the words."

My arms started to burn, sweat rolling off them. The sack felt heavier. Saito puffed out his chest and tucked his chopsticks under his armpit and pretended to be a drill sergeant. He barked incoherently and the soldiers roared in laughter at his mimicry of Takagi. He placed a hand at my chest level, palm facing down. "Here! Here!" He thwacked the bottom of my thighs upwards and I raised my knees higher so the top of my thighs slapped his palm, trying to meet his standard of marching. Then I forgot the words.

"Don't stop! Start again! Start again!"

I tried. I forgot. More laughter revelled around me. Saito clapped his hands to time the beat of my marching and my legs, leaden, struggled to keep up with his furious pace.

"Louder! Faster! Louder! Faster!"

I was yelling what I knew of the anthem, a burst of a word here and there, when my arms crumpled. The sack dropped onto my head with a painful *thump* and then fell to the floor. I collapsed to the ground with it. Saito shook his head, feigning disappointment. He raised a finger. "He's bad, huh?" The soldiers laughed and rose, gathering their mess tins. The evening entertainment was over. They entered the house, leaving me on the street.

Nakamura lingered outside. He grimaced at me and said, "It's okay, Nanban. Return the rice and go home." Then he went in too. I obeyed his instructions. It spoke to the height of my fear that I was actually relieved Saito had not punished me further for not remembering the *Kimigayo*.

From then on, I told myself to stay out of the soldiers' sights. I made it a point to eat dinner behind Kurosawa's house, in the verdure of the trees where it was safer, and tried to keep away from Jalan Besar Road in the evenings. But this was not always possible, especially when I was walking back late from Headquarters. So to make it easier on myself, I started singing the *Kimigayo* during the morning assemblies, singing this ode to the Emperor, wishing he would reign over Japan and Singapore and me for thousands of years. With more help from Saito, I memorised it within two weeks.

But after that, Saito made me carry a six-kilo sack, then an eight-kilo sack. He clutched my mouth open in an O and poured rice beer down it. As a child, the beer was bitter and it stank. He ordered me to walk a straight line on Jalan Besar Road and the soldiers laughed as I sashayed and swayed and tripped into the drains before blacking out. I woke up outside Kurosawa's house with a balakkoo on the back of my head, the *kamidana* watching over me. Yamashita had kicked me awake.

Just once, Saito smiled pleasantly, knelt and stuck a hand out to me. This made me even more terrified. Hesitantly, I reached mine out, wondering if this were a new compromise. He grabbed my right arm, turned his back to me and threw me over his shoulder. I catapulted over and fell on the flat of my back, the shock tearing through my spine. With a yell, I thrashed on the floor as laughter echoed around me. Saito smiled even more pleasantly. After a while, the laughter faded, the pain left and Saito disappeared. I lay on my back, staring at the night sky, blinking and waiting for my body to settle. This was my introduction to the famed world of Japanese martial arts, or *budō* as they called it. Later I learned that Saito had treated me to a famous judo throw called the *ippon seoi nage*, and I wondered why a man so much older and bigger—decidedly stronger—felt the need to use such a technique to incapacitate me, or why he needed to incapacitate me in the first place. But like Mango girl, I was entertainment fodder for the Jalan Besar soldiers during their free time, letting them do what they wanted to me. And I counted the days till I escaped, when I would no longer be at Saito's mercy.

But the soldiers bullied their subordinates too, and I believe that the Japanese soldier dreaded facing his officer more than his enemy. Platoon Sergeant Takagi, who was in charge of the soldiers' discipline, gaffed the troopers with a baton for every mistake. The soldiers like Saito merely closed their eyes, steeled their bodies and muttered repeated apologies while he berated them. Once, Takagi ordered two soldiers to punch each other in the face, alternately, at his command. First they swung crosses at each other's cheeks. But Takagi shouted at them to punch each other's jaws and noses. He commanded them to punch harder and harder. Finally, one of the soldiers collapsed, concussed, bleeding below the eye. Takagi left the other soldier, also bloodied, to tend to the comrade he had knocked out.

But a crucial difference existed between them and us: The Japanese could thrash an inferior soldier because of the hierarchy they had already established amongst themselves. The Japanese soldier could only establish his hierarchy in Singapore because of his ability to thrash us if we refused to obey. The gun gave them power over me, let them treat me like an *eta*. I started considering whether power was cruel, or if cruelty was power, and if this was what it took to survive in this world. For if saving Appa required me to be cruel, I was prepared to do whatever it took.

...

Every Saturday evening, Kurosawa hosted dinner in his house, and Yamashita and I rearranged the desk in the middle of the room, propped up on its bricks, and I sponged away the table marks left against the wall. We rolled up Kurosawa's documents inside my mat and Kurosawa's mat, and kept them neatly in the corner with his field pack and uniforms. His guests were usually officers of the Japanese military of equivalent or higher rank, for Kurosawa never fraternised with anyone of a lower rank. They sat with folded knees around the table, and the most important officer and Kurosawa sat across each other in the middle. The least important sat on the fringes, almost without a table to eat from. Yamashita prepared the food.

I sat next to the bottles of Japanese sake, either of *nihonshū*, which is less strong, or *shōchū*, which is Japan's hard liquor. I learned to listen carefully if anyone needed a refill, and poured the right drink. Some of the soldiers called me the ugliest *oiran*, or courtesan, they had ever met. Apparently this was so funny it bore repeating and more repeating. Yamashita explained the joke to me.

Once, a lieutenant of Kurosawa's age shouted at me for potato *shōchū*. He was red-faced and rambling on with Kurosawa, gesticulating enthusiastically with his hands. I knelt by his side to pour into his ceramic cup, holding the bottle with both hands as I lifted its bottom, as Yamashita had taught me was the respectful way to pour a drink. Then the Lieutenant accidentally swatted my hands and the colourless liquid started spilling onto his lap. He shouted and reeled back. The officers roared cheerily at his misfortune.

I was stunned and stood there like an idiot, holding the bottle downwards as if I was still pouring him a drink, the clear liquid pouring onto the tiled floor and seeping into the cracks and soaking his socks. The officers cheered some more. Then the bottle disappeared from my hands as Kurosawa snatched it away. The wet Lieutenant had risen now and was dabbing at his soused trousers rather uselessly with a handkerchief. Another pink-flushed officer pretended to lick the alcohol off at his nether region and they laughed some more. Kurosawa handed the half-empty bottle to the drenched officer, telling him to keep it. Then he curled a finger at me as if to say, "Come here." He still wouldn't say a word to me.

He took the rotan and I followed him outside while the banter and drinking resumed inside the house. Kurosawa motioned for me to face the wall and I knew what he would do, but decided then that I wouldn't scream and beg for him to stop the way I had the first night. I would be as cool and stoic as Mango girl had been. When the pain slashed through me, tears fell from my eyes but that was out of my control. I just didn't scream. After caning me five times, he went back under the *kamidana*. Although I was trembling, I quickly followed as if nothing had happened, returning to courtesan duty. But from then on, I didn't yell or beg at his canings, like when he caned me for collecting the wrong folder or leaving biscuit crumbs by the door or staring at him from outside as he was talking to an informant. It was my own little stubborn resistance. It was the only thing we fought back with in those days—pride.

But I was glad when Kurosawa chose to bring girls to serve during the Saturday dinners, for he and the other officers were happier socialising with womenfolk. The women sat in between the men, all pained smiles as they piled rice and pickled vegetables onto the men's plates and poured sake into their cups and carried out simple conversations in Japanese, as if the soldier was interested in talking. But they certainly put on a better show of enjoying it. The men put their arms around them, touched them, kissed their cheeks like goldfish as the women turned their lips away. When the girls were around, I was allowed to sit outside. Through the doorway, under the orange light, I watched the soldiers eat and drink until two or three in the morning, loose and merry, a bacchanal celebration. They laughed and stood and chest-thumped at each other over the table, stumbled out drunk, and occasionally fell asleep amidst the angsanas thinking they were home. I considered urinating over their unconscious bodies but I am afraid to admit that I couldn't find the temerity to do this. But they were the complete opposite drunk from what they were sober.

This way, over the days and nights, over the passing weeks, over the armed Japanese soldiers ruling over the other peoples, over the Japanese soldiers drinking alcohol and eating food and smoking tobacco that the rest of us could not afford, over the British soldiers who had lost the War and now laboured to complete the war projects of their victors, over the locals running to and fro at the behest of their new masters and the locals hiding in their slum houses and scrimping for rations, over the black crows on heads on poles, over the half-built memorial, over Headquarters, over Kurosawa's house, over and above all of this, a white flag, with a red sun in its middle and thick, red rays streaming out of the sun like a glorious cartoon image, fluttered proudly on the courtyard, announcing that it was the real sun.

After two months of captivity, having delivered a note from Kurosawa to Uchida, I was walking in the hallway of Headquarters when someone behind said in Malay, "Oi, wait." I saw a local man in his forties looking around, worrying if he had spoken too loudly, as if fearing so would save him now. He was what I like to call an idiot. Then he advanced towards me. He glanced at me cursorily and hurried past to talk to another man by the door. They lowered their heads, muttering into each other's ears. But in the echoes of the hallway, I heard them talking in Malay.

"Don't forget to collect the new passes for the drivers. Security is tight across the causeway. We don't want any problems as they cross over into Johor. You understand?"

The other man nodded seriously and I headed for the entrance again and his voice blossomed in my ears. "You've arranged the drivers for the second leg into Burma?"

"Yah yah, don't worry about that. You just make sure the drivers are at the prison by seven. If they are late, we are dead. And remember the new passes. Don't forget."

I stopped, barely a metre from them. A prison. Appa was in prison.

"I know I know. I'll have the drivers at Changi by six-thirty. And I'll have the passes ready too. No cockups. I promise."

I picked up the word "Changi".

"There better not be."

"What are you looking at, boy?"

The men were glaring at me.

"You want something?"

"N-no, sir."

I bowed my head and stalked towards the entrance, feeling their stares follow me until I pushed the heavy doors open and gladly left. A thunderstorm raged outside, pounding Headquarters and the courtyard like an air raid, having cleared the open plaza and roads of people. The sky was low and grey, occasionally breaking apart in white flashes. The storm encouraged me into thinking that this was the moment. I knew where Appa was and wanted to save him. He wouldn't be in the prison come dawn the next day if they took him into Burma. And I thought that Kurosawa

WARRAN KALASEGARAN

would assume I was waiting out the rain at Headquarters and wouldn't look for me unless it subsided, which it didn't look to do for a few hours.

It is of course laughable that I assumed one prison held all the detainees. But it is also even more laughable that as a nine-year-old, I thought I could single-handedly rescue Appa. But after singing for the Emperor to rule long over me every morning, after praying to the *kami* and bowing and scraping for the occupying soldiers on a daily basis, it became apparent that what was laughable could also be real. And I intended to make it so. I bowed to the guards as I showed them my pass and ran down the stairs, thinking it was the last time I would bow to them. It was time for me to escape, and I decided to run for Serangoon Road.

6

Tailored Revolutions

Every illiterate person living around Serangoon Road gathered on the second floor of Papatti's house that Saturday, crammed around the dining table, unromantically pressed against each other inside the bedrooms. Their chatter swirled and tea boiled over the stove, the Ceylon smell engulfing them, repulsing Papatti, who had never really liked tea—a quirky distaste for a local to have. Lalitha fried vadais, a spicy South Indian doughnut, and the oil in the pan sizzled and crackled to Papatti's approval. Her amma poured the tea . into stainless steel tumblers and arranged the vadais on trays. Children distributed the refreshments to the adults, nipping deftly through the bodies without spilling the tea, running back for more. Papatti knew that some of her guests could read and write far better than she could, but they had turned up anyway. The embroidering had turned from a way out of memorising letters into an excuse to gather old friends.

The evening before, Papatti had carried her unfinished garments down to Govinda mama's backroom for safekeeping.

She had returned her bobbins, pincushions and legions of safety pins into their knobbly drawers and hidden the metre rule behind the machine. She scrubbed the sewing tabletop with a rag until it was a spotless brown, and left only the polished needle perched there, its tip glinting, ready for business. Papatti joined the sewing table with an extra desk to create a longer work surface and placed the stool opposite her, arranging it like an interview that she would control.

Intent on being thoroughly professional, Papatti invited her guests to sit in front of her one by one and asked what letter they wanted. Always, they asked for "A", some having already drawn a pattern on the back of their callused hands like henna. They stuck out their collar undersides, shawl tips and blouse bottoms, and pointed at the precise spot they wanted the alphabet embroidered with furtive whispers, as if someone might rat on them during the vote. Papatti refused more complicated requests, like from Singham, who wanted a lion to bellow the "A".

They babbled as she sewed, telling her they had bought kuehs from the Nyonya shops as house gifts, told her that as they had walked to Serangoon, they had called on Ravi on Lavender Road or Ilamaran at Bugis Street and dragged them along. "There he is, you see, showing off his letter. He was so lazy just now, telling us he knows how to read and write and is an educated man and all that. He said he taught your father and wanted to sleep in. My daughter also knows how to read, but she is here. Right or not, Papatti? What do you say?"

Papatti nodded, absent-minded. In her sewing chair, she was in the position of authority, and the customer needed her. It was the only time she felt safe in her dealings with the outside world. She glanced at Ravi, who had asked for the alphabet "A" on his shoulders like military epaulettes. He was showing them off to Wei Liang. But of course, Ravi was the sort to strip off his shirt in the voting booth, hang it up for the next guy to copy from, and walk out half-naked to grab a Tiger beer, braggadocio all the way to the coffee shop. Wei Liang, for his part, was competing with Ravi. He had demanded that Papatti sew the letter on his bottom, over his back pocket, because he wanted to say goodbye to the colonisers in his peculiarly emphatic way. Wei Liang had lain over the stool like Superman while Papatti threaded the fabric of his bottom regions without poking his skin, not because she did not want to hurt him but because she did not want to think she had even indirectly grazed his bum. It was quite an accomplishment, for every two seconds someone slapped Wei Liang on the buttocks or tickled his toes. He scolded her for not guarding his decency and honour until she threatened to pierce him with the needle and leave it shuddering there like a flagpole. After this, he sulked and grumbled about how rude women were these days and so she "accidentally" pricked him twice as she wove the "A" above his backside.

As she watched them now, Ravi and Wei Liang shouted at each other, fighting over whether Papatti was *one of theirs* or the *others'*. She became annoyed that this mattered, as if she could be treated like some inanimate possession, as if she could not just be her own person. But she could also not help smiling. People wanted *her*. And so far, no one had even mentioned Muthu & Co.

This gathering had not been difficult to organise. Rajpal had flitted from house to house showing off the "A" sewn into his shirt until Lalitha forced him to wash it. Papatti had quietly encouraged her appa to continue touting, and persuaded her amma that this would eventually increase the footfall to Govinda's Textiles Emporium and would help to pay the bills. In fact, she even proposed charging ten cents per stitching, but the night before, Rajpal had said, "I will not hear a word of it."

"Appa, I should charge more than a tattoo artist. I stitch for them and it doesn't even mar their bodies forever. If they change their minds, they just need to buy a new shirt. And if they like it that much, they can put it up in their house, like a trophy."

"That is your amma's side of the family talking. Only her brain thinks like that. Trying to milk money out of everything."

Lalitha shouted from the kitchen, "At least I have a brain. We could do with the money anyway. Listen to your beiti. Who's going to pay for all the thread we will end up using?"

"That's exactly what I mean. No no no," He unrolled his mat to lie on, offended on behalf of his embryonic nation. Papatti would have appreciated the extra money, but she didn't mind. She savoured having a crowd in her house, people struggling and shouting over each other to catch her attention, then sitting suddenly quiet and obedient while she stitched.

Velu fell onto the empty stool and shouted for both floors of the shophouse to hear, "Don't sew anything! I want to spoil the vote!"

The room booed. Gales of laughter as someone chanted, "Sabo!" "Communist!"

Velu clapped, relishing the attention. Then he cupped his mouth and said, "Who say I Communist? Ravi you idiot! You are a Communist! I never sabo! Wei Liang, I tell you! You dare to come here and make fun of me!"

They riposted back and forth, and when the spectators grew bored and Velu could tell, he turned to Papatti. "I'm just kidding girl. Come, give your uncle an 'A'. Let's see why my wife keeps spending all my hard-earned savings at your shop." Papatti fiddled in her spool drawer until she unearthed a matching colour.

When she was finished, Velu looked for the next person to bother, and Papatti tried to spot Rajpal's head wafting above the crowd. His colleagues huddled near the cupboard but he wasn't with them.

"Is it my turn then?" Karnan smiled at her and occupied the stool, tapping on its legs rhythmically. His dark eyes glinted like her needle. If anything struck Papatti about Karnan, it was his hirsuteness. Many times Papatti had wanted to ask him what brand of coconut oil he used to sweep his hair so smoothly to the side and back. His sideburns were evenly razored off at the earlobes, and what was left was so thick it looked stuck on. He sported a fiery black moustache that faded like two triangles beneath the ends of his lips. His mouth was always slightly parted, as if perpetually on the verge of saying something. "I came for a letter but I don't mind if you just want to gawk all day." He laughed at his own joke.

"I'm surprised you didn't come because your shirt was torn for the what, fiftieth time?"

"I didn't need that excuse this time, did I?" He seemed surprised by his own words, this sudden abandon. Then he smiled sheepishly.

Papatti raised an eyebrow and sat up straighter. "Well, your business pays better than your jokes."

"What. That hurt, but I guess I deserved it. I just hope you won't tell your amma what I said?"

She narrowed her eyes, letting him simmer in fear of Lalitha. Finally she said, "I won't. So how is this shirt holding up?"

He looked relieved and the twinkle returned to his eyes. He was wearing a grey-striped white shirt that she had not mended before. Despite the maddening heat, he hadn't rolled up the sleeves. Instead, he now tugged the cuffs downwards and the cloth stretched around his big arms. Karnan was short, but he had the low-centred, stocky strength of a labourer used to walking a narrow plank between boat and shore carrying steel plates and gunnysacks from dawn through dusk. He said, "This is my one good shirt. I don't wear it to the docks. But the rest are fine too. Still holding up—don't worry."

"I'm not worried. I'm happy for them to tear. Like I said, it's good business for me." She mimed counting change with her fingers.

He beamed, and she found it strange—how happy he was to part with his hard-earned salary. Did he think she was joking? He said, "What's happening outside?"

They turned to see a cluster of uncles and aunties swarming the door, craning their necks to peek through, murmuring gossip to each other in fascination. Papatti shrugged. "So are you going to work after this?"

"Are you chasing me away already?"

She laughed. "No, no."

He laughed as well. "Well, I actually did expect to work today. We had a big shipment of rubber come in this week from a plantation in Ipoh, but we managed to load everything onto the ships by last night. It's a shame though. I earn more on the weekends."

"Papatti."

Rajpal stood over them, wearing the shirt she had first embellished. That morning, as they had waited for the guests to arrive, Papatti had inverted and sewed the end of his shirt into its body, so the "A" would show proudly along with a triangular patch of Rajpal's stomach. Karnan stood and said in Malay, "Hi, uncle, sorry I didn't see you on my way in."

"Karnan, please sit, please. Papatti, our Assemblyman is here. He's come to see this…" He paused to consider the room. "…event? He wants to say hi to you. He's outside talking to the guests now and will come in soon to talk to you."

"An Assemblyman. An Assemblyman wants to talk to me? How did he find out about this? Appa, you see, I'm going places. I'm famous!"

Rajpal raised his hands victoriously. "I know! I am so proud of you. You have my genes, Beiti. But I just came to give you a heads up. Now, no smart talk you understand? No talking back."

Karnan said, "That might be a bit difficult for her, uncle."

Rajpal nodded with resignation. "I know. She doesn't get that from me. Now Papatti, just smile, show some respect and get a good name for yourself and the family. You understand?"

"Appa, must you lecture me in front of others? I know."

Rajpal was sincerely sorry. "It was an emergency. Sorry. Okay, I need to go see to the Assemblyman now. But remember: behave."

"Appa!"

Karnan sat down as Rajpal left and she asked him, "Which Assemblyman is this?"

"How would I know?"

"I thought you are some harbour union leader? You always give us pamphlets and tell us to attend rallies and come support this and that. What's the point of all that if you can't even tell me who to support?"

"I'm not hearing the respect."

"Yes, that's what's important now."

"I thought you're not supposed to talk back either?"

"To the Assemblyman, not to you."

"So much for post-colonial equality. Well, I know my Assemblyman. This is Serangoon so it should be...Arjun Kandasamy, right? Never mind, I think we are about to find out."

A man had walked backwards into the room, his silver camera plastered to his face, its broad black strap falling behind his neck. The camera shutter snapped away and the crowd behind the photographer widened to gave him space. Arjun Kandasamy entered, oblivious to the photographer, a tall lean man smiling widely for everyone in the room, for the customers in the Ah Hock Stainless Steel shop across the road, and maybe even for the hidden cameras in heaven to see. It was the largest smile Papatti had seen, made more brilliant by a face so clean-shaven she suspected that he scrubbed it with bristles and whitening detergent daily. His eyes shone, happy to see everyone. His nose looked wonky, as if it had been broken, and she had a strange desire to test its elasticity, to pull it to one side and see how far it bent. His hair was short on the sides and he combed it back slick. The Assemblyman wore his trademark red shirt tucked into grey pants, starched like they had dropped onto him from the sky, and his party's ensign was pinned to his left side of his chest. She admitted that he was a handsome man, and appeared very sure of himself. She was not sure if she sighed.

A little entourage followed Arjun into the room, led with smug satisfaction by Rajpal and Lalitha, and her amma shot Papatti a stern stare. The crowd pivoted around Arjun's movements. Arjun cast his Colgate smile on the guests standing in a huddle nearest to the door and stuck out an open hand. The man closest grabbed it and they exchanged words. Arjun lodged himself squarely in the circle, as if he had belonged there all along . His gaze turned like a clock's hand as he asked each person a question.

The photographer crabwalked around this ring, snapping as many pictures and angles as possible. He bumped into Poonitha and finally appeared to realise that there were other people in the room. He went up to Lalitha and whispered into her ear, whereupon she frowned and pointed Papatti out. Lalitha stared distrustfully at Papatti, and Papatti glared back. The photographer walked in between, interrupting this staring contest, asking, "Are you Papatti?"

"No, I am."

The photographer put his hands on his hips. "Don't joke, Karnan. I'm working here. Papatti, I just wanted to give you a heads up. I think the Assemblyman will come, shake your hand and talk to you a little. Then I'll take a photo of the two of you for the papers, probably the *Tamil Murasu*. Is that okay?"

She nodded circumspectly, but wished she could jump around and hug Rajpal instead. First, the Assemblyman's visit, and now, a feature in a national newspaper. The day was turning out better than she had ever dreamed possible. If this did not demonstrate to everyone that she was a unique brand of seamstress, she did not know what could.

Karnan said, "What about me? I'm not a bigshot Assemblyman or tailor or anything, but I'm a voter. I'm a constituent, man."

"Karnan, not now."

"I'm just joking, Rafi. Relax."

Rafi sighed. "I know. But I want to spend Saturday with my family, not work here. Come, take photos and go. I promised my wife. Besides, you know boss is strict when it comes to work. No fooling around." He thumbed in Arjun's direction.

Karnan said, "I'll take the camera off your hands, but I don't know how to operate it."

"It's okay. You'll damage it and then I'll spend more

weekends working to buy a new camera for the department. Anyway, why am I talking to you? I came to talk to her. Papatti, okay, just relax. He's a strict boss but very friendly outside of work. He likes talking to people. He will probably ask you a few questions, congratulate you, maybe make some small talk. Relax and have fun. Okay? Good. Don't let this clown distract you." Rafi slapped Karnan's shoulder and walked away, hoisting the sweat-lathered camera back to his face.

Karnan said, "He's right. Arjun is a friendly guy, a good, hardworking, serious Assemblyman. I've worked with him a few times. But he's wrong about something. I am *not* a clown."

They watched, captivated, as Arjun strode over to the wardrobe. He stared it up and down, and then turned around. The crowd re-pivoted into a semi-circle facing him, blotting out Papatti's view of the Assemblyman with the many colours of their clothes. She noticed that Jamuna's pink Punjabi suit had a white zipper garishly tracing her spine. The tailor should have hidden it. She would remind Jamuna to come see her tomorrow.

Arjun's voice wafted over the heads of the audience, towards Papatti. His voice was not particularly deep, but had a seductive husky tang to it. He was using some mathematical theorem to explain the impact one person's actions could have against the combined weight of the actions of a billion others living and dead, and how through this arithmetic, he had calculated that Singapore would be better off freeing itself from the British and joining the Federation of Malaysia. The Assemblyman dove into his geometry proper and Papatti dove into it too, his voice a conduit, and she swiftly lost track of the maths and the words. Subramaniam said to Jamuna, "What is he saying? I thought I understood everything about the referendum until he opened his mouth. He sounds like a girl. I don't like him. You know, they say he's a Sri Lankan Tamil."

Govinda, standing on the other side of Subramaniam, said, "You grouch. Where do you think your tea's from?"

Subramaniam said, "Why didn't they give us the Benjamin guy?"

Jamuna said, "Lower your voice, dear. The Assemblyman is talking."

"I don't understand a hair of what he's saying anyway."

"So you rather a Tamil Christian than a Sri Lankan Tamil?" asked Govinda. "Tell me the difference."

Retnam stuck his head into the conversation. "Subra, at the end of the day, he's a party man. You should worry what party he's from, not what paati he's from." Paati was Tamil for grandmother, and Papatti clasped her mouth just as a little laughter squeaked out. Retnam said, "And it's a good party. I support them. Which means, I support him, whether he's Sri Lankan or Indian or African. Don't be racist."

Papatti found herself liking Retnam. Why did it matter what race the Assemblyman was? He was an Assemblyman. He had proven himself. He deserved Subramaniam's respect. And what was wrong with sounding like a girl? Papatti started to think that Subramaniam made the same disparaging comments about her whenever Jamuna visited Govinda's Textiles Emporium, making crude remarks about why they were paying money to someone like Papatti. Subramaniam probably said that Muthu on Buffalo Road was a Chettiar and a man who knew business like only a man could, and that Jamuna should go there instead. Papatti became even more motivated to tailor Jamuna a brand new Punjabi suit that would impress Subramaniam into acknowledging that she was the better seamster and deserving of Jamuna's business.

She would show him.

Subramaniam said, "Don't act, Retnam. I'm not a racist. My neighbour, Nathan, you know him, he's a Sri Lankan Tamil and we celebrate Deepavali together. How can I be racist? Look, I see what you're saying about party and all that. But even then, he's too young. He's not even thirty. You see how he sounds? Like a girl that hasn't reached puberty. How can he lead us? We are a generation that's survived hell. What has he been through? He cannot even talk to us, a bunch of uneducated chaps. I cannot understand what hair he's saying. Do you?"

"Don't stir trouble, dear. Leave him alone. He was nice enough to drop by and say hi. Why are you badmouthing him? How do you know what he went through?"

Subramaniam said, "We can find out. Wait. We will solve this now." He made to raise a hand to ask a question but Jamuna caught it and held it down. They struggled, their bodies shaking on the spot, pulling and tugging, slapping each other's hands, hissing at each other. Govinda and Retnam slunk away, leaving the couple in their struggle. Karnan laughed quietly. Papatti, who had moments ago wanted to impress Subramaniam, now found herself hoping that Jamuna would beat that incendiary husband of hers with her fake leather bag until he was purple.

Arjun said, "Uh, is everything okay behind?"

The smile vanished from Papatti's face. Subramaniam and Jamuna froze as heads turned and silence closed in on them holding each other's fingers. They transformed quickly, pretending to be a lovely couple holding hands. Then they pretended to be a couple that was shy about holding hands in public, as any self-respecting Indian couple should be, and released them. Jamuna pulled her tunic straight and adjusted her shawl. Subramaniam looked behind, as if searching for the culprit too with the crowd, and his accusing eyes found Papatti and she reached for her needle. Arjun said, "Maybe I'm being a bit boring."

Heads turned to the front. A thrum of agreement rose. Arjun laughed, nervously. "Okay, okay. Maybe more than a bit. I take the hint. Let me see. I once learned—We must lead with the head, but drive our power from the body, from the masses, from a strong base. We don't have that in Singapore. We are too small a country, too vulnerable, against much larger forces. And I can show it to you. If you can just indulge my math a little more…"

Groans echoed and Arjun laughed nervously. He said, "Please please. Just a little…"

Papatti said to Karnan. "He has difficulty holding our attention, doesn't he?"

"He's intelligent. No doubt about that. Maybe too intelligent. He worked for the British and went to the University of Malaya."

"What did he study? Maths?"

"How did you guess? Well I guess that's why he needs common uneducated folk like me to work the ground. He builds castles in the sky, we explain them to kampungs."

"Are you calling me a kampung girl?" She placed her hands on her hips, then broke into a smile. "I'm just kidding. Explain it to me then."

"You scared me there. What is it you want to know?"

"Whatever Mr Superstar is saying. I need to be able to hold a conversation with him later, right? I have a business to take care of."

He smiled. "Well, your Mr Superstar is saying that we are a small country with a small population and we cannot survive on our own. We need to rule ourselves, but we also need merger to survive. But the Communists are against merger precisely because they know that a Federal Government in Malaysia will be far harder to fight than a City Government in Singapore. So the Communists are going around telling people to oppose 'A'. In fact, they are telling people to oppose the entire referendum altogether. But they are only looking out for themselves because they want to take over the Singaporean government once the British make their exit. And so they are misleading people from the facts. Which is why your Mr Superstar is telling—"

"You must be Papatti."

She jerked up. Karnan leaned back and closed his eyes.

Arjun stood over them, smiling like everything was ordinary. The quiet of the room swept into her ears. Lalitha stood beside Arjun, eyes bulging, dark cheeks shining red, her lips having almost disappeared into that distended face. Papatti and Karnan stood swiftly to shake the Assemblyman's outstretched and waiting hand. The Assemblyman smiled wider, indifferent to the moments that had lapsed, and shook Papatti's. She could already feel the Pythagorean force of his personality drawing her in, overpowering her. "Papatti, hello. I'm Arjun."

"Vanakkam, Assemblyman." Extracting her hand from his grip, she pressed her palms together in a namaskar and bowed her head lightly. She wondered how much of their conversation he had overheard. This was supposed to have been her moment. She had wanted him to like her and support her business, maybe by recommending her to his important friends, or maybe by awarding her an accolade for her contributions to the Malayan sewing industry that she could put on a mantle above the Emporium for all to see. Now, she feared she had lost her chance. She should have listened to her Appa after all.

Arjun said, "Don't be formal, Karnan. How are you?"

Papatti thought they were the same age, but Arjun carried his youth with a gravitas of purpose.

Karnan said, "Good, Assemblyman. Thank you."

"Are we all set for tomorrow?"

"Should be, Assemblyman. We are bussing the union guys in tomorrow morning to set up. Their families will come in the afternoon."

"Good, good." He pulled Karnan closer and leaned into Karnan's ear. With his back to the crowd, Arjun's smile vanished, replaced by tightened eyes and thinned lips that only Papatti could see. His face had become so tight it reminded her of her amma. Arjun said in a whisper that she barely caught, "Next time, don't talk when I'm talking. Just because you're an idiot doesn't mean you have to make me look like one."

Karnan bowed his head. "Yes, Assemblyman, I'm sorry."

Papatti blinked, marvelling at Arjun's ability to scold someone so confidently, and to command Karnan's obedience that way. But his reprimand was unfair. *She* had started the conversation with Karnan and labelled Arjun "Mr Superstar".

She would not confess that though, or he would scold her too. The Assemblyman exuded a politician's pheromones that made her desire his approval, made her want to impress him even more than her business necessitated. In that moment, she decided to settle for mouthing "thanks" to Karnan, and having not done what she knew was right, tried not to feel too ashamed by her cowardice. Karnan smiled back as if nothing was wrong, his eyes and grin twinkling back to cheery normal, telling her to enjoy the moment, and she felt comforted by his ready forgiveness.

As Arjun straightened for the room, that luxurious smile swept back onto his face, dazzling her. He said, "Papatti.

How are you? Can we take a photo?" Without waiting for a reply, Arjun swung around to her side, facing the photographer. Karnan had backed into the crowd, giving Arjun and her a wide berth.

As they stood side by side, Papatti felt Arjun's smile grow impossibly larger next to her, somehow intruding into her vision, and she imagined it blocking her face from the camera. She could hear him breathe. She was that close to a politician, a celebrity of sorts. Now, she would be in the same picture as him. She had almost bungled her chance earlier, but was glad that it was not lost.

She took a deep breath, straightened her back, let her hands hang uselessly down her front and showed teeth, hoping she was doing this right as she stared into the round lens. As she decided to close her lips, a white flash sprung forth, a loud burst of sound, and it was done. Papatti blinked and in the time it took her to blink the Assemblyman was in front of her again, smiling, "Thank you."

Disoriented by how fast the photo-taking session had gone by, Papatti shook her head. "Oh no. Thank you sir."

She forced herself not to stare at his crooked nose, but to look into his dark eyes instead. He was handsome. "No, please, don't call me sir. I am too young for that. Just call me Arjun. And thank you for your service. It's a ground-up initiative, for an important cause, and gets the community together. It ticks all the right boxes. The *Tamil Murasu* will like it. The photo should come out in tomorrow's paper so please keep an eye for that." Arjun glanced around. "And this is quite a multi-racial gathering. I mean, just look at you. It might even end up in some of the other language papers. Maybe even *The Straits Times*. Do you subscribe to any of the papers?"

"My family can't read, sir. That's why we are sewing letters."

"Papatti!" Lalitha's hands struggled with her shawl.

She closed her mouth. She hadn't intended to talk back. But she had thought it was rather obvious, no? Her amma was going to make her roll around the temple in penance after this. Thankfully, Arjun thought it should have been obvious too. He smiled at Lalitha gently enough to calm her from tearing the shawl apart and said, "No, that's my mistake. I'm sorry." He turned back to Papatti. "You are very brave to point it out. I tell you what, the next time I meet my residents, I'll read the article out in Malay. Actually, I'm meeting them next week, on Thursday evening, around eight. Do you think you can make it? You can come later if you want. It will be interesting and I will introduce you to them too."

He had a way of bouncing from staccato phrase to phrase, as if each point was a launch pad to the next logical consequence, thinking as he spoke, his meaning unravelling into existence the same time it built up. Without the maths, it was far easier to follow. His husky voice did not sound "girly" to her either. "Yes, she will," Lalitha said and nodded firmly at Papatti, who in turn mirrored this nodding obediently, not wanting to rattle her amma anymore or spoil what goodwill she had left with Arjun. Anyway, why would she say no? Arjun was helping her. She only hoped that Kareena would open up *The Straits Times* to be surprised by Papatti's face in it, and wish she had been nicer to her classmate all those years ago. In Papatti's mind, she was already famous.

Arjun said, "Well, I wish I could stay longer. I would like to have my shirt inscribed with an 'A' as well. But I have another community engagement to attend. Thank you for having me. And thank you for your work. You are doing a great thing here and I hope you all stay involved in the cause. This is going to be a life-changing vote for all of us and we need all the support we can get. After the referendum, the real work begins." He swung around and raised a dramatic hand up so fast that it barely missed swatting her nose so it looked just as crooked as his. He waved and said, "Thank you! Thank you very much! Thank you!"

7

Dedicated to Papatti

I kicked off my chappals on the porch. Rainwater and mud got on them right away. For a moment, I told myself that I would have to scrub the dirt off that evening or Yamashita would be displeased. Then I reminded myself that I would not be in Kurosawa's house that evening. I would be free. I picked up the slippers in my right hand and sprinted into the downpour. I was drenched in seconds, rain pounding my eyes and ears, blurring my sight like a watercolour painting.

Usually, when I returned to Jalan Besar, I went south from Headquarters and turned east onto Bencoolen Street. This time, I ran north from Headquarters and turned east onto Selegie Road so I would hook behind Kurosawa's house, in the direction of Serangoon Road. Already, the plan was unfolding in my mind, ratcheting up my anticipation and hope. I would blend into Little India and then hitch a ride to Changi, where I would find a way—cut a hole in a fence, climb over a wall—to sneak into the prison camp and find Appa.

Few people stalked Selegie, walking hurriedly away from the city under black umbrellas, eyes cast downwards. Two old British soldiers shovelled dirt that was clogging the ditch running adjacent to the road, numb to the storm and chore, and a boy running from rain perturbed no one. Sophia Road cut across Selegie perpendicularly. Without checking for traffic, I leapt across it. The next major crossing was Rochor Canal. Past it, I would enter Serangoon.

Rochor Canal drew nearer like a finish line, and that feeling of being close to it surged within me. I reached the road that went over the canal I had once caught bugs in. I heard the water rush full-freshet beneath my feet, whipped up into a fury by rain, angry at being fenced in like this. But people took no notice of rivers once they'd caged them and built a bridge across and I too ran across the canal.

Ahead, two rows of shophouses were lined like soldiers. The deserted Serangoon throughway rolled out in between them like a dirty carpet, and its horizon, a thin strip of asphalt, beckoned. The road was empty; the rain had sent the hawkers and their boxes, baskets and mat spreads of goods packing. I reached Tekka Market, which used to be on the other side of the road then. My fever intensified: I was at the beginning of Serangoon Road, so close to freedom and rescuing Appa. I had suppressed how much I missed him the past days, but those feelings were returning fast in the anticipation of seeing him soon. I had so much to tell him. I dashed obliquely across the road, to disappear into the maze of sidestreets and shops that comprised Little India. I ran.

And then I was flying. Something struck my right side with great force and I rolled on the ground, scrabbling with hands and feet to halt my momentum. The rainfall drowned out my shouting, spattered around the bruising of my body against stone and tiles. I came to a stop as I crashed against the cement wall of a house.

A Japanese soldier held an umbrella over his head, pointing at me and shouting angrily. His Japanese was too fast, too enraged, for me to understand. He half-bowed, pointed at his ear, swivelled and shook that hand, then half-bowed again. He resumed pointing at me and shouting, working his anger up, face red and ears quivering. I scrambled to my feet. The skin on my left arms and legs were raw from the tumble and the rain singed them. But I didn't care. I bowed the way I would have if I had seen the soldier, wanting to appease him quickly and carry on running. He wasn't with the Kempeitai or the Jalan Besar unit and I didn't want trouble or to disrespect him, if only he could understand. I bowed as deeply as my vertebrae allowed, staring at the wet floor, water pooled in grey corners, slush soaked with dirt.

He upbraided me still, unappeasable by anything until his anger was all vented. Then he tapped my head. Holding my bow, I peered up. He stuck an open palm out of the shelter of his umbrella and rainwater splattered on it and he showed me it was raining, that I was inconveniencing him greatly. I lowered my head again to apologise for the fact that it was the monsoon season and that it was raining heavily and he grabbed a fistful of my hair and swung it in a circle. I performed a foxtrot with my feet to keep up with the soldier's hand so my hair wouldn't be pulled out at the roots. Then he slapped my cheeks repeatedly, left, right, left. It was more annoying than painful, as if waking me up, calling me to my senses.

"*Mōshi wake gozaimasen,*" I said. "*Mōshi wake gozaimasen.*"

A voice boomed, a voice that overrode rain, and the slapping stopped and I looked up. A grey figure approached us, holding an umbrella over his head, a white armband circling his bicep. The soldier stiffened upright and saluted Kurosawa.

When I met Kurosawa's inquisitive birdlike eyes, I thought I was going to end up a head on a stake in front of the Cathay Building. I considered bolting, but both soldiers would have easily caught me. I hadn't even been able to outrun Kurosawa when I had a head start from Headquarters. Kurosawa positioned himself between the soldier and me, planting his legs apart, declaring his authority. Kurosawa the father, the soldier the son, and I about to become the spirit.

Kurosawa held another umbrella limply from his right hand. His eyes narrowed as they took in the carmine patches on my arms and legs and I saw the choler rise into his face. He seemed about to spit something out.

Kurosawa shouted at the soldier, one finger pointed at me. His voice battled with the rain for superiority, but Kurosawa wasn't going to be beaten by something as insignificant as rain and Mother Nature.

The soldier remained in obedient salute as this orchestra of rain and yelling played around him, this sudden change in his fortune from abuser to abused. I stood by quietly, knowing my place and happy to keep it while I could, thinking, if only this soldier had realised we'd both have been better off if he had just let me go instead of scolding me because of a bow. Pride slayed men, and karma was a powerful equaliser.

Kurosawa lifted the limp umbrella and clubbed the soldier above his knee, at that soft spot of muscle tissue, and his leg bent in. The soldier winced but remained standing at salute and apologising. Kurosawa raised the umbrella higher and bludgeoned him again. His leg gave way inwards and the soldier pitched sideways, almost falling except that now he used his own umbrella as a leg to prop himself up. The rain bathed him.

　　　　　WARRAN KALASEGARAN

Kurosawa pointed towards Serangoon Road, the way I had wanted to go, and his voice escalated to its loudest pitch yet, the denouement, *"Totto to kieusero!"* The soldier leaned his weight against his umbrella to stand straight. Wet and shivering, he saluted and bowed and limped off, the umbrella a vital part of his skeletal structure now, like an old man with a stick. He didn't look back.

I knew it was my turn. Kurosawa considered me. Then he pointed the tip of his closed umbrella at me and I flinched and closed my eyes. He said, "For you. I brought this for you."

I opened my eyes, shocked, feeling stupid for not hiding my fear, thinking, *of all times for him to speak to me and be kind.* He stepped closer and remembering, I bowed. *"Arigatō gozaimashita,* Lieutenant Kurosawa."

He considered the vacant wilderness of Serangoon Road, Tekka Market, the shuttered shophouses. He contemplated me and turned both palms upwards, asking me why I was here. I wasn't sure what the right or safe or believable answer was, or if these three could coincide, so I kept mum, allowing his conclusion to arrive in its own time. He drew a tall paper in front of me and indicated writing on it. I pointed towards Headquarters to demonstrate that I had delivered his note. Satisfied with this priority, he nodded. Then he stabbed at the ground with a finger and showed two open palms again. The same question: *What are you doing here?* He spoke in Japanese, less harshly, and I caught a few words. I knew he had realised it when he frowned at me and dread filled me with a sick fear. He cycled two fingers alternately like a running man on air and arched an eyebrow.

I lowered my head and nodded.

He tapped my crown. "Why?" his palms said.

"There?" his finger pointed at Serangoon Road.

I tiptoed, soles stretching, and raised an arm as high as I

could and faced my palm downwards, pretending to hold a ball from above, as he once had. It said, *Appa*.

"*Ahh. Sō desu ka.*" He took off his cap and wiped his bald head and his lips slid towards the right as he thought. Then he wore the cap and dropped the closed umbrella onto the ground, where it lay discarded. Kurosawa adjusted the rifle hanging behind him and bent down, locked one arm around my legs and lifted me. I expected to be treated to another painful judo technique, but he just threw me over his shoulder like a fireman, his rifle butt bumping into my face. The rain fell outside the halo of his umbrella and I didn't feel its patters anymore. But I was wetting his uniform.

Kurosawa walked back to Rochor Canal, to Selegie Road. I craned my neck upwards and watched as Serangoon Road and its two fences of houses retreated into the distance, as if fated to fade away. Kurosawa turned the corner and Serangoon disappeared. Gone. We turned onto Jalan Besar and Kurosawa walked into his house without taking off his muddy boots. He set me down in front of the desk and I looked for the rotan.

But Kurosawa snatched a rolled-up scroll from the corner and unfurled the tea-coloured paper on the empty desk. He knelt next to me and he was so close I could smell his stale sour breath, like clothes stored in the cupboard while wet and taken out later. His eyes were level with mine, but staring at the paper. He stabbed it with a finger. "*Miro.*" Look at this.

A wide diamond filled the paper, outlined in thick black ink and scrawled all over with incomprehensible but threatening-looking Japanese words. The artist had scattered smaller diamonds around this big diamond. It seemed carelessly sketched and I thought he couldn't have been a very good artist. Kurosawa stabbed at the bottom of the wider diamond. He pointed at me with the finger, pointed at himself, and pointed at the same spot on the diamond. "We are here," he said. The realisation that I was staring at a map for the first time suspended my sense of captivity. It felt like the world was laid out in front of me, a world larger than Singapore, Malaya, Britain and Japan, a world to escape into from this hell. Enthralled, I held my breath and edged closer. Appa had once told me that if the world was flattened, it would look like a broad and rectangular cobweb. But the map was nothing like a cobweb and I only wished Appa could have seen it. Then I remembered that I had failed to escape or rescue Appa, and that this world of hope, however large, remained elusive. I was still stuck in Kempeitai-controlled Singapore. I stepped back, disappointed, and then afraid that sooner or later Kurosawa would punish me for trying to escape. Later I would recognise it as a map of Singapore. But at that moment, in my wisdom of nine years, I thought it was a map of the world.

Kurosawa pointed at the northeastern edge of the wide diamond, of mainland Singapore. His finger prodded the beachfront, likely Punggol beach, although I thought then that it was the territory Appa had told me was most northeast on the cobweb: Japan. Europe, everyone knew, was in the centre.

Pointing at this northeastern brink, Kurosawa made the arm-raised motion that had come to represent *Appa*. He sat two fingers on where we were, walked the two fingers up the map, like a marching toy soldier, he marched the two fingers up to Japan, where he jabbed at the spot his fingers arrived at. He did the father sign. Then he cut his neck with his hand.

I shook my head.

He nodded and performed the slicing-the-neck motion again.

I shook my head adamantly, furiously. I stared hard

at the map. I pretended to judge distance and angle from our position to Japan. As if Kurosawa was the child playing the fool, as if I was the serious adult trying to decipher where my father was located on the map. He rotated my shoulders to face him but I turned back to the map. I only knew cobwebs then, not cartography or geography, but using that tea-coloured, pristinely maintained paper, I tried to chart a trajectory from my position to Japan, estimated the time it would take (a few days maximum by my calculations then), decided what I would have to bring along for this odyssey. Kurosawa twisted my shoulders again, pulled me towards him and held me so I couldn't turn back. Shaking my head, I stared at the ground I had swept cleaner than clean that morning. There were big and small mud prints around me. I refused to entertain Kurosawa's childish nonsense.

He stuck two hands into my vision, palms down, and swiped them in opposite directions. *It is over.*

I shook my head, down-staring still.

He dipped his head so his eyes looked into mine, so I couldn't avoid him. He performed the swiping motion, eyes speaking to me, telling me to see and to accept. I shook my head.

He nodded once, firmly. *"Hai."*

"No!" I shouted in Tamil. *Illai!*

He regarded me solemnly, deciding to pretend that I hadn't shouted at him, that I hadn't insulted his superiority. He nodded once, firmly, to restate his point.

I grabbed his cheeks, my hands tiny and weak on his large strong cheekbones. He was alert, but he didn't flinch. I leaned closer and our eyes were inches apart. I yelled into his face, "No! No! No!"

His expression didn't waver. He didn't even remove my hands from his face. He just gave me one firm nod.

"You are lying!" I swung a fist at the side of his head, my first ever punch, a neophyte attempt. My right arm rounded an arc, sailed towards him, and the soft side of my bunched-up fist connected with his cheek. His cheek appeared to merely shudder superficially, whereas the shock of the impact coursed through my arm, reverberating. His eyes widened. I blinked, fist still shaking on his cheek. We took in the now established fact, let it sink in. I had hit him, and he had let me, both of us wondering, why?

Then my shock gave way to an intoxicating feeling of rightness, a feeling of fairness and justice in having punched Kurosawa, that he deserved it, that I deserved it, and this feeling surged into me and I remembered him saying that Appa was dead and I became angrier and I started raining a flurry of chopping movements onto his face, as if I was striking down at him with two hammers instead of the soft fists of a nine-year-old child.

He opened his palms in front of his face so my blows rained on them and I didn't care—I hit his palms instead. I hit and hit and he watched through his fingers. Soon, my arms felt heavier and I began wheezing until with one final punch, I could throw no more, and I stopped and my fists rested in his palms, my weight leaning against him. He watched me catch my breath for long moments of quiet.

Then Kurosawa curled his hands around my fists. He pushed them so I stepped backwards. But he gripped my fists firmly and didn't let go and my arms extended in two straight lines in front of me. He pushed my right hand back to place it by my right cheek, balled up. He pushed the left arm so the elbow bent as it retracted, and then he snapped it back towards him. It felt like a spring had been compressed at the elbow and it now popped and sprung forcefully forward as my left fist landed on his forehead. This time, I hit him knuckles-first, cushioned by Kurosawa's hand wrapped around mine like 16-ounce gloves.

He ran his palm over my extended left arm to show how it had straightened from my shoulder to his face, the shortest distance, instead of the hammer-arcs I had been throwing. He moved my left fist back and forth, from my cheek to his forehead, to show me how it travelled that straight line. He did this again and again to make sure I learned. After this, he set the left fist by my left cheek and pulled my right hand towards his forehead and left it there. He twisted my hip so I felt the power drive up through my shoulder and jerk the fist further forward, further into his face. He held a palm open upwards, jerked it up and towards him. *Drive it up and forward.*

Then he began pulling on both fists alternately like two slings, pushing back the right and pulling the left jab, then pushing the left and pulling the straight right. He picked up speed. He pulled my fists faster and faster, helping my muscles memorise and internalise the form.

With growing momentum, adrenaline rushed into me, epinephrine surged and took over. I leaned forward and flung my weight into the punches and started slugging with abandon again. He let go of my fists and put his palms in front of his face again for me to aim at. I had lost the form he had so briefly taught me. Uncaring, I punched faster and faster, aborted technique for rage. He watched through his fingers and made an *"oosu"* sound as each punch landed, commending the punch, encouraging me to throw another one, until I got it all out of me. I was unaware that tears were running down my face and dropping onto the floor with my sweat. *"Oosu,"* he said, as I just kept hitting.

It felt like we spent the whole night with him kneeling in front of me, two hands open in front of his face, and me standing opposite, eyes level, punching his hands again and again. Again, my arms felt heavier. I widened my feet and flung my shoulders forward, twisted my hips left and right, closed my eyes and socked and smashed as blindly and as hard as I could.

There were no punches left in me. I leaned my hands on Kurosawa's face, wheezing in and out, sobbing long breaths, staring down at the drops of tears and perspiration that blackened the grey concrete around my bare, muddy feet.

I had lost Appa forever. I was as hopeless and powerless as I had accused him of being. I wished I had never accused him of anything less than being the best Appa to me. I didn't deserve to be his thambi. I wanted him back. How I wanted him back. Then Kurosawa hugged me, wrapping his arms around my body and holding me close to his chest, and I fell asleep on his shoulder.

8

The Republic of Families

The next day, the *Tamil Murasu* ran Papatti's story and Rajpal brought ten copies back from his early morning shift, much to Lalitha's ninefold chagrin. On page seven, lines and lines of text surrounded a pocket-sized, black-and-white photograph, the only part of any newspaper her family could understand. Papatti's face peered out, eyebrows arched, eyes wide open, lips half-parted, looking stupefied. Next to her, Papatti realised that Arjun's smile *had* grown wider. He had stiffened upright and locked his arms by his sides with supreme practised confidence, almost standing at attention with a grin, making her look even more neanderthal in contrast. But Papatti didn't care that she looked silly. A national newspaper had featured her. She was officially a celebrity now. As the news sunk in, she jumped. "Appa! That's me! That's me! I'm famous!" Rajpal held her hands and hopped with her. Lalitha ordered them to pipe down.

According to a literate tenant, the headline read: *A-Star Seamstress campaigns for Independence and Merger.*

The article called Papatti a staunch and dedicated anti-colonialist, anti-communist and a patriot (well if a national newspaper said so, then she was), and said that she had spent her entire Saturday campaigning for the Serangoon community to turn out and vote 'A' at the referendum (it would have been nice if the newspaper had added that she hadn't even asked for money for rendering this service). Legislative Assemblyman Arjun Kandasamy had dropped by to speak to Papatti and his residents and endorse the event. His quote on Papatti ran: "Papatti is intelligent, passionate and proactive about the issues (she didn't know what particular 'issues' Arjun was referring to but was happy to find out some day). I thank her and her family for their initiative and the residents for their support (she did not understand why he thanked her family when she had done all the legwork). In fact, her family is an example of the progress we can achieve if we work together (there, she led by example). She's the best tailor on Serangoon Road in my eyes. If you don't mind the pun, she's A-Star."

The best tailor on Serangoon Road.

The-best-tailor-on-Serangoon-Road.

She asked her tenant to say it again and again. Then she whooped as she ran around the dining room table with Rajpal, the other tenants clapping politely while Lalitha banged her forehead against the cabinet wall. Papatti wished she could cartwheel as she had as a kid. If an Assemblyman said so, then it must be true, everyone—Subramaniam, Muthu & Co., whomever else—would have to recognise that she hands down trumped the street's dressmakers and outfitters, that she deserved their respect. The good people of Serangoon would have no excuse to visit any other store anymore. In his exuberance, Rajpal tried to lift and spin her as he had when she was a child, but he sprained his back.

The best tailor on Serangoon Road. Papatti pestered her amma to repeat those words until Lalitha slapped her away and went to lie in the room, washing her hands of caring for the two overgrown children. Papatti accused her amma of jealousy, a most unbecoming trait. People were reading about her. An important person like Assemblyman Arjun Kandasamy was talking about her, complimenting not just her sewing skills, but recognising Papatti's involvement in nationwide "issues", a change agent. She had gone from seamstress to best seamstress to heroine, the way Arjun bounced from a phrase to a conclusion.

Her Saturday guests returned on the Sunday, papers in arm to show her the photograph and share the news, each thinking they were the first, and Papatti let them leave with this illusion intact. Rajpal hid every additional copy inside their cupboard and the secret pile grew and grew until Lalitha flung open the cupboard doors, threw a fit at her husband and called for the karang guni man to tow away the papers in his cart.

Rajpal took this as justification to pronounce to everyone who knocked on their door, "This is my side of the family! My genes! My beiti!" When Papatti dragged her rattling iron wire trolley on its two wheels to Tekka Market to purchase chicken meat from the butcher, neighbours shouted through their windows across the road, "Oi A-Star Seamstress! Yes, you, Papatti! Or should we call you the new Serangoon Sensation?" Papatti blushed, and their warm adoration made sure that the humdrum chore of visiting the wet market did not bring her down to earth.

But then she bumped into Jamuna, who was pulling a trolley with fresh green celery plants sticking out of it. She said, "Papatti, come here. You must see this," and with their two trolleys and vegetables and chicken rumbling side-by-side on the broken road, Jamuna led her to the freshly painted light blue shophouse of Muthu & Co. The "MNC" was in brackets. Inside the store, Papatti saw Muthu, wearing a flashy violet shirt that bulged at his paunch and spilled over black pants. He was laying out sarees on a long counter. There was a new signboard outside the store, surrounded by trinkets on mats and pineapples in rattan baskets. A newspaper was tacked onto the signboard, showing Muthu and Arjun smiling and shaking hands. Jamuna said, "The chalk writing on top of the newspaper says, '*We are not on Serangoon Road.*'"

The preposterousness of Muthu and the company he kept! Papatti was tempted to snatch the signboard and run off, if only she wouldn't knock all the fake gold and silver necklaces and rings into the drains. Jail garb would not suit her.

She tugged at her plait, hard. She took it personally that Muthu would not let her enjoy her moment. He was attacking her, trying to put her in what he thought her place should be, a place where people would deny her talent and she would have no customers, where she would be teased in private, ignored in public. He would win, and as an uneducated girl without a livelihood, she would become a pariah.

In fact, as a woman, she was also envious. She could not imagine shaking hands with Arjun with as much ease and comfort as Muthu exuded in the newspaper, the way only men could when they grasped hands. It would feel weird for her, perhaps even be considered inappropriate or rude, or too manly.

No. She tossed her plait over her shoulder. She would be as unexpectedly defiant as Muthu had turned out to be. She would show him. She would become more than just a "Serangoon Sensation". She would get Arjun to declare to all the *Whatever Times* available that she was the best seamster in the entire country.

And she had her opportunity on Tuesday night, when a tall dark man dropped by their living room. He had a white crown of hair, rectangular spectacles framing his eyes, blue and red pens sticking out of his breast pocket, and a brown notebook in his hand, all signs of a respectable education. He said in Malay, "I hope you don't mind, Rajpal. Govinda let me upstairs."

Rajpal threw his hands up. "Moorthy! Long time no see! Come in! Come in. What are you doing here? Come, come sit." Rajpal dragged out a chair, the legs screeching, as Lalitha took a coffee order and boiled milk over the stove. She instructed Papatti to retrieve the coffee powder from the cabinet, and when Papatti asked for a coffee too, she said, "No! Stop drinking so much coffee! You'll ruin your health." They argued briefly over whether they should argue in front of a guest. Then they made coffee to ruin Moorthy's health instead.

By this time, Moorthy had settled comfortably into the chair and opened his notebook on the table. "I'm actually here for your daughter. My editor sent me to interview her for a follow-up piece on the *A-Star* article. Write about her views on the hot issues. We think readers might like to hear a layman's perspective. What do you think? Papatti, what do you think?"

Papatti wondered whom he was calling a layman. Did any Thambi, Dev and Hari get featured in the *Tamil Murasu* these days? Lalitha said, "You already wrote a piece about her, Moorthy. What more can she tell you?"

"Amma! I want to." Layman or not, a whole article dedicated to her, not even shared with the Assemblyman, that would be a triumph. Even Muthu could not beat this. Perhaps in his quote this time, Arjun would proclaim her the best tailor in the city for her continuing good work on his "issues". She could already see the article fully-formed in her mind's eye, the way she saw the Punjabi suit product she wanted to sell before embarking on the first stitch—a photo of her with one triumphant fist raised, clutching a needle, leading a charge towards some horizon where the issues abounded. She began pulling her nose so it looked sharper for the camera and felt a desire to practise smiling in front of the mirror.

"Papatti, stop that! Pass me the tub."

"Amma, are you going to let me do the interview or not?"

"I'm not sure. Ask your appa first."

"Appa?"

Rajpal was already vacating the chair opposite Moorthy. "Why not? I don't see the harm." Her love for Rajpal surged at times like these, and she felt bad for not being kinder to him more often. Setting aside her guilt, she uncapped the Milo tin that was filled with arabica filter coffee powder, and raced to occupy the chair across from Moorthy.

Moorthy picked up his blue pen. "Okay, Papatti, I have a list of questions and we will go through them one by one. You can take all the time you want to answer the questions and I will write as you speak. Basically, you tell me what to write. How does that sound?"

"That sounds okay to me, Moorthy mama."

Lalitha set a tumbler of coffee before Moorthy and sat between him and Papatti, at the head of the table. The steam slowly began to dot sweat marks on his balding crown. "Have you eaten, Moorthy?"

"Yes, I ate and came, Lalli, thanks." Moorthy slurped the coffee. "Now, let's start. Tomorrow's a working day and I don't want to keep your parents up too late."

Moorthy asked his first question, which she didn't understand. She didn't understand his second or third either, each loaded with one-hundred-dollar words like Factors of Production and Common Market and Autonomy, words that dissolved over her head in indecipherable clouds of issues. Papatti blinked, issued *umms* and *ahhs* and other phonetics of ignorance to buy time, and looked to Lalitha for guidance. She took comfort in her amma's baleful frown at Moorthy, Lalitha obviously unimpressed with these questions too. Rajpal rubbed Papatti's shoulder and whispered, "Just try your best, Beiti. It's okay."

Moorthy, on his part, kept his eyes fixed on her. He said, "Papatti, what do *you* think? I want to know *your* thoughts on the issues. This piece is about *you*." You-issues. You-issues. If only she could find a way to cross the hyphenated bridge between them.

A mortifying self-consciousness crept over Papatti, as she absorbed the increasingly likely possibility that Arjun and Moorthy must just have been being nice to her in the article, as she realised that Moorthy was about to expose her true idiocy to the world. For in all honesty, she didn't know the first thing about any "issue". She had not been avidly campaigning for *A* based on some in-depth understanding of the anti-colonial struggle, the Communist threat or the History of the Japanese Occupation. She liked sewing, had the talent for it and had helped her appa out with his request. She had managed to persuade her appa to spill that over into a fun Saturday that won a little attention in the press. But that was that.

But she—the great competitive seamstress Papatti—had wanted to be in the broadsheet newspapers, had wanted to prove Kareena and Muthu and all the invisible naysayers wrong, and had let this business of publication go right to her head, hopping on one foot to do this interview. Now, Muthu would be tacking this second article onto his signboard, letting her ego defeat her. What would the neighbours and the aunties at Tekka Market say? The Serangoon Shamestress? Papatti might as well move house. Amma was right, she was a silly Papatti.

Moorthy scribbled away her non-answers and she became confident he would write his next article about her appalling ignorance. An article about how she didn't deserve that lofty accolade of A-Star. After all, she was a school dropout who had not even passed a class, let alone mustered an "A" grade. She could see the headline now: "Is this the future of our nation?" The lede: "Papatti is an asinine and spoilt girl, more interested in fame than her country, and an example of the miserable quality of the education system the British have left us with." Papatti bowed her head, scratching the tablewood with a fingernail until Lalitha held it still.

Moorthy took his time reading his notes, the soft flipping of a page occasionally interrupting the quiet interlude. Somehow, Papatti had filled four pages. For the first time, she was glad not to be able to read. As she waited for Moorthy to leave, he said, "Okay, Papatti. Why don't we talk about your family and you? Rajpal, Lalitha, you can chime in here too."

Lalitha said, "Talk about what?"

"Well, I need material to write an article and for that I need something more...substantive. Or my editor will cut me up and cook me in curry and serve me to *his* boss. Arjun was interested in your family. He talked about you as an example of social cohesion. So why don't we talk about that? Talk about how you and Rajpal met. How the two of you adopted Papatti. We could make it a personal family feature. What do you think?"

"I don't know. Why must we talk about ourselves for the world to know?"

"Lalli, it's just a small article and people would like to

read about you and your family. Besides, you probably know everyone who reads this paper, and they know all about you too. What could go wrong?"

"Well, if we say something stupid then the whole country will laugh at us. And you are asking questions about politics and economics like we went to university. Yes, we are not educated, but there's no need to advertise that to the world."

"No, no more questions on politics or economics. I swear upon God. Only on the three of you."

Moorthy glanced at Papatti, a knowing look. She could tell that he was being deliberately kind, giving her a second shot at redeeming herself. She could still save some face, *and* put out her article. But for this to happen, Moorthy needed her to make sure that Lalitha did not squander this opportunity. Papatti said, "Amma, please. If we don't do this, nothing will come out of it and they'll write something bad about me tomorrow." She grabbed Lalitha's hands, ready to use the key word. "Amma, if people read this they will come to our shop. We will make more money."

Lalitha bit her lip, uncertain. "Moorthy, if I tell you not to put anything in, you won't?"

"I swear upon God."

Lalitha nodded. Papatti wished she had clarified these boundaries as well. *Yes, you may ask me about the issues but only write about the issues that I know the answer to, like, is Arjun Kandasamy's nose bigger than Singapore? Did I like that one family holiday when we had all taken a coach to Johor Bahru and eaten nasi ayam penyet and chendol and visited the temple?* Why was it always her amma who was mature and on point, a true worn city survivor, while she, the young upcoming starlet who had had almost one year of schooling in total, behaved like some yokel from the village? Lalitha said, "Dear, what do you think?"

Rajpal said, "I'll let Papatti decide. It's her story more than ours."

Lalitha had been seven years old when her family migrated from a village near Muthupettai town in South India, a three-hour bus ride from Chennai. Her family had rented a room in the shophouse on 107 Serangoon Road, which the Chettiar family owned. Her father worked as a coolie loading and unloading spices onto ships at Keppel Harbour, while her mother laundered clothes for money as a dhobi, together making barely enough to pay the rent and raise one child, which they had hoped would be a boy. Either way, they neither had the heart to let Lalitha go nor the money to risk trying a second time.

Rajpal was born in Singapore and liked to claim that he was the true local in their family, even if his parents had migrated from what was now Punjab state in North India. His father had used their savings from India to lease the entirety of 111 on Serangoon Road. They had occupied one room, and rented the rest of the rooms out for a monthly fee that allowed Rajpal's mother to be a homemaker. Meanwhile, Rajpal had wanted to contribute to the family as a boy and so at eight, he followed his father into working at the *Straits Times* distribution centre, stock-taking the print that he could not read and delivering it by bicycle. By the end of his second year on the job, Lalitha and family had moved in down the road.

Rajpal was a Punjabi Sikh and Lalitha was a Tamil Hindu, but that hadn't stopped their families from arranging their marriage in 1924. This marriage took place because their fathers had enjoyed drinking cheap illicit brandy together late into the nights and their mothers had bonded by first badgering them to stop drinking alcohol, and when that hadn't worked, by whinging to each other about their husbands' objectionable drinking problems. Marriage could only bring their families closer together, a very agreeable proposition for all parents involved. Besides, Rajpal and Lalitha were the same age, spoke Malay and liked each other enough to be able to at the very least tolerate a marriage, so their consent was taken for granted.

Lalitha told Moorthy, "In those days, there were not as many women as there were men in Singapore, so he was lucky I chose him."

Rajpal said, "She is right. I didn't have much of a choice."

"Don't write that, Moorthy. He doesn't know what he's saying. Write my version."

They had two small wedding ceremonies, the first one at the Veerakaliamman Temple. Then they'd walked down Serangoon Road to the gudhwara on Towner Road. Per Indian custom, Lalitha moved to 111 the night of the wedding to join her husband and in-laws. Over the next days, she met Govinda and developed an interest in his textile business. Partially out of fear of being a financial burden to her in-laws, she taught herself to sew, bought the Singer sewing machine, and started helping Govinda's shop for a monthly commission. Of this, she gave half to her in-laws as rent, a quarter to her parents as a good filial Indian daughter, and saved a quarter as a fiscally conservative wife and hopeful mother. Before long, Lalitha's parents couldn't stand to live so far away from their daughter and left 107 to rent a room at 111.

Lalitha's and Rajpal's parents lived long enough to watch their only children fail to produce any grandchildren. Rajpal said, "We used to sit around this table and eat dinner together every night. It was cheap food, Moorthy, maybe rojak or some bee hoon. We even bought two extra chairs for Lalitha's parents and every dinner was like a fiesta. After that, the men, we went into the room with a bottle of whiskey or brandy, some ice and water, and we sat on the floor and drank the whole night. The old men told stories about Punjab or Tamil Nadu and sometimes the other tenants joined us and it was a celebration every night. What a time, I tell you. What a time."

Lalitha said, "No wonder we never managed to make any babies."

"Amma!"

"What? It's the truth. They drank so much. Your father will die of a liver disease or something. You just watch and see. Mark my words."

"*Amma!*"

Rajpal said, "You are going to talk about our love life to a journalist? You want this to come out in tomorrow's paper?"

"Moorthy won't write that. Cancel that Moorthy. Remember our deal."

"Okay, Lalitha." Moorthy made a diligent and obedient show of drawing horizontal lines across his penmanship. "Now, what about Papatti's mother?"

"I am her amma."

"I mean, you know, her biological mother."

"Oh."

...

1939: the zodiac year of the rabbit. Mei's parents stowed her away on a ship packed to the gunwales with coolies and migrant brides and refugees, and hybrids of all three social classes. She was nineteen years old. The steam-powered vessel left port from Fujian province in southeast China, sailing down the South China Sea in the pelagic blue framed by the chilli outlines of Vietnam and the Philippines, to arrive in Lilliputian Singapore. In China, civil war between the Communists and Nationalists had been interrupted by an even more brutal Japanese invasion from the northeast. As the Japanese lapped up Beijing, Shanghai and Nanjing, Mei's parents had told her that she was the unlucky one because she was born on the fourth day of the fourth month.

She had always been unlucky because she was a girl, the only daughter in the family. As her mama and papa used to say, the family breath ends where a girl's begins.

As a girl:

Mei could not perpetuate the family name.

Mei could not plough the fields or wield a sickle as well as her brothers.

Mei was of little use to a mama who could thresh the rice, cook porridge and launder the family's few clothes with one hand while she wagged the other and admonished Mei for being useless, spoilt and a girl. So mama and papa favoured her two older brothers. Growing up with these surname-perpetuating, field-ploughing, sickle-wielding alpha males, Mei felt like the tree that stood next to their farm. There was no point in chopping it down, but everyone attended to the crops.

After the Japanese invaded China, most of the men in her village in Guangdong in southeast China marched north to fight the Japanese. Her brothers marched with them and Mei never heard from them again. Mei was the only child left and her parents were not sure if that was a good thing, especially since no eligible village men were left to marry her off to. Struggling to feed an extra mouth, and fretting about Mei's future if the Japanese advanced further south, Mei's parents decided to find a groom overseas to take care of her.

A broker found a few Teochew men in Singapore who were willing to marry Mei. There were no photos, no legal or forged documents to validate the men's existence, only paragraph-length oral descriptions of each man that the broker assured Mei's parents were fact. No need to assure Mei of anything either. He described Li Chang as twenty-four years old, tall, handsome and healthy, evidence that Li could look after her for a long while. The broker said that Li was hardworking and rented a flat, evidence of a stable income that could also look after Mei for a long time. Li owned a bumboat and ferried textiles, vegetable oil, beer kegs and other goods up and down the city's chief river, a vital job, further evidence of stability. Her parents selected Li Chang.

Mei asked to marry the broker instead. He was unmarried and had a face and more than one paragraph to lead on. But mostly she wanted to stay with her parents near their farm. She wanted to show Mama and Papa that she was just as useful as her brothers, if only they gave her a chance. But her father said that the broker was unmarried enough to have worked for the Imperial Qing Court. They purchased her boat fare to Singapore the next day.

Li Chang existed. He received Mei at Tanjong Pagar harbour on the southwest of Singapore. He was a tall sinewy man with thick hair that captured all the heat. His nose and lips were faded, as if the heat had melted them into his bronzed skin. He held up a photo of her and shouted, "Li Mei! Here! Li Mei! Oi! Yah you! Here!"

She was overwhelmed by the clamour of steamboats trumpeting, trishaws tooting, men carrying gunnysacks on their backs, hunched over, hollering at her to get out of the way, swinging their arms violently when she didn't understand, women standing behind wheeled carts and touting their boiled peanuts and corns, fish flopping on newspapers lining the streetsides, throngs of people bumping into her, knocking her valise so she gripped it tighter. The crowd blocked her vision of Li Chang. She saw southern

Chinese faces, olive-skinned faces, darker brown faces, heard coarse alien languages flap about her like the chatter of bees. The faces stared hostilely at her. In her village, everyone knew everyone and at the least acknowledged each other, if gruffly. She hurried to Li, the nervousness of their first encounter overcome by the relief of knowing someone in this strange country. He appraised her. "You know who I am?"

She nodded. She held his gaze but didn't dare speak.

He held out a char siew bun. "You must be hungry." She accepted the fluffy white ball stuffed with seasoned pork and he took her small suitcase. She had gripped it so tight her fingers still curled. No introductions were needed. He turned and blew a piercing whistle at a rickshaw puller nearby. "Oi! Yah you! Stop slacking and work! Come here!"

He treated her to a rickshaw ride to their shophouse in Bugis. Sitting in the enclosed wooden chair, he pointed and swore at how sluggish their ageing rickshaw puller was, how noxious the Singapore River was, how the British needed to wake up their idea and clean the river. He said, "But listen. It's good to work in Singapore. Here, you can be the King's Chinese and the Qing's Chinese! No. There is no more Qing, right?" Even his questions were declarative rhetoric, for he laughed to himself.

Mei shrugged her shoulders.

He clapped his hands. "Never mind. Even the Qing weren't Chinese! Right?" He laughed all the way to Bugis. Mei quietly munched on her char siew bun. Her parents had told Mei that Singapore was a small township, but it was jam-packed and overflowing with colour, noise, people and life that zipped and whirled past the rickshaw.

Their shophouse turned out to be a mini Teochew ghetto built of concrete and painted in pastel pink and green, crammed between a row of sapphire, yellow and cerise shophouses. The first-floor shop sold light bulb tubes and filaments and power sockets. A young boy called Chee Keen manned it and said "Hello" to Mei and she was relieved to be able to understand his Teochew. Li said, "Come upstairs. You can meet everyone later." On the second floor, they crossed a tidy kitchen with a dinner table to enter a room. Li rented a shoebox, a room split in two by a stained flower-patterned curtain, like a crass massage parlour. He possessed few belongings. A thin mattress, a little shelf with a golden Buddha statue and burnt incense sticks, some unfolded clothes piled on the floor, and a half-empty bottle of Chinese liquor. He put the valise down by the mattress and turned to stare at her.

"Okay?" he said.

She nodded.

"Okay." He left for work.

And Li was indeed hardworking. Over the next months, he disappeared before dawn and returned home after nightfall. He worked overnight for some special shipments. Only on his off days did Li teach her Malay and how to take the bus so she could explore Singapore independently. But she was content to stay home when he was away. So when he found the time, he took her to pasar malams, night markets and the occasional Chinese cinema treat too.

She felt he was rough around the edges, especially his tongue, because he swore in Hokkien often and was a forceful kisser. He swore because his friends and certain matters, like the arrogant British who thought they knew it all, irked him. Li felt he always knew better than the rest and Mei quickly picked up the vulgar argot of the Southern Chinese dialect from him. And he kissed forcefully because he was an eager lover and wanted a son. But Mei felt that a reservoir of a good man welled inside. She trusted him.

Li put food on the table and in two years he put a baby in

her belly. He was her family now.

So when the Mitsubishi bombers flew in from the north, whistled over and bombed Singapore, and Mei and Li crawled under the dining table with the Teo and Loh families, legs and arms and necks squeezed together like a box of eels, Li cussing in Hokkien, Mei realised that having fled war in China, war had followed her here too. The next evening she said, "Sorry."

He lit his Lucky Strike cigarette, the match hissing. "What for?"

Mei was sitting on a squat wooden stool and said, "It's my fault they came here. Mama and Papa said I'm unlucky. I have two fours in my birthday."

"So?"

"*Si. Si.* It sounds like you are saying death twice. Death follows me."

He took a drag and considered this information. He blew ashen smoke, stubbed his cigarette on the table and rested it delicately on the wood. "If you talk rubbish like that again, I'll slap you. Look." He was already topless and now he unbuckled his belt and dropped his shorts and he wasn't wearing underwear. On his left thigh, above the tattoo of a koi fish, he had tattooed eight small vertical lines. The black ink still seemed wet beneath his finger. "Have I shown you this before? See, four and four is eight. It's a lucky number. Brings money. Prosperity. The only time you bring bad luck into the house is when you talk about it and if you talk about it, I'll slap you. You understand?"

"But I'm a girl. Mama and Papa used to say boys were better. They can work, they can fight."

He was pulling his shorts up and he stopped and put two hands on his hips and his shorts fell down. "So? You want me to have sex with a boy is it?"

Her eyes widened and she shook her head.

"You see." He was pointing at her bump. "You are pregnant. You carry my son. You are lucky what."

Her husband fixed his belt. For the first time, Mei felt lucky too. She thought that maybe after two years, she was starting to love him. It wasn't the sort of swooning romance, but it was a solid, stable faith in her husband. She stood up from the stool to thank him. He had relit a Lucky Strike and waved it at her and said, "Sit down and eat before you hurt yourself and my son. Then I will really slap you." She smiled. He never slapped her, and would never hit her. He just liked to talk rough. Mei started praying even more fervently that she could give him a son to show just how grateful she was.

Then the Japanese seized Malaya.

The Japanese strafed Singapore even more ferociously, preparing for a ground invasion.

The Japanese troops encroached on Singapore.

By the time the surrender was announced, Mei and Li had left the bomb shelters to find that their Bugis house and their savings had become flattened rubble of pink and green mortar bits and dust. Mei was seven months pregnant. They found a slum next to the Kallang River and Li built a shanty there. Initially, he caught herring and green chromide fish in the river and roasted them. But the river was overfished and as the days passed, he caught fewer and fewer. He was too proud to beg and hunger started to sicken Mei, throwing her into fevers, causing her to vomit bile, paring her body to skin and bones and leaving her lying curled up at home. They worried for their son inside her. Finally, Li went to the screening centre to collect ration cards and save his family. Then Mei's water broke. It was 1942.

...

She wanted to throw her head back and scream into the night. But they had anticipated this and wedged cloth into her mouth. She bit on it hard, exhaled in furious breaths. She sat on a towel, slumped against the cardboard and mud wall, sitting up on her elbows. Her long pyjama nightgown was pulled over her bloated belly to her chest, her legs open. Her old neighbour, Soo Hock, squatted in front of her. Her wide heavy-jowled peasant face seemed indifferent to Mei's tortured panting. Soo Hock had come over upon hearing Mei's cry when her water broke. Now, while they waited for Li to return, she squatted there without touching Mei, sly eyes staring between Mei's legs like a perverted Imperial Japanese Army soldier.

Occasionally, Soo Hock said in Teochew, "Breathe," "Push," and "It will be over soon." In response, Mei groaned into the wringed cloth to show she was doing her best, and willed whatever body her nerve centre found responsive to obey Soo Hock. She tried so hard her hips thrust at the old woman's face and Soo Hock sighed and pushed her waist back down onto the towel. Mei felt like she was trying to push her brain out of her body. She wanted Li. She wanted him to sit behind her, his cheek pressed against hers, the Koi fish and eight lines smiling on her left to give her luck and support, the dragons on the other thigh to give her courage. She wanted them to go through this moment together, create family together. She wished he would hurry home.

"Push," Soo Hock said and dragged her back into her suffering body and the dark four-square walls of their hut. "I see it I see it. Push, push." Mei bit harder and shut her eyes. She pushed with all her concentration and might and it felt like her body might explode.

"There. There. Push." She felt it come out, felt the empty sense of nothing, absurdly different from that full weight and pain she had been struggling with a moment before. An instance of dark, shuddering emptiness pierced only by a child's cry, and she slumped.

When Mei came to, Soo Hock's rough palm was on her sticky forehead. Mei turned her head to see a tiny babe cradled inside the old woman's arm. Fatigue throbbed inside Mei and she groaned and sat up sluggishly. She realised she was half-naked and hastily pushed her blouse down and then leaned back against the wall. "See," Soo Hock said. "See."

Mei was faintly aware that Li wasn't back yet. She felt like collapsing but forced her eyes to stay open. She focused on the infant, its body a structure of separate balloons attached at the joints, a balloon foot to a balloon calf, to a thigh to a stomach, as if it might pop in Soo Hock's arm. A delicate balloon of life that was so obliviously asleep, so angelic, so useless. Mei felt her cries come up. She ducked her face between her knees, suppressed her moans, and let the tears fall noiselessly onto the floor. Soo Hock continued to rock the baby, unperturbed by Mei's convulsions.

The sight of her baby had forced Mei to confront the truth that Li was not coming back. She had made excuses, postponed assuming anything, convinced herself she had time until her baby arrived. But now she had to take responsibility. Li had gone to the screening centre three weeks ago. No one took more than six or seven days to return, if they returned, and her husband wasn't returning. The Japanese had taken him. She should never have let him go to the screening centre.

She knew his proud past: boycotting Japanese exports, not ferrying them on his boat, not buying anything that was made in Japan, not even allowing her to visit the Japanese-run ten cents store on Middle Road to save some money. She knew the Japanese were hunting young Chinese men and they would have easily spotted and nabbed Li Chang, who had been so open and virulent about his anti-Japanese activity. But she had been too weak and too tired and too sick to stop him. He had left to try and save his son.

Now, she had a child to take care of. But Mei was just a girl, barely twenty-one years old, with no husband or parents, no job, no money, in a land she still found foreign and had become even more foreign after the Japanese invaded. She would starve to death and her baby would die of hunger. Or the Japanese soldiers would find them, which was worse. Mei remembered her mama telling her stories of Imperial soldiers shoving bayonets and pipes into babies' ends in Nanjing as she convinced Mei to take the boat to Singapore. She knew what the soldiers would do to her and her baby. She muttered, "Li. Li. Li." The cockiness with which he squared off against life, the attitude that everything would be fine was like a vacuum she ached for. "What can they do?" he would say, thrusting two fingers into the air. She wanted the security of that confidence back. Thinking of him, occasionally bursting into stifled sobs, Mei woke up with her head between her knees.

Her biggest worry was still there. Li had left after all, to save his son. But now her little daughter was ensconced in Soo Hock's arm. Soon, Mei would have to take her back, take responsibility for her, pick up the mantle her husband left behind. She considered the useless angel and thought, what would she do with her? What would she do with a *her*?

9

Dedicated to Papatti

The morning after my foiled escape, I was shaken awake by Kurosawa's hand on my shoulder. I jumped to my feet. He was dressed not for his morning run, but in his military uniform, smart shirt and shorts, without his sword. "Come," he said and walked outside calmly. It was four in the morning and dark out and only the sentry enlivened Jalan Besar. It dawned on me with a sense of wariness that he was talking to me again.

The night before came to me in a viscous, bleary memory of Kurosawa pointing on the map and showing me where Appa died, and I felt a familiar searing hole emerge within my chest, but just then Kurosawa fell onto his knees, sitting back on his heels, and I stopped, confused. His back was arched upright and poised. Watching me coolly, he patted the stone floor next to him and I knelt by his side. Folding my legs like that stretched them to the point of discomfort but I tried to emulate Kurosawa, whose breathing I could hear, slow and deliberate. The sentry watched us curiously.

Kurosawa stood, pressing my shoulder down to stay knelt, and stood in front of me. He said, "Say: Lieutenant Kurosawa, *onegai itashimasu.*"

I said it.

"Once more."

I said it again, louder, with more emphasis, worried.

"Okay, come in, Nanban."

I gazed around at the grey kerb and the dark crowns of the angsana trees and the emptiness of Jalan Besar Road, wondering what he meant. Should I return into the house? He tapped my armpit upwards impatiently and I scrambled to my feet like a horse unfolding its legs, clumsy.

He said, "*Kamae.*"

I blinked and he saw that I didn't understand and smiled. Kurosawa assumed his morning fighting position. His left foot stepped forward and his right foot back, his shoulders rolled forward and hung loosely, his chin tucked in so he stared at me from under his eyebrows, his hands came up and guarded his cheeks. "*Kamae,*" he said, as if it were self-explanatory, that this was *kamae.*

With his right hand, he drew a straight line through the middle of his forehead, down through his lips and chest to show me his weight was centred and balanced. He snapped to stand stiff at attention, arms pressed to his sides, feet together, shoulders drawn back, chin up, like a rod pulled upwards to the firmament by a taut string. Then he said, "*Kamae,*" and bounced back into his fighting stance, string released. "*Wakatta? Kamae. Kamae.*"

I nodded slowly.

"*Kamae,* Nanban."

Unsurely, I mimicked his fighting stance, separating my legs and raising my hands and stooping my back, hoping I remembered right.

Kurosawa grunted. He pushed my elbows outwards so they weren't glued to my sides. He knocked the top of my head so my chin lowered even further into my neck. He pushed my stomach in so it sucked inside, muscles tense and braced for impact. Then he grabbed my shoulders and turned me like a steering wheel so we stood side by side, one arm's length apart, facing the trees. I held onto my pose tensely, afraid to lose and forget it and be scolded.

Kurosawa jabbed with a left hand as if the fist shot out from his shoulder, the jab he had taught me the previous night. Leaving his arm extended, he looked at me expectantly. I struck out with my left hand, trying to remember the movement, feeling amateurish next to him. Then he retracted the left hand and punched with his right, leaving that arm stuck out. I copied that too. He pointed at his right heel and repeated the movement. The heel lifted and his hip twisted forward to drive the strike from below. "Remember? Last night?"

I tried again to show him I understood.

He released his *kamae* position and folded his arms, giving me a commanding look that said, *Carry on.*

Uncertainly, with trepidation, I threw my punches. He circled me in silence, observing, judging, waiting to swoop in when he spotted a mistake. I focused on the vertical dark ruts of the tree bole ahead that I was punching at, ignoring Kurosawa's legs in the corner of my eye, shrugging off his gaze scrutinising me from behind. I felt that if I punched the way he wanted and demonstrated that I was putting in effort, I would be okay. But I also wondered uselessly if I was punching correctly since he didn't interrupt. I twisted my fist downwards to see if this felt better, reverted to what I did before because I couldn't tell the difference, and before long he stopped and corrected me, to remind me not to lift my chin to watch my punch travel. At the end, he made me fall on my knees, bow my forehead onto the floor and thank him before he dismissed me to start the day's work. And during that morning, so caught up in moving my hands right and worried that I would anger Kurosawa, I am ashamed to say I forgot about Appa.

And so it came to be that every morning at four, with only the sentry and the moon presiding, beginning with my kneeling and asking for permission to join, Kurosawa taught me *kyoshokan* for thirty minutes.

With irony I soon realised that while the first batch of Japanese words I had memorised was the most polite set you could find, *pleases* and *excuse mes* and *sorrys* and *thank yous*, intended to show deference and respect to appease the soldiers, the next batch of words I memorised were words used to order an attack to obliterate a man. It was a dichotomy that matched the contrast between the Japanese soldier's rigorous social courtesy and his ruthless efficiency at waging war.

My first word in this violent spectrum of the vernacular was *kamae*. Always, in the middle of my punch, Kurosawa stopped me mid-motion like a still frame snatched out of continuous time, my hip twisted, arm halfway retracting. As I struggled to hold that pose for him, he patted my unguarded cheek or tapped me on the shoulder with a strong pair of fingers so that I toppled to the floor in the painful discovery that my weight was off-balance. When he was satisfied that I understood, he folded his arms and stepped back and said firmly, "*Kamae*," watching me. I returned to the *kamae* stance and we started from scratch.

When he taught me *tsuki*, he made me practise the punch a thousand times with each hand. He kept saying, "Lead with the top but drive your movement from the bottom."

So I threw the entire weight of my body from ground-up into every strike, once trying so hard that I flew into him like a missile child, and apologised profusely as we disentangled and I picked up his peaked cap for him and ran back to my spot, hoping he wouldn't cane me.

He wanted me to wield my legs effectively, become just as comfortable brandishing them as I was throwing my hands. The first time he taught me *keri*, he knelt in front of me and I could see the top of his cleanly shaved head. He placed a flat hand against my hipbone like he was about to cut it, and another hand next to my feet. He extracted both hands to show me how long my legs were, as if his hands still bounded the distance between my hip and feet. He stared at this bounded space and opened his mouth like an *O* and said with that impressed patronising way you speak to a child, a way my appa consciously avoided speaking to me in, "They're long, aren't they?"

Then, with the back of a straightened arm, he smacked the side of my body, pretending the arm was a leg delivering a roundkick. "*Keri*," he said. He darted at my stomach with it, sudden stubborn darts, pushing me back to show that my long legs gave me reach from an opponent, no longer treating me like a small child. I grunted and stepped back so they hurt less. "*Mae keri*," he said. Front kick.

Kurosawa rose to his feet. He pretended to grab the back of a man's head with both hands and said, "*Hiza*." He brought the invisible head down, invisible body with it as if forcing his adversary to bow to him. Kurosawa raised his right leg off the ground and thrust his hips out forcefully so his right kneecap dove forward like a bullet head into the poor bent opponent's gut. Kurosawa held the pose, knee jutting out like a mechanical crane. Then he hugged his stomach and winced and groaned, appearing to be in devastating pain, as if he had just been delivered the knee strike to his own gut. He stumbled in a circle, left leg stuck behind the right, and he extricated that leg and crossed it over only for it to entrap the right. He brayed like a goat and stumbled cross-legged like one of his disoriented drunk colleagues on Saturday nights. He collapsed to the ground and rolled. The sentry scratched his head. I laughed.

I had forgotten the ringing peal of that sound, like bells chiming. I had forgotten that it uplifted you, transplanted you for those moments into a blissfully forgetful place. Kurosawa stood up and dusted his uniform and put his hands on his hips. He stared at me amazed, me forgetting my *kamae* and falling onto my buttocks, trying not to topple backwards, holding my sides, trying to say *shitsurei itashimasu*, laughing convulsively. He watched me, stunned beyond belief, until he tilted his head back and laughed too.

And for that moment we were nothing but a man standing and a child on his bum, alone in the early morning dawn save for a perturbed sentry and an uninterested moon, laughing. We let it last as long as it would on its own, we did not hurry it, we did not stop it, we did not stretch it out. We only enjoyed what the laughter could give us, and after it had exhausted its supply, he walked over and extended his hands. He said, "You are a funny boy. Come Nanban, you have been doing well so far."

It was the first time he had complimented me, that anyone apart from Appa had said anything nice to me. I grabbed his hands and said, "*Arigatō gozaimashita*, Lieutenant Kurosawa." He pulled me up and we continued training before the other soldiers woke up and the day's official work began.

...

WARRAN KALASEGARAN

In the beginning, I played along with Kurosawa's martial arts training because he said so and my survival depended on doing what he said. But one evening, as I served miso soup to Saito in his bunk, he twisted my nipples, like turning two taps tight. I clenched my teeth at the pain, not wanting to scream. I held the cold metal bucket in one hand and ladle in the other and Saito laughed, knowing I wouldn't dare drop either. As expected, I gripped the hard metal tighter, more afraid of being caned for wasting the rations. Still, I refused to scream, and it was pointless asking Saito to stop. He would stop when he wanted to.

Finally, satisfied that my skin had ruptured and that blood stained my white shirt in two red dots that I would have to wash off, Saito gave my nipples one final wrench and released me with a casual smile. I sputtered backwards. He patted the top of my stubble to say I had been a good boy and slapped my arms encouragingly. Then he shared a joke with Morikawa, having forgotten about me already. I was humiliated, and anger at Appa's death bubbled back up with the humilitation and shame of being mistreated and molested and not being able to do anything about it. I blamed Saito and people like him for Appa's death. Saito, a bully who picked on weaker people going about their day just because he could. People like him had killed Appa. It was cowardly of me, I admit, to lay all the blame at Saito and the rest since Kurosawa had become my guardian of sorts. But from that moment, in my mind, Saito became responsible for Appa's death.

Saito said, "Eh, what are you looking at? Go back to work."

I walked back to the kitchen. But as a nine-year-old, I decided that every dog has its day and if the Japanese were to stay in Singapore for one hundred years then I would not escape. There was no one to escape for anymore and I would likely be caught again. No. I decided to stay in this camp and learn to fight from Kurosawa because one day I would grow up and one day I would be bigger and more powerful than Saito and then I would be cruel to him and everyone else who tried to mistreat me. I would hurt Saito the way he hurt me. The next morning I woke up earlier and was boxing the air and practising my kicks with a vengeance by the time Kurosawa joined me, to his apparent surprise.

...

Kurosawa soon made punching pads by stuffing damaged field packs with soil and wastepaper. He tied the tentacle-like coils dangling from the packs around his forearms so that when he knelt in front of me and held his arms up, I only saw two boxy brown pads waiting to be hit, hiding his face. The first time we practised with them, Kurosawa moved the left pad to my left hand so I understood to jab it. Then he held both pads by the side of his waist and at that height and angle, it seemed natural to throw a round kick at the pads. Once, he put my hands on the back of his head and placed the pads in front of his chest so I would knee into them repeatedly. Soon, he started saying, "Five times," or "Ten times," and I knew how many times he wanted me to kick or knee consecutively. By ten, I would be winded and gasping for oxygen, but he always expected me to have my guard up and to continue until he declared we were done for the day. He said, "Breathe. Breathe." He jabbed the air twice and made an, *"Oosu, Oosu"* sound to show me how to exhale upon impact and keep my breathing constant. If I were to perform combinations on the pads, I simply had to remember what each positioning of the pads required and to execute that as he positioned and repositioned the pads, so that by the end of keeping up with the pads, I would understand the combination he wanted me to learn. Then we would repeat the combination faster so it flowed.

He started hitting back too, first slowly, and then more suddenly, without notice. His blows weren't painful because they were padded and I believe he controlled his strength, but they were disorienting and made me want to cover my face and curl up, not duck and slip and fight back with confidence and ease, having forgotten everything I learned in one unexpected onslaught.

Sometimes, we miscommunicated. One morning, I was throwing myself at the pads and he said something as my fist connected with the rough canvas and produced a thud. I thought he wanted to teach me something new so I put my hands down and stood upright and looked at him. A pad hit me in the face. I fell backwards, dizzy, vomit threatening to rise through my throat. He pointed out later that he had said, "*Banzai.*"

Kurosawa had taught me the *banzai* action of hailing the Emperor. I was to raise both arms straight into the sky, then bring them down together with my head and chest in a bow perpendicular to my standing frame, the way the soldiers had cheered every victory from Manchuria to Singapore. But I was to move forward in this position to duck a punch and grab Kurosawa, closing the distance to disable him from striking out, and grapple from there. After some practice I learnt to do this without raising my arms into the sky and making a show of it. It was just a pedagogic device. But it took time to internalise the movement, and till then, he caught me offguard as he did that morning.

In those moments, as I blinked my eyes clear, he watched me blankly, expecting me to recover and continue as per normal. The pads were ready for my left roundkick. He said, "*Ganbatte,*" that Japanese universal expression for fight on. If I fell, *ganbatte*; if I was ill, *ganbatte*; if I was just going through life, *ganbatte*. And when that wasn't enough,

I remembered the Kempeitai dragging Appa away on his bum and Saito knocking the butt of his rifle into my head and laughing at my pain while I had to apologise for bumping into his rifle. I remembered this and remembered that I did not want to be weak anymore and so picked myself up and threw myself at the pads.

Throughout the day, when not scribbling at his desk or leaving for house inspections in the jeep, Kurosawa taught me his language with as much ferocity as he taught me *kyoshokan*, and my Japanese vocabulary started swelling with sedate, functional words in between the spectra of courtesy and violence. I had less and less time to fret over Appa, which I felt guilty about but also relieved, to be spared this futile agony. When Kurosawa was bored lounging on his mat, he pointed at the trees through the window and said, "Nanban. That. See. That is *mado*." It took me a week to understand that the window was *mado*. At night, he pointed at the fluorescent tube fixed to the ceiling, emitting a staccato orange glow, and said, *denki*. Then he said *kesu* and turned it off. He said *tsukeru* and turned it on and said *kesu* and turned it off again.

Once, a lady clad in red knocked on the door and Kurosawa raised two hands as if he had just realised something terribly important. He pointed at her and said, *onna no hito*, and pointed at himself and said, *otoko no hito*, and then waited for me to repeat it, the elegant lady watching our exchange bewilderedly at the door. Then he pointed at me and said *kodomo*. Then he said, "You are a fast learner but are you eager to learn everything today?"

I frowned.

He laughed and pointed outside and I left his house quickly. Those were the few times Kurosawa didn't keep me busy.

In the evenings, instead of letting me wander outside, he sometimes instructed me to carry his maps and notes and follow him to Headquarters for a night meeting. Along the way, he pointed at the houses and said, *ie*. He pointed at the clothes hanging on bamboos and said, *fuku*, and pointed at the road ahead of us and said, *michi*. Once, he saw someone scurrying away as we approached, feet scuffling against the floor. Kurosawa pointed at the fleeing grey silhouette and said, *Shōnanjin*. The silhouette dived into a doorway and only darkness remained. Kurosawa pointed at me and said, "*Shōnanjin*. Nanban is *Shōnanjin*."

Struggling not to drop the scrolls in my arm as I kept up with his brisk long strides, I conjugated the word and said, "*Shingapōrujin*, Lieutenant Kurosawa?"

Walking still, staring straight ahead, he shook his head and said as if it were matter of fact, like naming houses and bamboo poles, "No. *Shōnanjin*. You are *Shōnanjin*." The Japanese had named Singapore "*Shōnan*", and I assumed that if he called me *Shōnanjin* and he held the gun, then I was *Shōnanjin*.

"Lieutenant Kurosawa, what does '*Shōnan*' mean?"

"Light of the south. Now, look, the word for that is '*sora*'." He pointed at the stygian sky.

In time, when he gave me an order, he no longer just said an officer's name or signposted hastily and relied on our settled understanding from past experiences that I knew what to do. Instead, sitting at his desk, he stopped working and faced me solemnly. He tapped a report with a hard finger and said, "*Hōkoku*. Say it."

Hands behind my back, chest out, I enunciated the best I could. "*Hu-Ko-Ku*."

"Good." He put the report in my hand. "Now, what is '*motte kuru*'?"

I frowned. I knew it meant "to bring him something", but I didn't know any other Japanese words to explain it with. I only knew *motte kuru*. I walked to the door and U-turned and handed the report back to Kurosawa. "*Motte kuru*, Lieutenant Kurosawa?"

His eyes widened and he laughed. He put the report back on his desk and sipped his green tea, composing himself. He smacked his lips. "You are intelligent for a *Shōnanjin ne*, Nanban. We will make a soldier out of you yet. Now, go to Private Uchida and bring me the report on criminal activity in the fourth month."

It shames me to admit that I started to feel proud whenever he complimented me. "Yes, Lieutenant Kurosawa," I said. I bowed and ran out of the house, muttering the exact words of the report's title so I didn't forget it.

If he didn't have a meeting to attend, Kurosawa changed into his white T-shirt, still wearing his military trousers and socks. Then we sat cross-legged, a few papers and pencils lying on the floor between us, and he taught me to write and read in the three Japanese scripts, the *hiragana*, *katakana* and the *kanji*. The *hiragana* and *katakana* followed a grid alphabetical system similar to Tamil, with columns of vowels intersecting with rows of consonants to produce merged sounds, like "A" plus "S" to make "Sa". The *kanji* were abstract assemblies of long and short strokes and curlicues, like Chinese characters, each character assembly representing the same meaning as a word strung together by *hiragana* letters. Kurosawa made me write the letters, words and characters again and again on paper to rote memorise them.

But I found the *kanji* terribly difficult. Once, Kurosawa told me to draw the two *kanji* characters that represent Tokyo. I remembered that they looked like two distinct temples of the same size standing side-by-side. But I couldn't recall the details making up the two temples, as if its little lines had receded to the darkness of my conscious, and every time I reached it fearfully shrunk farther back. I gave up. I put my pencil down and stared at Kurosawa, my only hope left being his showing me the drawing again at which point of time I would think, *I knew that!*

But his obsidian eyes did not relent. He said, "I will wait for you to sing, little bird."

Sometimes, he said things whose words I knew but meaning I didn't understand. Later I learned that the phrase was used to lionise the patience of one Tokugawa Ieyasu, a 16th century Japanese warlord. You can understand why Kurosawa identified with him. In fact, Kurosawa called Tokugawa a great unifier of Japan. Apparently, feudal Japan was a hotpot of fighting fiefdoms and provinces before Tokugawa and two other leaders came along to put an end to it and attack Korea, which only goes to show that a race is just a group of people who were fighting each other until another group of people came along for them to fight. Of course, Kurosawa didn't see it this way and in any case, I didn't question his theories on race and religion and the nation. It was not my place to question anything.

I waited further, but then Kurosawa chuckled and his expression relaxed. "It's okay." He stabbed at my paper. "Draw something you like. You've been working hard so let's do something different, okay? If not you only spend your free time outside and what are you going to achieve that way? Here, take this. Draw anything you like."

He nudged the pencil lying on the floor and it rolled lazily towards me. I was confused by his sudden and strange nonchalance. Our conversations were always didactic, he telling me what to do and I doing it. Uncertain, I did the safest thing, which was to quietly twist the pencil in my hand

and stare at the paper, half-filled with squiggles and dashes, a memento of the battle I had lost to my memory, while waiting for him to clarify his instructions.

Kurosawa chuckled and picked up a piece of blank paper and spun around to sit next to me, our knees touching. He plucked the pencil from my hand and leaned over his paper. The black lead hovered over its surface momentarily. Then he sighed and slowly started applying strokes to his paper. He sketched an index finger, soft, tender, solitary. He was a good artist, shading in the chiaroscuro, strengthening its outline like a marker, as if the finger were his masterpiece, his world. Finally he leaned back and stared at it. He tapped the eraser of the pencil against the paper. "Do you know this?"

I showed him my index finger.

He chuckled and shook his head and smiled at the paper. It was a sad and lonely smile that only he understood. He said, "This belonged to my younger brother. Six months ago you threw it into the river and I was very angry with you."

10

A-Star Seamstress

Papatti contemplated another black-and-white photograph in the *Tamil Murasu*, but this time of her, Lalitha and Rajpal standing by the Singer sewing machine in freshly-ironed Deepavali-worthy clothes, ogling at the camera like aliens, the family as a whole uncomfortable with the photo-taking experience. Papatti only wished the splendid greens and blues that she had decked her family in could have shown in the photo. The bold black headline read: *A Singaporean Family's History*.

It was not dedicated solely to Papatti, but sharing the spotlight with her parents had its own satisfaction of a team victory. Besides, she looked less idiotic in this photo, her fingers interlocking with her parents' instead of hanging awkwardly, her teeth slightly bared and curved enough to pass as a smile—although far from as radiant as Arjun's, whose photo presented itself for comparison on the other door of the cupboard. Rajpal had cut out the new article and the days-older *A-Star* report and taped them onto their cupboard doors, so that anyone entering their bedroom would see them first and be immediately "amazed", as Rajpal put it, by the "brilliance" that was his daughter. The only disappointment was that Moorthy had not asked for a second quote from Arjun, but she would find another way to extract that conclusive accolade from him. Besides, this was already a reprieve from the slander Papatti had initially been expecting Moorthy to write.

Lalitha called from the kitchen, "Papatti, you better hurry or you'll be late."

"I have more than an hour, Amma!"

"You can go early. He's an Assemblyman and he was kind enough to invite you. If you are late it'll only be disrespectful. Go now, you stubborn girl, before you tarnish yours and this family's name. I don't know which is worse."

Papatti wanted to make a good impression too, but was there a need to be this antsy? Huffing exasperatedly for Lalitha to hear, knowing there was no point in arguing back, Papatti pulled the two doors of the cupboard open as loudly as she could. Inside, there was a white chest of four drawers and next to it, three piles of neatly folded Punjabi suits, shawls, sarees and trousers, all evenly aligned so the mass of cloth resembled one neat rectangle. Rajpal's shirts hung starched stiff from a horizontal iron bar above. She rifled through the middle pile to find the peacock blue shawl that would complement her teal Punjabi suit, colours the *Tamil Murasu* had been unable to display. Then she slammed the doors, stormed across the living room and banged the iron front gate shut.

The meeting with Arjun's residents took place in one of his volunteers' houses next to Tekka Market, and started at eight. Papatti arrived with forty minutes to spare, and by that time a long queue was already snaking to the pawnshop on the first floor, shuttered for business during these meetings. The appellants to the Assemblyman were engrossed in talking to each other, their backs tilted away from Papatti, heads lowered, and she could not help feeling a little affronted that no one had noticed her.

A cheery volunteer called Shah finally recognised Papatti and said that Arjun was preparing his interview notes upstairs. Papatti made to skip the queue and Shah grimaced. "You sure you want to disturb the Assemblyman, Papatti?"

"What else can I do, Shah mama? Wait here? I'm not here to ask him for anything."

"I know. But maybe come back an hour later? He doesn't like to be disturbed while working. He's very serious about work."

"If I go home my amma will just send me back. I'm sure it'll be okay. He invited me."

Shah seemed to be in pain considering this, saying things like, "I don't want to get into trouble for not crowd-controlling properly", and Papatti started feeling annoyed that she was a "crowd". Why, was she that fat? Or was she just one replaceable girl in this abundant herd? She needed to be clear: The Assemblyman invited her.

Did Shah not read the newspapers? He must have gone to school, for his smattering of English words in Tamil speech demonstrated that his parents had once thought educating a young Shah would be a profitable investment. He had all the perks of being an oldest son, a very straightforward Indian child to raise. He must have seen the photo of her and Arjun, understood the events that had led her to be there standing before Shah. She mentally scolded her amma for not having kept one of the extra newspapers to brandish like an invitation card. Papatti took a deep breath and said, "Uncle Shah, he's going to read about me. Imagine if it was you? Would you let someone stop you? Let me go upstairs please. I don't want to waste my time waiting around downstairs."

Shah deliberated this further, half-talking to himself in English, and soon Papatti grew flustered and ran up the stairs.

On the second floor, the living room had been cleared of any bric-a-brac, as if no one lived there. There wasn't even a dining table. Fook Weng, the scrawny silent-type man who owned the house, was setting up a wooden table and chair facing the staircase as Papatti came up.

Arjun leaned against the wall in his red shirt and grey pants, under a dead black clock, lips pursed, seriously flipping through a clip of papers. Seeing him so captivated by his work, she grew nervous. Perhaps she should have listened to Shah and waited below. What if Arjun scolded her? But she was already here and she decided that there was nothing to it but to step closer so her shadow could alert him to her presence.

Arjun looked up. He saw her and beamed, and his nose curved even more prominently outward. She felt relieved that he didn't look annoyed. *Silly Shah mama, there is nothing to bedevil yourself over.* Arjun rolled the papers into a scroll and said, "Papatti, you are early!" He stepped away from the wall.

She was going to scold her amma when she went home. Sounding rather silly about the platitude, she said, "I didn't want to be late, sir."

"No sirs, please. Just Arjun. Well, being early is a safe policy. And I'm happy to see you. But this might take a while. Even eight pm might have been early! I hadn't expected such a crowd."

"It's okay sir—Arjun. I'll wait. I won't disturb you, I promise."

"Here, you might as well be comfortable. Let me get you a chair." He pulled one next to the open window and she sat as primly and ladylike as possible, not wanting to deface the dignity of the occasion. She clutched her hands together. She was so used to holding a needle and thread when encountering anyone outside her family that her first thought in such social situations tended to be, *What do I do with my hands?* She had to stop her foot from tapping to Singer's rhythm. Through the window, she saw the blue neon lights of the Xinhui Clan Association across the street. Arjun said, "By the way, I read the second piece about your family in the *Tamil Murasu* today. I was riveted."

She glowed that an Assemblyman was riveted by her life story. "Thank you sir," she said. "I mean, Arjun."

Arjun smiled and nodded. Then he turned away, unrolled his notes, and returned to reading, leaving her alone. She tried to rationalise away the disappointment that rose within her. She had thought she would be worth at least ten minutes of his attention. She supposed that Shah was right. Arjun was unwilling to be distracted from work. She told herself that it wasn't her.

She asked Fook Weng if he wanted her help, but he gave Papatti the most cursory nod and continued to sweep the floor, as if to say that he accepted her presence as a matter-of-fact in the background, but much preferred that she remained there. So she watched him set a steaming pot of kopi on a cabinet, arrange Khong Guan lemon biscuits in a bowl next to it and wipe the top of the cabinet with a dirty rag. She didn't dare pour herself a cup until two minutes before eight, when Arjun sat behind the desk and waved a hand over. Fook Weng wordlessly went to the staircase to usher the constituents in. He stuck out a bony arm after each person passed to stop the rest, a stoic gatekeeper to that second floor of power, a floor on which Papatti had exclusive access to, a girl with a story that "riveted" an Assemblyman.

She couldn't wait to share the news with her appa.

The person at the head of the queue was a sixty-year-old man and Arjun knew his name, Kumaran. He stood to welcome him and asked after his wife and two sons with a familiarity that told Papatti they had met numerous times. Then they sat and Arjun listened intently as Kumaran appealed to relocate his family to a new government-built flat along Selegie Road "on a super-high floor". Kumaran suspected that his current neighbour was stealing chicken eggs from his coops, and wanted his sons' future wives to be able to move into a more comfortable house where they would not have to worry about thieves living next door. Arjun nodded at the appropriate junctures and dashed off quick scribbles on his paper before resuming the steady eye contact that was keeping Kumaran talking. When Kumaran finally wrapped up his request, Arjun promised to delve into the matter and Papatti was so convinced that he would overcome any and every obstacle to Kumaran's sons' future wives' happiness that she immediately started thinking of whether her family had any requests to make of their Assemblyman.

Kumaran, meanwhile, thanked Arjun and they rose together for a farewell that was as drawn out as their greeting, except it wasn't really a farewell, for Kumaran took a biscuit and coffee and hovered next to Papatti, apparently reluctant to leave.

The next constituent, Chun Han, complained to Arjun that his neighbour had a proclivity to urinate and defecate in the sidestreet between their houses. Chun Han extracted assurances from the Assemblyman to "look into the matter without involving the police because I like my neighbour and eventually want to buy *his* house". As Papatti wondered how Arjun would accomplish this 180-degree change in another man's excretive habits, Chun Han joined Kumaran in partaking in the Khong Guan biscuits and they bemoaned their uncivilised neighbourhoods, egging each other on to greater exaggeration.

Papatti recognised many of the constituents who came up, and they turned out to be regular attendees of these meetings, lingering after their appeals to tuck into the refreshments and banter about the latest gossip in the clearly scandalous Serangoon vicinity. They shared a camaraderie that Papatti was not privy to.

Arjun finished talking to the last visitor past 11 at night. With a tired sigh, he rolled up his papers, stood and pushed the chair in. By this time, a small cloister of constituents had gathered around Papatti. Having felt awkward being the only one seated, Papatti had given her chair to Kumaran at about nine pm and her legs ached. Kumaran was enumerating Suresh's gambling debt on his wizened fingers and listing the locations of the Secret Society gambling hideouts and mahjong dens that Suresh had lost his money at. Suresh had asked Kumaran to appeal to the Legislative Assemblyman on his behalf, but Kumaran had no inclination to intervene on behalf of a gambling addict. What would that say about Kumaran and his family? And why should he queue up for half an hour to spend his limited time with the Assemblyman discussing another man's problems?

No one had a chance to answer as Arjun cleared his throat. Fook Weng handed him a piece of paper. Kumaran's voice died away, much to Papatti's relief.

"Excuse me everyone. Thank you for coming. Today we have someone special joining us. Her name is Papatti and the *Tamil Murasu* featured her in an article that I promised to read. I hastily translated it into Malay, but I hope it's as clear as the original article. If I may have your attention, please. Thank you."

He began reading the "A-Star Seamstress" article aloud, his husky narration animating the article with vigour and filling her with anticipation—as if she didn't know the story already. But he read it far better than her tenant had. Arjun also occasionally glanced up at Papatti with a hearteningly familiar smile, those politician pheromones of sociability transmitting through each smile, and she dipped her head to acknowledge his brief but repetitive glances, forgetting her initial disappointment at being left alone on a chair by the window. When he finished with the journalist's patriotic conclusion, everyone clapped courteously in her direction, a timed polite beating of palms. Papatti, unsure what else to do, bowed her head meekly a few times in every which way and mumbled, "Thank you. Thank you. Thank you Kumaran mama." They stopped soon enough and she did not need to blush for long.

Kumaran shakily got to his feet and Arjun started mingling with his residents. Before Papatti could decide how to take her leave politely, the residents left to eat at the kopitiam nearby and Arjun spoke into Fook Weng's ear, whereupon the house owner gave Papatti another cursory nod and disappeared down the staircase, leaving her alone with Arjun and the table covered with crumbs and coffee stains. The empty living room became sound-swallowingly quiet. In the nervousness of those moments in which he approached her, Papatti blurted out what Lalitha had ordered her to say verbatim, "Thank you for reading that and inviting me, Arjun." She changed "sir" to "Arjun", and took some happiness in not having complied with her pig-headed mother's instructions in full.

Arjun wiped the sweat on his forehead back into his hair. "It's my pleasure. How are you?"

"I'm good. Thank—"

"I actually wanted to ask you for something, if you'll indulge me. I was very impressed by your initiative last Saturday. I thought it was creative and original. So, to get to the point, I would like to invite you to help with my campaigning team—for the referendum and after. We normally just order posters with our faces printed on them and march around with banners. It would be nice to have a breath of fresh air, a different vibe to our campaigning, some new ideas. What do you think? Would you like to help us? Join as a volunteer?"

"Oh." The opportunity flattered her, and she could already feel her expectations soaring. To Arjun, she was not just an ovum-producing tailor in a shophouse churning out bajus and babies, but someone who could make a positive difference to his political campaign. And joining his political campaign would give her the best platform she could ask for to reach out to the country with her ideas and skills. Besides, this was a cause that her appa and so many others felt so ardently about. It would be morally irresponsible of her to decline his offer.

But the memory of her disastrous interview with Moorthy crashed atop her and quashed her nascent expectations. What if Arjun was just being kind again? Was he only being kind when he said he was *riveted*? Or what if he had genuinely overestimated her intelligence and passion and whatever that third adjective was? Even the second article had been fascinating only because it was about her parents—biological and adopted—and unrelated to anything she had done as a conscious adult.

She was beginning to hate these fluctuations, so recently come upon, from periods of high self-estimations—where she thought she could achieve anything—to a lack of any confidence in her ability whatsoever. Now, presented with

Arjun's request, these opposing conceptions of herself collided head-on, and the pessimism she had inherited from Lalitha won and she said, "Arjun, thank you. But I must be honest. I don't really know much about any of this. Actually, I don't know anything about politics or economics or anything else. I didn't go to school and I just like to sew. I don't think I can help you."

Arjun's eyes widened and his smile, for some reason beyond its naturally aggrandising tendencies, enlarged.

"But I do want to be the best tailor in the city. It would mean a lot if you could tell people that." There. That was all she had come for.

He laughed, and did not seem to hear her plug. He said, "Well, that's a welcome change. Normally, people are very happy to talk coffee shop politics and tell me how to do my job. But Papatti, I think you do know politics, but maybe in a way that affects you personally, like whether you should have gone to school, or how much money you pay to the government from your work with Mr Govinda, or whether Mr Kumaran gets his Selegie flat. You know, I actually devised a mathematical formula to calculate a coefficient to multiply the effect your one vote has on the course of your life, depending of course on the size of the population you live amongst. Would you like me to explain it?"

She scratched her head. "Um, not really?" She laughed, and her laughter tumbled out and then died in the silence between them when he didn't laugh. His smile had departed the way she thought it should have an hour ago, replaced by an irritated gaze that intimidated her. She was suddenly afraid that he was angry. She made a mental note not to make any more jokes with the Assemblyman, to restrain herself, to conduct herself like a mature lady. She tried to make up for her mistake. "I'm sorry Arjun, it's just that I don't understand maths much either."

The dark clouds cleared from his countenance and good humour returned as he smiled. She felt safer for it. "It's okay," he said. "Forget about that. Let's look at it this way: I want to make people like you—people who think they don't know or care about politics—I want to make them care about the issues and support me. If you help me, I just need you to pretend to talk to yourself. Tell me if you understand what I'm saying, and if not, why? For example, you can tell me that my maths are confusing. Or tell me how else I can make you understand that something is important and win you over to my side. My team has been staring at the same things for too long. You'll bring a fresh perspective, and a new skillset. What do you think about it this way?"

"I think it makes sense." She bit her lip. In the quiet of the house, a car screeched and swerved on Serangoon Road; someone swore in Hokkien and someone swore back. She shuddered.

"I thought you might. And I promise you it will be fun. My team is motivated and although we work around the clock, we are very excited about the future. What do you say? Plus, as an added incentive, we'll get to work together." He winked at her, so quick she wasn't certain she had seen it, but it sounded alarms the same time it sent tingles down her body.

"Papatti," he said, "what do you think?"

About whether he had winked? The new tingles were spreading through her body, that's what she thought. As if reading her mind, he added, "About my request to join my team? We could use a spunky new volunteer like you."

Winks aside, Papatti knew that she could either refuse Arjun and disappoint him now, or agree and prove inadequate to the task and disappoint him later. All she had wanted was for him to settle the matter of who the best tailor in town was.

Remembering this, the latent optimism she had inherited from Rajpal stirred and charged, making its advance in the form of unstoppable possibilities. Wasn't this also a way to what she wanted? Helping Arjun campaign would win him over to her side, create a comfort level between them that allowed them to take a photo casually shaking hands to broadcast to the nation, perhaps even get her airtime on Radio Singapura; and he might offer to translate for that interview too. She might not even need that vaunted declaration from him by then. And her appa's dutifulness never failed to remind her that she would be involved in a cause that was very important to him and the country. Her amma's voice, never one to be sidelined, recognised the winning side and jumped onto the bandwagon, by admonishing her—Papatti had already insulted Arjun once today, and she should postpone upsetting him again in case he ended up giving Kumaran *her* house.

Papatti said, "Okay, Arjun. I will try my best." Immediately, she regretted her ready acquiescence when put on the spot. Amma would have stated a few conditions, even if Papatti didn't know what those conditions should be. Meekly, in a rush of absence of clear thought, she said, "But please don't be angry if I can't do it!"

He laughed. She wiped his spit from her eye as he said, "I won't if you try your best. Well that's good. Now that that's settled..." He checked the clock and frowned when he realised it was stuck at nine. "I must tell Mr Tan about that. I hate it when things don't work—"

"On the clock?"

He frowned at her. For God's sake, the first thing she needed to sew together were her lips. Ignoring her rude interjection, Arjun said, "Are you doing anything after this?"

She shook her head.

"Well, I am done for the day and hungry. Do you want to have supper?"

Papatti searched his imploring eyes, unsure what the invitation implied, unsure how she should interpret it or respond, unsure whether it was linked to the wink. He quickly said, "I just thought it would be nice to talk. But if you are busy, that's okay. I can meet my constituents at Tekka for supper too."

So he wanted to have supper *alone* with her. What was "nice to talk"? Talk about her joining his campaign or talk about something else? Did he really find her funny or did he want to talk despite her impudent interventions? The tingles returned, spreading fast, and she was flattered, excited, but cautious and uncertain. Even her parents' voices within her were confused, silent in their thoughts. Papatti didn't like being ambushed like this and later wished she had had the pluck to throw him offguard, with something like, "Only if you let me pull your nose."

But two problems confronted this course of action. First, this fount of confidence only seemed to spurt forth effectively when she was talking to her parents, where a single word could and would end the conversation decidedly in her favour. And second, when she did make these occasional comments to strangers, she instantly regretted them and had to try even harder to hold her tongue, as she had twice with Arjun tonight already. She had much to learn from Amma about dealing with people, if only the woman wasn't so difficult to deal with herself.

For instance, if Amma had explained to her nicely about what to look for in a man and how to approach such an invitation from a man to supper alone, Papatti may have known how to respond to Arjun. Instead, she didn't even know what she was allowed to want in such a situation, or want from a man at all. All her life, she had only had this vague idea that it was her destiny to one day be married, with little girls of her own (she had tweaked this from the standard destiny that prescribed little boys). She had always assumed that this destiny would fall into place without her intervention, settled by a combination of her parents and some man's parents and that omnipresent *fait accompli* so crudely referred to in Tamil as *that which is written on your forehead*, i.e., your fate. Hence, her mind now ran blank and dizzy with this proposal, the tingling surging, and she found another Papatti shaking her head furiously and babbling in a way she knew she would regret, "I'm sorry Arjun. It won't be appropriate for me to go out with a man at this hour of the night alone. Amma will scold me. I'm sorry. I need to go back home to Amma. She is waiting up for me. I need to be back. I'm sorry."

Arjun stepped backwards, showing two open palms. "Of course, of course. I understand." He paused. "It's just that— the day is difficult for me because of my work schedule. And of course it may create unnecessary rumours if I were to be seen with a girl in broad daylight. But you are right. What was I thinking? Another time. Maybe after the referendum would be better timing too."

Why would there be rumours? So he liked her? He did not want to wait for the writing on his forehead to settle everything on its own timeline? But Arjun's face was a smiling Great Wall again, unreadable. She felt a strong urge to pinch his nose and squeeze out a confession that she could discuss with her amma. No, she would not even dare recount this conversation to Lalitha because that incendiary woman would only berate Papatti for her meagre response to an Assemblyman's kind invitation.

Papatti felt like such a bumpkin, invoking what a girl should or should not do at night. She decided that the best recourse at this moment was to change the subject. Indeed, she should leave the matter of men and marriage to her parents. Her mind scrambled desparately, and she managed, "Does wearing an 'A' into the voting booth count as cheating?"

"Oh… That's a good question. I don't think so. If it helps you vote, I don't see why you can't carry a damn help sheet into the booth, pardon my language, although the Communists would kick up another dangerous fuss about that. But forget them, I think your way is more fun. Truth be told, I think we should do whatever it takes to win this referendum, if just for the mandate it gives us. We should be just as ruthless as the Communists have shown themselves to be." He became quiet, and he said coldly, "As ruthless as others have shown themselves to be. An eye for an eye makes the whole world equal, which, oddly enough, is what the Communists claim to want too."

"Do you think we'll win the referendum?"

"You can't tell for certain. But if we work hard and campaign hard, then yes, I think we will carry the Serangoon vote and hopefully the national vote and join Malaysia and become truly independent. And it will be thanks to you and good people like you, Papatti."

It was the textbook-perfect politician answer, noncommittal, plenty of "we"s, dispensing of credit, while stringing the words together with all his charisma. But it worked on her regardless and she forgot the wink and their awkward discussion about supper and instead, let the irresistible forces of the mathematical philosopher draw her inner Rajpal out, buoying Papatti with renewed pride about Arjun's offer, infusing her with a newfound zeal for the cause he wanted her to support, whose fate now lay in her hands as well. He said, "But I cannot stress this enough so please remember this too—the real work will only start after the referendum."

She nodded, persuaded, and said, "I promise to work hard for you, Arjun. Thank you."

...

Over the next months, Papatti baked sugary peanut-filled kueh makmur and kueh tarts glazed with pineapple jam and delivered them in silver tinfoil to Arjun's meetings as an occasional break from the Khong Guan biscuits, even if she stopped lingering to watch Kumaran kick-start the proceedings by asking for a permit to rear his chickens in the corridor of his new fifth-floor flat at Selegie. She used coloured chalk to recreate the "A" as mosaic kolam patterns on the pavements lining Serangoon Road, retouching them whenever people scuffed the chalk colours in their haste, or when she saw a football roll through the middle of one, sending her chalk colours merging like jetstream. Govinda donated excess lengths of red and white cloth, and she spent her lunch breaks and off hours sewing large crimson "A's" on white flags for her neighbours to drape from their windows. Serangoon Road became flanked by two rows of As, and Papatti felt a happy jolt knowing she had singularly revamped her street and given everyone a visual reminder of the crucial vote that lay ahead.

But she did not want to be caught off guard by another journalist, for she had decided that it was a matter of time before *The Straits Times* came knocking, or a guild of tailors invited her to speak to them about "political embroidery". Hence, at the rallies, she listened more than she cheered. While sewing, she turned on the black Sony transistor radio that sat on the windowsill whenever the hosts discussed the referendum. She sat in on Rajpal's occasional late night drinks sessions with his work buddies. Their heated political discussions sometimes led to blows and Papatti's expulsion because it was getting too dangerous for her, and Lalitha would scold all the men and evict them from the house, including Rajpal. Papatti would wait till the next day to ask her appa why a topic was so sensitive that they had fought over it.

Soon, she felt confident enough to go knocking door to door with Karnan along Serangoon Road, up into Jalan Besar, and past Jalan Besar to Kallang where the river remained brown and smelled of sewage. When the door opened she always said, "Hi, my name is Papatti. Don't worry, you don't need to know his name. But we would like to ask you to vote 'A' at the referendum." Karnan smiled, and she made sure to do all the talking.

She had four broad points that she listed out in Malay. First, she recounted Rajpal's story of Mr John Stevenson, and arrived at Rajpal's conclusion that they could only rely on themselves to survive. Then with a passion that could only be distilled from personal experience, she explained that with a common market, Govinda's shop could sell more garments to more people at cheaper prices, and in turn hire and train more workers like Papatti. She called the Communists misguided for thinking that they could decide whether Papatti should work as a seamstress or rubber tapper or homemaker, thinking they could dictate what she should sew, and above all, misguided in thinking they could murder and terrorise to achieve these totalitarian aims. Finally, she invited them to attend the Farrer Park rallies to hear Arjun elucidate these points with his mathematical erudition.

It was thus only reasonable that Papatti felt a strong sense of accomplishment when, at the end of two months, they won the referendum, unshackled Singapore from British rule and joined the Federation of Malaysia. She and the Serangoon contingent joined the dense throng of celebrators near City Hall, waving shawls and banners designed by her, watching feverishly as Assemblymen, Ministers and then the Prime Minister climbed the stage, grabbed the microphone, and led with their victory speeches, their electronically amplified voices booming out of the loudspeakers encircling the crowd. Papatti's contingent stood in one small tight body amidst a horde of free emancipated bodies, linked by common purpose, that roared and lurched forward when their favourite speaker mounted the podium, and ebbed back and settled when there was a lull, but through it all her contingent waved her custom-made banners, joining the chants, shouting en masse, cheering and shouting "Merdeka!" and "Majulah!" until their voices left them and they shouted only air. Still they shouted and when they woke up the next day, Lalitha fed Papatti and Rajpal honey to soothe their throats and Papatti applied Vicks to her dotted fingertips.

And of course, as part of a celebratory centrepiece, a journalist from *The Straits Times* turned up at 111 Serangoon Road to ask Papatti for sound bites from her campaign trail. This time, she was prepared, and she smiled well in the photograph, and the article made the seventeenth page. The journalist also quoted an anonymous customer, who said, "Papatti is easily the best clothes maker in the country. You must visit her shop." She paid no heed to the rumours, likely started by Muthu, that the anonymous customer was Govinda, and mounted the article on the cupboard above the two *Tamil Murasu* news reports. Rajpal even suggested hiring a photographer to take a picture of the cupboard in case the ink faded with time, but was dissuaded by Lalitha, who threatened to burn down the cupboard if he and Papatti did not stop with their nonsense.

And so Papatti had been utterly unprepared for the shock of Lalitha bursting into their living room one day, pottu fallen off and leaving a fairer patch of skin, shawl trailing behind on the floor and clinging to her ankle, panting in shock. Her eyes, hysterical, seized upon Papatti. Her nose ring flashed dangerously. "Wash your hands and come here."

Papatti was holding a soggy ball of rice mixed with sambar between her fingers, about to pop it into her mouth. "What Amma? I don't understand."

Lalitha vanished into their room. "We don't have time! Come here quick!"

Papatti splatted the rice back onto the plate, grumbling about wasting food. She poured water over her hands. As Lalitha shrieked, "Papatti!", urgency infused her and she rushed into the room to find Lalitha staring into their open cupboard.

Lalitha spun around. "Do you need to urine?"

"What?"

"I said do you need to urine?"

"No! What's wrong with you, Amma?"

"Papatti, go inside the cupboard. Don't talk back. Just go in. We must hide you."

Papatti stared at Rajpal's shirts, hanging in white and blue vertical lines. There was an earthy brown shirt that Papatti hadn't approved of in between. "I don't understand. Why, Amma?"

"Papatti, don't talk back! Just go inside now!"

Unnerved by Lalitha's batty shouting, wondering what had touched her amma off, she sat backwards on the fabric mound. Her butt sank in and Rajpal's shirts swarmed forward around her cheeks.

Lalitha's expression was tight and pitiless. Papatti said, "I'm scared, Amma. What's happening?"

Lalitha said nothing and lifted Papatti's calves. Papatti retracted them to bring her legs into the cupboard, sitting cross-legged. "Amma, tell me please."

"There are riots outside. The Chinese and Malays are rioting against each other. Now sit properly. Listen to me. Listen to me!" Their eyes locked. Lalitha gave her a fierce stare, gripping the doors on either side of Papatti, the moment pounding between them. Then Lalitha sighed. "It's probably nothing, Papatti. I ran here before even hearing everything and they said the rioters won't come to Little India but we can't take chances. I will find out what's happening and then come and get you. But until then, I want you to hide. I don't want you to come out. I need you to take this seriously until I understand what is going on. Do you understand? This is not a game. I'm going to look for your appa."

As Papatti opened her mouth, Lalitha shut the doors and the darkness swept in. Brisk footsteps petered away and the loneliness of her situation sank. No one heard her say, "But Amma…"

The clinical zing of mothballs, buried deep underneath, swirled upwards. Papatti's nose was what the radio host called a "price taker". Her eyes and ears were monopolists, trying to control her perception, trying to be responsible for every decision she made. Now that they had been starved, her olfactory receptors kicked in, and her nose smelled the herbal ayurvedic soap in Rajpal's shirts, the aroma of wood in the walls, the humid odour of her armpits, and the sambar residue in her fingernails. Papatti hugged her knees to her chest and rested her head against the wall.

Second by second passed in audible ticks and the occasional grumbling of her stomach, and Papatti wished she had brought the other half of her dinner into the cupboard. Where was Appa? How long would she have to stay in the cupboard? What were the people outside fighting about anyway? Wasn't fighting going to make them less safe than whatever they were worried about? She could not help becoming angry at the absurdity of it. Here she was, a Chinese girl raised by a Punjabi-Tamil family, knowing she was Indian, but now having to hide because others would think she was Chinese. She wanted to know what exactly counted in making people different enough that they would fight each other over that difference? She remembered something Rajpal used to tell her, "People are the same. Everyone different." She missed him.

Papatti dozed off and woke up intermittently, sleeping again, losing track of how long she was inside the cupboard. Only a whimpering cry woke her up. Papatti sat up, wiping the drool off her chin. She felt cold.

The doors opened and light flooded in. Cringing, she shielded her eyes, blinking furiously. She remembered the riots and fear entered her. Then Papatti said, "Amma?"

Tears ran down Lalitha's cheeks. "Papatti, they say he died. Tell me it cannot be. They say your appa is dead." Lalitha collapsed onto her.

11

Dedicated to Papatti

Singapore is separated from Malaysia by a slip of water called the Johor Strait, as if someone had taken a serrated knife and carved the smaller island out of the longer peninsula. Nobuo Kurosawa was an infantry soldier in the Japanese 18th Division and one of thousands of troopers crossing that strait between Johor and Singapore on their boats, one night in the February of 1942, about to storm Sarimbun beach on Singapore's northwest shore to begin the invasion.

When Kurosawa spoke of his younger brother Nobuo, he sounded at once tender and distant, and I imagined Nobuo as a youthful, fresh-faced version of Kurosawa. In the moonless dark, on silently lapping waters rippling with the adrenaline of a coming fight, Nobuo's assault barge managed to lurch into a swamp that was crusted with numerous mangrove tree trunks. Nobuo jumped onto a bog, which gave way and he dropped into warm water up to his thighs. Machine-gun fire roared from an enemy foxhole in the distance, its clack-clack-clack sparking off shouting and hollering and falling.

Nobuo plunged into the dark water, swimming and clinging to the mangrove hair roots perched off the coast, while his commanders around him bellowed orders to fire back.

He heaved himself onto wet soil in a gap between the dense and impenetrable trees, hidden by stems and darkness, camouflaged by the twigs and leaves he had planted on his helmet to break his shape, and fired back at the Australian and Indian soldiers hidden in the undergrowth ahead, hunting for the white sparks of their firing rifles. His platoon commander, lying prone next to him, ordered Nobuo to advance and just as he leapt to his feet to sprint forward and gain ground, Kurosawa said, "They shot him. Here and here and here. Three bullets, that's all it took." He pointed at his left chest, right bicep and right ear. He said it matter-of-factly, like reporting a stranger's death over the news.

The beach landing finished fast and during the regroup, the platoon commander found Nobuo's corpse lying boots-up, legs on land, chest and face half-immersed in the creek water, and dragged it out.

Sitting next to me, Kurosawa stretched out his right index finger stiff. He used his left finger to saw it at the second joint, pretending to cut clean through the bone, the way the platoon commander had used his bayonet to chop off Nobuo's finger. Kurosawa said, "I burned the finger, collected the ashes and tied them up in my handkerchief to bring back to my mother when I return to Japan. I put it in the mess tin and prayed to it every day. But," he said, eyes staring through me, "Nanban, you threw it into that smelly river." He shook his head as if disappointed with me, as if I had merely peed in my bed. He continued to smile sadly.

But I remembered Kurosawa desperately wading into the river to find what I had thrown away and caning me afterwards, and it made sense now. I became scared that he would become irate again and bowed my head, afraid of meeting his gaze. I had just been trying to clean the room thoroughly so that he wouldn't punish me. And at least, Kurosawa had known how his brother had died, had possessed his ashes for a few days, luxuries I did not have. He tapped my chin encouragingly. "It's okay, Nanban. It's over. Many months ago. And my brother died bravely, he fell like a cherry blossom. Do you understand?"

I nodded, still down-staring, while he hummed a tune, "If I die for the Emperor, there will be no regrets." I had heard the Jalan Besar soldiers sing the song several times when marching. They called it *Umi Yukaba*—if I go away to the sea. Kurosawa cut off sharply and said, "You don't want to draw? You want to learn more *kanji*?"

I shook my head and he laughed and clapped his hands. "No one likes to learn *kanji*. Come, draw something. Unless you are secretly Utagawa Hiroshige." I scratched my temple with the butt of the pencil and he laughed, saying, "An excellent artist."

...

If I needed to trace the beginning of the Japanese Occupation of Singapore, it began geographically with Sarimbun beach, but spiritually it began from the Emperor sitting on the Chrysanthemum throne in his Imperial Palace in Tokyo. Once, in the middle of another writing lesson, Kurosawa asked me to explain Hinduism to him. I didn't know much about Hinduism so Kurosawa said, "Good," and proceeded to lecture me about Shintoism and that was the end of Hinduism.

The Japanese Emperor was a descendent of Amaterasu, the Sun Goddess, and seemed to have inherited all the best qualities of his divine ancestor, such as infallibility and invincibility, to which he added more earthly expertise like American fighter jets and British gunships. Of course, divinity, like gravity, poured downwards and in the Imperial Army's hierarchy, a lower-ranking soldier obeyed his superior officer as if the latter channelled the unerring word and authority of the Emperor. As the Japanese military apparatus was decidedly male and the Emperor was also male, I sometimes wondered when they decided that the wellspring of their divinity should be a Goddess. Either way, the Japanese would do anything their Mikado commanded, including happily and honourably—for the two often went together—giving up their lives for him, which explained Kurosawa's calm acceptance of his brother's death. When inebriated, Kurosawa often declared in odd fits of passion, "Every Yamato man, woman and child will take up a katana, or a needle, or sharpen this pencil and charge to death before surrendering and dishonouring the Emperor! Do you understand? Nanban, you must too! Do you understand?" So when the Emperor ordered the Japanese military to march south, they unflinchingly followed his word, and took his approval as a blanket licence to do anything in his name. Kurosawa wasn't just patriotic, he was devout.

At the same time, because the Japanese claimed descent from the Emperor, they believed that his divinity had spilled over to them too, making them superior to the rest of the world, undefeatable. Through the Emperor, the Age of the Gods continued in Japan and spread from there to the world. Kurosawa told me that in ancient times, the Mongol Emperor Kublai Khan had amassed his fleet off the coast of Korea, poised to attack Japan and expand his empire to the eastern edge of the world. But as the Khan's fleet set sail, a typhoon wreaked havoc along the Japanese coastline, destroying the Mongol ships and drowning its sailors and winning the battle for Japan. The Japanese called this typhoon the Divine Wind, *kamikaze*, arriving in time to protect the sacred Japanese islands from the infidel Mongols. Kurosawa believed that the divine wind continued to protect Japan's people, and would secure her military's victory in any battle, and gave her the right to rule over any people.

Curious contradictions occurred to me that I dared not mention to Kurosawa. Where was this divine protection when his brother was shot? If Japan could not lose, why would it ever have to choose to die fighting? But I guess this is why faith must be infinite. Nevertheless, I found myself stuck between Japan's inability to lose and its unwillingness to surrender. But at the same time, I did not accept Kurosawa's myths about the Emperor and Japan at face value.

I wonder, if I had been born and raised during Japanese rule, would I have grown up thinking the Emperor's divinity was natural and Japanese supremacy inevitable, the way my appa had felt about the British colonialists? But this was always going to be impossible. I had observed the transition of power from the British to the Japanese, and in that instant the curtains lifted and I saw the barbaric human hand of power underneath these kabuki plays of authority and myth. There is nothing natural or inevitable to any rule. I was grateful to have three meals a day and lessons in *kyoshokan* and Japanese from Kurosawa, but I also knew that captivity had merely saved me from what captivity had endangered me with. I was as lucky as I was unlucky.

A week after our brief talk about Nobuo's death on Singapore's northern shores, Kurosawa called me out of his house in the middle of the day. I was washing his uniforms in the toilet and ran out, hands wet and dripping with foam, ready to bow. But Private Nakamura was on his knees, facing me. Kurosawa towered behind Nakamura, wrenching a tuft of Nakamura's black hair back so violently that Nakamura's head and spine arched backwards.

Later, Kurosawa would tell me that he should have known from Nakamura's hair that he was a troublemaker, the type who would tattoo his body and bring shame to his family. Nakamura's oval eyes brimmed wet with the stinging pain dancing on his scalp, his crooked teeth bared, sweat lathering his face. His knees trembled on the concrete floor, shaking even more vigorously whenever Kurosawa moved his knotted fist.

Kurosawa didn't seem particularly enraged. He was as solemn and inscrutable as he always was in front of the soldiers. But the sight of punishment meted out immediately frightened me. Despite the scorching heat, my insides turned cold and I braced myself that I could be next. No matter how many times I was punished, I feared it all the same. The Jalan Besar soldiers had scrammed into their houses and the road was deserted. I suspected they were afraid too. They must have also wanted to spare Nakamura the embarrassment of their watching his disciplining and punishment. Yamashita was standing beside Kurosawa and I glanced at him for comfort, but his skinny arms were crossed tightly and he only grimaced disappointedly at Nakamura, ignoring me.

Kurosawa said, "Nanban."

I remembered my manners and bowed. "Yes, Lieutenant Kurosawa."

"A boy knows better than you. You should be ashamed." He yanked the clumped hair harder and Nakamura's neck arched further. I began suspecting that Kurosawa must have wanted to discipline Nakamura in front of a child and compare him to a child to make his punishment even more humiliating and cruel, and thus a far better punishment. "Nanban, I want to tell you what Private Nakamura here did.

He has been stealing rice from the store every week. Rice meant for soldiers of the Imperial Army."

The Japanese soldiers adhered to their rules and customs so painstakingly that I found this unbelievable. After all, these were divinely ordained rules and customs. And if heavenly mandate failed (again another strange contradiction, for if it fails, is it heavenly?), the offenders were most mortally punished, another reason not to break the Kempeitai's laws. Kurosawa said, "Do you want to know why, Nanban?"

"To eat, Lieutenant Kurosawa."

He laughed, a forced laughter. Sarcastic. "No, Nanban. No. Private Nakamura has more than enough food for himself. He has been stealing the rice at night, putting it into his rucksack, and pouring the rice into the windows of houses from Jalan Besar to Mackenzie to feed civilians. Locals." He spat the last word out with disgust. Kurosawa had started speaking so virulently that Nakamura's knees levitated off the ground.

I was astonished that a Japanese soldier had not only stolen from the army, but sympathised with the locals enough to steal from the army to feed them.

Kurosawa said, "Private Nakamura thinks he is Shinozaki Mamoru. But there is no Navy to help him disappear. He will be punished for his irresponsibility. Do you understand, Nanban? Do you understand what I am saying?"

I didn't know a Shinozaki Mamoru and when I asked Kurosawa about him another day, he curled his nose in disdain and refused to divulge more, and I left it at that. But on that day, I nodded agreeably with Kurosawa.

"But that's not all, Nanban. No, no. Apparently, Nakamura here is in love with a girl who lives along that street. Can you believe that? He is a romantic thief. He stole rice to steal her heart and she stole his heart to steal our rice.

Does he deserve to be punished?"

I nodded, which was expected of me if I wanted to stay safe. But I agreed with Kurosawa too. I admired Nakamura's bravery and didn't buy into this Emperor nonsense. But the rule of law was as arbitrary as any rule, and theft was theft. Why should Nakamura be made an exception? The rest of us had gone about with our heads down, surviving day by day, but Nakamura had tried to be a hero. And in so doing, he had turned the spotlight onto me, whoever his lover was, and everyone living on that hungry street. He had brought on unwelcome attention and put us all in danger. What was I doing in this courtyard, watching Kurosawa punish Nakamura, afraid of what could follow? What would happen to that girl and the rest of the people who had taken the rice? If Nakamura had felt that some residents didn't have sufficient food, he should have just lodged a complaint with their district heads. These were selfish thoughts, a selfishness I had abhorred in Appa. But I was making progress in this new world called *Shōnan* and I didn't want Nakamura to derail this for the sake of his romantic dalliance.

Kurosawa said, "Nakamura chose to break the law, to be special. But the nail that sticks out is always hammered back in. How shall we punish Private Nakamura, Nanban?"

"I don't know, Lieutenant Kurosawa."

"It's okay. I know. Do you remember your right roundhouse *keri*, Nanban?"

"Yes, Lieutenant Kurosawa." Understanding overcame me. "No, Lieutenant Kurosawa."

"Yes, Nanban. Yes. Here." He slapped Nakamura's left cheek twice, hard. The tears that had pooled in Nakamura's eyes tumbled over and fell onto the grey floor in black spots. But Nakamura didn't resist the wrenching and slapping. Instead, he closed his eyes, as if that would whisk him away to a more peaceful place. "Strike him here. Do you understand?" Kurosawa slapped his cheek again to make the point and I wished he would stop. It was terrifying me even more.

"No, Lieutenant Kurosawa. Please."

"Yes." He rose even taller and said, "Nanban, repeat after me: *Jakuniku kyōshoku*."

Afraid I was testing his patience too much, I said, "*Jakuniku kyōshoku*." It sounded familiar.

"It is a proverb that means the strong devour the weak. You must always remember it. You can either be strong like the eagle, or weak and eaten up like the mouse. But you must choose. Japan chose to be strong so other countries wouldn't devour us. Now, Private Nakamura could have been a soldier of Japan, leading us to glorious victory, upholding our Empire, but he chose to be weak, to dishonour the Emperor who has led us so far. Now you choose, Nanban. Are you strong? Or are you like Private Nakamura? Weak."

"Yes, Lieutenant Kurosawa. No, Lieutenant Kurosawa."

"Then come forward."

I shook my head adamantly, but his stern gaze compelled my feet to shuffle forward. I believed Nakamura should be punished, but I didn't want to punish him myself, I didn't want to beat him. Training *kyoshokan* with Kurosawa every day, I was used to punching air and kicking his pads, and I remember punching Kurosawa when he wanted me to practise on him, but he had been strong and braced for impact then. I didn't want to hit a man when he was down. Not like this. I was no bully. I started hating Nakamura, kneeling there with his eyes closed like a Mahatma after all the trouble he had created with his memsahib.

"*Jakuniku kyōshoku*" was one of many slogans I learned during the Occupation, a pithy strings of words that Kurosawa hurled out to justify the Emperor's rule or his own commands, as if those few words could summarily justify another man's death. Like: "Rich Country, Strong Army"; "Heaven's Work"; "All the World Under One (Japanese) Roof"; and of course, "Asia for Asians". Sometimes, I overheard soldiers in the Cathay Building discussing the efficiency of these slogans, quantifying the simplicity of the words and the time required to hear them, creating an index of the effectiveness of these slogans based on this quantification, a mathematical precision that I grew to admire. In fact, a few days later, I remembered why Kurosawa's proverb sounded so familiar when I heard a soldier singing:

There is a Law of Nations, it is true
But when the moment comes, remember,
The strong eat up the weak.

But the proverb, while catchy, also made being strong sound very insecure, as if one became strong by being eternally afraid of getting eaten up.

I was an arm's length away from Nakamura now, standing a little above his eye level. I could see the individual sweaty strands of black hair tangled and wrapped around Kurosawa's tanned fingers, like a tiger's stripes. He reeked of urine and sweat. When Nakamura opened his eyes, they were swollen red, but he stared at me coolly. As Kurosawa waited quietly, Nakamura said, "Just finish it, Nanban. It's okay." Saliva sputtered out of his parched mouth.

Kurosawa pretended not to have heard the private speak below him. Instead, as a non-response, he slapped Nakamura's cheek again, where he wanted me to kick, and Nakamura winced. But Nakamura kept his eyes fixed on me, and did not let the humiliation show. He gave me one firm nod. "It's okay, Nanban. Just do it."

Kurosawa's eyes were stern. There was no hope I could back out of this.

I was gripping my fists tight; the sun was baking my neck. I told myself to be done with the deed. Nakamura deserved it for the crimes he had committed. As Kurosawa had said, this was how the world worked. And if Nakamura's marauding military had taught me anything, it was indeed that the strong devoured the weak. Their cruelty had served them well. And for once, I was the stronger one. This was right.

I pivoted on the ball of my left foot, my right leg curling and swinging in the air like a bat. Nakamura closed his eyes and took a breath. I swung both arms out toward my oncoming leg like a fan, jerked my hip out to snap my right leg like a whip. As that leg extended and straightened, parallel to the ground, I closed my eyes too. My shin bone crashed into his cheek with the sound of a cracking branch. Pain shot up my shin as I heard a hoarse cry. Saliva splattered my thigh. And then I heard Kurosawa clapping.

12

My Jewel Inheritance

Her appa died, they told her. But Papatti hated the word *died*, as if her appa had chosen to execute the verb, had deliberately and consciously *died*. He had been killed and found dead. Rajpal had been cycling home, trying to make the nationwide curfew the government had introduced after the first spate of riots, being an obedient citizen, a conforming member of society that should have rewarded him for this agreeability. But a getaway car had swerved out of a slip road and hit him and hadn't stopped. It had fled, shambling on its way and leaving her appa thrashing and moaning in pain on the road as his blood trickled after the car. They found her appa in the morning, dead in the middle of the street, the bicycle a crumpled heap metres away. They said, "He died like an orphan." Another man was found hacked to pieces in a drain in the alley around the corner.

Her amma had hugged Papatti and cried on her shoulders for hours as if someone had taken a sledgehammer to her tight façade. After the coroner released the corpse,

Subramaniam and Jamuna washed it and applied talcum powder and make-up to the abrasions and cuts before calling Lalitha and Papatti, to spare them the further anguish of seeing a wounded cadaver, and only then did Lalitha stir and let go of her daughter. But when she saw Rajpal's peaceful form, eternally reposed, no longer jubilantly running and excitedly jumping around with Papatti and giving Lalitha an excuse to scold him, Lalitha tearfully fell to her knees, gripping his dead arm, beating her chest and forehead, saying, "You are supposed to be the dramatic one! You are supposed to be the dramatic one! Not me!" She fell asleep there and remained heavy with sleep for days.

Papatti postponed her own grieving and took charge of organising the funeral, asking Wei Liang and Subramaniam, who worked in the death industry, to help her hold the wake. Wei Liang reserved a space at the funeral parlour along Lavender Road, which was filled to capacity that week, and ordered the van to transport the casket from the morgue to Lavender. The funeral room was a simple but elegant white room on the second floor and Wei Liang set up circular tables, arranged chairs around the tables and bought coffee for the guests. He also helped Papatti buy an affordable coffin, while Subramaniam bought marigold garlands, vibhuti, milk, ghee, and helped Papatti clean and dress Rajpal's body again and instructed her in performing the Hindu rites throughout the funeral.

The day of the wake, Lalitha was a crippled and exhausted white shroud, white gown hanging over the stool next to the coffin, reflecting her husband's lifelessness. An old aunty or grandma would enter the funeral room and pay their condolences to Papatti, kissing her forehead and calling her things in Tamil like "My golden girl", or "Diamond", or something like "My jewel inheritance". Then they sat next to Lalitha, peeked into the coffin and set off into a terrible wail. With their palms faced up to the heavens, heads tilted back, they ululated in horrifying waves as they bemoaned Lalitha's loss, lamented the injustice of Rajpal's death and demanded explanations from God since they could produce none. This catlike bawling sparked Lalitha back to life like a spring rapidly unwound, and she joined in the caterwauling, her tears gushing again, as they sang together in waves of grief until Papatti ran over to shoo the dramatic old women away from her amma.

Karnan offered to take over this important watch duty for Lalitha's health and Papatti's sanity. But physically he was far stronger than Papatti, and once he used a little too much force on Whampoa athai who, mid-flight, appealed to God, and who in His divine mercy answered her prayers by providing her forehead with a hard landing against the wall. She complained to Papatti, but Papatti didn't care. She was having enough difficulty preparing for the following day's cremation, tracking expenses and welcoming the guests without dramatics straight from the Kollywood film industry. If Papatti had allowed herself to be rude, she would have said, "Serves you right." But she knew her appa would disapprove.

So for the rest of the wake, Whampoa athai sat in a corner, holding a tumbler of coffee in one hand and a small bag of ice to her head in the other, scratching the white plaster paint from her forehead and telling anyone patient enough to listen that it was deplorable that a girl—Papatti—was performing funeral rites normally reserved for a man. Papatti had half a mind to walk up to her and tell her she was on her period too, but she didn't want to handle two dead bodies.

Arjun entered, dressed in a white shirt tucked into high-waisted black pants, with a photographer trailing behind.

His smile was tempered. "I'm sorry about your appa," he said. "He was a good man." He held one of her arms comfortingly and a few eyes turned before he let go. Over Arjun's shoulder, the photographer signed at Papatti, using his fingers to make a clicking of a camera motion to ask for permission. Papatti tightened her jaw and and threw her gaze away from him. She smiled weakly at Arjun, and said, "Thank you."

"I am going to talk to your amma for a bit. Stay strong." As he walked away, Papatti poured Arjun coffee and reluctantly poured the photographer a cup too. When Arjun returned, he sipped it and stared around and she started suspecting that he wanted to ask for something. She made to walk towards Subramaniam. But Arjun said, "Papatti, wait."

She didn't want to broach this topic now. "Arjun—"

He cut her off. "I know this isn't the best time, but I guess there is no such thing as a good time for this. Papatti, we need to try even harder to bring people together. We don't want more riots to happen. I'm trying to organise a peace procession for the day after tomorrow and I want to invite you and your family and friends along, ask you to help us with the procession. Will you join us?"

Now, Papatti understood that this was a matter of grave import, a matter of life and death for the country. And she knew that it overrode her comparatively self-interested and perhaps even trivial anguish over her appa's death. But she didn't care. Did he have to bring this matter up now? She would have thought he'd be more sensitive. Couldn't he at least wait for her to cremate her appa's body? It was insulting.

Arjun said, "I know what you must be thinking. Like I said, I know this isn't the best time. But I have a larger duty and I'm just trying to do my job. I hope you understand."

To hell with him and his job and trying to please him.

When they were preparing her appa's corpse, Subramaniam had volunteered to fetch Rajpal's best set of shirt and trousers to dress his body in. Papatti had demurred and returned home alone while Lalitha kept mourning vigil over Rajpal at the funeral parlour.

With only the flickering of an orange candle and the vibrating sounds of the Singer machine hard at work through the night, Papatti had sewn a long flowing azure tunic and tapered trousers and matched them with a blue turban to dress her father in, knowing this would be the last time she ever sewed again.

She could not shake off the distasteful realisation that ever since Lalitha had taught her to sew, she had been sewing to endear herself to others. As she had grown older, the number of stitches she had made and the number of customers entering the shop asking for her had increased pari passu, but it was the latter that gave her the greater happiness. And even then, she had not been satisfied. She had wanted national fame, wanted to beat every competitor from Muthu to Changi, wanted to prove every itsy bitsy nobody naysayer wrong, and had even joined a good cause for the most selfish of reasons.

But now she had ended up losing the one person who had actually tried the hardest to endear himself to her, the one person who cared for her above everyone else and whom she loved more than anything, whose opinion alongside her amma's was the only one that should have mattered in the first place. If only she had understood this earlier instead of dismissing it as a symptom of parental love that she could take for granted. And to think, when her appa had needed her the most while bucking in pain in the middle of the road, she had not even been there. Rajpal had rescued her as an orphan and kept her from dying alone; she had not been able to do the same for him. Now, people said that he died like an "orphan".

With the sober and cold clarity that comes in the wake of severe loss, sewing seemed so pointless, and so wrong and twisted in her hands. She had taken advantage of an honest profession for all the wrong selfish reasons, taken advantage of a good cause for all the wrong selfish reasons, and ultimately forgotten what—or who—really mattered. For in the end, only the people who chose to stay could matter.

She would bury the needle with Rajpal. Of course, her appa would disagree, tell her to do what she loved, to stay with the cause he so fervently believed in, to listen to the Assemblyman and to fight for the values her appa loved to espouse during dinner talk. But she wished she had never sat on that stool before the sewing machine or stitched any letter into her appa's shirt. She wished she had shown him more affection when he was alive. It made her hate everything else that she had given more attention to, including the needle and the Singer machine. By the time Papatti finished sewing her appa's last jippa, apricot sunlight had started cracking through the shutter windows and the buzzing of the sewing machine had grown tired and weaker, as if it needed sleep too. Papatti returned her needle into its drawer, closed it and draped the excess blue cloth over the Singer machine so it echoed her mother's ghostly image. She fell forward on it and cried.

Now, confronted with Arjun's request, Papatti found that his logical rationalisation had no effect on her. She said, "No, I understand. You are doing a good thing, a great thing. I know that." She pointed at the egg-shaped coffin. "But I'm sorry. My appa's death has started me thinking. I don't want to sew anymore. I don't deserve to sew. I just want to take care of Amma. She is the only person I care about. I need to be there for her. I'm sorry Arjun, but I can't help you anymore."

Arjun frowned, displeased by the sudden tack the conversation had taken. "Papatti, how can you say that? You have a real talent in sewing. How else are you going to make money? This doesn't make sense."

"I don't care about money. I don't care about anything. That was my problem—I cared about everything that didn't matter. But I couldn't even protect my appa. I couldn't even be there when he—" Her throat choked. She shook her head. "I don't want to sew. I don't deserve to. I just need to learn to take care of my amma. I need to learn to do the right thing for the right reason. This is the only way I can prove it." She was rambling. She felt the onset of tears, mounting with grief. She had never spoken to Arjun so freely, but she couldn't be bothered. She was taking advantage of his compassion and tolerance during her period of mourning, but she didn't care. Loss made her care less.

Arjun narrowed his eyes. "Papatti, you don't need to prove this to anyone."

"I need to prove it to myself."

"Papatti, stop. Trust me. I lost my appa a long time ago. The Japanese killed him. But you must carry on with your life. That's what your appa would want too. Be sensible. Your sewing has nothing to do with this. You will not make any point by giving it up. You are just being emotional. Try to think rationally. You have such a talent. Don't waste it."

She folded her arms. "I can always find another talent."

He frowned. Then he downed the rest of his coffee and plonked the cup onto the table. "Okay. I understand that you are upset. But just think about it. Can you do that for me please?"

She gritted her teeth and nodded. But she had made up her mind.

"And if you really don't feel up to it, in the worst of cases, let me know. I'm sure our team could use the sewing machine. They can't create new ideas, but they could replicate yours."

She almost lunged at him to strangle him. He could be importunately and persistently insensitive. And now that he had asked for her sewing machine so callously, Papatti found herself not wanting to give it away, not so soon anyway. Even though something told her that Arjun was right, that she was just being emotional and would pay a price when his patience ran out. If she had determined not to use her machine anymore, she should stick to her guns, be just as dogged as he was, and give it to someone who would use it. Arjun didn't have time to deal with her flippancy. She gritted her teeth and nodded once, reluctantly.

Arjun checked his watch. "Okay. I'm sorry but I have another engagement to attend and will take my leave. Take care of yourself and your amma, okay? I will see you soon." He gripped her shoulder in an awkward attempt to be consoling and then left, photographer trailing after him.

Karnan, who had just finished cheering Whampoa athai up, came over and said, "Are you okay?"

She told him what transpired, and he said, "Of course you are grieving and you need time to work through your grief and figure out what to do next. You have no time to think about anything else."

"So I was right, right?" she said.

"Yes. But he is also right in saying that you have a talent and giving it up would be a waste, and that he could use your talent. I won't deny that. I guess someone needs to do his job and you have to take care of your amma."

"You are not saying or denying anything then, Karnan," Papatti said, feeling her exasperation rise at him too, wishing he would be more reassuring.

"I think the both of you are just trying to make the best of the situations you are in. Aren't we all?"

...

From Punggol beach, Papatti waded into the great green sea until the cold white rollers broke against her waist. She upturned the golden urn in her hands and strewed her appa's ashes over the rolling waters, watching as the grey cloud drifted into the curve of the sky that joined the water. She climbed ashore, avoiding broken glass and cracked shells and torn corals that were swept ashore by the waters and abandoned, and helped lift her amma up from the sand and took her home.

Climbing upstairs and taking in the empty living room, Papatti noticed the sobering absence of the shouting over each other, Amma nagging Appa, his rushing to Papatti for protection, or cheering Papatti up whenever Lalitha scolded her. The loving, avuncular living space she had always taken for granted was replaced by an empty stranger she was nervous and unwilling to meet. She handheld her mother through the desolate living room, into their bedroom, and closed the door to keep the stranger out. She rolled out Lalitha's mat and unfurled Rajpal's onto it, and Lalitha slept on her side, digging her nose into the rattan weaves for solace. Papatti swept Lalitha's cascading hair away from her eyes and rubbed her back and massaged her neck, wondering in silence if Appa missed them too.

But Rajpal's passing demanded not only an emotional adjustment. Without him to collect rent, Papatti soon realised that her tenants were less forthcoming with their monthly payments. They were mostly single men sharing the other rooms, with a little age over Papatti and an increasing excess of creativity that they deployed to test her resolve. Whenever she knocked on their room doors, she faced a new excuse:

"The work has stopped because of the riots, Papatti. I am

not being paid. By next month, it should be settled."

"I can't even afford to go to work, Papatti. Give me time to recover my losses."

"They are forcing us to pay higher union fees, Papatti. Give me until next month and I will have enough money."

"My amma is ill, Papatti. I remitted the money to Chennai to pay for her hospital fees. She will be discharged by next month and after that I will be able to pay again. I promise."

They always promised to pay, and Papatti trusted them because after all, why would they lie? They had always paid their rents punctually before. She was sure Appa had encountered these very ostensible reasons once and showed them some flexibility. Rajpal had always encouraged her to be kind and understanding. So she and Lalitha, who was still unable to do any sort of work, pawned away the small number of gold-plated chains and bangles that represented their bank savings, liquidating the gold to cover their payments to the landlord until their tenants could pay them back. Having quit her job at Govinda's shop and being determined to stick to her guns to quit sewing altogether, Papatti took up a job as an ah ma at the Tan Tock Seng Hospital along Moulmein Road, cleaning the hospital wards, changing the bedsheets, bathing the patients, helping them urinate during the morning and afternoon shifts for a regular income. It was weary work, and she took her time to adjust to it, but she forced herself to diligently see it through every day. Her amma was too exhausted to protest against her career choices.

As the months wore on, the excuses persisted:

"My company's still suffering, Papatti. It's not paying me a single cent. Do you want to talk to my boss?"

"Some hair stole my bicycle, Papatti! All my savings have gone to buy a new one. I'm broke myself. Some more time, please. I promise I'll pay you everything back."

"My amma's condition has worsened, Papatti. Please give me more time. I promise I'll pay you by next month."

Papatti had no gold left to hock and even the better-paying night shifts at the hospital were insufficient to cover the lease she owed the landlord. She regretted ever allowing her tenants to postpone their rent payments, for now that she considered threatening to kick them out, she realised she couldn't even afford to do that because she needed the money they owed her. Now, they held power over her. And where would she find new boarders and how would she make *them* pay?

The only tenant paying punctually was 111's longest lodger, Govinda, until he asked Papatti to meet him behind the cashier after closing time. Swivelling on his stool like a child, he stared at the ground and said, "Papatti, how are you? How are finances?"

She shrugged to express that there wasn't much she could do about them. "Difficult, mama. The—"

"Papatti, I'm going to shutter the shop."

"What?" He refused to meet her eyes. "What are you saying, mama?"

"I'm sorry child. It's just that, it's too unstable here. There is still fighting on the streets, and the bus companies and dockworkers are striking, and it's not good for business. No one is coming to buy anything. The bank also doesn't want to lend me any money to refinance my business because of how sour the market is. It's no wonder the tenants can't pay you, even though yes, I know some of them are not being honest. But I've tried talking to them for you."

"But what will you do?"

"I'm going to go meet my wife and children in Selangor, and then we're going to move back to Chennai."

"Mama!"

He glanced at her, fear of another person's reproach clouding his eyes, embarrassed at taking flight. "I'm sorry, Papatti, really, you know I adore you and Lalli. But I'm a family man and a businessman, and I must look out for my family and business. You understand, right? Please?" He squeezed her hands.

Papatti understood where Govinda's interests lay, but also recognised that he was leaving her in the lurch. She became jealous he could even afford plane tickets, an escape route, a new start. "I'm sorry Papatti, please believe me," he said again.

"I know, mama. I know." There was nothing else to say.

After that, every night and every morning she returned home from work, entering through the store front, she noticed its walls emptying, the long colourful rolls of sarees replaced by monotonous brown wood. The readymade shirts and Punjabi suits disappeared from the racks and the hangers hung empty, and the mannequins were denuded into lonely beige plastic. Bulging cardboard boxes began to pack the floor and a week later, the boxes disappeared too, garments shipped off to Chennai. The store became barren.

Govinda gave her a token sum of thirty dollars inside a red packet and kissed her on the forehead before dragging his suitcase out to take the morning bus to Selangor. Lalitha did not want to say goodbye and stayed upstairs as Govinda shouted from the road, "Lalli! See you! Write to me! I've left the address with Papatti!"

It hurt Papatti to know how lonely Amma must feel, now that an old friend, one of her oldest friends, was leaving, abandoning them. That evening, she took Lalitha to the Perumal Temple, where Lalitha's friends would be present for Tuesday prayers and might cheer her up. But even they couldn't. Lalitha came home and screamed at the only tenant in the house, Arul, her hair open like a devouring Kali, raging at him in glittering language.

But Arul just said, "What are you going to do? Kick us out yourself? Stop shouting and act properly like a woman. You could learn a thing or two from your daughter." Then he slammed his door close on Lalitha's astonished face. Lalitha was not used to being spoken to this way and became possessed, banging his door with her fists until Papatti, afraid her already distressed amma would collapse, towed her away. She undertook to handle the problem of rent payments herself and exhorted a promise from her amma not to intervene on this anymore, for the sake of both their healths.

The next day, to buy them more time, Papatti found a second job as a cleaner at the new Japanese department store that had opened on Orchard Road, a ten-minute bus ride from Tan Tock Seng Hospital and a twenty-minute bus ride from home. But it was not enough and they were still four months behind payment.

Their landlord was a bald and fat man, who in his white shirt and veshti reminded Papatti of the quintessential movie villain, especially when he lifted his chin and stared at her from the bottom of his eyes and smirked. He sat while she stood across his large desk in his Little India Arcade office and she felt like a criminal hauled to court. The landlord threatened to expel Lalitha and Papatti and replace them with more "dependable" and "reliable" and "trustworthy" leaseholders, as if the words meant different things. Even his voice had a nasal villainous quality, issuing snarky comments like "So I'm supposed to collect the money, is it?" All Papatti had done was to ask him to speak to her tenants and judge for himself who was to blame. He continued, "That's your job, Papatti. It's called a delegation of labour. That's why I let you inherit Rajpal's lease. Unless you are telling me to revoke it?

Legally, I am allowed to."

"No," she said.

"Then find a way to cough up the money. I knew Rajpal for many years, and his appa before that, and I want you to continue staying at the house. I really do. But I have a business to run and I need your cooperation with that." He said "cooperation" in English, pronouncing the "co-op" like "cooorp". "Do you understand?"

Of course she understood. She had always understood. But what could she do with this understanding? Put it on top of her head and dance? Make the tenants pay? Papatti gave him a flip of her braided hair as she stormed out of the office, feeling good in thinking, "Understand that!" even though she only felt safe being sassy because he had already buried his reprobate nose into his papers and files. In fact, if she recalled right, he hadn't even attended Rajpal's funeral. Damn all these businessmen with their businesses to run. It was enough to make her consider learning about Marxism.

But since everyone was being difficult, she decided to take a leaf from her tenants' books and be just as difficult herself. Papatti decided to pass the problem of dues on to someone else. She found a moneychanger called Vinodh near Bugis who apparently did not read the *Tamil Murasu*, did not know her family and thus could not report these unwelcome tidings to her amma. Papatti borrowed money from Vinodh to pay off her rent to the landlord, and when the monthly collection date swung by, she took satisfaction in relaying her tenants' excuses to Vinodh and asked him to speak to them instead.

She gladly passed the buck like this for several months, understanding first-hand how her tenants had found it so easy, so addictive, to simply *not pay*. Once, she returned home in the evening to find a skinny teenager, about sixteen years of age, sitting by the porch, massaging his foot into a stray cat. He stood up to examine her. "What do you want?" she said in Malay as she fidgeted with the side door.

He was a most polite teenager and worked for the moneychanger. He was here to collect the outstanding payments.

Papatti said, "I can't pay you. Do you want to know why?" She did not care that he backed away fearfully and the cat scrammed as she opened the door and stuck her head into the house and shouted in Tamil, *"Because no one has paid me! Ask them! They are upstairs sitting in the rooms they have not yet paid for!"* She turned around. "Do you understand?" She smiled, feeling as deranged as she must appear.

He likely did not understand, but nodded regardless. Heartened by the respect this teenager showed his elders, Papatti slammed the door on his face. Fuming, she climbed the stairs and bumped into Lalitha. "Amma!"

"Who were you talking to?"

"What are you doing here? Aren't you supposed to be at work?"

"Papatti, don't change the subject."

"Nothing."

Lalitha glared. "Then why were you shouting at the tenants?"

"I was bugging them to pay."

"Ah." Lalitha turned swiftly, grabbing her hand and hurriedly leading her into their room. She shut the door and pulled Papatti down to sit on the floor. "I think we have a way to solve all of this."

Papatti became nervous. "What?"

"You have a marriage proposal."

"What?"

"You have a marriage offer, and it's a good one."

"From whom?"

Lalitha said, "From the Assemblyman, Arjun Kandasamy. He came by the house in the morning and said he likes you and that the two of you talked quite a bit while you were still helping him with the campaign."

"Amma, that was almost a year ago. Before Appa passed away. And we barely talked. I was only working for him."

"What does it matter? He's been very busy with merger and all the problems after. But now he said that he sees he will always be busy and wants to settle down with a wife while he can. And he said he likes you a lot. He thinks you are smart and funny and brave. For a moment, I was confused about whether he was talking about my daughter. Okay, anyway, he's a sensible boy. He was also very honest—he said it's good for a politician to be married. It will make him look conservative and responsible."

"That's romantic."

"Be practical, Papatti."

"Why didn't he ask me then?"

"You were out!"

Papatti said, "Amma, he's only asking you because he is unsure of what I'll say. We didn't have a pleasant conversation the last time we spoke. He's trying to get to me through you! He really is a good politician."

"Don't talk nonsense. He told me he doesn't know what *you* think, but he came here because his parents are dead— the poor thing—so they obviously couldn't make the offer themselves but he still wanted to do it traditionally and properly. In fact, he said he'll return shortly to ask you. He just ran to Fook Weng's house for some urgent matter. Anyway, he said he'll give us time to talk first."

"So you can convince me."

Lalitha leaned forward with eyes too earnest and grabbed Papatti's knees. "Don't be silly. Now, tell me what you think."

"Amma, you clearly want to tell me what you think. And let go. Your fingernails are cutting me."

Lalitha caressed her hands, too tender. "Papatti," she said in that about-to-deliver-a-sermon tone. "Let's look at the facts. Your appa is gone and who knows how long more I will be around. You are twenty-three now and we have all these money problems that I don't want to leave you alone to handle. I was married by the time I was your age. I just want to see you married and taken care of before I die. Arjun has a stable income. He can provide for you and even this house. Who knows? I told him that if you two marry, he can move in here if he wants. And he's an Assemblyman. I'm sure the rest of the tenants will start paying up. Everything will be taken care of and I can die in peace."

"Amma, you told him to move in?"

"*If* you marry."

"And you want me to marry him to solve our financial problems? So he can intimidate the tenants into paying their debts? So we can keep the house? So he can put food on the table for us?"

Lalitha threw her hands off, annoyed. "Eh. That's not what I'm saying. I'm just saying that I want to see you married and taken care of. Papatti, if your appa can go like that, imagine when my turn will come? Tomorrow? Next week? How can I leave you unmarried and homeless before I go? What will your appa say when I finally meet him?"

It was Papatti's turn to reach for Lalitha's hands, gather them in hers and try to impress some courage into them. "Amma, you are not going anywhere. Don't say that."

"That's what we thought about your appa. You see what happened? I just want you to be well."

"And I am well. And we will be well. Am I not earning enough to pay for the house for now? Don't worry. I promised to take care of you. And I will."

"You just shouted everyone's ears off trying to get the tenants to pay. What do you mean don't worry? We have no money left for ourselves."

"I will get another job."

"You already have two jobs. What about the marriage offer?"

"Amma, I don't like him."

"Why?"

Papatti stopped. "Must I give an explanation for this?"

"Papatti, you can at least be a practical adult about it."

She sighed. Why did being an adult come with all these clauses and qualifiers? "I don't know, I've never thought about it properly."

"So why don't you think about it properly now?"

"He sometimes puts me off, Amma. You know, he once asked me to have supper with him late at night, alone."

"When? What did you say?"

"This was after one of his meetings at Fook Weng's house. But I turned him down because it was inappropriate. And I guess I didn't know how I felt."

Lalitha slapped her shoulder twice. "On these things you finally listen to me. You should have gone! Why didn't you tell me earlier?"

"Amma! You would have scolded me if I went alone."

"I must beat myself with a slipper first."

"Don't."

"Papatti."

"Amma, I'm sure he's a good man, okay? He's a good Assemblyman, and he is honest. Maybe too honest. You know, he asked me to continue helping his campaign the day after Appa passed away. But I don't like him and I don't want to marry someone to pay my bills. I want to marry someone because I like him."

"So the offer?"

"No, Amma, it's a no."

Lalitha said, "We are going to be cleaning toilets forever, aren't we?"

No; she was going to have to borrow more from a different moneychanger. Rising to her feet, Papatti said, "Well since you have wasted my time and spoilt my appetite, I might as well go see if there are any other jobs out there that pay better. Don't you have work?" After Lalitha had started feeling better, she had tried once and failed to persuade Papatti to start sewing again. So instead, Lalitha had decided to help with alteration services at Muthu & Co herself. This had not troubled Papatti one bit. She no longer cared about the workings of the company at Buffalo Road as long as they treated her amma well.

Lalitha said, "I changed my evening shift to tomorrow because I thought we'll be making nuptial arrangements. But it looks like I'm going to die before seeing you marry."

"Amma."

"Where are you going to find a job now?"

"I'll ask around, don't you worry. Why don't you just go to work then."

"Well, someone needs to wait for the boy to come here to tell him the news. Unless you want to do it?"

Papatti shook her head, noticing that the moment she refused to marry Arjun he had become "the boy". Lalitha said, "I'm going to take a nap. Hopefully, God takes me while I'm sleeping peacefully so I don't have to deal with any of your nonsense anymore."

So much for not wanting to die before seeing Papatti married. Rolling her eyes, Papatti left the room and threw on her slippers. She rushed to open the front door, where she saw two men standing outside, equally surprised to see her. They were tall, wore white polo T-shirts tucked into pleated black trousers, and carried thin moustaches above their lips. They also had blue bands wrapped around their wrists. The man closer to Papatti held up a badge that she struggled to read. He said in Malay, "Madam, we are from the police. My name is Inspector Chee. This is Constable Vikram. This is 111 Serangoon Road right? Are you Madam Papatti, daughter of Rajpal? This is you?"

Inspector Chee unfolded an aged, grey newspaper for her to see, a page out of the *Tamil Murasu*, a page she recognised as once plastered on her cupboard door. In the centre, the black-and-white photograph of her and Arjun leapt out, a supremely happy smile scotch-taped onto his face, whereas she looked puzzled and caught off guard. Papatti became embarrassed by the photo, that reminder of how desparately she had wanted attention and fame. But why were the police holding onto it? Was it that bad a photo? Was she being arrested for a bad photograph?

Still holding onto the door's edge, she nodded vacuously, unsure what answer they wanted to hear since they should recognise her in the photo anyway. She noticed that, across the road, people continued to briskly walk past the shuttered Ban Keng Furnishing Pte Ltd shophouse and the Ah Hock Stainless Steel store, occasionally overtaken by rumbling carts and cars and lorries. The hawkers had packed up for the day. Her corridor was empty, the teenage boy had disappeared, and she couldn't even see people spilling out onto the road from the kopitiam further down. She had forgotten the time, and no one seemed to notice the two policemen standing at her doorway.

"Madam, is this you?"

She jerked. Clearing her throat, she nodded more

vigorously and said, "Yes, yes. That's me."

Inspector Chee folded the newspaper piece and passed it to Constable Vikram, who tucked it under his armpit. "Okay, madam, we just want to ask you a few questions. Can you come to the police station with us?"

"When?"

"Now, madam," he said, as if it were obvious. Did she look like she had spent a lifetime in the Law Ministry?

"Why?" she asked.

"It's nothing major, madam. It's all very routine. Mr Vinodh has lodged a complaint that you have been behind on your loan payments for four months. Is that correct? Yes, yes, we understand that you cannot pay up now. But we just need you to come with us to make a statement. This is to make sure that we have the full facts of the case for our records. Don't worry, we won't be taking any action against you, we consider this a private affair. But now that a complaint has been lodged, we just need to do our due diligence. We would appreciate your cooperation in coming with us."

Then they stared at her blankly, as if Inspector Chee's words would explain themselves better the longer they gazed at her. But Papatti didn't understand what the Inspector was saying. What statement could she give? Why would Vinodh lodge a complaint against her if the police could not do anything about it? And most importantly, if they could do something about it, would they also collect money from her tenants if she lodged a complaint? She would have done so earlier if she had known. She had been the first person to be wronged.

For an instant, she wished Arjun were there to explain the situation to her and speak to the officers, and then felt guilty about thinking of taking advantage of him as suited her whims and fancies. She truly was spoilt. Her eyes flitted from Inspector Chee to Constable Vikram and finally she mustered enough control of thought and speech to say, "I'm not planning to run away without paying." Had she sounded too defensive? As if she had something to hide?

The policemen laughed, smiling at each other. Inspector Chee said, "Madam, of course. And we are glad to hear that. But that's why I said it's a routine follow-up. If you come with us, it'll be a quick questioning and statement-recording and then you'll be free to go. We just want to take down your statement."

Questioning? Why was there a questioning now? What did she need to be "free to go" from? Wasn't she freed when the British left? Again, she wished she had completed her education, perhaps studied something useful like law so she would know whether she was allowed to be whisked away like this. She asked, "Should I tell my mother first?"

Inspector Chee sighed and tapped a foot on the ground. He checked his watch. He and Constable Vikram started to seem like a pair of local ah bengs or anjacks. But Inspector Chee did not refuse her request, and he seemed so official. After a few moments, he said, "Madam, have you decided? We do not have much time."

Why hadn't he just replied then? She decided against irritating him and making the impending questioning worse for herself. Besides, if she told her amma about this, she would have to explain borrowing from a moneychanger too. "It's okay. I can tell her when I come back."

Inspector Chee smiled and patted himself on the heart. He said, "You are a smart girl. I give you my word, madam, you'll be back chop chop, very fast. Come, let's go then."

As she turned to pull the door close, she heard a shout of "Papatti!" From Tekka, Karnan half-jogged towards her, shouting in Tamil, "I wanted to ask you something." He pulled up to her quickly, moustache brimming with excitement.

"What?" she said.

"Who's this?" Karnan stared at the two men and then switched to Malay, "Who are you?"

Papatti faced the three men, back against the unclosed door as Inspector Chee straightened, an upstanding police officer, and said, "Sir, we are with the police. My name is Inspector Chee. This is Constable Vikram. We are just here to ask Madam Papatti a few questions." He took out his badge and stuck it into Karnan's face. Karnan, like Papatti had, jerked his neck back, trying to get a read of it from a legible distance, frowning at it until Inspector Chee finally retracted his hand, and Papatti felt a bit better that she wasn't the only one who had been stupefied by all this rapid badge flashing. Couldn't they at least read out from the badge for her illiterate sake? Then, she suspected that Karnan didn't read either.

Karnan said, "Why don't you just ask her your questions here then?"

"Sir, she's a suspect and we are entitled to take suspects away for questioning and to record their statements. Please don't interfere in police business."

Suspect? What was she suspected of? Inspector Chee had said this was a routine statement and that she could go home soon. Why had he suddenly escalated it? He hadn't meant "chop chop" literally in the sense of her returning home in a body bag, had he? She tried to interject, to tell Karnan to leave and not get himself into trouble as well, that she would talk to him later, that she would be fine and that she just wanted to get this questioning over with so the police would know she was innocent. By the end of next month, she would pay Vinodh all his money back, including interest payments. She would work triple shifts. She hated her tenants for coercing her into borrowing money in the first place.

But before she could summon the words, Karnan said, "You should know all about being taken in for questioning." Papatti became annoyed. She wanted to be finished with the inquiry, not watch another interrogation before that. At this rate, he was only going to dig her grave deeper. "Karnan…"

Inspector Chee raised a palm and said, "Sir, I don't understand what you're trying to imply. But please, don't interfere with our job or we will have to take you in too."

He said, "Who are you trying to kid, you lowlife? You think you can cheat me? You think I don't know who you are, you ruffian? Are you trying to bully an innocent girl? What for?"

Papatti stepped back at the meanness in Karnan's voice and the accusations he was hurling at Chee and Vikram. The door creaked open under her weight. Inspector Chee, if he was an Inspector, said, "Sir, watch it." He sounded so professional and well-rehearsed, he must be with the police. What lowlife? Constable Vikram stepped forward to stand beside Inspector Chee, thumbs tucked under his belt.

Karnan said, "You should leave."

"What did you say?" Constable Vikram said. He put another dangerous foot forward, chest swelling out, very anjack-like indeed. And then Papatti screamed but only air came out as the door swung in and she fell onto her buttocks while Karnan swung a punch, hitting a stunned Constable Vikram in the chin. The Constable staggered backwards and the back of his head struck the corner of the colonnade and his eyes rolled up. Only the whites showed. His body slid to the ground, back supported by the column, legs splaying out as if he were just sitting down. But then his torso fell from his hips, fell sideways onto the pavement and Constable Vikram's head lopped forward onto the concrete. Blood had followed his head in a crimson line down the wall and the more Papatti stared at it, the fainter she felt, but nothing came out of her mouth as she just stared at Constable Vikram, stooped over like a sleeping drunkard with blood dripping around him.

Inspector Chee roared and charged at Karnan, raising his right arm to punch. Karnan kicked him in the stomach to break his momentum. As Inspector Chee buckled, Karnan used the same leg to knee him in the nose. Papatti heard a thunderous crack, the sound of cartilage breaking, and with a yell Inspector Chee rolled to the ground, tongue lolling out next to the Constable's black leather shoe, the blood from his nose dripping into the cracks along the concrete, creeping along them like red veins on the stony floor. Papatti tore her gaze away and stared at Karnan, trying to process what had just happened. She became terribly afraid for Karnan and herself.

Karnan stood over their fallen unconscious bodies, fists clenched and quivering by his sides, face scrunched up and ugly in wrath. She had always thought he was like Appa, incapable of a bad mood, let alone anger. But now an alien contemptuousness blanketed his face, unbecoming of him, as he contemplated the two comatose men. He said, loud enough that she could hear and be surprised by the vehemence of his scorn, "Where was your gun, *officer*? Police my foot." As he turned, he saw her and his face transformed. Contempt vanished, replaced by concern and sympathy. He rushed to her and knelt and said, "Papatti, are you okay?"

She shook her head and he helped her shuffle back on her bum to sit against the wall, out of view from the doorway. "I'm sorry," he said. "I didn't mean to frighten you." She could already hear people murmuring outside and calling friends over. Karnan walked to the edge of the doorway and watched through it. He said, "Don't worry. The real police will come soon enough. They'll sort it out. I'm so sorry."

"What do you mean they weren't the police? Who were they then?"

"Papatti, what happened here? Karnan? What are you doing here?" Arjun stood in the doorway, flustered, gaping at the unconscious men behind him and staring shell-shocked at her and Karnan. Recovering his senses, he darted into the house, into a blind spot to hide from the swelling crowd outside.

Karnan said, "Loanshark runners. He showed me some fake card and pretended to be the police to take Papatti away. But I saw them at Suresh's house a few weeks ago, hanging a pig's head at his door. Besides, you could tell from one look that they were lowlifes, not police officers."

"Papatti!" Arjun said. "You borrowed money from a loanshark?" He shook his head, and she immediately wished that she hadn't disappointed him.

"I'm sorry, Arjun. But why would they take me away?"

Karnan said, "For no good reason."

Arjun said, "To rough you up, intimidate you, scare you into coughing up your money. What else? You must think straight. How could you be so hopelessly naïve?" He jerked a thumb at the two fallen runners. "Now what are you going to do about this mess? People are gathering around the bodies."

She didn't know.

Karnan said, "Assemblyman, you shouldn't be seen here. People will think you were part of all this hooliganism. It's not good for your reputation. The police will be here soon and I can handle this. Leave by the backdoor."

Papatti wanted to take some responsibility, to prove she could take care of herself, to defend Karnan. "It's my fault, Arjun. I'll take the blame. Karnan was just helping me. It's not his fault."

"They're lowlifes and thugs and they were trying to

pull one over you," Karnan said. "This is no one's fault but theirs."

Arjun said, "There might be a way for all of us out of this. Since I'm already here, we might as well take advantage of it. Karnan, will you do me a favour?"

"Tell me, Assemblyman."

"Why don't we make the best of this situation. I have spent all my political capital and could use the publicity. Let me take the credit for beating them up. The story will be, they came to take Papatti away, I was stopping by and helped her and knocked the two men out. They are gangsters and they'll be put away and even when they get out of jail, who's going to believe their side of the story? Meanwhile, I'll get some good press and you'll get off scot-free. What do you think?"

Karnan raised an eyebrow. "I'm not worried about myself, but you want to wayang, Assemblyman? You want to lie to the press?"

"Call it whatever you want, Karnan. But if you want the credit and publicity, you can take it. I just thought that I could use it to do some good. This would be the perfect soapbox. But it's up to you. I know you deserve the credit too. You tell me what you think. What do you want to do?"

Papatti could not help but feel impressed as well as shocked by the ease in which Arjun had proposed this third way, and understood why he was the savvy politician and she the uneducated shift-to-shift worker in hospitals and department stores. There was a disarming ruthlessness to his honesty, as if explaining away every fault with clear honesty would justify it. She had to admit, there was an allure to such cold-blooded efficiency. He possessed a charming pull, that mathematical vortex of forces, making it sound as if it were up to the other person. Up to Karnan to make the decision, even though Arjun had already predisposed this choice by stating that Karnan would be taking credit for credit's sake, whereas Arjun would use that credit to achieve something greater than them both, something greater for society.

Karnan did not take long to consider Arjun's proposal. "I really don't care about the press and whatnot, Assemblyman. If you want it, you can have it."

"I want it for something bigger. You can try getting out now if you want."

"It's okay, I'll stay with Papatti. Don't worry, Assemblyman, I'll vouch for you. You have my word." Karnan walked over to sit next to her, sliding down against the wall, pulling his knees up. She could hear the quickness of his breath from the adrenaline of the fight. Papatti wondered if Arjun would ask for her cooperation as well or simply assume her compliance in the matter.

Arjun said, "Good. Well, I might as well go out and calm the crowd before the police come, try and explain the situation to them." So, she was worth marrying but not consulting.

As Arjun left the house, she asked Karnan, "You are really going to let him take all the credit?"

He looked at her over his shoulder. "I have no need for the publicity, whereas he does. So he might as well take advantage of it. He's right in saying that."

"He is honest about being dishonest."

Karnan chuckled. "He is honest about being dishonest." He cracked his knuckles, the bones clicking one by one until she grabbed his hands to stop them because it was too soon for her to be hearing any part of any body cracking. His calluses were red and warm from the fight. He didn't shrug her hand off but said, "Anyway, the Assemblyman will seize any opportunity he sees, whether you let him or not, so we might as well pretend that we've let him."

She nodded and let go. From outside, Arjun's voice

wafted through the doorway, speaking with as much high-pitched gusto and impact just as when she had first heard him in the room upstairs two years ago. She could already see him gesturing with his hands, flinging them in wide orbit, his throat husky with highfalutin logic. He was saying, *"Please, listen. Thank you. Calm down. Thank you. The Japanese had a saying:* jakuniku kyōshoku. *The strong devour the weak."*

Papatti straightened her legs. "He asked me to marry him."

"Did he?"

She nodded.

Karnan said, "What do you think?"

Papatti shrugged. "Amma says it's a good offer. She wants to see me married. She is getting old and clearly finding it more urgent that I do. And we do need the money. Arjun says it's good for his career."

"Papatti, I said what do *you* think?"

"It means that we can be strong and survive; or weak and be devoured. I learned at a young age that this is the way the world works. But we can choose who we want to be."

Papatti realised that she was starting to like him. No, she decided that she liked him, regardless of what parents and fate had to offer. He did care about what happened to her, in his own way, and his sincerity was truly disarming. He had a soothing reassuring tone and she wanted it to last longer, to hear him and talk to him longer. Her presence of mind returned, and she turned to Karnan and said, "I guess it is a good offer."

"It is."

She smiled gratefully, feeling even more certain in her opinion. "By the way, what did you come to ask me?"

"Can you do me a favour?"

"What's that?"

"I learned young that every man is an island and I must

stand up for myself. Britain was not made any less by this clod being snatched away. I had to fend for myself. I had to be strong. But how?"

Karnan said, "The police will probably take me in for questioning. But if I am not released by tomorrow, do you think you can explain what happened to my amma and brother and ask them to bail me out? The real version. Actually, don't tell my amma. She worries easily. Just tell my brother please."

"Why would anyone need to bail you out? Arjun said you won't get into trouble."

"You know—if you see someone drowning and jump into the river to save him, he's more likely to try and drown you to save himself. I'm happy for the Assemblyman to take the credit, but I'm not an idiot. If you marry him, I'll be the weak link who knows what really happened today. What if he tries to put me behind bars to silence me as well? I don't want to be stuck there without my amma and brother even knowing where I am and what happened. Could you do that?"

"I learned at a young age that we survive by our punches and machetes, by guns and the cane. I learned that we survive by our willingness to jump into the trenches and fight."

Papatti asked, "Where can you learn to be that cutthroat?"

Karnan shrugged. "From being ordered around by the Japanese? From opposing the Communists? I guess we can never judge someone until we face his options. Besides, maybe we need people like him to keep us safe, someone who can be tough and cold when necessary."

"True. But you were the one who beat the rowdies up. Not Arjun. You seemed to hate them quite a bit."

"I don't like bullies. They were trying to cheat you and hurt you and it made me angry. But I know that violence isn't right. I'm no Gandhi. I just don't like bullies."

"You would look horrible bald and in only a veshti."

He smiled, a yellow wall under the black moustache.

"Today, I see that the world remains the same. These two ruffians tried to hoodwink an innocent girl. They tried to kidnap her, to rough her up, to extract money from her. They only dared to try because they were stronger than her, because they thought no one would stop them."

She said, "Anyway, I wasn't judging you. I'm thankful to you. Thank you."

"It's okay. Can you do me another favour please?"

"I'm going to start charging per favour. What's this one?"

"But I know their world well, and I was willing to beat them at it. I fought to make sure that they, or anyone else, could not harm good, innocent people. You tell me: was I right?"

Half the crowd cheered "Yes!" while the other half jeered at the motionless thugs on the floor. Sirens called from the distance and someone shouted, "Now you have it! Hair!" Papatti could already see the blue and red flashing as the real police cars swerved onto Serangoon Road. The sirens drowned Arjun's continuing speech.

Karnan said, "I know you've given up sewing. But do you think you could lend me your kit? I want to sew cigarettes into my trousers before I go in for questioning, just in case they put me in lock-up." He reached into his dark brown pocket and pulled out a cigarette box. He pulled out six soft sticks, one for each pleat, and laid them side-by-side on the cold tiles. Lifting up a fold on the thigh of his trousers to create a slit, he tucked a cigarette inside and covered it with the fold and smiled at her triumphantly, as if he had shown her the greatest legerdemain.

She said, "So while I was fighting for independence you were inspecting my sewing skills to see if they could brighten up your jail stint?"

"Like I said, you cannot judge a man until you face his options. And if I remember right, *I* just saved *you*. Didn't you just thank me?"

"Well, let's see who saves who in the end." She ran upstairs to find her amma asleep on the floor, snoring in tired sputters, oblivious to the drama and commotion downstairs. Rajpal's death had really transformed her.

Papatti threw back the azure garb on her machine and pulled open a drawer. Finding a spool of umber brown thread, she grabbed her needle and ran downstairs, where the police cars had pulled up outside and the sirens had died. She could only assume that they were real policemen. Sitting down, she said, "Each pleat is five cents."

"Each hour in custody is 50 cents. Deduct your commission and tell me how much you owe me when I'm out."

She laughed and handed the needle and spool to him. "You should know that I only opened that sewing machine for you, because I owe you. Just this once."

"Well, I'm honoured," he said.

"Consider us even."

He snorted. She watched as he gingerly and uncertainly poked the skin of his trousers with the needle, the needle disappearing inside the beginning of his pleat. He grunted before the needle poked its head up at the other end of the pleat, and the connecting thread pulled the two ends of the pleat together up like a crooked pyramid, making him look incredibly aroused with a squashed cigarette peeking out of the erected pleat. Papatti laughed and shook her head. Searching for an excuse to turn away from that obscene-looking spectacle, and to resist the urge to grab the needle and sew for him, she picked a cigarette from the floor, feeling the soft ductile white stick, smelling the nose-curling zing of dried tobacco. "You shouldn't smoke. It's a bad habit."

"Thanks, Amma Theresa. But smoking is the only time my supervisor doesn't shout at me to get back to work. It's considered as precious as going to the loo. Can you blame me if I got addicted after that? You see? Facing my options."

Reluctantly conceding this point, just this once, Papatti watched him destroy another pleat. "You are really bad at this."

Holding up the needle like a knife, he said, "I swear I will poke you next."

She smiled at the memory of her appa. Then her thoughts were interrupted by Arjun talking to a policeman for the street to hear.

...

The police turned out to be real, while the fake policemen really did turn out to be loanshark runners. Karnan and Arjun dissuaded the real police from hauling Papatti to the station to take down a real statement. Karnan said, "Give her some time to recover. The Assemblyman and I are witness enough for you for today." Arjun agreed and Inspector Saleem, whom Papatti actually knew, acquiesced to their request and asked Papatti to drop by the station the next day.

When the police left with Arjun and Karnan and the ruffians, the neighbours offered to mop and sponge the bloodied corridor and column, insisting that Papatti rest, refusing to let her even touch a rag. So she decided to update her amma upstairs instead. Lalitha said, "Where have I been the entire time?"

"Sleeping, you old woman."

"So all it took was an organised crime syndicate for you to be okay with marriage?"

"Not marriage, Amma! And you aren't even worried that I was almost kidnapped!"

"I wish they had taken you, they would have sent you back in a day."

"Chopped up!"

"Good, I'll make curry out of you. At least that way you'll be of some use. Who asked you to borrow money without telling me? From a loanshark!" Lalitha slapped her thigh.

"Stop it! I didn't know he was a loanshark."

"You don't know anything. If he's lending you money when he's not supposed to, of course he's a loanshark! Loansharks don't have signs over their shops saying 'Loanshark. Please come and borrow from me.' You are a silly girl."

"I'm sorry, Amma. I just wanted to look after you."

"Yes, now one job has become four. I would have been mad if you hadn't agreed to marry someone. So do you want me to tell him?"

"No, Amma! It's not a marriage!"

Lalitha grunted, unhappy at being denied control over this important and delicate family matter, unhappy that this matter was less of a matter than she wanted it to be. Papatti could see Lalitha's mind bulging with the question, "Why just go out with him if you're not going to marry him? You'll only make the neighbours ask unnecessary questions." But Lalitha said, "What date is it?"

"Why?"

"It must be an auspicious date."

"Amma! It's not a marriage! Stop it!"

Lalitha grunted again. "Fine, this marriage is all up to God now."

"There is no marriage!"

The next morning, Papatti went to Serangoon Police Post, where Inspector Saleem told her that she didn't need to give a statement. The police had enough eyewitness accounts, including that of an Assemblyman's, and plenty of outstanding issues to resolve without spending unnecessary time corroborating statements. And he assured her that his colleagues were dealing with the loanshark runners as they spoke.

"Who are they, Uncle Saleem?"

"Just hoodlums, Papatti. Small-time errand boys working for a big boss, that moneylender you had a run-in with. Don't worry about them. They won't be disturbing you anymore. Okay?"

"Thank you, Uncle Saleem."

"Don't worry. Next time, talk to your amma before making these types of decisions. I know money is hard. I understand where you're coming from. But you must be careful, girl."

"Yes, Uncle Saleem."

"Good. These are uncertain times. We must all be very careful. I am only expecting work to pile up."

"Sorry, Uncle Saleem. Can I ask about Karnan?" She hoped intensely that Arjun hadn't betrayed Karnan's and her trust.

"He left yesterday," the Inspector said.

So Arjun had kept his side of the bargain after all, Papatti thought as she left the police post and waited at the bus stop. But that was because she hadn't agreed to marry him and so he wouldn't know if he could trust her to take his side. She shook the Machiavellian thoughts out of her head. They were an easy habit to pick up in the midst of such uncertainty and gloom. But she didn't want to be naïve either. She had to find a way to reconcile her Rajpal-induced optimism with Lalitha-esque pragmatism, an impossible deadline in the time she had to wait for the bus.

She alighted at Tanjong Pagar and found the address easily. The door opened and Karnan stared at her, pleasantly surprised until he realised he only had a purple sarong wrapped around his waist and legs. His chest and arms were darkened, stocky and hairy.

"You're like a hairy Gandhi in purple," Papatti said.

"I'll change. Give me a second."

"Don't bother. Wait. Just listen. This is unconventional, and I may be wrong. But I think you like me?"

His eyes widened. Then he smiled brightly, even brighter than Arjun, which infuriated her and she struggled not to yank his bushy, infuriating moustache. "You really can't just be the traditional Indian girl who lights the lamp in the house, can you?"

"What? Anyway, yes or no?'

"Go on," he said.

"Yes or no?"

"Go on, please. I want to know where this leads."

Flustered, she rolled her eyes as exaggeratedly as she could. "Well, I'm not marrying Arjun and thought you should know that. And I think I like you, or I like talking to you, and am happy to go drink tea with you, or coffee, or whatever you like to drink except alcohol, if you ask, nicely that is. And go out in the daytime."

An arched eyebrow. "You mean, go out? Like they do in the films? What will the neighbours think?" What was he? Her mother? She made to yank at his sarong and he jumped back to protect his modesty. "Now what will the neighbours think? Besides, you make it sound like you're doing me a favour by going out with me."

"Okay, I'm going," she said, and turned on her heels. The films didn't teach her how to deal with obnoxious idiots. She would throw her lot in with fate instead.

Behind her, she heard him laugh and stumble out of the house without his shirt or slippers, saying, "Yes, I will. Let's go drink tea! I'm coming! Let me get a shirt! Wait!"

13

Dedicated to Papatti

It was not a surprise that retribution awaited me the next day. In the end, Nakamura was a soldier and Yamato, and I was not. It was that simple. The soldiers of the Imperial Guards, led of course by that simian Saito, waited for the day's work to finish, waited for Kurosawa and Yamashita to return to their rooms, and then dragged me before them to hold court in their bunk. Some sat on the cots and some stood around me, having closed the door. I think it speaks to their insecurity that they needed to encircle and intimidate a ten-year-old boy like this, but they considered it strength simply because they demonstrated power over me.

Saito was sitting on Nakamura's cot. An unsheathed Type 30 bayonet, with a long thin blade and a short dark hilt, lay next to him. I tried not to glance at it. Saito leaned forward with a smirk. "Nanban," he said. "You look as scared as a girl being interviewed by her future husband's family."

Sniggers flew around me. Saito felt encouraged. "We haven't seen you in a while *ne*, Nanban? You've been busy. You are learning *nihongo*, *kyoshokan*, working for Lieutenant Kurosawa. You are a big man now. You don't need to see us anymore. Are we too low rank for you now? You only spend time with the officers. Why are you scared?"

"No, Private Saito." I stared down meekly. There was nothing else I could say, and Saito didn't care for what I said either. This was not a trial. It was a sentencing, and I thought the less I said, the less worse-off I would be.

"Nanban, we want to ask you something. Where is Private Nakamura?" I kept staring down. His finger entered my vision and prodded my chest. It hurt.

The shoes and slippers and field pack underneath Nakamura's cot and the photos pasted above it had vanished along with the soldier, leaving a barren bed and empty wall in that part of the room, a warning for the other soldiers, a warning that was now being used as evidence in my sentencing. But Kurosawa hadn't been thinking about me and what the soldiers would do to me when he had instructed me to kick Nakamura.

I said, "I don't know, Private Saito."

"You don't know? You don't know? Tell me—what is this then?" He rested a finger on my bare shin, where a blue bruise had flowered into a mushy patch that Kurosawa had said would heal in a week. Saito pressed his finger into it like it was playdough, kneading the patch with the finger, pressing sharp jolts into it that made me want to grab that area tightly and seal off the blood. But all I could do was wince and hold myself steady and upright while he said, "Private Nakamura is gone because of you, right? You told on him. You are the tattletale." He pulled his finger away.

I shook my head furiously, more aghast by the spurious accusation than the shooting pain in my leg. Appa had called snitches and informants, "scoundrels" and "bastards", and

I might have been a lot of things, but I was no tattletale. I wouldn't rat on anyone. "No, Private Saito. I am not a tattletale, Private Saito."

"Let's see. You fetch the rice for Corporal Yamashita, you help Corporal Yamashita count the stocks, you clean the storeroom. Who else goes in there? Only you could know. It must be you. You told on him."

"No, Private Saito."

"You think I am stupid, Nanban?"

"No, Private Saito."

"And you dared to hit an Imperial Japanese Army soldier, a Yamato man, a servant of the Emperor. You, a boy from *Shōnan*."

"I did not want to, Private Saito. Lieutenant Kurosawa ordered me to. I am sorry, Private Saito."

"So? You had a choice. You could have offered to kill yourself instead of hitting Private Nakamura, right?"

I blinked.

"Right?"

"Yes, Private Saito. I am sorry, Private Saito."

"You are sorry?" he said, voice escalating to a high pitch. "Let me tell you what you are." He yanked my left arm, jerking me towards him, his grip painful, his breath hot and moist on my face. "You think because Lieutenant Kurosawa spends time with you, you are a big man? You are better than us? You want to know what you are? This is what you are." He hawked, and his throat gagged with a deep guttural sound that rose up and he spat phlegm onto my left eye. I barely blinked in time.

I did not dare to wipe it off and so did not open that eye. I let that belittling thick wet glob stay there. But as happens with being humiliated, I felt angry, a rage I couldn't vent, the impotency of that anger compounding my humiliation.

In those moments, I could only retreat into the sovereignty of my mind to wish that I was big enough to fight back, to be able to spit at him and hurt him myself. I imagined choking him by the neck, watching as he gasped and clawed my arms for breath, fear entering his eyes as the light dimmed in them, knowing he was about to die, knowing he needed my mercy to breathe and seeing him beg for it. Then he would know how it felt to have your life in someone else's hands and be tyrannised for it. I would be his bodhisattva and guide him to eternal atonement, devour him indeed.

But I hadn't grown up yet and Saito was twirling his bayonet, expertly looping the flat of the blade around his fingers as the hilt whirled, his face smirking in ugly superciliousness. Seeing me watch the blade, he said, "I am not going to scare you with it, Nanban. We all know that has become too boring for you already."

There was nothing boring about fear; in fact, fear was always crippling. The knife had assumed Shobun's sinister smirk, looping around his hand. I said, "I want to go back to Lieutenant Kurosawa's house please, Private Saito."

"You want to go back to Lieutenant Kurosawa's house? You still have work to do. You see, we are not sure if our bayonets are sharp enough. What will Lieutenant Kurosawa say? If our bayonets are blunt, we are poorer soldiers for it. If we are poorer soldiers, the Army is weak. If the Army is weak, Japan is weak. Can we allow that?"

"No, Private Saito. But I want to—"

"Good answer. Don't talk anymore. Listen. We are also your seniors. Just because Lieutenant Kurosawa teaches you, doesn't mean you don't listen to us. Do you understand?"

"Yes, Private Saito."

"So, I want you to test our bayonets. Since you were willing to hurt Private Nakamura to uphold the Army's good standing, I am sure you will allow us to hurt you just a little for the glory of the Army too. Right? Stick out your arm, Nanban."

I gripped my hands tightly behind my back, pulling them down so hard I was afraid my shoulders would pop. "No, Private Saito," I said, "I don't want to, please."

"Stick out your arm," he said, cautioning me by raising the bayonet.

"No, Private Saito. Please."

He reached around me to grab my left arm and draw it out. I resisted, clasping my left hand with my right tighter, pulling down harder, leaning away from him. "Come," he said, still smiling, still tugging, a bit harder, then a bit rougher, until the smile left his face and he was now angry, unused to being said no to, unhappy that I, a ten-year-old local boy, was disobeying him, a grown-up Yamato soldier. He wrenched and he was strong and my feet dragged towards him but I still tried to heave my weight the other way, like we were playing a tug of war over my left arm.

I started using my right hand to push Saito's arm away, but it felt like stone and wouldn't budge and only escalated his ire. "What do you think you are doing? Let go of my arm, Nanban."

But I pushed and struggled and tried to throw him off. "Please Private Saito, no!"

"You are lucky I don't just chop off your hand! Now, obey me! Don't make it worse for yourself!"

Another soldier tried to drag my right hand away now, trying to give Saito free and ready access to my body, and I squeezed my eyes shut and shouted, "I said stop!" And it was accidental, a kneejerk response to my intense burning desire to not be touched or hurt, and in that despair I headbutted Saito in the nose.

The room quieted. His nose turned pink as salmon and he let go of me to pat and feel it, incredulous, eyes wide open, staring astonished at the nerve of me. All of a sudden, no one held me.

Someone behind me warned, "Eh, Nanban."

I wiped the wet sputum from my eye, knowing I was done for, and that there was nothing I could do to salvage this situation. I just had to wait for how Saito would respond. I was so afraid that I wanted to cry.

His eyes narrowed. Then he kicked me in my stomach. With a choked sound I fell to the ground, nausea rising in me. I held tightly onto my abdomen and curled up on the floor like a foetus, trying to suppress the pain. But out it came, a pile of vomit full of noodles and tea and biscuits. The soldiers moaned at the milky slush spilling onto their pristine floor.

I could hear Kurosawa's voice in my head saying, "Your guard was down. *Kamae. Kamae,* Nanban." Groaning still, I rolled onto my back, telling myself to stand and defend myself but unable to. Besides, how could I fight an adult, a soldier? A tall figure stood over me. Saito sneered at me in cold and clear contempt. It was awfully quiet. "I was just trying to frighten you but you really think you are a big man now huh, Nanban? You think you can do anything you want with us? You are nothing. *Wakaru?* No matter what Lieutenant Kurosawa or anyone tells you, you are nothing. Remember that."

He lifted his boot, and the ridged black sole blocked my vision, blocked out Saito and the room. Kurosawa's voice throbbed in my head again, *"Kamae! Kamae!"* I wanted to bring my hands up, to roll sideways to protect myself. I heaved and tried to wheel over and had barely managed to summon the strength to close my eyes and turn my head aside when I heard a slamming noise. Something broke and collapsed and then quiet thundered.

WARRAN KALASEGARAN

I was surprised to open my eyes. Kurosawa stood over me. Saito was sprawled on the floor, spread-eagled against the wall, half-conscious, and Nakamura's cot lay crumpled and flattened beneath him. The soldiers had already backed up against the walls in two lines, bowing and clearing a path for Kurosawa, who was flushed red and angry. I hadn't seen him this mad since I had thrown Nobuo's ashes into the river. He raised a shuddering finger and screamed at Saito, yelling at him so furiously and rapidly that I didn't catch what he said and don't think Saito did either.

Saito was dazed. He blinked as if to clear his vision and mind. He tried to lift himself up but was slow and shaky and collapsed again with a tired grunt. Kurosawa realised that Saito didn't understand him and stopped shouting. His eyes cast around the silent room in a fluster. Then he found a boot and flung it at the private as if this would knock it into his delirious senses more efficiently. The boot bounced off Saito's forehead, made Saito's bleary eyes roll up again. Then Kurosawa hurled the second boot.

I managed to find my feet. I stared at Saito as the boot crashed into his chin. He no longer looked strong, or proud, or snooty. He seemed pitiful, in pain and vulnerable, with the face of a helpless chimp stunned by what was happening to him. I must have always looked like that to him. Something came over me, something that took me a while to understand.

I rushed over to Saito and kneed his face, knee flying into his nose. He cried out and reeled back and his head hit the wall. Rage and a powerful sense of justice rushed into me in a torrent and I grabbed the back of his head and thrust my knees into his face again, fast and hard as I could thrust. Kneed him again and again, left and right, *hiza keri*, *hiza keri*, inflicting as much damage to his ugly face as possible. I wanted to do this while I could. While I was stronger than him and had the chance, while he was as weak as I had been all this time.

Kurosawa grabbed me from behind, lifted me off the ground by the chest and carried me backwards. Even then, forgetting myself in fury, I resisted Kurosawa's pull. I fought hard to cling to Saito's neck and knee him some more. Eventually I was forced to let go, but I still kicked with my feet, managing to punt his chin before Kurosawa lifted me out of reach entirely. Still I kicked in the hope of hitting Saito.

I shouted at him, and Saito watched me with wide and stunned eyes, struggling to understand what was happening to him, blood dripping from his nose onto the floor. I shouted, "I will kill you! I will kill you, you stupid, stupid, stupid! I will kill you!" It was the only bad word I knew in Japanese: *Baka. Baka! Baka!* I shouted it at him, going mad with rage, until Kurosawa carried me out of the house and across Jalan Besar Road, which was when I realised that my dark knees were red with the blood from Saito's nose.

Just as incredibly, when Kurosawa set me down, he seemed amused instead of angry. He smiled and peered at me like I was a curious fellow, as if I had simply poured good sake down a drain to prove a point (although later I decided that this would have made Kurosawa much angrier than beating Saito). As my breathing slowed, I tasted puke and felt sick and quickly wiped my mouth before it made me barf. He tapped my chin. "Nanban, I see you took my lesson to heart."

"Sorry, Lieutenant Kurosawa."

"Eh, I have never liked that boy. He probably deserved it, yes?"

I waited to see if he was sincere, then I nodded.

Kurosawa chuckled. "I will make sure he doesn't disturb you anymore. You don't have to worry about him anymore. If you were older, I would have given you a cup of sake to celebrate your bravery. But we can wait for that. We have time. For now, here." He pulled the white armband down his sleeve, the red calligraphy of the Kempeitai stark and clear as it slid off his wrist, and he passed it to me. "You can't wear it, but you have earned this, I think. You are a good student. Almost too much for your own good. You surprise me for a local." He chuckled some more.

...

Saito did not disappear the way Nakamura had. He continued to serve with the Imperial Guards at Jalan Besar, albeit with a bandaged nose for a few days. I did not know how I felt about this—whether I would have preferred it for my sake if the Kempeitai had disposed of him like they had Nakamura, or that I should have been glad out of a certain selfless respect for life that he hadn't been killed on my account.

To be honest, my selfish first thought frightened me more than any of Saito's beatings. For Saito's bullying had been externally and physically inflicted, and I knew I would recover from it and grow stronger some day, but this thought suggested a deeper, darker transformation within me, a remaking of my soul.

By attacking Saito so viciously, I could not help feeling that I had crossed a line, become willingly complicit in the brutality of the Occupation. Kurosawa had commanded and forced me to kick Nakamura, but no one had compelled or even so much as asked me to knee Saito. I had done so of my own accord and could blame no one else for my actions. I had no excuse. I had become as much culprit as victim.

Which made me think, had I become a culprit as soon as I started working for the Kempeitai? Directly or indirectly, I was contributing to the Occupation and the Imperial Army's rule over Singapore for the sake of my own survival, even if through this I had also been contributing to my own enslavement. I baulked at being called a tattletale, but as an errand boy, I was no better than the informants Appa had once insulted.

Kurosawa had once told me a famous Japanese story, about a poor starving man who spotted a witch at the base of a Shinto gate in Kyoto. There were corpses dumped around the gate and the witch was cutting their hair off. The man threatened the witch to stop this outrageous defilement of corpses, which was when he realised that she was just an old woman, also penniless and hungry, and trying to make wigs to sell for food. Wasn't she just trying to survive? Trying to get by? Yes, the man realised, she was just trying to survive. She was in the right, and he could be too.

So he pounced on the doddering old lady, killed her, stripped her of her clothes to hawk them, and tossed her naked old figure onto the rotting cadavers and left, secure in his newfound righteousness.

Kurosawa was very proud of the author of this story, probably because he was Japanese. So I didn't tell Kurosawa that the author made men sound like prurient foxes to this ten-year-old, for why couldn't the protagonist have just taken the hair the old woman had, perhaps snipped off her hair too? Why strip the poor old lady? What value did that add to the story? What happened to selling wigs? Either way, I saw myself becoming this man, thinking that I too could do anything to survive, no matter how terrible. Beating Saito made me realise that I did have a choice, and I had been making my choices all this while. After all, hadn't Saito been right when he said that I could have killed myself if I felt guilty enough? Instead, I had let life as an errand boy under Lieutenant Kurosawa make me a far worse person.

And as if to affirm this feeling, a week later, Kurosawa brought me along for a house inspection.

He told me that the Kempeitai had a lead on Nakamura's lover, who had apparently run away. This was not surprising. One does not have a dalliance with a soldier of the Imperial Japanese Army, collude with him to steal their rice and then stick around when he's gone. Kurosawa said I should finish what I had started with Nakamura and that it was time for me to earn my food and board, which only heightened my guilt that I was complicit in the Occupation. He also kept calling this lover a comfort woman, and I didn't know if he referred to her job or her love affair with Nakamura. Again, I had no choice but to join the inspection, but I had been telling myself this about many other things during the Occupation as well.

Before the inspection, Kurosawa checked my attire to make sure I looked my neatest and smartest. For him, creating the image of a sharp and disciplined unit that acted as one body functioned as a deterrent, less costly than having to put down rebellions that might have been inspired by a less-threatening-looking Kempeitai. Trouble, Kurosawa used to say, was contagious. Once uncorked, it was difficult to shove the stopper back into the bottle. So he didn't want me to hamper their image. As my hair had grown out pointy in all directions like a durian, that king of fruits, he also ordered Yamashita to buzz my head again. He became vexed when they couldn't find shoes my size, which set off a flurry of shouting and searching before Yamashita came running from the distance with a pair of black sneakers in fulfilment of the Mikado's request. Kurosawa gave me a quick briefing that culminated with, "Follow my instructions and don't do anything else", and then ordered me to climb into the first army jeep.

I squatted against the partition that separated the passengers from the driver. The Jalan Besar soldiers poured in after me, cramming themselves on the benches on both sides of the jeep. They held their rifles between their legs, muzzles pointed up, and sat in silence. Some nodded off during the jeep's journey and drooled onto the soldier next to him until he was elbowed awake. Saito sat at the end of the bench, staring through the square entrance that swelled with the moonless night as the engine revved and the jeep made off.

If Saito was resentful or hateful, he didn't show it, and I knew that Kurosawa had kept his word—Saito wouldn't disturb me anymore. I believe Saito's sense of shame—knowing that I was inferior to him, yet untouchable—had convinced him he was better off pretending I didn't exist at all. I also suspect he was insulted that I hadn't been made to apologise to him. Shame and honour, shame and honour, that was all that mattered to the Japanese soldier. Even if it was more a sham honour.

But to him, I was an *eta* and our interactions needed to reflect that hierarchy. So whenever our paths crossed, I performed the right rituals of respect to help him save face, lest he thought I had become complacent and decided to take his chances with Kurosawa and put me in my place. I would bow and say, *"Osaki ni dōzo,"* and show a hand to let him walk across first, and only after he passed without a word or a glance would I continue on my way. This simple accommodation of each other's existence suited me, and I did not care whether it appealed to His Excellency's rump honour or not.

The two jeeps did not travel far. They shifted onto Serangoon Road, my first time seeing that street since I had tried to escape. The street disappeared as we turned left onto Balestier Road and then we turned left again onto the long Race Course Road, the old British horse racing grounds that were now dotted with a series of shophouses. As the two jeeps sped down the road, I saw people running into their houses and bolting the doors. I didn't understand what the point of that was, since the jeep had already passed them. But I guess that is easier to say from within the jeep than outside.

The jeep screeched to a halt outside an orange shophouse with grey awnings and windows. The second jeep pulled up behind us and I saw Takagi seated at the front. On the roadside, a man had been pumping air into his bicycle tyres. He quickly climbed atop the bicycle seat, but he was not quick enough. Takagi leapt out of his jeep and demanded the man's papers.

The soldiers in my jeep clipped their helmets, hoisted their rifles and quickly formed three sharp, straight lines on the road, facing the house. I took a nondescript spot behind them, stood like they did with my feet together. The ground floor of the house operated as a bicycle shop, which explained the pump outside. The storekeeper, an elderly man with wispy white hair, came outside wiping his greased hands on a black rag. He wore a singlet and a sarong and his collarbones jutted out dangerously. He had a songkok on his head. Kurosawa pointed into the house and the old man led us in.

In the shop, bicycles were packed side by side so tightly that their handlebars overlapped and their pedals stuck into the spokes of each other's wheels. A few bicycles hung from the ceiling like hung corpses, swivelling dangerously whichever way the wind blew. Black tyre tubes hung on the walls, elongated by gravity, and leather seats, wrenches, pliers and other metal tools were slotted into gunmetal shelves.

Kurosawa ignored the man and squatted in front of the standing bicycles, disentangling them to inspect their sizes, feel the weight of their steel frames and test their brakes. I didn't know if this nonchalance revealed a deeper interest in cycling or was meant to give time for fear to set into the storeowner, but the old man just watched Kurosawa, as if Kurosawa were just another customer. The old man looked as untroubled as Kurosawa, and I admired and respected him for that.

Kurosawa wheeled a road bicycle out and said, "Nanban, ask him how much this bicycle costs."

I quickly translated in Malay. When I relayed the old uncle's answer, Kurosawa stared at the old uncle, then nodded. He shook his head and slid the bicycle back into its place. He asked about a few more bicycles, and I helped to translate. None of the bicycles lived up to his expectations. Finally, he pointed upstairs.

The uncle led the Jalan Besar soldiers up to a living room that stank strongly of fish and cat litter, and this was because three sardine cans lay open with two tomcats licking out the last of their contents. They glanced up with crimson whiskers at Kurosawa before ignoring him and returning to their cans, a luxury only critters could afford.

Sarongs were spread and arranged in rows across the hall like tuna fish at an auction, doubling as mattresses, creased and used. A sack of uncooked rice stood in a corner beside a makeshift stove like the one Appa and I had built. A frame of black Arabic lettering was hung up on the wall, the only ornament. It was very quiet. The three doors that encircled the hall were shut.

Kurosawa said, "Nanban, come here."

I came out from behind the soldiers.

"Tell everyone to come out. Say, 'Kempeitai' and 'come out' in Malay."

I said it.

"Say it louder, Nanban. With more force."

I shouted, "Kempeitai! Come out!" My voice had not

even broken yet. I felt and sounded rather feeble, and nothing happened. Kurosawa chuckled. Then Takagi banged one door with the butt of his rifle, a loud reverberating boom. Someone inside yelped.

Life roared back into the rooms as sounds of hushing and footsteps emerged from behind the closed doors. Shadows assembled in that slit of light beneath the doors and for one moment, the house quieted again as there was silence, the taking of a last breath.

Then the knobs creaked and turned, the doors swung inwards, and men and women and children came out of the rooms and formed a long line looping around the hall, around the sarongs, exchanging glances to comfort each other. I counted 24 people and thought it was a miracle that they had all squeezed into the house. There were also four children my height.

"Ask them for the census card."

"Can you give me your census card," I said. A few heads swung towards me, looking at me strangely. A man, wearing only a pair of shorts, stared at me hatefully. The rest kept their heads down.

"You must learn to speak louder. Don't be scared. You work for the Kempeitai, not the comfort station."

"Sorry, Lieutenant Kurosawa." I shouted, "Can you give me your census card."

The old uncle had the standard orange paper ready and handed it to Kurosawa. The Lieutenant told me to read out the names. I said the first name, and was surprised when a tenant automatically raised his hand. But I did not doubt that the hand was answering to the Kempeitai, not me. I continued the roll call until the last name. It turned out the old uncle owned the house. Kurosawa said, "Is everyone present then?"

I counted 28 names again and said, "Yes, Lieutenant Kurosawa."

Kurosawa appeared relaxed and insouciant. This was nothing new to him, probably just another humdrum procedure for him, even if it must have been the most petrifying experience the tenants must have had. He said, "Okay. Nanban, now follow my instructions and we will look for this girl. Do not be afraid. It's just a girl, probably your size. Are you prepared?"

"Yes, Lieutenant Kurosawa."

He directed me to check the first room, which had one bed, a cupboard and a bicycle, which were all shoved against the walls to create more space in between. I assumed it was the old landlord's.

Kurosawa stood lazily against the doorframe and told me to check under the bed and in the cupboard so I crawled to the floor and underneath the mattress, found cardboard boxes and jerry cans and a stack of papers. I opened the cupboard doors to find rows and rows of haphazardly folded clothes and Mango girl sitting on top, hand cupped to her mouth.

When she saw me, her dark eyes grew in recognition. But she clasped her mouth tighter, pinched her nose with thumb and finger. Her other arm wrapped her grey knees close to her chest, and I could see rings of blood around her yellow nails. Her head had been shaved, days-old stubble dotting her scalp. Her face looked rounder for it, and dirty with oil. She wore a T-shirt and shorts with tattered holes in them. She looked boyish, and I could smell that she hadn't showered or changed out of her clothes in days. Trying to be ugly, manly and smelly were known tactics for the local girls in those days to throw off lecherous Japanese soldiers who wouldn't take no for an answer.

It was also well known that the Japanese tended not

to disturb the Malays, whom they tried to set against the Chinese locals they were actively targeting, and I could understand why Mango girl had taken refuge here. But did she know the danger she had put this house—the old man and the 27 others—in? That they were going to die because of her and her foolish romance? I grew confident that Nakamura had deserved the kick I gave him.

"What is it, Nanban?" Kurosawa said.

Mango girl's eyes grew larger and more frightened at hearing the Japanese lieutenant at the door. They seemed to question me, asking me what was happening outside. Then they started to mist and a tear rolled down her grey face, into the grey hand clasping her mouth.

I said, "It's smelly, Lieutenant Kurosawa. The clothes were wet."

Her eyes trembled. She didn't understand me.

He chuckled. "You are getting spoiled *ne*. Come and check the other rooms."

"Yes, Lieutenant Kurosawa." Her eyes grew even larger, and I started smelling urine as I slowly closed the doors. Then the doors shut and she was gone. I made sure the doors were closed properly.

I left for the next room, praying that Kurosawa could not hear how loudly my heart had started to stammer. My legs shook and threatened to give way, and I forced them to work, to put one step after the other. I tried to appear calm on the outside, tried to be normal.

But I was desparately hoping that Kurosawa would not search the room after me. By closing the doors of the cupboard, I had put my neck on the chopping board, put that lease of life and trust that Kurosawa had given me on the line. I could lose everything I had slowly built up with Kurosawa, and more.

But I could not snitch. I could not be complicit in so obvious a way in someone else's demise, could not tattle on someone whom I had even the slightest chance of keeping hidden, could not send a houseful of people to the firing squad. I would not be that *Rashōmon* man.

Now, I didn't think that this exonerated me. I knew I was still a culprit. They say that heroes die first and my long life has only affirmed for me the fact that I am no hero. If one day I meet the Maker and she turns out to be the Japanese Goddess, she will damn me to hell for what I did that day, and if she turns out to be something other than Japanese she will damn me for what I did the rest of the days.

But I had also liked Mango girl, who seemed sincere. She had had a gritty attitude towards a gritty life. And she had more guts than I.

I slowly searched the other rooms, putting on a show of following Kurosawa's instructions to the letter. And indeed, I told myself, I had answered his question truthfully. I had not lied. The cupboard *had* been smelly. I told myself that I hadn't saved Mango girl nor informed on her. I had merely let her be. Like Appa had always advised me to—I had minded my own business.

By the third room we had found nothing else and Kurosawa said, "There is nothing in there, Nanban?"

"No, Lieutenant Kurosawa. Is it your turn to check?"

"That is strange." His eyes honed in on me, considered me. I met his hawklike gaze as clearly as I could, my body somehow still holding up. I wished I had kicked Nakamura harder. I had the conviction for it now.

Kurosawa swung his gaze away and said, "Stupid informants. You can never trust them. Sometimes, they just tell you what you want to hear. I did not sign up with the Kempeitai to go around chasing comfort women. I don't want to waste anymore time. Sergeant Takagi, tell the men to fall in outside now."

Takagi immediately barked his orders and the men rushed in single file after single file down the stairs, their boots rhythmically trotting down.

Kurosawa clasped my shoulder before I could follow. I didn't know what was running through his mind, whether or not he believed me, or why he would let me go if he didn't believe me, but I stared at him as plainly and clearly as I could. He was poker-faced and I think that if I ever played cards with Kurosawa, I would lose all my money. He said, "Good job, Nanban." *Good job.* I thought he actually looked proud.

"Thank you, Lieutenant Kurosawa."

He smiled. "Now go join the rest."

He let go and I ran downstairs, hoping I never saw Mango girl again. The man in shorts still stared at me with all the hate in the world.

14

Raindancing

Papatti enjoyed drinking tea with Karnan. She found him a thoroughly good person and a funny one too, always smiling and laughing and asking if she needed help at the hospital, as if nary a bad or depressing thought could invade his mind, even if sometimes he fancied himself funnier than he was. Now, all the years of growing up with Lalitha had taught Papatti to suss out flaws from the deepest cavities of a person's character, no matter how good he was, and so if Karnan had a flaw apart from his frequent overestimations of his sense of humour, Papatti decided that it was a streak of vanity that revealed itself in the way he constantly adjusted his shirt to make sure that it was tucked in perfectly, or in the way he kept a comb on standby in his back pocket, or trimmed his moustache to a hair's detail every morning and kept touching it as if extra hairs would sprout out and upset its balance before sunset. He was like a child on the first day of school and Papatti finally understood why his moustache always seemed to bristle so angrily. If someone kept fiddling with her so constantly, she would be furious too! In their numerous meetings after that first tea, it seemed he never changed out of that one good shirt with vertical grey stripes, and good moustache, and good hair, so he always looked his best.

Papatti was not one for going out to restaurants or cinemas because she didn't like spending money frivolously, and Karnan concurred with her thriftiness and visited her at 111 Serangoon Road every weekend instead. He would come to her house properly dressed this time, without rips and tears in his trousers or shirts, and bringing with him kuehs and tiffin for Lalitha. Once, he bought her a wreath of puffy marigold flowers. But Lalitha pointed at the photo of Rajpal hanging in the cabinet and told Karnan that these were the type used to garland the dead, including her husband, and asked if he was trying to send her off early. Mortified, he stopped experimenting with house gifts, even if Papatti never stopped teasing him about it.

He helped Papatti to finally move her sewing machine out of the house, calling his colleagues to drive it away on a rented pickup truck. The wooden machine, draped in light blue garb, stood tall and wobbled away on the back of the truck down Serangoon Road like the finale of a good but long Hindi movie. With the money they received from selling it, she paid off the moneychanger's wife. Vinodh was behind bars, but Karnan said that it was not good to have bad blood with anyone.

In the seemingly small and tightly-knit circle of union leadership, it turned out that Karnan knew the others who supervised Papatti's tenants, whether at the harbour warehouses, cargo companies or construction sites. He collaborated with them to dam the tenants' salaries, threatening to unilaterally siphon all of it to Papatti unless they monthly and incrementally paid up their debts and met future payments a week before they were due. He took this initiative on his own, without her asking, and when she confronted him about it, he merely said, "I hate bullies."

She felt a spasm of angry dependence about his helping her without asking, as if she needed him to take care of her and Amma, but couldn't also help guiltily feeling grateful because the payments had tided her over the distrust the landlord had been accumulating towards Papatti, and he let her keep the house. But Papatti, feeling rather fatuous and inane at this point, nonetheless ordered Karnan not to interfere anymore, and she kept her two jobs at Tan Tock Seng Hospital and the Isetan mall because she didn't want to be dependent on any man, woman, shopkeeper or tenant.

Regardless of Papatti's opinion, this initiative of Karnan's endeared him irrevocably to Lalitha. She had always accepted him because she wanted Papatti to marry *somebody*, but now that Karnan had proven that he could be useful too, Lalitha felt fiercely that he was *the one*. She was a very bribable mother-in-law. After she'd set out dinner—rice, chicken curry and fried bananas, a Queen's feast—Lalitha gave Papatti a deliberately violent nudge, muttering about how God was going to whisk her away soon and she would love to see her daughter married, and with some luck even see her grandson, before this untimely reunion with her husband.

Karnan was polite enough to turn his head away and pretend he hadn't heard Lalitha, and he endeavoured so strenuously to behave normally the rest of the evening that for five minutes he stopped speaking to think about how he would normally answer a simple question about his day that Papatti had asked him. But she liked Karnan even more for his courtesy in this matter of dealing with her most indelicate mother, and for putting up with Papatti berating Lalitha for exhibiting a preference for a grandson over a granddaughter.

By Papatti's account, they fought thrice. The first was over the amount of salt that Lalitha should pour into the rasam soup she cooked for dinner. Karnan argued for two scoops on the grounds of taste, but Papatti demanded for half a scoop because it was the healthier choice, obviously. To resolve the issue and shut them up, Lalitha separated the gravy in half and added the salt separately. But Papatti could not help wishing that she had won the argument more decisively—by making Karnan take less salt in his soup too.

They fought the second time when Papatti asked Karnan, with the sincere and honourable intention of caring after his health, why he drank beer every Saturday and Sunday when alcohol was damaging to the liver. He answered that he couldn't drink from Mondays to Fridays as well because he was working on those days. These were the sort of poor jokes he made that she simply could not tolerate. So Papatti stopped talking to him the rest of that evening, and when he didn't betray the littlest ounce of contrition at her obvious silence, the slightest hint of admitting that he was wrong and she right, Papatti reached across the table and snatched the frosted glass bottle of Tiger beer and gulped it down to show that she at least had tried to understand the case championed by the other side. As the yellow fizz galloped down her throat faster and nastier and more bitter than she had expected, Papatti hightailed it to the sink to throw up the liquid, grateful that her amma was asleep. Karnan helped her clean her chin and the metal basin and after she felt better, she asked him how he managed to drink such vile stuff, and he said, "You see. It builds character." So they had their third fight.

But the next day, they reunited without words, her arm strung through Lalitha's, as the radio announced that Singapore would be separating from Malaysia to become—truly—independent. In those moments, she asked Karnan,

"Will we be okay?"

"I think it will be difficult. What do you think?"

She met his gaze. "Yes," she said. "But we will be okay. I will take care of my amma and you. I have faith."

He smiled. Lalitha climbed into her rattan mat to retire from another day, and Papatti and Karnan held hands for the first time in the kitchen, and she held his hand firmly. They remained quiet, as the radio translated Prime Minister Lee Kuan Yew's speech into Malay. The radio host began speculating about the days to come.

Whenever Karnan swung by her house, Papatti felt an unnatural lift at seeing his lambent eyes and electric moustache and hearing his sonorous voice embark on his next flat joke. She enjoyed whinging to him about how unaffordable and ugly most of the clothes at Isetan Singapore were—not that the two were related of course—and how she would have been able to do better. He shared with her his dream of starting a small business built around his passion, and his fear of leaving an iron rice bowl to bet on something new.

It was evidence of the growth Papatti had experienced over these years that she agreed with his pessimistic outlook towards starting a business. It was better to be safe than sorry. After all, she too missed the empowering and cathartic connection that came with doing something she loved, of being involved in a business enterprise that she could call her own. She wanted to feel that again, but was unwilling to leave her shift-to-shift jobs in search of a calling other than sewing. She had to be mature and responsible, and he did too.

And every time they met, Papatti's dread grew and grew as the time he needed to leave for home drew closer—always ten minutes past eleven so that he could catch the last bus to Tanjong Pagar. Therefore, when he took her to a religiously commendable vegetarian restaurant called Komala Vilas on Serangoon Road and nervously tested the waters by asking how she felt about marrying him, Papatti smiled and said, "I can tolerate you."

He beamed. "That is an accomplishment." He asked her to marry him right away and she said, "Yes."

The next Sunday, Karnan brought his mother, Saroja, and older brother, Murugan, to Papatti's house to ask for her hand traditionally. Saroja was sticklike but strong-boned, with a strong face and strong arms hardened from years of single-handedly raising two vigorously animated boys, both prone to a cheekiness that Papatti concluded was a sometimes endearing and sometimes tiresome family trait. After all, Saroja only appeared strong the way muscles are strong *after* the heavy lifting is done. Murugan was as tall as his older brother, with a bit more give around his cheeks and waist, a largeness matched by a jovial smile that Papatti always welcomed with Murugan's favourite dish of hers—chicken feet cooked in masala.

Karnan officially proposed to Lalitha while Murugan gawked excitedly at his brother's jittering and "uh"-ing. Saroja watched on impassively, eyes like hollowed-out round candleholders, unsure and thus unconcerned about whether her oldest son was simply playing another practical joke. Over the years, Karnan had whittled away Saroja's trust by persuading her that he liked some girl or was courting some other, only for Saroja to learn that his professed loves were merely lies, ruses for him to avoid her nagging that he marry before he turned thirty. As far as Saroja was concerned, attractiveness was the great equaliser among sexes, and despite the differing biological timelines of male and female fecundity, boys and girls became similarly white-haired and ineligible after thirty.

But Saroja's eyes lit up—as if some wick and wax remained in those candleholders to be struck with hope—when Lalitha grunted a few times, grumbled louder under her breath, and finally declared, "I wish the decision was up to me. I would have said yes two years ago. Well, girl, what do you want? You've been seeing this poor boy, leading him on, but you don't say anything to him or me about your intentions and now he's had to bring an army to support him. Do you have an answer or not?"

Papatti slapped her mother's thigh under the table. "I've already said yes, you old woman. We are only doing this for you." Papatti tried to restrain her mother from performing a weird rain dance of happiness around the table, but Lalitha sprang free and gripped Karnan's shoulders with her talons, oblivious to his squirming in pain. "You will stay with us. You will stay with us," she said gleefully.

Papatti realised then that she should have asked Karnan about this. It was Indian custom for the woman to leave her parents and move in with her husband and in-laws, but she couldn't leave her amma behind, alone without her appa. As Lalitha mentioned this, Papatti watched Karnan's reaction for clues. It was a deal breaker, after all. In Tamil, there wasn't even a bye, let alone such a thing as a *good* bye, only an "I'll go and come", or a "See you". And Papatti could not say any sort of unqualified bye to her own amma.

Karnan smiled at her. "Of course," he said, as if she should have known all along that he didn't care for these customs and only cared about her. Her love for him soared, if it were possible. This was far better than the sense of fate she had grown up with.

Saroja breathed a sigh of happy relief and reclined against her chair, as if a lifelong mission had finally been accomplished. She said, "Take him. Take him. Good riddance. I'm tired of looking after two buffaloes." She gave her younger son a slap on the shoulder. "Now I only have one."

"Don't talk about my mapillai like that," Lalitha said. "But I will. I will." She walked to the altar to thank God and pressed vibhuti to the foreheads of the soon-to-be newlyweds. They touched her feet for blessings.

...

They married in the December of 1965, which according to the local astrologer and his parrot, was an auspicious month for twinning their horoscopes. It was a small family ceremony with only a little rice thrown at them in Perumal Temple. Lalitha's exceptional elation that day was only eclipsed over a year later when Papatti gave birth to a baby boy. They named him Raj, and Lalitha saw her husband live on in name before passing away in her sleep while Papatti was pregnant the second time.

After her wedding, Papatti felt—with relief—that they had automatically settled into an equilibrium of humdrum family bliss, filled with weekend walks around Haw Par Villa or the Botanic Gardens, and the occasional birthday dinner with the in-laws at a South Indian restaurant on Race Course Road that was for some peculiar reason named after a Greek God. But Karnan loved their fish head curry even if Papatti found it a little too indulgent.

This equilibrium was sporadically buffeted by the exasperation she felt from repeatedly failing to persuade him to quit his drinking and smoking habits at the Tekka Market hawker centre, but they always moved on from these. In fact, apart from these instances, Papatti counted that they only disagreed thrice as a married couple.

After Rajpal's accident, Papatti hadn't liked the idea of Karnan cycling. He argued for the 24-hour availability and the frugality of the humble working-class bicycle, but in the end, they came to a compromise. He agreed to hop onto the lorry that picked up the dockworkers from Cuff Road and drove them to the port every morning, but would cycle to run his weekend errands. In said compromise, they nipped their first disagreement in the bud. Meanwhile, Papatti quit her day job—temporarily she insisted—to care for Raj, working the occasional night shift at Tan Tock Seng to maintain some measure of financial independence.

The second time they sharpened their swords, Papatti had just taken a half-year-old Raj to Ravi's clothes store down the road. Although she had quit sewing, she continued to detest spending on the imperfect, defective and criminally expensive products of other garment stores. So to save money, she bought shirts a few inches larger than Raj's size so he could grow into them.

When she returned home, Karnan's jaw dropped at the sight of Raj wearing a dotted white shirt like a dress, its short sleeves dangling over Raj's fingers and its hems swimming around his toes. Karnan took Raj from her and said, "He will never grow into this!"

Annoyed at her husband's complete disregard for the value of money, Papatti said, "What are you talking about? He's growing faster than your brother's tummy. He will fit into it by next month, you just see. Until then, I can roll up the sleeves."

"Roll up the sleeves? They are not even long sleeves! We named him king but he looks like a princess. My poor boy." Karnan lifted Raj into the air and fit his head into the opening at the shirt's bottom, nuzzling his nose against the baby paunch. "Oh God. It's like a cave in here. I thought you were the one who said that if the clothes don't fit, nothing else can make you look good." His voice echoed inside the acoustics of the shirt.

"He doesn't know how he looks. The boy doesn't care, why do you? You are the only vain pot in this family."

Karnan's face reappeared into view, Johnson's baby powder splotched on the button of his nose. He shook his head sadly. "This is what happens when someone else makes decisions for you, thinking they know what's best for you."

"Well I do know better."

"Dictator! My son and I outvote you. Revolution! Merdeka!"

"Too bad," she said, rubbing the white powder off his nose.

While this particular conversation and disagreement had ended there, Papatti also became more willing to indulge her son's aesthetic and some other luxuries after the September of 1967, when Karnan ran home to proclaim that he had been awarded a raise. Papatti had been nursing Raj in their bedroom, his eager suckling at her teat causing her to picture herself as the Lord Krishna's favourite cow, when two gentle knocks sounded on the door. Upon receiving permission to enter, Karnan bounded in with two fists pumped up, arms curled like the horns of a bull, and Papatti decided to stop breastfeeding Raj before she started mooing as well. She was feeling all too bovine.

He said, "I got a raise! A raise, dear!" He rushed over to take Raj from her so she could cover herself up, and she said, "Wait, I thought you couldn't get promoted anymore?"

They had discussed this. As a result of his lack of any academic qualifications whatsoever, Karnan had hit a paper ceiling. To climb up the ranks any further as a supervisor or a clerk, he would need to return to school, which was difficult because he had never even entered school in the first place and had no inclination to take the risk of trying now. He said, "Question a good thing, will you. You are just like your amma. But yes, I thought so too. But apparently, they can increase my pay *without* promoting me. Who would have thought?" He held Raj overhead and spun him in a circle, Raj's shirt swishing like a frock.

Papatti didn't dare interrogate their good fortune any further, in case that really did chase it away. After all, they had another child due the next month. Overcoming the gravity of her pregnant stomach, Papatti lunged at Karnan, hugging him and promising to buy Raj a better fitting shirt for the coming Deepavali. Before this auspicious, sartorial occasion, she delivered their second son, whom they named after Karnan's father, Krishnan. They decided to stop at two.

As the first sign of their upward mobility, Papatti and Karnan exchanged their rattan mats for two single-sized mattresses that they joined and shared with the children, although these futons were not without disadvantages. For one, the stuffing sagged underneath Papatti whenever she rolled, which was neither comfortable nor flattering to her weight. And Papatti could not simply roll up the mattresses and store them away at daybreak as she could the mats, causing their room to appear cramped and slept in throughout the day, until she decided to lean them against the wall. But this also had the downside of showing their moulding underbellies and she was never truly content.

They also installed an electric fan in the corner of the room, but Papatti tormented herself so much with nightmares of Raj poking his fingers through the grille to touch the revolving blades that she finally unplugged the device from its socket and they stopped using it altogether.

As she began grousing about these small things to Karnan, Papatti realised with horror that she *was* becoming like her amma, finding fault with everything. Finding this idea particularly disagreeable, she ceased both the carping and the buying of new furniture immediately, deciding instead to save the extra cash for the inevitable rainy day.

And of course, like all good things eventually do, this swelling surge in their good fortune encountered a sudden roadblock when Murugan stopped by the house during the May of 1969. This was to be the third fight of their marriage.

"Anni," he said, addressing her respectfully as sister-in-law in Tamil, "I just came to drop this off for Annae. I keep telling him to change his mailing address but he's so lazy about these things sometimes." He plopped a plain white envelope on the dining table. Having only ever received the routine bills with their standard black government lettering and round official-looking stamps, Papatti found it refreshing to see a blue handwritten address and a stamp decorated with a pink plum flower.

"Who's it from?" she said.

"I don't know these things. Annae has become very secretive about his mail lately. He doesn't like us opening them. So you might as well ask him when he returns." No, she hadn't realised this at all, for she had never seen Karnan receive any personal correspondence. Intrigued by this supposed secrecy, she picked up the envelope, turned it in her hands, curious about what was tucked inside its soft opaque walls. Who would write him anyway? She examined the return address, but could not understand the words and gave up. Murugan said, "Anni, I can see that look in your eyes. Don't, it's dangerous, I'm telling you. Annae once saw Amma opening his mail last year and shouted her head off. And you know how calm and composed he always is. And Amma can't even read anything! I don't even dare."

Karnan—shouting? This surprised her, intrigued her even more, and she traced a finger along the edge of the sealed flap. What was there to hide? And how angry would he be if she just peeked into the envelope? She snapped at Murugan without thinking, "He won't hide anything from me. There are no secrets between us. He won't shout at me." Right?

"Okay, Anni, if you say so. But this is between you and Annae. Leave me out of it if he asks."

"You don't want to eat?"

"No, I'm going to play cards with the boys. I'll see you, Anni. Take care. I'll see you."

She wished she had controlled her temper. Murugan was so sincerely kindhearted, bubbly, warm, like a brother to her. And she was lucky her short fit of pique had not woken up her boys, who were napping inside the bedroom on the spongy mattresses.

But she was alone with the envelope now, and felt drawn to it. Why did putting it down seem so impossible? *Be practical*, she told herself. There were two ways this could go: If it was nothing, Karnan might protest and she would apologise and that would be it. He loved her enough to forgive her; she knew that. And if it was something, then he should have told her earlier and a tough conversation needed to be had anyway. They had only disagreed twice since marrying. Once more wouldn't hurt badly.

With this conclusion, Papatti tore away the sealed flap, opened the envelope, and found an American hundred dollar bill inside.

Immediately, her fingers trembled on the white and green colonial palace printed across the paper. She struggled to process the small fortune denoted by the imposing number "100" emblazoned on its four corners, and her mind panicked with the possibilities that could have led to the mailing of this note to Karnan. She scoured the envelope's insides, turned it inside out, hoping to find clues but encountering only illegible alphabets on the cover. No letter accompanied the money.

The burning question: Was this the vaunted raise? Was she

somehow married to a criminal who had been moonlighting on illegal ventures so they could procure useless fans and unflattering mattresses and custom-fit Deepavali clothes? Why else would he be receiving foreign currency? It must have been a way to launder cash. She did not know the foreign exchange rate, but one hundred Singapore dollars was two months' worth of rent from a tenant. She was sure the figure would be worth far more in American dollars, and that neither she nor Karnan made this type of money.

But this was impossible. The man she had fallen in love with and married was so thoroughly good, so impossibly honest and decent and kind, that she couldn't see him lying to her, couldn't see him stealing or cheating or breaking the law. She couldn't be married to a criminal.

But if she was, she realised, in their society, it would be far easier, far more honourable to wish one's spouse dead rather than divorced. It would be more respectable to be a widow than a divorcee. If Karnan was a felon, she and her sons were stuck with him and his law-breaking ways.

Or not. She wouldn't let society chain her to a criminal by her thaali, if he was one. No, she was thinking too far ahead. She needed to step back and confront him first. She restored the envelope and set it on the table, the money atop it, and rested a silver tumbler on both like a paperweight, feeling lighter for having relinquished the money and envelope at a distance, as if they were ganja. But still, she needed, she *deserved* to know the truth.

As Papatti sat behind the table and waited, she played out the coming argument with Karnan in her head, anger mounting over their imaginary confabulation, as she imagined him talking back to her, trying to justify what she knew to be a wrong, knowing that at the very least, he hadn't been honest with her. The very qualities she had married him for.

And how dare he refute that in their imaginary argument?

She heard Karnan's voice, talking to the new shop owner below. Lee Jin, a purveyor and repairer of watches, had leased the storefront and moved in with his wife and four children soon after Papatti married Karnan, as if to physically remind them with his wares that the clock ran on every new beginning, and that they should maximise their time together, not lie to each other during this limited time about the money they were earning. Karnan kicked off his flip-flops and whistled like an innocent soul as he ascended the staircase, and as his happy face appeared at the head of the stairs, his eyes fell on her and he smiled wider. But she maintained her angry and clenched frown.

He noticed the green bill lying on the table and his smile departed and he stopped walking forward. "Where did you get that?"

Immediately, she felt guilty having to admit to opening his mail without his permission, but then she became angrier at having to feel guilty when she was clearly in the right for discovering that she had been lied to. "I will ask the questions," she said quickly. "What is this?"

"Papatti."

"Don't *Papatti* me. What is this?" She rose and stabbed a finger into the heart of the note, the tumbler falling on its side and rolling. "Is this how you are earning money?"

He frowned. "Of course not. Where did you get it?"

She picked up the thin paper and flapped it like a bus ticket. "Where did *you* get it? Have you been lying to me this whole time? I thought you were a good man. Even that Arjun got what he deserved when the party expelled him for lying about beating up those rowdies. That man is still struggling to put his life back together, to even find a job. What about you? I loved how good a person you were, I wanted to marry that person, but was all that just a front, just so you don't get caught? Was marrying me a front? This is a lot of money, dear. Who sent this to you? Why?" She tossed the paper back on the table and it skimmed to a halt against a splinter of wood.

"What rubbish. What are you saying? The party learned that he lied and they didn't want to run a party with crooked people. What does that have to do with me? Stay on point."

"I don't want to run a family with crooked people either."

"I am not doing anything illegal or crooked. Are you happy now?"

"No," she said. "Then tell me where this money comes from. How long have you been getting it? What do you do with it? It didn't even come with a letter. If you have nothing to hide, tell me then. I deserve to know. I am your wife." She folded her arms across her chest and glared at him expectantly. She heard only her angry breathing. Karnan stared resentfully at the green American note, as if he wished it had never existed. She wondered if it was a look of guilt.

Finally, he exhaled a deep sigh and released his bunched-up hands. Staring at the note and saying in a tone so soft it frightened her even more than if he had shouted, "I've been getting the money every year for the past four years. This is the fourth time I've gotten it."

"And what do you do with it?" she demanded.

At the impatience in her voice, his eyes narrowed and his fingers curled again. "You want to know what I do with it? Is that it? I can show you. I'll show you."

He spun away, mumbling to himself in a fit, and walked over to the sink. He plucked a frying pan from the drying rack. The stainless steel plates that had leaned against the pan clattered sideways into the sink, clinking and clanking in metal bangs, and Papatti jumped in fright.

Having not heard her yelp, Karnan stalked towards her,

hand wrapped around the pan's handle, its plate dangerously large, round and black. Something about his rapidly oncoming figure, his distressed eyes, his hand clenching the handle of the pan so tightly his knuckles had turned white, made Papatti step back and she bumped into the chair. Karnan stopped. His eyes were wounded. "You think I would hurt you?"

He sounded so surprised that she felt foolish for a moment. Then seeing how saddened and stung he seemed and pitying him for it, Papatti said, "I'm not scared of you." She righted herself and folded her arms as confidently as she could manage and stuck her chin up, a most artful diplomacy, communicating simultaneously that she trusted him and wasn't afraid of him but still hadn't forgiven him. He shook his head to himself and picked up the crumpled note.

"What are you doing?" she said.

He turned and even though she was unnerved, she stalked after him. "I said, what are you doing? Where are you going?"

He stopped at the altar. Horrified, she watched him stick the edge of the note into the fire. When he pulled the money back it carried the flame dancing atop the one hundred figure at the corner. He threw the immolated money into the pan. The fierce orange momentarily shrouded the black rectangular border on the reverse side of the note. Then the number and border disappeared and the fire moved inwards to eat the large balding head with round eyes peering at her, an American with a strong nose and pursed lips and long hair. Then the man curled up and vanished too. The flame ate the rest of the paper it needed to survive before it whittled up in smoke, leaving behind ash on a charred black pan.

Papatti blinked, started consciously breathing again, released from the spell of money burning. This was unacceptable. Money and books were sacred. If she had accidentally stepped on either, she would have touched the paper and touched her heart thrice in apology before picking it up and restoring it to an elevated table, out of reach of disrespectful feet. Now, too late, she said, "How could you burn money?"

He was staring at the black pan. "You wanted to know what I do with it. This is what I do. I throw it away. I don't steal or embezzle or whatever it is you have clearly convinced yourself that I do. And I certainly don't spend this money. I want nothing to do with it. You are right about one thing. It is not good money."

"Whose money is it then?" she said, feeling like her high ground had just been swept from underneath her feet. But he walked to the sink and tossed the pan inside. It landed on the plates with another bang and he slapped a hand to stop it with a ringing hum, despite how hot it must have been. With his back to Papatti, he slowly replaced the plates on the rack and said, "It doesn't matter."

"You owe me an explanation," she said, grabbing his arm. He ducked his head away from her and she thought his eyes were misted. Was he crying? Had she made him cry? She had never seen him cry before. She'd rather he fought her, argued with her, screamed at her, than cried. He flicked his arm to shake her hand off and, having set the last plate back, walked to the stairs, still hiding his face, his hands reaching up to cover his eyes.

"Where are you going?" she said.

He didn't reply, only disappeared at the turn, leaving her alone.

15

Dedicated to Papatti

Over the next weeks, Headquarters recalled a few Jalan Besar soldiers back to Japan's Pacific territories and I didn't know why, and believe most of the soldiers didn't either because the Imperial Army operated on a "trust me and obey me" basis and everyone just followed quietly. After all, by simply opening our mouths to question orders, we would also have been questioning a God-sent, faultless Emperor. In all honesty, I'm surprised it didn't strike Emperor Hirohito that he would probably sound more infallible, and be more infallible, if he admitted that he wasn't infallible.

But it suited me to complete my tasks without poking my nose into extra business, especially since Saito had also left with the repatriated soldiers. Then a few more troopers left in a second batch and only two sections of Imperial Guards soldiers were left on Jalan Besar Road.

Meanwhile, during the day, Kurosawa calculated that I had memorised a little over two hundred *kanji* and taught me to piece them together with the *hiragana* and *katakana* to create phrases, which demanded more rote-writing practice. In the mornings, he trained me to spin and kick with the back of my heel, which initially I found awkward. After constant twirling and kicking, I held my knees and waited for the ground to stop swaying. Kurosawa said, "Nanban, are you dizzy?" He chortled. "You become dizzy very fast *ne*. Well, you are not Japanese. Maybe we should focus on the standing and striking movements for you, like a boxer, less spinning. We should focus on your strengths."

"Yes please, Lieutenant Kurosawa."

"My father grew up learning karate. But he created *kyoshokan* after watching an American boxing match. Karate doesn't allow you to hit the enemy's face during a competition. In karate, you can only hit the body. So the training also focuses on hitting the body. But my father saw these two big *kurombo* American boxers punching each other—here in the jaw, here in the temple—until one was knocked out on the mat. My father called it 'realistic'.

"The head is vulnerable. Therefore, it is important to learn to attack and defend the head when fighting. So my father modified his martial art according to Western boxing rules, although of course, *kyoshokan* allows you to kick too. It is a full-body martial art, so you must learn to use all your body can offer. Even if we focus on standing and striking in the future, it is good to have a few surprises in store for the enemy. You must still learn your *ushiro keri* well. Do you understand?"

"I understand, Lieutenant Kurosawa." I rose upright. "Where is your father now, Lieutenant Kurosawa?" *Otōsan*, the Japanese word for father. We all have one.

He frowned. "You have stood up. Are you okay now, Nanban?"

"Yes, Lieutenant Kurosawa."

"Then why are we still talking? Do; don't talk. Practise the *ushiro keri* again. Train to surprise your opponent."

"Yes, Lieutenant Kurosawa." I returned to *kamae* position.

"Hurry up, Nanban, practise as much as you can before it is time for work."

"Yes, Lieutenant Kurosawa."

Later in the evening, I asked Kurosawa about his father again and he put down the book he was reading and sighed. "Don't ask pointless questions, Nanban."

"Sorry, Lieutenant Kurosawa."

"Are you very free there? Here, take this and copy the *kanji* fifty times. Memorise them. Use your energy more constructively. Do you understand?"

I took the paper, a single page from a report he was reading, and sat by my mat. He always circled the *kanji* I was to learn in red.

I had begun trying not to think about Appa because I felt that I was betraying his memory every additional day that I worked for the Kempeitai, felt more and more like the "scoundrel" and "traitor" that he had accused informants of being, helping the Japanese in exchange for keeping my life. I wondered if Kurosawa felt guilty or ashamed thinking and talking about his father too, and why. But having to write *kanji* in exchange for asking questions put me off from broaching this subject with Kurosawa again.

Instead, I said, "Lieutenant Kurosawa, can you tell me more about the Sumo wrestlers?" Large rotund men slamming against each other, like fleshy pots and kettles wrestling on tatami, appealed to my imagination more than writing exercises.

He slammed his book shut. "Are you trying to avoid practising *kanji*?"

"I want to learn more about Japan, Lieutenant Kurosawa."

"Nonsense. You are a mischievous boy. I know what you are trying to do."

I kept quiet, but he stood and set his feet wide apart and squatted low, his bum bouncing on air. I had learned by now that one of Kurosawa's flaws was that he was unable to resist teaching me about Japan. He raised one leg at a time to show me how the Sumo wrestlers trained, first his right, then his left.

I copied him and shifted my weight from leg to leg, but it was fast tiring on my legs and also difficult to squat that low with my back upright.

When I tumbled backwards and fell on my bum, he said, "Wow. Are you dizzy doing this too? That's bad. We must improve this situation. We must improve your flexibility, Nanban. Come, stand up. Do it again." But I was happy to practise this amateur sumo instead of penmanship. It was a success, relief and wonder that we made it through the evening without another writing lesson—or another lecture on the Emperor's beneficence—but I continued to feel increasingly undeserving of my good fortune and despised myself for it. I hoped that Appa was not watching from above.

...

Kurosawa didn't take me on any more house raids and I told myself that this was simply because it was not my job. Everyone had his role to play and I was no soldier. My armband was titular and that's why I kept it at Kurosawa's house instead of strutting around with it like a red-and-white peacock.

Besides, Kurosawa hardly went on house raids anymore himself. There were only so many people the officer could imprison or execute before having to transplant the whole population from some Japanese village in Kyushu.

Kurosawa started giving me the new currency, with its images of banana trees, coconuts, and a promise from the Japanese government to pay the bearer on demand. Kurosawa allowed me to go farther afield alone to buy him and the other soldiers fruits and food that were not on the currency, like papayas and jackfruits, as well as kuehs from the mama shops around Little India and Bugis. Sometimes, Kurosawa asked me for recommendations for food or a particular hawker who specialised in making you jia kueh, or he wanted me to explain the colourfully layered peels of the kueh lapis or whether cendol was made from matcha. And thus I fed the hand that held me.

One evening, as Kurosawa was tippling his sake and thinking to himself in front of his desk, he opened his glassy eyes—I think he might have had one too many cups—and stared at me. He said, "Nanban. You did not find that comfort woman in that house, right?"

Till this day, I wonder what he wanted me to say or what he *didn't* want me to say. Back then, I concluded that we were both better off if I said, "No, Lieutenant Kurosawa. Why, Lieutenant Kurosawa?"

I truly believe that you can do whatever you set your mind to because I tried super hard to look truthful and sincere and finally Kurosawa nodded and a faraway expression returned to his eyes. "I see. I see." He closed his eyes and leaned back on his hands, his fingers outstretched like two webs. A little relief overcame me. Then he started talking, eyes closed, and relief drained in an instant, I grew nervous again. But he said, "Nanban, I want you to teach me to cut and eat a durian. I cannot stand the smell, it is like the drain, but I should try it once. I don't want others to see and laugh at me. So we must do it inside here. Do you understand? Will it make my house smell?"

...

A few air raids blitzed us in the November of 1944. In the early mornings as we awoke, B-29 bombers soared under the dark dawn sky, like black flying crosses. I stood outside Kurosawa's house and tilted my head back to watch the planes, worse angels inspecting the earth, and closed my eyes at the terrible roar that blasted over me and flew onwards. I wasn't afraid because we all knew that the jets were targeting the harbours, including—as I heard from Radio Syonan— the Naval Base at Sembawang. The Japanese used it now.

Kurosawa dismissed the bombers as piddling attempts by the British to stay relevant, a child's tantrum. I imagine that when he saw the planes tearing across the sky, all he saw was the word LOSERS streaking through like clouds. After the second wave of bomber flypasts, he said, "This is a *Japanese* territory. *Shōnan*. The British should realise that instead of giving us unnecessary work. They are not achieving anything. Nanban, I want to take you to Ise shrine one day, where we will offer our prayers to the Imperial Regalia. Once this is over and I am recalled home, I will take you to offer thanks to the Emperor for our decisive victory. Then you will know the might of the Emperor. Do you understand?"

I couldn't imagine leaving this small island; I had never known anything else and I had buried everything here. The land can be our father and it can be our grave and it can be all we need to know. But I said *yes* and *thank you* and that was that.

Kurosawa's dismissive attitude was vindicated when the air raids stopped and they disappeared from the front pages of *The Syonan Times* and life became normal, or what had become considered normal. For me, I didn't bother thinking about other possibilities because I saw no point. But perhaps we should have paid closer attention to who flew the planes.

During one clear and quiet morning, Kurosawa left for a meeting at Headquarters and I finished my chores and cooked lunch. He had given me money to buy his favourite tropical fruit, mangosteens, and I procured a bunch near Serangoon Road.

I carried the five purple grenades in a bag back to the house, only to find Kurosawa on both knees before his empty mess tin. Even with his back to me, I sensed his severe sobriety as he offered prayers for his brother. I bowed to the *kamidana* and waited for Kurosawa to finish before asking for permission to enter the house, but as minutes passed and he didn't budge, the feeling that something was wrong came over me.

Yet across the road, two Jalan Besar soldiers milled about carefree and laughing and the sentry was on his routine duty and here I was carrying mangosteens. I surmised therefore that nothing could be wrong. Most importantly, I did not remember doing anything to cross Kurosawa. So I said, "Lieutenant Kurosawa, *ojama itashimasu.*"

He didn't hear me. He didn't even waver. I raised my voice, a little, and said, "I'm sorry. Excuse me. Lieutenant Kurosawa, *ojama itashimasu.*"

Slowly, his head turned and his eyes were bloodshot and wet, like two open wounds, not seeing me. Kurosawa's face was wan and white, like the blood had run from it into his eyes. Immediately, I wished I had walked away when he hadn't responded the first time. But it was too late now and Kurosawa waved a hand and said, "Come in." He sounded croaky.

I glanced at the rotan, leaning upright against my coiled mat in the corner. Kurosawa planted his ashen knuckles on the floor and touched his pale forehead to the cement.

He stopped in that kowtow for seconds, taking his time, and then righted himself, wiped his sweaty face and stood up. I set the bag down in the doorway, already thinking of how I could leave politely. "Your fruits, Lieutenant Kurosawa," I said.

He considered the slouched bag. Then he tore his gaze away and paced the room, patrolling the sterilised floor between desk and mat, desk and mat. He clutched his hands behind his back, to stop them fidgeting, and stared at the ceiling as he paced. He did not look in my direction.

Then a thought struck him, a thought that obviously buoyed his spirits. He jogged over to pick up my clothes, neatly folded beneath the rotan, and presented them like a gift to me. "Take these with you, Nanban." He dropped the light parcel into my arms. The red and white *kanji* of the Kempeitai sat on top. He saw it, and said, "No no." He plucked the armband and tossed it onto his desk. "Ah!" He raced outside and returned as quickly with one green punching pad. "Here, keep this. A keepsake, yes?"

Once inside the house, the pad's sweat-soaked acetic stink was overpowering. Kurosawa flinched and wrinkled his nose. He hurled the pad through the door and it rolled towards the trees. He stared at his empty hands, wondering what to do with them. "No, no," he said. His eyes searched the spartan house and finally he shook his head and said, "No, no. It will be safer if you don't take anything." He grabbed the clothes in my arms and tossed them onto the floor.

He dug into his pocket and pulled out a batch of finely folded banana currency and stuck them into my open palm instead. "Buy new clothes, Nanban. Change and throw away these clothes immediately. Wait, I'll give you more money. First, buy new clothes, then change your clothes and then buy food. Spend the money fast. Do you understand? You can take the mangosteens with you. Do you understand?"

WARRAN KALASEGARAN

"I don't understand, Lieutenant Kurosawa."

He stopped. Then he knelt and gripped my arms tight, reddened eyes searching my face, searching for an answer, still avoiding my eyes. He smiled, a fragile smile loaded with effort rather than sincerity. It was a sad smile, and just as tears welled in his eyes, he hugged me tight. "It will be okay. It will be okay, Nanban."

My chin stuck out over his shoulder and I didn't understand which of us he was talking to. He clutched me so tightly it hurt into my skeleton. "Lieutenant Kurosawa, what happened?"

It took a few quiet moments before he pulled away from me. The wet streaks splashed across his cheeks told me he had wiped his tears away in a rush. He was always either superbly stoic or violently angry and I had never thought he was the sort to cry, the sort to break down, and I was frightened of what could have snapped him this way. He still did not look at me. He said, "I don't know."

To be unsure, and to admit it, was equally unlike the Lieutenant I knew. I became even more worried. "Lieutenant Kurosawa?"

He stared downwards and his lips trembled and finally he said in the smallest whisper, as if the wind was supposed to carry his words and chuck them into the depths of the Rochor River, never to be heard hence, "I need to tell you that the war could be over."

I thought I hadn't heard him correctly, or that my Japanese was floundering. He finally met my eyes. The piercing redness of his gaze stays with me till today. When he spoke, he had steeled himself and his words were strong and clear again. "As far as you should be concerned, Nanban, the war is over. As far as you need to know, Japan has lost the war." His face scrunched up and his hands covered it. He released an animal sob.

"They will hang you for saying that, Lieutenant Kurosawa. Why do you say that? There is no war."

His hands slid down his face, wiping the tears off entirely so I wouldn't see them. "There are other battlefields where the war was taking place, Nanban. Battlefields bigger and more important than *Shōnan*, and Japan may have lost them. Can you understand this?" I nodded, although I was absorbing the news that Japan was still fighting. Whether or not the Emperor hocus-pocus had destined Japan to win wars forever, I had assumed from Kurosawa's unparalleled confidence and the years gone by during the Occupation that Japan had already won decisively the world over.

He saw my confusion and his face darkened. "The Emperor declared that the war is over. He declared it and I heard him declare it and his word matters above us all, doesn't it? It is all that should matter for you. The war is over. That is all you need to know. We must bow to the inevitable. Japan must endure the—" He dropped his head before his voice could crack and his tears could fall again.

He took a large breath to collect himself. "No. The Emperor is safe. He is trying to save us, trying to save the *kokutai* and civilisation. Do you understand this? He has a larger plan, a strategic design that we do not know yet. Soon, we will find out, and Japan will continue to be glorious. Do you understand? But, as far as you need to know, the war is over. Do you understand?"

Then as if a Zero bomber had blitzkrieged my mind, it struck me that the Jalan Besar soldiers hadn't fought. Thousands of Imperial Japanese Army troopers still stood guard at Headquarters and patrolled Singapore, alive, healthy and armed. Kurosawa was here, unscathed by war, struggling not to cry instead of taking up his rifle or needle or pen and charging at the enemy, as he had declared he would.

Carefully, cautiously, I asked, "Lieutenant Kurosawa, did Japan surrender?"

Stillness shrouded the stooped figure of Kurosawa. His head lowered, and I no longer recognised the authoritarian in this pitiful state. Down-staring still, he said, "As far as you need to know, yes, Nanban. I have been ordered not to fight. I have been ordered not to commit *seppuku* and kill myself. I have been ordered to stand down. Japan will hand over its territories peacefully to the Allies. I must endure the unendurable. That is all you need to know."

"Don't kill yourself, Lieutenant Kurosawa. Why do you want to die?"

He sniffed a little sincere smile and looked up. His eyes had cleared a little and some white showed in them. "Nanban, you are so mature for your age, sometimes I forget that you are still a child and I have so much more to teach you. But we won't have that opportunity anymore."

"What happens to us, Lieutenant Kurosawa?"

"For now, the Imperial Army will hand over to the British and we will see what they want. You will become a British subject again. Do you understand? This is why you need to learn that the war is over and Japan lost."

"So we both go to work for the British now?"

He laughed and clapped his hands, a little of the old sensei Kurosawa coming to life whenever he was amused by me. "We won't go together Nanban. I still have orders to follow from Headquarters. But you must go alone, and soon. When the Allies start telling the people that Japan has lost, they will be angry, they will take revenge on the soldiers and anyone who worked for us. And that includes you. They will drag you through the streets if they know you worked for the Kempeitai. If we disarm, there will be chaos. A lot of chaos. You must not tell anyone that you worked for me or the Kempeitai. Go quietly, buy new clothes and spend the money on food. Spend the money fast, before the handover. Do you understand?"

"I understand."

"Remember what I told you from the start, Nanban. This is not your war. You have no price to pay. Just be careful until you find someone you trust and who will take care of you. You will find someone else. I promise you. Do you understand?"

"I understand."

"And do not worry. We will come back. I will come back for you. The Emperor has a larger vision that we cannot see yet. But you don't need to worry about this. You must only worry about your survival. For now, all you need to know is that the war is over and you must survive. Do you understand?"

"I understand."

He took a deep breath. Instructing a subordinate, performing his authority reminded Kurosawa of who he was. He seemed calmer and certain, more himself for it. He narrowed his eyes at mine with a sombre gravity and that gravity pulled his head down in one firm nod. "Therefore, this is it. You must go now, before the people start finding out. You cannot waste any more time."

I lowered my head.

"Nanban."

"I don't know where to go."

"You will be okay, Nanban. I have given you money that will last. You cannot be seen with me. It is not safe." He shook my arms vigorously, trying to shake me to life and out of his house.

When this didn't work, he said, "Nanban," and shook me even harder, like beating a carpet. I didn't move. He rose to his feet and towered over me and planted his hands on his hips. I could feel his severe Imperial gaze frowning upon me.

"Go, Nanban. Go." *Ike*.

I hadn't moved.

"I said *go*, Nanban."

I felt a strong stinging on my cheek where he slapped me, a strong hard one. He pointed an outstretched finger at the door. "You must obey me. Now go, Nanban."

The old Kurosawa was back in full force. The hot throbbing on my face made me angry, made me hate Kurosawa. I stared at him balefully. "You have no right to order me or to hit me anymore. You lost the war. I don't serve you anymore and I don't serve anyone."

He slapped me again. My cheek danced ablaze. Kurosawa was shaking, fists clenched, red. "Get out of my house. Leave me in peace. I am tormented enough. I am forced to live with this situation, but not with your insolence."

"If you want to die, I wish you will die. I will kill you myself."

Kurosawa blinked. Surprise replaced anger. Then his face etiolated with grief, like when I had found him upon returning to his house. He was sad. "You want to kill me?"

"Yes. I hate you," I said, meaning every word of it. "You took everything from me, for nothing. I hate you. I hate you!" The money scattered like leaves around me as I stabbed a finger at him. I didn't care.

Kurosawa stuttered but nothing came out.

Then he clamped his lips and wheeled around. He strode to the bottles of sake and uncapped one with black *kanji* lettering that I could not read. He downed large gulps from it before slamming the glass bottle down so hard I thought the bottom would shatter. He marched to his backpack, rifled it and pulled out a brown leather-bound dagger. He unsheathed the knife, the slender grey blade shining out dangerously, and fell onto his knees before me. He was so close I could smell the turpentine breath of rice wine from his heavy breathing. He grabbed my right hand and wrapped my fingers around the brown leather handle, blade pointed at him, and did not release that hand. He said, "Therefore, do me a favour, Nanban. Do as you want. Do it please."

He grabbed the blade with his free hand, clutching it so tightly that wine-dark blood emerged from the cracks between his fingers. He pulled the blade into his abdomen in a rough tug, seemingly oblivious to the blood and pain. "Here. You push it in here hard. You push it in like one straight jab. Next, you pull it this way." He dragged the blade across his stomach in one horizontal line, and it tattered the shirt to reveal pale untouched skin. Finally, he took his hand off the blade and as he flicked his hands up, blood spattered my face and red tributaries trailed down his wrists, following his veins into the mouthlike cuff of his uniform, blotting it sanguine. He pressed a finger into the vein on his jugular, leaving a large vermillion dot. "After that, you cut me here. Like this." The side of his palm sliced his neck, drawing a thick crimson line across his neck. "Here, like this. Do you understand?" He grabbed the blade again and repositioned it back at his abdomen and regarded me mournfully. "After this, Nanban, leave immediately. Talk to no one, buy new clothes, buy food, spend the money and stay low. Remember everything I am telling you. Do you understand?"

"Why do you care?"

He sighed. He drew both my hands onto the hilt of the dagger, and then let go of me. The handle was warm with Kurosawa's blood. The back of my hands were red and I could feel his blood dripping from my wrists onto the floor. "I always did."

He set his palms on his thighs. His brown uniform was flecked in crimson spots and handprints, crimson dashes covered his stomach and neck and face. The metallic smell of blood was rising. He closed his eyes and took another long deep breath. When he opened them, they spoke of acceptance. He looked weaker from losing blood. "Now, Nanban, do it."

I gripped the hilt tight and instinctively pushed it on command, widening my feet to lean my weight against the dagger. If I killed him, I wanted it to be swift and immediate, like squashing a cockroach. I didn't want to torture him. The blade pushed into Kurosawa's stomach and he grunted. An awareness came over him at the pain and he closed his eyes. His face became a blank parchment, pale and pure, as if this is all it took to wipe away his sins and shame. He was going to a peaceful place. He said, "Now, please do it, Nanban."

He had never said please to me before. I stood staring at this man, knelt before me, reduced to my height, vulnerable. The sword was finally in my hand and at my command. Kurosawa's life lay in my hands. The tables had turned. Eyes still closed, Kurosawa said, "*Sayonara,* Nanban. *Tennō heika banzai.*"

"Stop calling me 'Nanban'," I said. "My name is Karnan." I hurled the dagger with both arms and it crashed against the rotan. They fell to the floor together, tumbling the open sake bottle over and breaking it into a thousand shattered jewels, clear liquid spreading out and drowning and curling up the banana notes so they would never be used again. The rotan rolled back and forth in the colourless rice wine before coming to a halt, immersed, the smell of sake blooming. His eyes opened, stunned. I turned and ran out of his house for the last time. Outside, B-29 bombers flown by Americans were soaring overhead, yellow leaflets were falling from the grey sky, the soldiers were staring up and shouting, people were staring openly through their windows at this most aberrant autumn, and the sun was slowly sinking into the land.

16

Radio Age

Papatti sponged the frying pan clean, washing the ashes of one hundred US dollars down the drainage pipes. Since her boys were still so obliviously, blissfully comatose, she stayed in the hall and turned on the Sony radio, hoping it might lighten her depressingly heavy mood. The Oli station was playing the song "Ullathil Nalla Ullam" from the Kollywood movie *Karnan*.

Papatti sat and rested her sweaty forehead on a fist, thinking that only a few weeks ago, she had been joking with Karnan that they should go to the Rex Cinema to watch the rerun of the movie, based on an old Indian mythic poem, and glean similarities between the eponymous protagonist and her husband. Karnan had feigned offence, arguing that he was far more handsome than the lead actor, Sivaji Ganesan. He also happened to find Tamil movies fake, consistently ridiculing the idea of one man beating up a hundred while delivering punchlines, and so snubbed Tamil films and preferred to watch the Chinese kung fu movies that he averred were far more realistic and entertaining (as if one man beating up a hundred without punchlines and with fancy tricks were more realistic). But he had good-naturedly agreed to come along for *Karnan* because she so badly wanted to watch it and, as she had accused him, because deep down he was vain and narcissistic and couldn't resist watching a flick with his name on it. They had bought boiled peanuts, rolled up in a newspaper cone, from the vendor outside Rex and laughed throughout the serious period drama about the brazen overacting, thrown peanuts at the screen, and ultimately agreed that he was indeed far better looking than Sivaji Ganesan.

She missed that ease between them now—all because of one random envelope. They had never fought this seriously.

The lyrical melody surged forth from the radio, and in the movie, Krishna sang the song to the dying warrior, Karnan, who had been orphaned and lower caste and doomed from the start, telling him to keep striving, at which point her husband had told her a Japanese word that apparently conveyed the same meaning. Papatti remembered telling him not to show off. She also remembered sharing the most jokes with her husband during this scene too, as Sivaji's character died from the arrows sticking out of his chest with all the delay and drama that was to be expected of a Tamil movie.

The song finally swelled to its resolution in 111 Serangoon Road, and static caught in the net of the black speakers and crackled as the station abruptly switched from songs to the news, as if even the radio knew something was wrong, and was corrupting its transmission.

A man calmly delivered the headlines and Papatti recognised Prasad's voice. The anchorman lived nearby on Kitchener Road and they had grown up together. He was a bubbly man with a thicker moustache than Karnan. Papatti always marvelled at how different Prasad sounded over the radio—monotonous, robotic, detached, as if he would never be affected by the news he delivered. When he said, "Riots have broken out," Papatti jumped to her feet.

Her first instinct sprang to Karnan, likely cycling around town like her appa had been, distracted by her harsh words, consumed by his hurt, not paying any attention to his surroundings, not knowing the latest news, not knowing to stay indoors and safe. Papatti wanted to go to him, tell him to postpone their fight and return home first. But she couldn't leave her sons alone in the house; not like this. She needed to be faster than her amma had been. She didn't have time.

Prasad started diving into the details of the riots and in her haste to turn off the radio, Papatti knocked it off the windowsill and the black box fell with a loud snapping crack. The sound fizzled into a noisy, antsy and jarring loop. Papatti cursed and left the radio as it was humming in the background to hurl open the doors to check the other rooms, leaving the doors swinging against the walls as she darted from room to room. No tenant was in. She shouted, heading for the staircase, "Uncle Lee! Uncle Lee!"

"What, girl?" came the response from his wife, Li Hua. "What's that noise?"

"There are riots!"

"What?!"

"Riots! I heard from the news. Close the shop and hide in your room! Now!"

To the noise of Li Hua shouting at her children and husband, Papatti dashed into her bedroom. Below, she heard the metal shutter reeling and rumbling as it slammed down. She opened the cupboard doors, which were now a barren yellow. Papatti had torn out the silly articles of her sewing escapades and only some difficult tatters of tape were stuck to the door, resistant to further peeling. To think she had once been so enamoured with those reports. How many riots needed to occur, how many more needed to die before the country finally puked them all out, got them out of its system? This was still the age of hiding in cupboards.

Having opened the doors, Papatti gently picked Raj up by the armpits and leaned him against a corner of the cupboard, under the eave. At being seated upright on the clothes, he stirred, eyes dewy while Papatti tucked Karnan's hanging shirts around him to hide him. "Amma, what are you doing?" he said in Tamil, eyes clearing and growing big and round.

"Keep quiet and sit still, boy. For your amma, please." She scooted over to Krishnan and carried him, still asleep, to the cupboard. Raj was sniffing by the time she returned, confused. "Don't cry Raj, please. For Amma."

"I want Appa. I don't want to sit here."

She wanted him too. If only to know that he was safe so she could upbraid him another day. "Appa will come home soon, don't cry. Don't worry."

She spoke to her own anxieties as much as she spoke to Raj. Fearing for Karnan's life, knowing he could become nothing, dead in an instant, or lying in pain on the road helplessly like her appa had been, made their fight over one hundred dollars seem so ridiculously petty, so narrow-minded, so stupid. She should never have opened that envelope and she should never have confronted him about it. She should have trusted him from the start.

At the very least, she shouldn't have ambushed him and made her own husband, a grown-up, cry. She wasn't fighting a war against an enemy here. A hundred dollars, in American currency at that, was a Queen's ransom. Any other wife would have been overjoyed if that sum had dropped into her lap, and spent it on 4D lottery tickets and lavish family dinners and clothes for the children and kept the rest in a bank. Only the great Papatti was stupid enough to accost and interrogate him without even finding out the facts first. He must think she was a ruddy fool. Why was she as shrewish and fault-finding as her amma? Hadn't she always wanted to be more like her appa? Now, she was about to become responsible for her husband's next cycle of reincarnation.

No. She would go to Karnan, bring him home safe, be there for him the way she hadn't been able to for Rajpal. She would make it up to him. They would never fight like this again.

Cradling Krishnan, she said in the most serious teacher voice she could muster, "Raj, I need you to do something for me. I am going to go find your appa and I need you to be the man of the house. I want you to stay inside this cupboard with your thambi. I don't want you to leave this cupboard or your thambi, no matter what. Can you do that? You are not to open this cupboard until I come back. Do you understand, Raj? Can you be an adult for me, please?"

He was about to blubber. Papatti didn't even know if her three-year-old understood her fully. She couldn't even blame him if he did not understand. But finally, Raj nodded tremulously, and Papatti took what she was could. "Good boy. Come, move over, I will put your brother here, on top of all these clothes. That's it. Put your hands here. Yes, to keep him from rolling. Good boy. You understand? Just make sure Thambi doesn't wake up. Okay? Hold him and don't disturb him and he won't wake up. Okay? Good boy." Raj's two arms angled sideways to hold Krishnan's waist while he looked to her for guidance, for consolation.

"You will be safe here," she said, as she had been during the first spate of riots. It was Karnan, cycling outside, who was in danger, like her appa had been. "Amma will be back soon with Appa. Okay? Don't be afraid. Be very quiet and look after Thambi. Okay, Raj?"

"Yes, Amma." He sounded so uncertain, so wet behind the ears and in the eyes, but she had no choice. She kissed him on the forehead. "Now, I'm going to close the doors very slowly, okay? Slowly, slowly," slowly, and her sons disappeared, hidden behind the yellow doors. Silence echoed from inside.

With a deep breath, Papatti closed their room door and ran across the hall, noticing that Lee Jin's door was shut, likely locked. She was descending the staircase when the main door creaked open and voices emerged, men, chattering in Malay, and she stopped.

Papatti sprinted back up two tiptoe steps at a time to the kitchen drawers. She pulled out her long butcher knife and darted into her room. Holding the knife behind her back, she opened the cupboard door again and exhaled with quiet relief when Raj merely jumped without yelping, one hand shielding his eyes from the light and the other guarding his thambi. She put a finger to her lips right away and mouthed, "Good boy." Raj started to speak and Papatti said, "Don't say anything."

She brought out the knife and that silenced him effectively. *Perfect*, she told herself, *you've just threatened your son with homicide to shut him up*. She picked Krishnan up in one arm, careful with the knife, and sat inside the cupboard, feeling her weight sink into the fabric pile as it had years ago. Papatti retracted her legs and pulled the doors shut, hearing the Malay words grow louder outside as men tumbled up the stairs. In the hall, a muffled man said, "There's nobody here."

"Shh," she said, holding out the knife, its tip lanced at the strip of grey light between the doors, shaking.

"The radio's broken," someone said.

"Let me check the rooms."

The chairs were pushed roughly. A slam. "No food!" one said, and the rest laughed.

"Anything?"

"No!"

"This one's locked." That must have been Lee Jin's room. She had forgotten to lock their door!

"Amma, cockroach," Raj said. Head tilted back, he was staring at an engorged bug crawling on the cupboard ceiling. "I want to go out." Papatti gave Raj her most murderous stare to demonstrate that he had far more to fear from his mother than a cockroach, and this time she sincerely hoped that the butcher knife heightened this effect.

A silence had descended outside the cupboard, the type of silence in which people exist but are quiet, where hearts could still be heard beating, that of hers and her sons. The cold knife shivered in her hand, nervously aimed at the door. Then the cupboard doors opened and she couldn't even see her knife or what was outside as the light blinded her. But she screamed with terror and lunged out with it anyway, with all her might. Raj screamed too.

"Oi, watch that. What are you doing?"

"Appa!" Raj said.

Karnan had glided aside, hips swinging back, a matador deftly sidestepping a bull's charge, the perfect veronica. He was examining his shirt incredulously, which thank God, remained pristine and white, unblemished by injury.

Papatti said, "I'm sorry! I'm so sorry! I'm sorry!"

He snatched the knife from her and threw it to the other end of the room where it smashed against the barren wall the sewing machine had once stood against. "I knew you were angry with me, but I didn't think you were that angry!" he said.

Careful with Krishnan, she jumped out and leaned sideways into him. "I'm so sorry, dear. I'm so sorry. Please forgive me. I didn't think it was you."

He wrapped his arms around her. "What were you doing in there?"

"Riots. In the radio, the news, they said there were riots. Amma made me hide here during the riots before and I wanted to keep the boys safe. I've told you this before."

"Okay, well, there are no riots taking place. Where did you hear that? Are you sure he said the riots were taking place *here*?"

It dawned on her that she had not listened to the entirety of the newsreel. She sheepishly shook her head in his chest.

Karnan said, "So you just assumed there were riots here. You can be quite foolish for such a smart woman at times, you know that? Is that why Uncle Lee's door is locked? Did you convince him there were riots taking place too?"

She nodded sheepishly as well. Then she felt angry at being called foolish. Fear was fear and she of all people had good reason to be afraid.

She pulled away from him. "How was I to know where the riots were taking place? I got scared and wanted to hide your sons and come find you. You should have been here to take care of them, not gallivanting around outside just because we had a tiff. Where were you? How could you just storm off like that? Who's in the hall then?"

"My workmates! Who did you think they were? You always complain about how Saleem talks for his mother in Pahang to hear. Couldn't you hear him? Murugan is here too." He laughed and took Krishnan from her arms. "This one could sleep in an ambulance on call."

Papatti agreed. Eunos stuck his head into the doorway and said, "You found them? Guys, he found them!" A cheery roar went up in the hall. "Disband the search party! Recall the scouts!"

Saleem inserted his head into the doorway too, above Eunos', and jabbed his chin at the gaping cupboard. "Were you in there? Why? How could you fit all three of you? Also, your radio's broken."

Karnan said, "She thought she was hiding from riots. Can you tell Uncle Lee that he can stop hiding and reopen his business?"

Saleem frowned. "Riots? What riots?"

"Exactly. She heard something over the radio and thought you guys were rioters. Now go call Uncle Lee."

Saleem burst out laughing. He tilted his head back and shouted, "Oi Murugan! Tell Uncle Lee he can come out! Be gentle ah! He thinks we are rioters!" Some hooting and laughing and banging of tables answered Saleem's call, which couldn't have made Lee Jin feel any better and Papatti sank lower.

Eunos said, "Alamak, Papatti. I tell you: rioters are idiots. The first time I heard about riots was right after the Occupation ended. Someone ran around my village shouting that the war had ended and that everyone should pack their bags and run because the Chinese were burning Malay villages and killing Malays in revenge after the Occupation. He said they were coming to my village. The radio also said the same thing. In the end, half my village moved and half stayed, including my family. My father was the village chief, how to move right or not? The next day, we saw Chinese people coming down the road, carrying parangs, so we went out to confront them. We stopped, maybe the size of this room apart, and my father asked what they wanted. They said someone had told them to run from the Malays and they had left their village also! Crazy. So we took them in and they filled up the other half of our village and Chinese, Malay, Indian, Alien, we never let any rioter touch our village. We told them to keep their problems outside. That's when I learned: the country is not divided among Chinese, Malays and Indians. It is divided between people who just want to fight and people who want some peace. So don't worry. If anyone tries to hurt you, we will protect you. Anyway, your husband here is the kung fu specialist right. Who can touch you?"

Now she felt even more embarrassed, afraid of having offended Eunos and Saleem. "Of course I don't think you will hurt me, Eunos. But I guess I was scared of the people I don't know. I'm sorry."

Eunos smiled. "Nothing to be sorry for. That's the problem, right or not, it's always strangers attacking strangers, people they don't know. What's the point? Don't worry, Papatti. Anyway, I'll give you guys some time alone. Can I make tea?"

"I'll do it," Papatti said, adjusting her hairbun.

"No need. No need. We can handle it. Take your time." Eunos' head vanished from the door, yanking Saleem's along with it.

"The tea's under the sink!"

"Okay thanks!"

"Appa! Amma!" Raj had about-turned and was struggling to lower his feet onto the floor.

Cradling Krishnan, Karnan sat inside the cupboard, where Papatti had sat, and patted the clothes next to him. "Why don't you sit with Appa?" But Raj's toes had just touched ground and he shook his head. Karnan gazed at Papatti. "So this is what this is like."

"What is?"

Raj said, "I don't like it. There is a cockroach there." The light had chased the arthropod away and Papatti made a mental note that she would have to remove all the clothes and blitz the cupboard with insecticide later. She would drown the critter if she had to. Karnan said, "There was a time when I found a woman hiding in a cupboard."

"Did she like cockroaches, Appa?"

"Why?" Papatti said.

"It was during the Occupation. She was hiding from the Kempeitai, the Military Police. I worked for them as an errand boy and happened to find her."

"And what did you do?"

"Left her the way I found her, I suppose. Appa used to say, keep your head down, do your work and disturb no one. And that's just what I did."

"You saved her?"

"No, I just let her be. I was no hero. I was an accomplice to very bad things, Papatti."

She recognised the leaden heaviness in his voice. He had been just as distressed when they had argued about the money earlier. She wondered if she should, and quickly deciding said, "Does this have something to do with the money?" She bit her lip.

"Papatti."

She knew she was being an idiot, twice over. She had just regretted confronting him and was repeating her mistake. "I'm sorry," she said. "You don't have to say anything. We don't have to talk about it. I'm just being kaypoh. I don't care. I'm just happy to have you back." She sat next to Karnan, their shoulders squeezed together, legs hanging out, Karnan tapping a foot on the room floor.

Raj, standing in front of them, cocked his head and said, "You are like kids." He laughed, tickled by his own joke, a guffaw that ended with him sitting on the floor and waking Krishnan up. Karnan cooed so the baby didn't cry and

Papatti pushed Krishnan's hair back as gently as she handled a thread.

Karnan smiled and said, "I know you care. And yes, it has something to do with the money. And one day, I'll tell you all about it. Okay? And answer all your questions. In fact, I'll give you a long letter on it and you might have to ask your son to read it for you but it will all be there. In fact, I'll have to ask our son to write it for me too. But for now, it's just very raw and I don't even know how I should feel and I don't want to think or talk about it. I'm just trying to put it behind me. Just trust me that I'm not doing anything illegal or corrupt or anything of that sort. Please?"

She nodded because she had faith in him. After all, she was the one who kept telling him that faith must be infinite. If only she listened to her own advice at times.

"Is this when your amma took you in?"

"Yes."

"Did you ever talk to her about the Occupation? Or to Murugan?"

He shook his head slowly. "We never spoke about it or what happened to my appa or her husband. We didn't ask questions. We just started from zero and built our family from scratch. But I'll admit—I worried that if I told her, she wouldn't want me anymore. What if she accused me for what happened to her husband? That guilt has never left me."

"Don't say that. She would never. Saroja Amma loves you. And I don't know what it is, but it's definitely not your fault."

"I worked for the Japanese. For the occupiers."

"Dear, like I said, I don't know what happened, but those were the 1940s. You were a child. It was all out of your hands. Nothing was your fault."

"I could have tried harder to escape maybe. They dared to do this thing called *sepukku*, and I could also have committed suicide to deny them my service. I was always safe and well-fed and didn't deserve to be."

She would have slapped him if he was not carrying Krishnan. "Don't talk rubbish. You were a child. What could you have done?"

He smiled sadly. "That's what my appa used to tell me."

"Do you miss him?"

"Yes. I remember every detail about him."

He turned his head away. She wrapped her arms around him and rested her head against his shoulder. She could feel his chest swell and ebb against her arm. "Well, he was right and you cannot blame yourself for what happened during the Occupation." And then, because Papatti was Papatti, she could not resist saying, "You know, if you tell someone like me what happened, you might feel a lot better."

He burst out laughing and held her forearm. "You don't give up, do you?"

"No."

But she could tell that he remained unconvinced. She was no priest to lead an absolution; she was just his wife, but that was enough to try and make him feel better. She pulled back and said, "You know what I think, dear?"

"I know you will tell me what you think, dear."

She slapped his shoulder, not caring anymore about whether Krishnan was in harm's way. "I don't think anything was your fault, but if you don't believe me about that, then fine. But I can tell you that today, you are a good man. You don't talk badly about anyone, you don't hurt anyone, you love your amma, and Murugan, and your sons. And the fact that you feel bad about something you had no control over shows how good a man you are, and that's all that matters."

"Are you trying to save me now, Papatti daughter of Rajpal? Psychiatrist specialist."

She slapped his shoulder twice. "I'm talking seriously here."

"Okay, sorry."

"You know when I stopped sewing after Appa died— everyone else we know told me that it didn't make sense. But I couldn't understand them. I just felt like I needed to quit sewing because it was the right thing to do. And now that I'm talking to you, I understand what the rest must have felt like trying to convince me otherwise. You just don't make sense to me. But I guess you feel like you're right and no one else will understand. But it's time to move on dear, to listen to reason."

He smiled. "So you will start sewing again?"

She straightened herself and frowned. "Will that help?"

"Papatti, you don't have to."

"No no, I'm trying to make a point here. Can you let me?" She said, "You wanted to start fresh, so let's start fresh, again, properly. No more blaming you or me, no more baggage, no more fear, nothing. Let's start from scratch. We have two sons and I want to raise them to be better than us. I want to send the boys to school. And you know what, I'm going to change my mind. I think you should leave your job and start your kickboxing gym. And I will save for that too. We will build our family from scratch, like you wanted to with yours."

"I want to with this family too. But Papatti, you don't need to start sewing again for me."

"Well, I want to do it for you, and I think I want it for myself too. And I think I've changed enough to try again. I forget sometimes that I really loved to sew; I just need to focus on each stitch and gown instead of worrying about each customer and his opinion. I think I can do that now. I will sew to enjoy it and to make enough money to raise our boys and help you start your business. That's enough. What do you think? Do you want to move on with me?"

"I'll make money, Amma," Raj said, standing up aggressively, chest puffed out. "I don't need to go to school."

She reached for his ear but Raj ducked her hand and stepped away. "Naughty," she said, "you will go to school. And you will stay there, Kareena or Mangatta or whoever comes. Dear, I'm serious. I'll sew, but you must promise too."

"Promise what?"

"Promise that you'll aim to leave your job in three years to start your gym. That'll be your promise to move on."

"Three years? Papatti, the money?"

"Well, sewing pays better that my current jobs, and I can always work harder. But I want this for you. I want you to focus on doing what you love. I want you to move on. But first you must promise me that you will try."

"Papatti, but the kids? Their school? The house?"

"Dear, I'm not asking you to leave your job and wallow around in beers and cigarettes for three years. I'm asking you to plan and work for it with me. If you want it and work for it, you will get it. That's what my appa always said to me."

"Three years?"

"Three years."

He nodded. "Okay. I promise."

He met her gaze again. "Thank you." He leaned forward and kissed her forehead.

She said, "You know, we could have used that American money now. I just realised that I'll need to start saving for another sewing machine. I mean, it's okay, I'll do it. Just that it'll be harder. But we'll manage. I promise too." Papatti had already calculated how much money they would need to send their two boys to school and keep them there. Besides, the new government had made it compulsory. But Papatti also wanted to buy a television set so they could learn to speak the

Queen's English from it. After which they would teach her and Karnan to read and write so their entire family would be educated. And then her boys would find secure well-paying jobs with good reputations that they could bowl over the landlord with (she couldn't resist being a little competitive) and finally buy a new and better house, maybe like that Selegie flat that Kumaran had always talked about, one they could not be threatened with eviction from.

But Papatti groaned at the thought of splurging on a new sewing machine and then having to laboriously scrimp and save all over again, especially when she had once owned a perfectly functional one. But she would, because she felt excited about this reset of their relationship, about making a plan as a family, and because she wanted Karnan to feel better.

He said, "I still have your sewing machine."

"What?"

"It's in the warehouse at the dock. Dear, I would never sell it off. It's your passion. It's your talent. I've always hoped you would sew again, sometime or another. Everyone who knows you hoped that, even if you didn't want to yourself. You thought you were doing it for all sorts of reasons, but we all knew that deep down you loved doing it and were good at it and we wanted you to eventually pick it up again. That's all we cared about."

"But the money we paid that moneychanger's wife?"

Karnan chuckled. "I had a little saved up; it was enough. Your amma helped as well."

"Dear."

"Three years, dear. Three years."

The wood creaked under Papatti, like a branch cracking in half. Grabbing Karnan's shoulder, she made sure he held Krishnan securely and shouted at Raj to back away from them. Papatti sank a few inches, feeling Karnan sink in next to her too, and then stopped, wondering if that was it. Raj looked puzzled at this sudden anti-climax, having wanted something more explosive, perhaps something that blasted his amma into smithereens for another laugh.

Relieved, Papatti breathed normally again. Underneath her and Karnan, under the drawers and clothes, the floorboard must have given way, breaking inwards in half. Karnan chuckled. "I thought it was an earthquake. Thank goodness. Why don't we just buy a new cupboard and nobody sits in it anymore?"

"Thank God," Papatti said. "Yes. Let's do that. It wasn't built for your weight. This is what happens when you drink and drink beer. You end up breaking my cupboard." She stepped out of it and took Krishnan, amazingly still asleep, from Karnan's arms so he could push himself out. But before he did, she slapped him on the shoulder and pushed him back into the cupboard. "That is for lying to me about the money. I will pay you back every cent in three years when we open your gym."

Raj ran to his father and held two hands out. "Are you okay Appa? Let me pull you out."

Karnan clasped his hands and said, "Okay, Thambi."

Epilogue

It was the year 2001 and Professor Kurosawa Takeshi slowly ambled out of the arch of the crimson Akamon gate, that majestic west entrance into the University of Tokyo. Cameras shuttered all panicky as tourists posed before the Meiji-era edifice, holding up fingers in the V peace sign. Takeshi was inured to these sights. A lady said, *"Hai, chizu!"* Big smiles dawned on a group while Tōdai students brisk-walked around the lady and her models to enter campus. A few zoomed in on bicycles. But Takeshi was 84 years old and white-haired and moved laboriously, so students and tourists alike stopped what they were doing and parted to give way, even if he would rather they could take care of himself. He was not an invalid. Regardless, in the space that swelled around his senescent presence like a spotlight, he waddled to the traffic stop.

It was three in the afternoon and although the September sun spilled like an open wound, its nucleus was hidden behind tall buildings and the whistling wind required a jacket.

Takeshi wore the standard salaryman black suit with a thick Prussian blue tie. If he had listened to his daughter and worn his Asics track shoes, walking would have been much easier and more comfortable. But Takeshi had wanted to look sharp and dignified and above all, able. So he had chosen his heavier and tighter leather Hush Puppies and his feet now shuffled as if he were skating on concrete rather than walking. He knew he would reach home; he always did. He just needed to keep moving his Hush-Puppies-swaddled baby feet one half step at a time. At least his backpack, carrying only the notes of a speech he had just delivered and two pens, sat lightly on him.

The light turned green and Takeshi crossed over to the Darjeeling Indian restaurant that served a reliable naan and curry lunch deal before hobbling down the pavement, venerable spotlight protecting him better than any Kempeitai entourage could have. He marched past a Chinese restaurant that had once sold him frozen prawns underneath a hot sweet chilli sauce. He passed a MOS burger. Tokyo was now a cluster of mini-cities connected by *izakayas* and Starbucks, and Takeshi went past both before he reached the Hongō-Sanchōme metro station, which serviced the mini-city of Hongō and its mainstay, the Tōdai campus.

He whisked out his Suica card, readily prepared in his blazer's inner pocket on his daughter's advice, and tapped it at the turnstile before taking the lift down to the Marunouchi line. Two minutes till the next train. He found the sweet spot that would release him exactly at his exiting station's gate and waited patiently.

Takeshi used to study and teach Political Science at the University of Tokyo. Today, his younger colleagues had invited him back to speak at a conference. Despite his age and difficulties walking around, he had been unable to turn down the invitation. So Takeshi had sat amongst a long panel of professors inside the Yasuda auditorium at Tōdai. History, that recidivist intruder, manifested itself in their stooped vertebrae, silver hair, stuttered speech and the defiant passion, borne by the conviction of their age and experiences, which they extruded into low-placed microphones. They spoke about the War.

A roar announced itself in the dark tunnel and yellow lights flickered against the murky shaft shadows. A metallic square face surged forward, and the train slid to a smooth halt. Takeshi boarded and a schoolboy rose to attention, saying, "Please," and pointing at his seat. Takeshi shook his head and motioned for the boy to sit down, unable to muster the energy to talk. The boy remained standing and Takeshi held on to a metal bar for support. It was just one stop to his exit. The seat remained empty.

The bespectacled boy was about nine years old, dressed in a long-sleeved black blazer with gold buttons, black shorts, black socks pulled to the knees and black leather shoes similar to Takeshi's. A peaked cap with a gold star in the middle sat on his head, far less menacing without the red band—simply a brighter innocent star, a new star. The old star was a dead sun now. He reminded Takeshi of another boy. The last thing Takeshi remembered of that boy were the words, "*Boku no namae wa Karnan desu.*" Takeshi had opened his eyes to see his short sword smash against the wall, breaking his backscratcher and shattering the sake bottle. The lanky boy fled into daylight, vanished from the doorway, gone forever, as American B-29 bombers drummed overhead.

The Marunouchi train lurched into Ochanomizu and Takeshi cautiously hopped the gap while the schoolboy sped around him and raced up the stairs. Takeshi queued at the escalator and by the time he arrived on ground level, this boy was gone too. He crossed the impressively large bridge over the Kanda River, the bright pink billboard of Sakura Pharmacy beaming down at him from across, near the Ochanomizu JR station. Further down the street, garish signboards and bright lights of shops selling used guitars and trumpets and snowboards jostled for his attention, a multi-tasking he could no longer sustain, indication that he had grown too old for the city.

The aged station building had no lifts, and as Takeshi detested the ceremony of station officers helping him down the staircase, he went it alone. He gripped the handrail and suddenly worried that vertigo might drag him down the staircase much faster and much more painfully than he desired. But he didn't want to resemble a toddler climbing down backwards either. Compromising between progress and dignity, Takeshi walked sideways, scolding himself for not listening to his daughter and taking a taxi. But taxis were eyebrow-raisingly expensive in Tokyo and Takeshi would have lost a preposterous 10,000 yen cabbing home. Whatever for? He could do this.

The handrail divided the staircase for commuters to walk up and down without bumping into each other. As the way down was large enough for only one person, people behind Takeshi leapfrogged to the other side, unwilling to hurry an old man. He apologised profusely to whomever might be listening, but focused on crab-walking step by step until his feet finally touched the platform. Sighing with relief, he moved out of the queue formed up behind him, like a cork pulled out of a bottle of people.

The Chūō Rapid rail was due to arrive in four minutes and Takeshi joined another line where the train doors would open. The metallic train that arrived was older and heavier and noisier than the Marunouchi, vibrating clumsily to a stop. As Takeshi boarded, a young lady, a professional like his daughter in a white blazer and green skirt and carrying a Louis Vuitton tote, asked him to take her seat. It was a 25-minute journey minute journey to Kichijōji so Takeshi thanked her and she helped to unsling his backpack. He sat and tenderly pulled the bag onto his lap and on cue, the train rumbled onwards. It was quiet and only two men with heads full of youthful black hair and wearing pinstriped blue suits spoke in serious, nod-provoking tones. The lady appeared to keep an eye on Takeshi, smiling pleasantly every time he stared back at her, even though he was actually willing her to stop watching over him. Finally, he gave up on his ineffectual eye power and closed his eyes, resting them instead. Age might cripple his body but it could never cripple his pride. Only the modality of his ancient memories could inflict that kind of pain.

Takeshi had read about work done by the United Nations, SOS Children and other humanitarian organisations that treated child soldiers for war trauma, re-educating them to overcome their brainwashing and move on, helping them to re-join society. Now, whenever Takeshi thought back to the end of the war, in those moments when he was ordering Karnan to leave the house, Takeshi realised that at that ripe age of 28, as an officer of the Imperial Japanese Army, he had been the brainwashed, indoctrinated one who had needed help rewiring his brain, who had needed reformation and support to metamorphose into a new social being for a new normal world. He had been the duped, not the enlightened.

To 2001-Takeshi, 1945-Second Lieutenant Kurosawa Takeshi was a separate ontological being altogether, twice soul-vacuumed and removed entirely. 1945-Takeshi was now a part of 2001-Takeshi as much as an important lesson from a book he had read, but separate from *this* Takeshi's consciousness and *this* Takeshi's identity and this Takeshi's sense of self-worth. Otherwise, how could he live with *this* Takeshi daily?

Sometimes, Takeshi obliged himself to remember these ancient memories, and remember that these memories, dredged up from the graves and ashes and blood of others, were *his*, that he was talking about things *he* had done, and reminding himself of this, spasms of grief and regret would crash onto him and immobilise him until they buried his 1945-alter-ego again.

Takeshi's healing process had begun in the August of 1945 with shock therapy. An eerie chanting, like a mantra being recited at a Shinto shrine, high-pitched, feminine, antlike even, was emitted by a puny silver radio. He had struggled to hear and struggled harder to accept that that voice, transmitted by the Japan Broadcasting Corporation, chanting that strange indecipherable Classical Japanese, belonged to His Majesty the Emperor Hirohito. Takeshi had been among other junior officers pressed to the back of an overcrowded conference room in Kempeitai Headquarters, having been summoned for an emergency meeting, hands squashed to his sides, feet melded together, while the Colonels and Generals of the Southern Expeditionary Army Group sat around the mahogany table, leaning forward, drawn to the tiny radio in the centre. Finally, that fitful agony stopped, and a radio announcer dared to replace the Emperor, this time speaking in clear and understandable Japanese, declaring that Japan would accept the terms of the Potsdam Declaration and end the War. This announcer was even more terrible and blasphemous to hear, and as Takeshi bowed his head and his tears of humiliation and sorrow fell and the soldiers next to him wept, Takeshi hated the announcer with all the depths and recesses of his soul even as he clung to every syllabic letter he pronounced, trying to process what was happening.

When the announcer finished with *keeping pace with the progress of the world*, a junior officer down Takeshi's line shouted, "Treachery! Hang that announcer for treachery!"

Another soldier shouted, "I don't believe it!"

"What is this weapon? It's a fake broadcast!"

"We have 70,000 soldiers in Syonan! We have 700,000 soldiers in the south! We can still fight the decisive battle!"

"Strike now!"

"I still have my life to give!"

"It is a betrayal of the Emperor!"

"I will fight!"

"I will fight!"

"*Tennō heika banzai!*"

"*Tennō heika banzai!*"

"Silence! Silence! Silence or I will court-martial all of you!" Marshal Count Terauchi Hisaichi, commander of the Southern Expeditionary Army Group, slammed his fist on the table, lodging it there like a shuddering hammer. The Marshal was commanding enough to have managed to threaten to hang soldiers who wanted to die. He glared at them in their eyes, scanning the walls of junior officers, daring anyone to talk back to such a senior and decorated commander. The senior officers rose to support him.

Slowly, the pumped and raised fists lowered, squeezed back into the pressed bodies. Heads bowed. Stifled sobs escaped into the silence. Death was preferable to crying in front of an officer like the Marshal. But in these circumstances, it was too difficult to be the exemplary dry-eyed and stony Japanese man of *bushidō*.

As the Marshal shellacked them for their shameful behaviour, as he told them that Prince Kan'in Haruhito would fly into Singapore the next week to confirm the Emperor's rescript and that he expected Shōnan to be ready to accept

His Imperial Highness, that he expected his junior officers to conduct themselves befittingly and not to shame him before the Prince, as he ordered them to stand down and accept their orders and trust in His Majesty the Emperor the Almighty, trust that this was all part of a glorious plan they could not yet see, Takeshi remembered his arrival in Singapore.

He had been greeted sombrely at Headquarters by Nobuo's platoon commander, who wordlessly handed Takeshi a mess kit. Takeshi pulled out the mess tin to find a cold blue finger wrapped in a green leaf. The platoon commander apologised for Takeshi's loss and hurried off, afraid that Takeshi would seek retribution through him. But Takeshi had not been able to think that clearly then. Instead, he had stumbled home to cry in private, knowing he had betrayed Nobuo, knowing that Nobuo's death was his fault.

He spent the next days crumpling unfinished letters into a growing pile of paper because he could not tell his mother that Nobuo was dead, and because he quailed at the thought she might write a letter back blaming Takeshi for killing her younger son. Takeshi took out his grief and rage on his soldiers, sending them on fast marches around Singapore in full battle gear until one died of heat exhaustion. And then he flogged Takagi and Yamashita for not having trained their soldiers better. He took it out on his interrogation victims, whipping them harder and harder with knotted rope lashed with water as they hung from the ceiling whenever the rage engulfed him. He drank himself to extreme states of forgetfulness in the evenings, hating himself even more when he woke up bleary, groggy and depressed. But in moments of sober clarity, he consoled himself with one undeniable truth: Nobuo had sacrificed his life valiantly for his Emperor and Japan. It was not a vain death.

But as the Marshal evicted the junior officers from the conference room and Takeshi lowered his head and balled his fists and walked out, he realised that the undeniability of this singular overarching truth, the force of its consolation, had been ripped from him in an instant.

Takeshi tried to trust that the Heavenly Sovereign still watched over him and his dead brother and the *kokutai*, that the Emperor saw a bigger picture and envisaged a grander plan that the junior officers were just not ready to know yet, some form of strategy above Takeshi's paygrade. But the nagging doubt had been seeded in his mind, and it had begun to tear at him. What if Nobuo had died in vain after all? And back in Jalan Besar, swept up in this pain and confusion, treading to stay afloat, Takeshi botched explaining the new situation to Karnan.

The small boy had never been his enemy. Having trained to melt searing candle wax onto men's matured privates, to insert pencils into their auricles and burst their eardrums, to pump water into their stomachs through their noses and mouths, to order them driven to Changi beach for Harsh Disposal, Takeshi had been wholly unprepared for a malnourished and motherless boy of eight years old fighting against soldiers and all possibilities of divine mandates to save his *otōsan*, loyal to his father despite the risk to his life, staring up at Takeshi with terrified but defiant eyes, refusing to stop fighting. It reminded Takeshi of Nobuo in 1936, when the Kempeitai had arrested Takeshi's father in his home in Hiroshima.

Takeshi had been nineteen years old then, when five Kempeitai policemen, without even taking off their shoes, barged into his porous chestnut wood house wearing the only warrant they needed—white armbands with two red *kanji* characters for Kempei—the Military Police. They arrested Takeshi's father, Yasu, for avoiding conscription into the Imperial Japanese Army. A policeman started reading the charges, and Yasu remained a blank face, unperturbed by the allegations. Tall and muscular, he sported a black moustache and goatee that turned heads. It was well known that the local women were attracted to him and jealous of Takeshi's mother. When the policeman finished, Yasu said plainly, "You are all just kids. You should ask your fathers. Any man with a good brain who lived during the Taishō era knows that the Emperor is neither infallible nor a god…"

"Shut up, old man! Shut up!" The policeman raised his baton.

"…He is certainly not a model for you kids to follow. I will not fight for him. I will not follow him. He will take us nowhere."

"I said, shut up! Or I will beat you!"

"…You are just a small kid. You won't understand. But don't expect me to join in your stupidity."

They began beating his hips and legs and Yasu's knees buckled. But Yasu didn't fight back, and instead still tried to lecture them. Later, they added the charge of lèse-majesté.

Meanwhile, Takeshi clasped Nobuo around the chest and clamped his mouth to restrain him from fighting the police or saying something stupid. He grappled Nobuo into their room, where just minutes ago they had been competing to throw out winter poems. They knocked a standing ceramic vase onto its side, its ferns and sand fillings toppling out. Takeshi sank into the dirt, using his weight to drag Nobuo to the floor, and like a spider he locked Nobuo within his arms and legs. Nobuo struggled against his older brother's grip without success. Takeshi kept silent and still, protective of Nobuo, and ashamed of his father. Disgusted, he watched through the doorway as Yasu, his face blotched red with the beating, stood up straight and limped out of the house with the Kempeitai, thinking he knew how to protect the nation better than the Emperor. Takeshi's mother gave chase in bare feet.

Takeshi disowned his father right away. He talked to Nobuo through the night and past sunrise, explaining to Nobuo that the police were not the bad men. *Otōsan* was in the wrong. Yasu just didn't understand the world situation.

In their dojo, Takeshi had once supervised a sparring match between two juniors. He barked at one, a skinny, feeble and demure fifteen-year-old who had started learning *Kyoshokan* six months ago to improve his confidence. "Motohiro, keep your guard up! *Kamae*! *Kamae* Motohiro!" But Motohiro, panting, kept lowering his tired arms instead of protecting his face. Takeshi wanted badly to help him. He hollered and hollered, "*Kamae*! *Kamae* Motohiro! *Kamae*!" trying to teach Motohiro to defend himself, trying to scream his lesson into Motohiro's head if that's what it took. After all, Motohiro's first tournament was next week. Did he not want to win?

Takeshi shouted more and more, growing vexed, his throat running sore. "*Kamae*! *Kamae*!" Then he ran into the fighting circle and high-kicked Motohiro, dropping the junior to the mat with a split ear, shouting, "This is why you must keep your guard up! Do you understand? Defend yourself! Now you will learn! Now you will learn! *Kamae*!" Motohiro lay unconscious on the tatami, his white *dōgi* turning red at the scapula.

Yasu never caned or beat his sons. His sanctimony believed that *budō* mandated the strong to protect the weak, not devour them. So he had given Takeshi a verbal thrashing, upbraiding him for a relentless one hour for bullying Motohiro, for not behaving with the compassion expected of a senior student, a *senpai*. He commanded Takeshi to apologise to Motohiro, take him to the doctor and pay for his medical bills, tasks that Takeshi found completely unpalatable, but somehow managed to complete without saying a single word to the useless junior.

But in and out of the dojo, Yasu just didn't understand that a real fight, like the fight Japan was being slowly sucked into, demanded ruthless strength to protect Japan from the colonising-addicted Westerners. If Japan didn't learn and become stronger quickly enough, it would be eaten up, just like Motohiro, who (thankfully) never returned to the dojo again. He was weak. The choice, between being Takeshi or Motohiro, seemed obvious to Takeshi.

So after Yasu was arrested, Takeshi did not even give the Imperial Japanese Army the opportunity to draft him; he enlisted immediately and convinced Nobuo to follow him once he turned eighteen. The Kempeitai, highest on the Imperial pecking order after the Emperor, enlisted Takeshi and he excitedly transferred to Tokyo, recently renamed from Edo, to train at the Koho Kimmu Yoin Yoseiji. A year later, the 18th Infantry Division enlisted Nobuo and Takeshi promised to look after him. Most importantly, Takeshi assured Nobuo that the Emperor would watch over the both of them.

Only their mother, ever loyal, visited Yasu at the prison south along the Ōta River. Despite her pestilential overtures, Takeshi refused to write a single letter to his father or call on him during vacation breaks.

So as Takeshi intercepted Karnan from running to his father, he had remembered restraining Nobuo in Hiroshima too. And when Karnan had crumpled to the floor under Takeshi's gun, unconscious and bleeding from the nose, Takeshi knew that when the boy woke up—if he woke up—there would be no one, no older brother, no money, no food, no army. He couldn't even work as a comfort woman.

When the sun rose and the firing squad forced the father to dig his own grave before blindfolding him, ordering him to sit and shooting him into it, the sunrise and the fatal bullet would strike the death knell for the son. Against his better judgement, not knowing what else to do, Takeshi carried Karnan back to Jalan Besar Road. The boy wasn't the enemy. This wasn't his war. He had merely been betrayed by his *otōsan*.

But at war's end, Takeshi had been unable to explain that he was still trying to save Karnan. That if Surrender did loom close, that if his agonising doubts were correct, a local boy could not be seen with the Kempeitai, or any Japanese soldier for that matter, let alone wearing his hand-me-downs. Takeshi could not protect him any longer. Takeshi scolded him and slapped him to try and chase him out of the house, so that Takeshi could also be alone to resolve his own confusion and wait for Japan to recover. But instead of accomplishing this, he had managed to become quickly and stupidly hurt by an eleven-year-old's words. Enraged, he had challenged Karnan to help Takeshi commit *seppuku*, to put an end to the doubting and grief. And Karnan refused to kill the man who had orphaned him. Alone on his knees, staring at the empty door with the sun pouring in, Takeshi wondered for the first time if killing Karnan's father, imprisoning Yasu and sending Nobuo to an early death were in vain, or if he would soon discover the Emperor's higher purpose and be renewed by it. He had never prayed as strongly as he prayed on his knees that day, forehead planted to the cement. He prayed to the Emperor that Karnan would find someone to take care of him, prayed that Karnan would survive, prayed that the higher purpose would reveal itself soon.

Then, a week after Karnan left, Takeshi was treated to his second electric shock when Major Okamoto Hideaki stopped by his house. Before Takeshi could salute, the tired Major said, "Let us go inside, Kurosawa-san."

"Of course, Major Okamoto. How can I help you? Any news on the ceremony?" He took a ceramic cup from the floor to pour the Major a drink.

"No, that's okay. Kurosawa-san, listen please. I must- I am sorry to tell you, and I don't know how else to say this: Your parents are dead."

The cup broke into tiny shards, splintering against their pants. Hideaki was unfazed. Instead, he bowed his head. "You have my condolences and the condolences of our superiors."

The Americans, those usurpers, had bombed Hiroshima with the new cruel weapon the Emperor had mentioned in his Jewel Voice Broadcast. Fear coiled in Takeshi's guts as Hideaki, educated in agriculture and forestry, tried to explain the term "nuclear", which didn't even have a Japanese equivalent. Takeshi found it difficult to visualise this bomb that could fit inside the weapon bay of a plane but had evaporated his entire city at a button's touch, blasted its life-channels of schoolchildren and fathers and mothers, the Shima hospital and Hiroshima castle, into a black barren desert, raging with uranium fire, hellish monads of burning ash and death. The bomb sounded more divine and more Godly than the Emperor, and stoked Takeshi's confusion that such a superhuman, supercharged force existed that was not the Emperor, that could force the Emperor to bended knee. And to think that the Americans owned this weapon, possessed it so confidently and smugly that they could call it *Little Boy*, as if simply to spit into his face. *Little Boy*, some *Little Boy*, had flung his city off the universe. It dawned on Takeshi that he was in the same state he had put Karnan in: orphaned.

Takeshi fell to his knees and asked Hideaki for permission to take his life. Hideaki said, "No, Kurosawa-san. Don't be stupid. We still need you." He grabbed Takeshi by the armpits and with an animal grunt tried to haul him to his feet. But Takeshi was so heavy and inert that Hideaki sank to his knees too, holding Takeshi there. Takeshi wasn't crying. He was blankly staring over Hideaki's epaulette, dreading that Yasu was right—for if a man-made weapon cowed the Emperor and if the enemy possessed that weapon, there could be no grander plan, there would be no decisive battle. This was the decisive bomb. It was surrender, plain and simple, even if the soldiers avoided the word, and Japan's fate now belonged absolutely to the victors. Yasu was right. The Emperor was not infallible, and they had been led nowhere. The Major was crying, salty tears drenching Takeshi's moribund uniform. He had come to this conclusion too.

Everything that constituted Takeshi—the soldier, the Shinto devotee, the Japan nationalist, the responsible older brother leading Nobuo to war, these structures of identity that were entwined around and built upon the divinity of the Emperor—were collapsing into the cold blood trails he had spilled from Japan to *Shōnan*, a long death march. If there was no ultimate purpose, if the Emperor was not the infallible monarch for whom anything could be done and for whom everything should be given up, why had Takeshi torn families like Karnan's asunder? On whose unfailing authority and to what higher end had Takeshi conducted Operation *Dai Kenshō*, the Great Inspection, and imprisoned, whipped, starved and summarily executed countless men and women, merely to throw their disfigured corpses into mass graves? The Emperor's soldier could do anything, be denied of nothing in service of the cause. Was this all wrong? Why had his parents been ground into the nothingness of arid black Hiroshima soil? As the bomb had dropped from the plane, falling through the clear and blue and empty sky, as during this free-fall its gun had automatically fired to activate another process as inexorable and unstoppable as gravity, unleashing uranium to charge and break uranium to create a compounding series of explosions to the exponent of 15 kilotonnes of trinitrotoluene, as this process had unleashed itself in nanoseconds, the bomb had said, I am death, shatterer of worlds. And then it blew.

And to think, as the shock explosion blasted the firmament over Hiroshima, puncturing the heavens, as its raw power swept through earth and vaporised buildings and people, as its black fires and scalding heat raged in pursuit to melt whatever was left standing, his mother and father had had to endure the shock and pain and death alone, apart. As he had forced others to endure. Takeshi pushed Hideaki aside and vomited bile onto the dirt. He wondered: what had he done?

...

The rail reached Kichijōji and the unnecessarily solicitous lady smiled brightly as 2001-Takeshi hugged his bag and gladly departed the train that was starting to feel like an old folks' home. On the platform, he put one arm through a sling, hoisted the bag, then slid the other arm in. He stood by the left of the escalator, tucking his hand into his pocket as another woman made fast downstairs, the stilettos of her heels rapidly drumming the hollow metal steps.

Kichijōji: another mini-city in the west and a refuge for students and artists fleeing the skyrocketing rental rates of central Tokyo, like Takeshi had done years ago when he chanced upon his first apartment here. The station was located inside the trendy Atré mall and Takeshi wobbled out and passed a McDonald's, convenience stores, ramen joints and a British pub before reaching the main road. The seven floors of the Marui department store rose before him and at the bus stop, the red digital clock told him to wait for eight minutes. Takeshi shed his backpack to be ready. Having to take a twenty-minute bus ride at the end of a long train journey used to be the worst part of his daily commute, and he realised it still was. But his younger self had stomached it better. These days, he stayed at home reading and writing, leaving the house only for his weekly doctor's appointment and medically mandated walks around Inokashira Park.

After the official surrender ceremony at the Municipal Building, 1945-Takeshi had confessed to the British that he was Kempeitai, hoping they would court-martial and hang him, meting out justice and giving him that quick release from the agonising guilt and futility of it all, saving him from grappling with it and trying to make sense of it for the rest of his life. But the Allies weren't interested in a junior officer like Takeshi. They wanted his commanders.

So Takeshi had drunk *shōchū* and put his pistol inside his mouth, the cold iron barrel resting on his tongue, shouting in his head to pull the trigger. A few Japanese officers had planted a timed bomb underneath a house in Bukit Timah and drank themselves silly with sake until the bomb exploded. Three hundred Japanese soldiers had stabbed or shot themselves since the surrender.

But Takeshi put the pistol down, sobbing. He couldn't, but not because he didn't want to die. Death was lighter than a feather. He would happily join Nobuo and his parents. But that was the problem. Although Takeshi wished that someone would take the matter into his own hands and hang him or shoot him, Takeshi didn't deserve to exonerate himself from his guilt that easily. It would have been cowardly. What's more, *seppuku* tasted too closely of the old way, of the way before the surrender, of Emperor worship, a way that had led to Takeshi's parents dying in Hiroshima and Karnan abandoned and wandering the city.

He would have to find a way to live with his guilt. In the obstetric sentence the British pronounced upon him, to work as a prisoner of war for the very British he had once abhorred for two years, living out Karnan's occupation *lex talionis*, a new Takeshi was slowly born, the Takeshi that would grow up into 2001-Takeshi. An undernourished British private, once a prisoner of war himself, gleefully stripped Takeshi of his weapons, and ordered Takeshi to remove the barbed wire around the YMCA building and pluck out the heads lined in front of the Cathay Building. Day by day, Takeshi filled out potholes cratered into Tengah Airbase by Allied bombings and cut the grass on the grounds of Sembawang Naval Base. The day after Emperor Hirohito publicly renounced his divinity, Takeshi was building the Royal Air Force a church near Lim Chu Kang.

He found refuge from guilt and grief in his work, and so threw himself into it. But he would not forget; he could not forget. In the evenings, when he was allowed to visit the library, he would pick a book but his mind would leave the story and wonder about Karnan and if the boy was even alive. He would start wondering how many boys like Karnan were wandering around without their parents because of Takeshi, for no good reason. *Hamlet* would lie there, open, as the tears came up and Takeshi started crying and slapping the table until a guard rushed up to escort him back to his bunk. *And let me speak to the yet unknowing world how these things came about. So shall you hear of carnal, bloody, and unnatural acts, of accidental judgements, casual slaughters, of deaths put on by cunning and forced cause.*

In 1947, the British dispatched Takeshi with the last prisoners of war back to Japan, where Americans received, processed and then released him. He didn't bother with

Tokyo. He took the first 13-hour coach west to Hiroshima, where he debussed onto a wasteland. The absence of his mother waiting by the bus station smiling at him, and the knowledge that his father was not even in the vicinity struck him even harder. The guilt surged back and he vomited.

He looked up from his wretched state, his breathing slowing and calming, and he began to notice hope in the shape of sturdy makeshift wooden shacks and small shops and resilient older structures like the Bank of Japan and Higashi police station, symptoms of a city slowly and doggedly rebuilding its way back to life, with children running down the streets fearlessly, many tattooed with bloated keloidal scars of radiation. Takeshi stood up. The next day, he joined the Koya Construction Company and went to work with bricks and clay, rebuilding his father's city.

After a few years, the Mayor's aide, learning that Takeshi had been a soldier and a prisoner of war, asked for a favour. The local government was building a peace memorial park, and as Takeshi had seen the costs of war first-hand and lost his parents to the atomic bomb, the aide wanted Takeshi to tell his story in Tokyo to raise funds for the memorial. Takeshi said that he wasn't best suited to ask others to donate to a peace memorial, for he had been responsible for many of those costs of war, a litany of sins. He had not been able to forgive himself these past years, and struggled with guilt. How could he expect anyone else to forgive, let alone give charity to him?

But the aide shook his head and raised a firm palm. He insisted that Takeshi's contrition only strengthened the conviction of their cause to rebuild Hiroshima as a tribute to peace. They went back and forth, and Takeshi found it difficult to keep saying no to such a noble endeavour and to the aide's face. He ended up feeling doubly guilty. He started thinking that if the Mayor's office wanted him to help then he should at least try, and he took a two-week leave of absence from the Koya Construction Company and paid his way to Tokyo. This was in 1952. The Americans were handing government back to the Japanese. The occupation of Japan was ending.

Takeshi stood along the roads and under the railway bridges of the convalescent business districts of Marunouchi and Hibiya to ask for donations. To anyone who might listen, Takeshi couldn't bring himself to talk about Lieutenant Kurosawa Takeshi during the war, but he walked up to them and apologised for disturbing them and explained that his parents had died in the atom bombing, jogged alongside them while explaining that the *hibakusha* children were still suffering from blood disorders like leukaemia because of the radiation, held up laminated black-and-white photos to their faces to show that progress had been made like the reopening of the elementary school and that their money would not go to waste. "Will you donate please?" he must have asked a million times.

People in Tokyo were different from people in the country: busier, hustling in their teeming herds, almost sprinting once they had broken away from the crowd, as if worried the crowd might catch up and suck them back in to an average speed of movement. And they were even less tempted to stop for a lone man with long dirty hair and a scraggly beard, dressed in handed-down drabs smeared in mortar and paint, chasing after them talking rapidly with a strange countryside accent. They likely assumed that Takeshi was a deranged beggar, bereft of any family to support him, and right on one account. Then Takeshi met Professor Fujiwara Hiro.

...

The 01 bus arrived like an animation, narrow and boxy with lights smiling like a cartoon face. The doors opened automatically and the driver, seated with a white surgical mask protecting his mouth and nostrils from germs, asked Takeshi if he needed help. Takeshi shook his head and took a priority seat by the window, hugging his bag close. Through the glass, he saw a row of shophouses selling yoghurt ice cream and sushi and KFC. The bus started wobbling and then advanced. It turned left and blazed between award-winning hairdressers, whiskey bars and Inokashira Park.

Fujiwara Hiro was a short and slender man with flatly combed white hair and a respectably measured manner of speech that merely paused and waited for the train charging overhead to pass before speaking again. He was worried that Takeshi was freezing, standing there alone in a tunnel, touting at strangers while Tokyo funnelled its powerful winter winds through the arched passageway. Would he not freeze to death?

"No, I am okay," Takeshi said, shivering. "Thank you."

"I can tell you are not from the city. If you are here to eke out a living, I insist you take this. Or you'll die of cold before long." Hiro shrugged off his long black overcoat and held it out to Takeshi.

Takeshi stared at the coat, stunned. Then he recovered his senses and snapped his hands behind his back. He stepped away from that menacing coat, shaking his head furiously, bowing repeatedly. "Thank you. Thank you. But I don't need it." He refused to accept this charity. Others needed it more.

Outstandingly stubborn for his diminutive stature, a trait Takeshi would rediscover again and again about the Professor, Hiro patiently folded the coat and put it on the stool for diners near Takeshi and walked away. Takeshi grabbed the thick rich wool and ran after him, shouting, "I am not a beggar! I am just an old soldier trying to raise money for my city! Take your coat back please! Please! It's cold!"

Hiro wheeled around. "You were in the war?"

Takeshi jogged to a stop gratefully and held the coat out with a slight bow. "Yes. Please take your coat back."

Hiro ignored the coat. His wrinkled eyes assessed Takeshi's face with the gentleness of a glove. "How old are you?"

Takeshi let his hands fall to his sides. "Thirty-two."

Hiro smiled. "My son would have been your age. He died fighting in Okinawa."

Takeshi bowed deeply. "I am sorry for your loss."

"It is okay. It is over. At least, I tell myself, I have my wife. Some people have nothing. Who do you have?"

Takeshi stayed quiet.

"I am sorry for your loss too."

"No, please."

"So," Hiro said, "please tell me. What brought you here?"

"I am trying to help rebuild my city—Hiroshima."

"I see. But what brought you here?"

Takeshi blinked. Hiro was the first person to ask. Now, the older man's eyes waited patiently behind those spectacles. There was something like concern in them, a concern and gentleness for Takeshi that could not be overcome by the harsh Japanese winter winds whirling around them. His feet were planted firmly too. He was not going anywhere. Takeshi hugged his arms, shivering, the jacket dangling uselessly, but he felt a warmth and trust he had not known in a long time. The quiet between them had become comfortable.

As Hiro waited kindly, Takeshi soon found himself opening up into talking about his work for the Kempeitai, about the killings, the torture, Nobuo, his parents and his term as a prisoner of war. He could not bring himself to speak about Karnan. That boy had endeared himself to Takeshi and tormented him more than anything else, representing with a face and a story and the most personal of accounts every innocent life that Takeshi had wronged, and Takeshi could not bring himself to speak about him. Still, he told Hiro everything else, including the guilt and the grief that he was wrestling with since the surrender, glad that winter had chilled his tear ducts.

Throughout, Hiro listened quietly, nodded appropriately, patient as if it weren't bitterly cold at all, as if for those minutes, Takeshi's monologue had become a warm refuge. His silence continued coaxing the words out of Takeshi and when he finally stopped, Hiro merely stared at him quietly too, confirming in those further silent moments that Takeshi was finished talking.

Then Hiro said, "What are you doing now?" Takeshi soon learned that the Professor had an academic's knack for asking follow-up questions.

"I work for the Koya Construction Company but I volunteer with the reconstruction effort. That is why I am here."

"I see. Thank you for telling me your story. I was also drafted for the war effort. But I did not go to the frontline. I sat behind a desk, as a typist at the War Ministry while younger men like you and my son went to fight."

"A typist?"

"Yes. The office was not too far from here. I was comfortable. I cannot imagine what you must have seen. You seem in much pain."

"I hope that I am recovering through my work."

"Here." Hiro fished out a business card from his wallet. "Now, I teach political science at Tōdai. Have you heard of this institution?"

Takeshi nodded.

Hiro stuck the card out. "Take this. You are clearly smart. And you are doing good work, but your mind is not challenged. Hence, it is wandering everywhere. It is hurting you. I want you to consider studying at Tōdai. It will engage you and make you more productive. I think it will suit you. In fact, a lot of my research is about the war. It will be painful at first, but I think that as an academic, you will appreciate being able to control the lens through which you think about the war. It will help you frame and control your thinking. In fact, maybe one day, when you feel better, you can consider writing about your experiences during the war for other people to read. It will be like a new beginning."

Takeshi almost keeled over. "I am honoured, Fujiwara-san. Thank you. But I do not deserve your kindness. Besides, I am too old for school."

"Nonsense!" Hiro looked incredulous. "You are never too late for school! I am still studying every day."

"Sorry. I did not mean to insult—"

"No, please do not worry. What I am trying to say is, you are not too old. You are just alone. I want to help you. Please, let me."

"Thank you, Fujiwara-san. I appreciate it. But I am sorry, I do not deserve this. Besides, I do not want to disappoint you as a student. Who will want to read what I write? I am sorry."

"You will be surprised. There are many people who would prefer to learn about what happened from a soldier on the ground than a typist in the office. And I am confident that you will feel better penning it down."

"I understand you, Fujiwara-san. Thank you. But I am sorry, please let me think about this. For now, I want to return to Hiroshima. I want to finish the memorial. I have plenty of work in my city."

"Well, I understand that. Please, take this donation first then. It is partially for the city and partially for you to finish your work there quickly and come back to Tokyo. And you can hand the coat to me when you return to visit. I expect you to call me. Do you understand?"

Takeshi gratefully bowed as he accepted the money with both hands. He also realised with a slight smile that he could not argue with this old man. "Yes, Fujiwara-san. I will call you. Thank you, Fujiwara-san."

The Hiroshima Peace Memorial Park opened in 1954. Hiroshima had healed like scar tissue, different, stronger. It had blossomed, evolved into more than a city, a symbol, and this gave Takeshi some modicum of strength to believe that he could one day heal too, become stronger. He kept his word and called Hiro. The old man was equally stubborn over electronic communication and extracted another promise from Takeshi.

In the autumn of 1954, Takeshi returned to Tokyo. Hiro and his wife, Fujiwara Kaori, a lady of same height and soft demeanour as her husband, hosted Takeshi in their house in Nezu, a ten-minute walk from Tōdai's Hongō campus. Hiro showed Takeshi the university's Gothic architecture, Europeanesque statues, yellow gingko trees and green lake. He invited Takeshi to sit in on a class on Immanuel Kant. Then they sat on a park bench sipping coffee, and Hiro, like a magician conjuring up the excitement of Tokyo and the opportunities of learning at the country's best university, tried to prevail upon Takeshi into staying longer to prepare for the entrance examinations into the University of Tokyo. Hiro said that even if Takeshi did not want to research about the war, he might enjoy studying political science. Over dinner, Hiro and Kaori said that they had talked it out and they would furnish him with a bed and food if he was willing to study and help take care of their dog, a pretty brown shiba-inu called Umi, and water their patio garden. Oh, and they advised him to cut his hair and shave his beard. What did he say to that? Chewing his *daikon* as Umi danced around his chair, Takeshi demurred, but if it was difficult to say no to Hiro, it was impossible to refuse Kaori.

So a clean-shaven, blazer-wearing Takeshi moved in with Hiro and Kaori to study. Just as he had thrown himself at laying brick after brick for the Koya Construction Company, he now absorbed his mind in text after text, wrapping his brain matter around the words and opinions of scholars, thinking up arguments and counter-arguments for his essays, constantly scrubbing his writing to craft his points as succinctly as possible. Hiro guided him, recommended reading material, introduced him to the relevant professors who were experts in their fields, gave suggestions for essay hypotheses that Takeshi could explore.

Hiro had been right—studying engaged Takeshi's mind totally. And Takeshi steered clear of studying the war. In fact, he was drawn to political philosophy. When he read Hobbes' political geometry or Locke's theory of private property, contesting their ideas in his head, he realised that he was in fact enjoying himself. But when he eventually closed the books and sat alone in the cafeteria for lunch, or turned off the lights at night and lay in bed with nothing to read, guilt inevitably wound its way back into him, and he squeezed his eyes in the trauma and hoped that one day he would find some measure of peaceful reconciliation.

Takeshi was soon offered admission into the Faculty of Law at the University of Tokyo. Political science, not considered a scientific enough discipline and hence not respectable enough to stand on its own two feet, was constituted under the province of the Law Department to add esteem to the subject. He was given a small scholarship stipend to survive in Tokyo. At the age of 38, Takeshi was a first-year Tōdai undergraduate student.

Hiro had alerted Takeshi that getting accepted by Todai would be the most difficult part of his odyssey to graduation, and indeed, he now found himself slightly freer for time and went house hunting, which was when he discovered the mini-city of Kichijōji, a small apartment for rent in nearby Mitaka and the loveliest park in all of Tokyo called Inokashira Park. Two months after enrolment, Takeshi moved out of Hiro and Kaori's house. But he visited them and Umi every Sunday for lunch and dropped by the Professor's office over the weekdays. They and his books remained his sources of comfort. In another year, he introduced them to his girlfriend, Akira.

Akira, raised by a traditional conservative family in Saitama, had been dissuaded from attending university after finishing high school. It simply wasn't a girl's path. But as the war ended, seeing how massively men had managed to mess things up, Akira decided she at least deserved a shot at *not* messing up, and in categorical defiance of her father, enrolled herself at the University of Tokyo. She had been studying for her postgraduate doctorate and teaching an undergraduate seminar on the Morality in Adam Smith's Writings when Takeshi had popped in to try the first class. He was struck by her fierce passion for the subject, and immediately wanted to find out more about this one Adam Smith and the pretty tutor championing his work. Takeshi innocuously asked Hiro what Adam Smith's subject matter expertise was before signing up for the class.

Not many were interested in learning about Adam Smith's moral sentiments. But Adam Smith became Takeshi's best friend, his invisible hand guiding Takeshi to Akira's office one too many times to ask for advice on his essays before he finally decided to ask her out to coffee, then book-hunts around Jimbōchō, then dinners at Shinjuku. She had a peculiar ability to captivate his attention totally, to block his mind from thinking about anything else, as if transporting him into a different world, one dominated overwhelmingly by her distinctively positive and high spirits and the chemistry between them and the happiness she made him feel.

But when they kissed and parted in the evenings and he climbed the stairs down to the train station, the sobering memories returned, reminding him, shackling him again as he descended into guilt. With every date, Takeshi felt increasingly ashamed. He was living a lie, hiding his memories and who he was from her because he was afraid that the truth would repulse her. But once, they were talking on the sofa, and Akira suddenly pounced on his hands and said, "I love you."

He stared at her.

"You don't need to say it back, I think."

"No, it's not that. Of course I love you." Saying the words sent goosebumps popping all over his body. It felt right. He held her hands in his. She smiled happily, and he felt that happy lift. But it was time to come clean. And for the first time, Takeshi told someone everything about his time during the war, including about Karnan. As the words fell out of his mouth, he searched the tears that ran down her face for clues of how she felt.

The pause that followed was infinite, and as Takeshi prepared for the moment when she would rise from the sofa and walk away, she pulled his hand and admitted to being divorced. Her husband had wanted her to stay at home and raise a "wolf pack", not attend university.

"Akira," Takeshi said, "divorcing a man isn't as terrible

as killing him."

"If you must know, my ex-husband would have preferred that I had killed him."

"Akira."

"Takeshi."

"Tell me what you're thinking. I ruined so many lives. Karnan's face haunts me every night."

She sighed and let go of his hand. "I'm processing it myself. It is hard for me to digest."

"If you want to leave me, I understand."

"Of course not. I still love you."

"Really?"

"Of course. Takeshi, I don't have the right to pardon or punish you for what you did. But I can tell you this."

"What's that?"

"You are a different man now. It is no longer you. You have tried and are trying to be better. And I want to be part of your new life and support you with this."

He shook his head. "I don't deserve this."

She lifted his chin. "You deserve love."

He smiled tearfully. "Thank you."

Takeshi's favourite Saturday afternoons were spent strolling to Inokashira Park with Akira, sitting on the bench across the Benzaiten shrine, and reading and thinking up rebuttals to Clausewitz and Machiavelli with her, each exciting the other in their duet until they could read and think no more, at which time they went to the Standing Bar by Kichijōji station to drink cheap Hoppy beer and dull their thinking for the night and joke about how academically studious they were. After Takeshi received his undergraduate degree in the spring of 1959, with highest honours and an embarrassing mention for his special success as a mature student, they married each other.

After much deliberation with Akira, Takeshi applied to

study for a PhD and asked Hiro to be his supervisor, deciding that it was finally time to sit, research and write about the war with Hiro. Akira feigned insult that he hadn't asked her to be his supervisor, but they knew that he would not have had the strength to confront the old cause without her support.

Initially, it had been frightening to sit in front of a wooden desk piled with volumes and volumes of death statistics, propaganda analysis and memoirs from victims of the war. When Takeshi turned the first pages, he often flinched, stopped and walked out of the library to take in the cool air. But he went back into the musky space and persisted slowly. Soon, he jotted down notes, scribbled his opinions in the margins of his notebooks, drafted bite-sized paragraphs, and realised that Hiro was right—when he read and then wrote about the war afterwards, he crystallised his powerful but amorphous and unwieldy emotions into point-by-point logic destined towards a conclusion, and in so doing, was better able to understand his own thoughts and feelings.

He realised that he was not alone in his outrage, in his sense of betrayal, in his guilt, that there were other ex-soldiers who had written about the war too. He began co-authoring papers with Hiro, and before long, developed his own hypotheses. His doctoral thesis was part-memoir and part-analysis of the operations of power, distilling the lessons of his years as a Kempeitai Military Police officer and all the political philosophers he had studied into forty-thousand words. He did not include Karnan's story because that would have divulged details about the boy that Takeshi did not have the right to unilaterally publish. But pouring out the rest of that unfinished thesis gave him a sense of relief, and at the end of every writing marathon, he felt gratefully depleted of thought and feeling.

Takeshi received an A+ for his thesis and a book offer.

But the highest honour was seeing Akira close the booklet of pages and say, "I am proud of you, Takeshi. I cannot wait to read the rest of this."

And somehow, in the midst of Takeshi and Akira sprinting from office to lecture theatre and back to teach undergraduate lectures and work on research papers, between the microwaved convenience store *yakisoba* dinners they ate while rushing to meet submission deadlines, in the middle of sessions where each critiqued the other's presentation technique in preparation for conference presentations, Akira laughing at his self-conscious seriousness and urging him to smile more, despite all medical forewarnings and a complete absence of intentions, Takeshi and Akira had a daughter, whom they named Nanae. To celebrate his acceptance into the postgraduate programme, capitalise on the larger stipend and most importantly to make room for their daughter, they rented a bigger house in Mitaka, closer to Inokashira Park.

...

2001-Takeshi pressed the bell before a lady's mechanical voice could announce the next stop, Shinkawa, where the bus doors opened onto a newly developed condominium. Takeshi stuck his left leg into the air over the curb and lowered it slowly. With a grunt, his weight dropped onto that foot. His other foot followed and swung over and he almost fell forward. But he was on the kerb. Behind him, the doors took their time closing and the bus flickered its right signal and Takeshi wore his backpack again. As he put his left foot forward, it ached and he scolded himself to wear track shoes the next time, even if he knew that when next time came around (if next time would bless him by coming around), he would choose the Hush Puppies. The bus sped off.

In 1966, a friend of Takeshi's from his graduate school

days in the Law Faculty—who had since joined Japan's Ministry of Foreign Affairs—was assigned to a taskforce with the mandate of establishing diplomatic relations with a recently independent Singapore. Takeshi called in a favour. He asked the diplomat to scout the address of a Singaporean called Karnan s/o Krishnan, who should have been in his late twenties.

His friend and ex-classmate asked his local counterparts and after ample searching, returned to Tokyo and gave Takeshi an address and a page from the Singaporean *Straits Times* newspaper to corroborate his findings. The headline read: *A-Star Seamstress Marries Harbour Union Activist. Will multi-racial families be the new norm in a new Singapore?*

Underneath, in a black-and-white photo, an Indian man and Chinese girl stood side by side. The man behind the aggressive moustache, with his large dark eyes and parted lips, as if on the verge of making a smart retort, was unmistakeably Karnan.

His heart stammered and tears filled Takeshi's eyes when he recognised the boy he had last seen 21 years ago, when he read that Karnan was happily married. He showed the article, proudly, elatedly, to Akira and she let him frame it up, protecting the fragile recycled paper with glass. Whether what followed was a plea for forgiveness, an instrument of personal catharsis and atonement, or just an instinctive human need to reconnect and reconcile, Takeshi did not know, but his trembling hands picked up a pen and began writing a long letter to Karnan in English.

He first congratulated Karnan on his nuptials. And then Takeshi apologised. He apologised for taking Karnan's father away, for forcing Karnan to work for the Kempeitai, for caning him, for not having said a proper goodbye, for not having contacted him since. He could only apologise again and again. Takeshi then wrote about the atom bombing and his parents' deaths, his two years as a prisoner of war in Singapore, followed by his repatriation to Hiroshima and his desperate reconstruction efforts in that city. Takeshi detailed moving to Tokyo and enrolling at Tōdai, teaching Political Theory to a new cohort of undergraduate students every year, and researching and writing about the war with Hiro. He told Karnan he had married Akira, and they had a chubby little daughter called Nanae who was now seven years old and whom he spoiled too much. Takeshi concluded that he could not be the judge of whether this U-turn of a meandering life, this single-soma metempsychosis, was redemptive, but he was doing his best in remorse, and he hoped that it would add the force of conviction and sincerity to his apology.

A thought struck Takeshi then: How much did a dockworker in Singapore earn? His friend had said that Singapore's GDP per capita was abysmal. If Karnan was starting a family, would he need the money? Deciding to err on the side of caution, Takeshi ended his letter writing:

I do not earn much but I wanted to share this with you. Please use it for yourself and your family as you wish. I will send it to you every year. I think of you often and hope you and Papatti-san are well.

Best Wishes
Kurosawa Takeshi

And Takeshi included his home phone number, office phone, office fax, home address, office address and Hiro's house address for good measure. He rewrote the letter twice, neatening his penmanship until his hand stopped shaking so much and Takeshi was satisfied that the words ran exactly horizontally with sufficient white space to be easy on the reader's eyes. He asked Akira to proofread it, and then sent the letter and a US hundred-dollar bill off to the given address at Tanjong Pagar, Singapore.

The next morning, Takeshi woke up early, brewed a pot of coffee, called in sick and waited nervously on his couch for the reply. Akira had to return in the evening and cook him breakfast and remind him that the letter would take a few days to reach Singapore. She said that he should take his mind off it for at least three weeks.

Takeshi tried, but as the September of 1966 turned into October and November, and then December, Takeshi checked with the post office to see if the letter had gone undelivered or rebounded, asked his friend to confirm the address, and considered following up with a letter that said, "Did you receive my first letter?" But the mail had been delivered to Karnan correctly. There was just no response.

He asked Akira, "Should I have sent the letter at all? What if Karnan doesn't want to hear from me?"

"You had to try, Takeshi. And you've tried your best. Don't think about it now, let it go."

It took a complete unearthing and exhumation of Second Lieutenant Kurosawa Takeshi for new-Takeshi to rationalise, with great sorrow, why Karnan would not bother replying at all, why Karnan would not feel the same way about Takeshi reaching out. He felt so stupid. Of course Karnan would not want to hear from him, let alone forgive him. Who could, when even Takeshi couldn't forgive himself? The pain of the past ran too deep.

But Takeshi had pledged to send money to Karnan annually. In hindsight, this was presumptuous. Yet if he broke this promise, thinking Karnan didn't want to hear from him, he risked making Karnan feel deceived or cheated, as if Takeshi would only send money on the condition that Karnan spoke to him, a transactional relation that was far from the truth of what he wanted. What if Karnan really needed the money?

On the other hand, if Takeshi sent the money and Karnan really didn't want it, Takeshi would become an irritant, aggravating an open wound, the last thing he wanted the new-Takeshi to do either.

"So you have a choice between being a flimflam and a pest," Akira said.

"What do you think?"

"You were quite pesky when you kept coming to my office, asking for my advice on your essays, browsing through my bookshelf and refusing to leave and let me do my work."

Takeshi was shocked. "You never asked me to leave, Akira!"

"Because I actually didn't want you to. On the other hand, if you cheated me, I would feel very hurt."

"But I did terrible things to Karnan," he said. "Maybe he will never forgive me."

"That is not for you to decide. That is for him to decide. You just need to give him time. Maybe the next time, send the money without writing a letter about you or me or Nanae or your job. He doesn't need to know all that. This way, at least he will know that you want to stay in touch and you will also be keeping your word. In the worst case, Karnan-san can just throw the money down the chute, yes?"

Takeshi smiled. He could see the spunky boy doing that and wished to know if he had grown up just as spunky. He certainly hoped so.

In any case, Takeshi sent a small portion of his salary to Karnan every year and felt a guilty gladness that he had a link, however minute, however one-way, to Karnan. Sending an envelope to his address every year was a connection, and Takeshi relished as much of that isolated connection as he could. Before sending the mail, he spent evenings folding and refolding a dozen envelopes like an origami aficionado, writing out the address longhand and printing it out on a sticker to compare to see which looked prettier, and ironing out a US one-hundred-dollar note so the wrinkles on Benjamin Franklin's face were only those of the original image and not because the paper had been sat upon. He then slid the bill neatly into the chosen envelope, nestling the note safely in the bottom right corner before sealing the envelope with UHU glue. He would turn the envelope in his hands for minutes, appreciating it before gently setting it down on the table without any paperweight. He made sure the fan was turned off.

Going to the post office was a ritual too, where he wore his lucky suit and tucked the envelope into the inner lining of his briefcase by seven am. Akira hugged him at the door as if he was going for a conference in Berlin or New York, and he didn't stop to talk to his neighbours, assiduously staring and marching straight ahead until he arrived at the Mitaka Shimorenjaku Post Office and deposited the envelope into the safe hands of the postal officer. After this, he sat in the French bakery next door and ordered a croissant and black coffee and pondered the myriad ways Karnan might react to this envelope before Takeshi realised with a start that he had a job he wanted to keep, at which point he paid the bill and met Akira and Nanae at Kichijōji station. He never stopped hoping for a reply.

But the reply, imagined and anticipated with relish, never came. After five years, Takeshi decided to stop, because either Karnan would go crazy from irritation at this yearly unwanted contact, or Takeshi would turn mad from the yearly cycles of nervous overthinking and suspense and the eventual depression of realising that no response was forthcoming that year either. Or maybe some guy in Singapore was collecting and cashing in a lot of money that didn't belong to him. Akira, as always, supported Takeshi one hundred per cent. He donated the annual sum to the Red Cross instead and on those mornings in September when he would have otherwise sent out an envelope, he, Akira and Nanae went for breakfast at the bakery.

...

One foot at a time, Takeshi-san, 2001-him said to himself as he walked past the daylight neon lights of the 7-Eleven convenience store and crossed the road. The traffic light started flashing maniacally as he was halfway across and if he had been younger, Takeshi would have sworn, and then run. Now, he had the inclination and energy to do neither. Perhaps he should not make such long journeys across the city anymore. Tokyo wasn't even a city, it was a cluster of mini-cities, a metropolitan area to be technically accurate. But this wasn't possible.

The conference organisers had invited Takeshi to speak about his work and his experiences during the war. The entirety of his life was connected to that chasm in history in so many ways that Takeshi could not refuse. And veterans like him were becoming fewer and fewer in number. Every year, the organisers said that they had fewer people to invite to speak about their experiences. What was it Akira used to quip? Old people were an endangered species.

Hiro and Kaori had passed on many years ago. Last year, in 2000, Takeshi had woken in bed and turned over to find Akira motionless, not breathing, unresponsive to his tender shakes and worried pleas of "Akira, Akira, wake up Akira," dignified to the end. His beloved Akira. How he missed her.

After his remedial walks around Inokashira Park, Takeshi bought flowers and stopped by her grave to tell her what he had read on the bench they used to debate on or ruminated about during his walk. Sometimes, when he was cooking or cleaning the house, he stopped and heard his voice fade away as he realised he had been talking to her as if she were still sitting on the long sofa in the living room with a book spread on her lap. He started placing her pillow on her side of the bed to fill that space. During the rest of the day, Takeshi worked, reading and writing and attending conferences like the one today to keep his mind occupied, to preserve the semblance of stability that Hiro and Akira had helped him earn over the years, to keep him a little more alive.

One of the last things Akira had said to him was to keep in contact with Karnan and to never lose faith. She hoped that one day, Takeshi would write about his and Karnan's story in the war to complete his doctoral thesis and share it with the world. Then, she wanted Takeshi to retire.

Takeshi had pondered this, knowing he needed Karnan's permission, wondering if he even had the courage to write about this immensely guarded and personal part of his time during the war, to share it with anyone other than Akira. He finally consulted Nanae, then walked rounds around the green lake of Inokashira Park and chattered to Akira's gravestone until he finally came to a decision, in Akira's words, to "Just try it, Takeshi." Her wholesome sunny voice still echoed around him, her spirits lifting his with hope.

Nanae sat by him, quiet with her hands neatly folded on her lap as Takeshi wrote, hand trembling, legs shaking, a letter whose first half-page was filled with apologies for intruding again after a hiatus of 23 years.

Afraid of incurring Karnan's wrath and afraid of being

disappointed, Takeshi recalled in writing that he had in his earlier letter mentioned that he was researching and writing about the war. He explained that Hiro and Akira had encouraged him to write down his experiences during the occupation to understand them better and to find use for them by sharing them. How every time the guilt and the pain came over him, he had spoken to Akira and penned his thoughts on paper. For his thesis years ago, he had written about his time as Lieutenant Kurosawa Takeshi of the Kempeitai, described how the Kempeitai had seized and wielded power, examined how they had abused it. But he had not written about Karnan. This time, he hoped to finish his written thesis. He asked for Karnan's permission to write about the two of them, to lay it all out. He would include or exclude anything that Karnan wanted him to, but hoped that this would round off that chapter of a terrible period. In a way, it was an end.

Takeshi mailed off the first honest draft of his letter, dispensing with the morning routine and the French bakery, telling Nanae and himself most importantly that a response was 99.9 per cent unlikely, even if Takeshi could not suppress that one percentage point from growing beyond its assigned weight and consuming his imagination and igniting his hope.

Of course, no reply came. But by now, time had seasoned and prepared Takeshi for the disappointment and Nanae was supportive to the letter, bringing her son and daughter over after school to play with him and cheer him up. She even bought him a new tie with shiba-inu pictures scattered all over it.

Along the narrow pavement, a boy on a bicycle snuck past Takeshi while the jetstream of his fast-rotating wheels almost smacked Takeshi off his feet. The boy vanished, out of grasp. Takeshi sighed and dusted his jacket straight and

WARRAN KALASEGARAN

turned into an alley.

His neighbour's brown shiba inu lay on its paws outside, crestfallen, lolling while waiting for company. Behind her, the door was ajar and her leash ran into the house. She spotted Takeshi and jumped to her feet, leash stretched tight, pink tongue sticking out. "Hello, Mori-chan! How are you doing today?" He petted her on the way to his door.

He fumbled in his pocket, heard the clinging and felt the cool metal as he pulled his keys out. He opened the metal mailbox by the door, noticing through the corner of his eyes that Mori was still standing, hoping for more backrubs. "Sit, Mori-chan. You will become tired. Sit please." Her tongue fell longer and Takeshi chuckled.

Opening the tin box, he found his pension and insurance notifications and a few letters from his various university networks and a telegram from an editor. Underneath them was a bulky yellow envelope. Takeshi curiously pulled it out and groaned as it sent the smaller snail mail in a scatter onto the road and Mori jumped side-to-side in excitement. Slowly, laboriously, Takeshi lowered himself onto one knee and gathered the small white envelopes and the big yellow mail into his arm, and by some miracle of stored energy, managed to rise and open the door to enter his home.

Akira had decorated the hallway with photos of Nanae's children and a photo of their small wedding, with Hiro, Kaori and Akira's mother by their sides. Takeshi, not one for décor, hadn't changed a chopstick in the house since Akira passed on.

He gladly took off his shoes, hung his keys and stepped into the living room. Takeshi dropped the stack of mail onto the coffee table and unharnessed his backpack onto the floor. He plopped himself comfortably into his thick one-man sofa, sinking into it. He had stopped using the long sofa since

Akira passed on because he didn't like sitting next to the empty space. He only ever sat in it when his grandchildren visited and they watched anime on the television together.

Takeshi pulled the yellow envelope to him, curiosity growing. The return address, in big black letters, was directed to Singapore. Takeshi's heart stopped. He bolted upright, the sofa trying its best to quickly adjust to his old, shifting weight. Tears sprang to his eyes like stars. He knew, he just knew. *Akira*, he wanted to cry out, *Akira! Akira!*

He recognised the name emblazoned above the address and his heart set off in a stammer, palpitating, too fast for his doctor's approval but Takeshi didn't care. His breathing had quickened, a windlike roaring had filled his ears, and his heart raced even harder. The stars melted into excited happy water flowing down his cheeks. Like a child once more, eagerly and earnestly opening a present, Takeshi tore at the glue-seal. He slit the opening and, trembling, pulled out a bound batch of papers like a booklet the size of his doctoral thesis, setting them on his lap.

Takeshi dove his face into his jacket sleeve so his tears wouldn't wet the paper. He scrubbed his eyes dry into the wool, took a deep breath to recover, and examined the missive again, his world shrinking to become the booklet, the noise in his ears becoming the words of the booklet. As a note fell out of the envelope in his hand, a lone letter falling gracefully onto the carpeted floor, Takeshi was reading the first line of the papers on his lap: *Dedicated to Papatti.*

Acknowledgements

I thank Epigram Books for receiving this novel as part of the Epigram Books Fiction Prize in August 2016. Thank you to the Epigram Books team—Edmund Wee, Jason Erik Lundberg, Yilin Tan, JY Yang, Yong Wen Yeu and Winston Tay—for making this happen, and for your valuable edits, advice and support. Thank you to the National Arts Council for its grant towards publishing the novel.

I thank the following people for their support in the early days: Charles Speller, Elizabeth Morris, Holly Wenger, Monique Perks, San Rajgopal and Thomas Preston. Thank you to Lynne Riggs from the Society of Writers, Editors and Translators of Japan. Thank you to John Gribble, Karen McGee, Marco Lobo, Sara Ellis and others from the Tokyo Writers' Workshop.

I wrote this novel while studying at the Graduate School of Public Policy at the University of Tokyo and am grateful to my friends and faculty there for encouraging me to pursue my interests. Thank you also to Iimura Kenichi, Ono Ryo, Nakajima Yuzo, Fukakusa Hiroyuki, Jason Angove, Yoshimoto Takuya, Yuta Jindai and the other members of Kichijo¯ji dojo for teaching me their beautiful martial art of kudo, on which *kyoshokan* is loosely based.

And of course, to my family, Chitra K, Kalasegaran Genkatharan, Meira Kalasegaran, Santhiya Kalasegaran, Parwathi Ramulu Bhaya, Krishnan Singaram and Miki Kobayashi.

This book is based on the Japanese Occupation of Singapore of 1942 to 1945. However, the characters and their stories are fiction. I have also taken some liberties with chronology and detail. The following books helped in my research and I am grateful to their authors:

Akashi Yoji and Yoshimura Mako (eds), *New Perspectives on the Japanese Occupation in Malaya and Singapore, 1941-1945*

Brian Ferrel and Sandy Hunter (eds), *A Great Betrayal: The Fall of Singapore Revisited*

Chris Brown, *Singapore 1942: Battle Story*

David Pilling, *Bending Adversity*

Donald Keene, *So Lovely a Country Will Never Perish: Wartime Diaries of Japanese Writers*. (The epigraph for this novel is cited from here)

Edwin O. Reischauer, *The United States & Japan*

Gretchen Liu, *Singapore: A Pictorial History 1819-2000*

Herbert P. Bix, *Hirohito and the Making of Modern Japan*

Inazo Nitobe, *Bushido: The Soul of Japan*

Jim Baker, *Crossroads: A Popular History of Malaysia and Singapore*

Jon Diamond, *The Fall of Malaya and Singapore: Images of War*

Lafcadio Hearn, *Japan: An Attempt at Interpretation*

Lee Geok Boi, *Singapore Under the Japanese, 1942-1945*

Lee Kuan Yew, *The Singapore Story*

Mark Felton, *Japan's Gestapo*

Okakura Kakuzō, *The Book of Tea*

Paul H. Kratoska, *Malaya and Singapore During the Japanese Occupation*

Richard Mason, *A History of Japan*

Roman Bose, *The End of the War*

Roman Bose, *Singapore at War*

Ronald Specter, *In the Ruins of Empire*

Ruth Benedict, *The Chrysanthemum and the Sword: Patterns of Japanese Culture*

Ryūnosuke Akutagawa, *Rashōmon and Other Stories*

S.R. Nathan, *An Unexpected Journey: Path to the Presidency*

Yasuo Kuwahara and Gordon Allred, *Kamikaze: A Japanese Pilot's Own Spectacular Story of the Infamous Suicide Squadrons*

The Singapore Infopedia website, run by the National Library Board of Singapore, is an encyclopedia on Singaporean history. The Oral History Interviews website, hosted by the National Archives of Singapore, is a repository of people's accounts of significant periods in Singapore's history.

Any factual discrepancies, intended or otherwise, are my own.

About the author

Warran Kalasegaran studied Politics with International Studies at the University of Warwick. He graduated with a Master of Public Policy from the University of Tokyo, where he wrote *Lieutenant Kurosawa's Errand Boy*, his first novel. He works at Singapore's Ministry of Foreign Affairs.

Fox Fire Girl

O THIAM CHIN

Derrick can't believe his luck when he rekindles a romance with ex-girlfriend Yifan. But Yifan remains aloof and distant. She confides to Derrick that in her hometown of Ipoh, she discovered that she is actually a fox spirit with mystical powers. But Derrick isn't the only person who has fallen under Yifan's spell. Unbeknownst to him, Tien Chen, a man with an unhealthy obsession with fire, has also been dating her. When Tien Chen eventually confronts Yifan about her infidelity, she tells him a story about her childhood in Ipoh to explain her actions. But is Yifan really the person she claims to be?

Once We Were There

BERNICE CHAULY

Journalist Delonix Regia chances upon the cultured and irresistible Omar amidst the upheaval of the Reformasi movement in Kuala Lumpur. As the city roils around them, they find solace in love, marriage, and then parenthood. But when their two-year-old daughter Alba is kidnapped, Del must confront the terrible secret of a city where babies are sold and girls trafficked. By turns heartbreaking and suspenseful, *Once We Were There* is a debut novel of profound insight. It is Bernice Chauly at her very best.

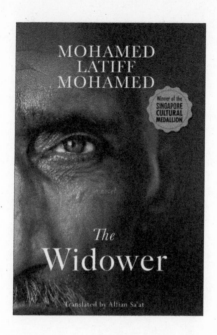

The Widower

MOHAMED LATIFF MOHAMED

Former political detainee and professor Pak Karman loses his wife in a car accident. The intensity of his mourning causes him to become untethered from his sanity. As reality, memory and fantasy become more and more blurred, he must come to terms with his past actions before his grief overwhelms him completely. Mohamed's novel, hailed as a landmark in modernist Malay fiction, is an unsettling tale of psychic disintegration and obsessive love.

The Tower

ISA KAMARI

A masterful tale of success and failure. A successful architect visits the new skyscraper he designed. As he climbs the tower with Ilham, his clerk of works, he reflects upon his life and spiritual journey in an increasingly materialistic world. As he struggles to reach the top, he is plagued by memories of a dark past. These memories are woven through the narrative as a series of fables and elliptical digressions, mirroring his own increasingly fractured state of mind.

State of Emergency

JEREMY THIAM

A woman finds herself questioned for a conspiracy she did not take part in. A son flees to London to escape from a father, wracked by betrayal. A journalist seeks to uncover the truth of the place she once called home. A young wife leaves her husband and children behind to fight for freedom in the jungles of Malaya. *State of Emergency* traces the leftist movements of Singapore and Malaysia from the 1940s to the present day, centring on a family trying to navigate the choppy political currents of the region.

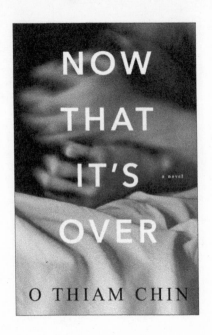

Now That It's Over

O THIAM CHIN

During the Christmas holidays in 2004, an earthquake in the Indian Ocean triggers a tsunami that devastates fourteen countries. Two couples from Singapore are vacationing in Phuket when the tsunami strikes. Alternating between the aftermath of the catastrophe and past events that led these characters to that fateful moment, *Now That It's Over* weaves a tapestry of causality and regret, and chronicles the physical and emotional wreckage wrought by natural and man-made disasters.

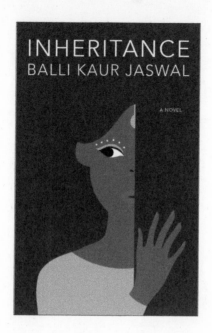

Inheritance

BALLI KAUR JASWAL

In 1971, a teenage girl briefly disappears from her house in the middle of the night, only to return a different person, causing fissures that threaten to fracture her Punjabi Sikh family. As Singapore's political and social landscapes evolve, the family must cope with shifting attitudes towards castes, youth culture, sex and gender roles, identity and belonging. Inheritance examines each family member's struggles to either preserve or buck tradition in the face of a changing nation.

Let's Give It Up For Gimme Lao

SEBASTIAN SIM

Born on the night of the nation's independence, Gimme Lao is cheated of the honour of being Singapore's firstborn son by a vindictive nurse. This forms the first of three things Gimme never knows about himself, the second being the circumstances surrounding his parents' marriage, and the third being the profound (but often unintentional) impact he has on other people's lives.

Kappa Quartet

DARYL QILIN YAM

Kevin is a young man without a soul, holidaying in Tokyo; Mr Five, the enigmatic kappa, is the man he happens to meet. Little does Kevin know that kappas—the river demons of Japanese folklore—desire nothing more than the souls of other humans. Set between Singapore and Japan, "Kappa Quartet" is split into eight discrete sections, tracing the rippling effects of this chance encounter across a host of other characters, connected and bound to one another in ways both strange and serendipitous.